BEFORE YOU START ... moment to think a punctum books, an i

@ https://pun

If you're reading the e-book, you can click on the image below to go directly to our donations site. Any amount, no matter the size, is appreciated and will help us to keep our ship of fools afloat. Contributions from dedicated readers will also help us to keep our commons open and to cultivate new work that can't find a welcoming port elsewhere. Our adventure is not possible without your support.

Vive la Open Access.

Fig. 1. Hieronymus Bosch, *Ship of Fools* (1490–1500)

PARIS BRIDE: A MODERNIST LIFE. Copyright © 2020 by John Schad. This work carries a Creative Commons BY-NC-SA 4.0 International license, which means that you are free to copy and redistribute the material in any medium or format, and you may also remix, transform and build upon the material, as long as you clearly attribute the work to the authors (but not in a way that suggests the authors or punctum books endorses you and your work), you do not use this work for commercial gain in any form whatsoever, and that for any remixing and transformation, you distribute your rebuild under the same license. http://creativecommons.org/licenses/by-nc-sa/4.0/

First published in 2020 by dead letter office, BABEL Working Group, an imprint of punctum books, Earth, Milky Way.
https://punctumbooks.com

The BABEL Working Group is a collective and desiring-assemblage of scholar–gypsies with no leaders or followers, no top and no bottom, and only a middle. BABEL roams and stalks the ruins of the post-historical university as a multiplicity, a pack, looking for other roaming packs with which to cohabit and build temporary shelters for intellectual vagabonds. We also take in strays.

ISBN-13: 978-1-950192-63-2 (print)
ISBN-13: 978-1-950192-64-9 (ePDF)

DOI: 10.21983/P3.0281.1.00

LCCN: 2019955875
Library of Congress Cataloging Data is available from the Library of Congress

Copyediting: Lily Brewer
Book design: Vincent W.J. van Gerven Oei
Cover image: Eugène Atget, "The Panthéon," Paris (1924). Collection of the J. Paul Getty Museum, 90.XM.64.34.

HIC SVNT MONSTRA

Paris
Bride

A Modernist
Life

John Schad

Fig. 1. Portrait of Marie Wheeler, Paris (1897).
Blocher Saillens Archive.

He said, Marie,
Marie, hold on tight. And down we went.
In the mountains, there you feel free.
I read, much of the night, and go south in the winter.
                                        — T.S. Eliot, *The Waste Land*

To Jacques Blocher

Contents

Acknowledgements

Many people have kindly helped me in the writing of this book or in some way supported me in it. These include numerous colleagues both here at Lancaster and elsewhere, including Jenn Ashworth, Rachel Bowlby, Isaac Cohen, Susanna Burghartz, David Bradshaw, Steven Connor, Valentine Cunningham, Roger Ebbatson, Niall Gildea, J. Hillis Miller, Jean-Michel Rabaté, and, last but not least, the admirable Mr. Hopper. I must also thank a whole number of archivists and librarians at the University of Lancaster, The British Library, The National Archives, Bishopsgate Institute, Enfield Library, Historisches Museum Basel, and Zentral-&-Hochschulbibliothek Luzern for their invaluable assistance. I am equally indebted to Anthony Grahame for permission to include a revised version of the opening chapter which first appeared in *Hostage of the Word* (Sussex Academic Press, 2013); to BBC Radio 3 for enabling me to read from that same chapter on "The Verb"; and to kind and helpful audiences at various universities, including those of Queen Mary's London, Malta, Nottingham Trent, South Wales, and York. Finally, I must thank the wonderful Jacques Blocher, formerly Président de la Société d'Histoire et de Documentation Baptistes de

France and great-grandson of Madeleine Blocher-Saillens; without him, this book would have been simply impossible.

The same might be said, albeit for different reasons, of a woman called Katie. Indeed, without her, I would myself be impossible.

— John Schad, Lancaster, January 2019.

List of Figures

Preface

On July 4, 1905, in Paris, an Anglo-French woman called Marie*
Wheeler married a Swiss émigré, Johannes Schad. Marie had
completed two years at dental school and Johannes was a clerk
with Chautard, a rubber-trading company. The two had first
met through the Paris Tabernacle, a small evangelical church
into which they had both been baptised as adults, and by full
immersion. Immediately after their marriage, Marie and Johannes moved to England, following his relocation to Chautard's office in central London. They settled in Palmers Green, a
north London suburb. Here they lived for nineteen years, during which time Johannes progressed through Chautard's ranks,
and both he and Marie became part of a large Baptist church in
nearby New Southgate. In 1924, however, something happened
to change their lives; and, as a result, Marie, in many respects,
simply disappeared.

Paris Bride is, then, an exploration of the lost life of Marie
Schad, of whom little is known beyond a few legal papers, a
number of letters, some photographs, the Tabernacle records,
the diaries of a friend, and an obituary. With so little else known
of Marie's life, I here seek to read her back into existence by
drawing on a number of contemporaneous texts—that is to say,

---

* Pronounced with stress on the first syllable; the 'a' is thus long, as in 'car.'

largely modernist texts. To be precise (and in order of focus) these are texts by, respectively: Virginia Woolf, Franz Kafka, the Paris Surrealists, Stéphane Mallarmé, Oscar Wilde, Katherine Mansfield, and Walter Benjamin.

These particular authors have been selected because they are each connected with Marie through some coincidence of time, place, or theme. Each chapter focuses on just one such coincidence and just one author—or, in the case of the Surrealists, one very particular movement. For example, the opening chapter seeks to read Marie's life via Virginia Woolf, in particular via her 1925 novel *Mrs Dalloway,* the cue being that just a year before, in 1924, Marie made a very particular visit to the exact same streets of the West End of London as those in which Woolf's novel is set.

This first chapter is related exclusively through the voice or consciousness of Marie. At the beginning of chapter two, however, the reader will find herself apparently being addressed by myself, or rather a version of myself. This "self" of mine will come and go several times throughout the book, as voices and perspectives continue to shift and change. But be assured, the voice of Marie will make many returns.

Much of what follows is, necessarily, imagined, and where that is the case it is, I believe, very obvious. It is, I think, equally clear when I am quoting—as is repeatedly the case, or the trick. If, though, ever unsure please refer to the notes at the end of the book.

Finally, and most importantly, I should add that, although I myself never met either Johannes or Marie, it is clear to me that both were my betters. By far.

A Prefatory Fragment

❁

Minutes of an Act of Marriage
— 17th Arrondissement, Paris, 1905 —
On the Fourth of July, at noon, Johann Jakob Friedrich Schad, clerk, born in Basel, lawfully married Marie Anne Wheeler, dentist, born in Paris.
(Préfecture du Département de la Seine).

Fig. 2. Portrait of Johannes Schad (c. 1900).
Schad Archive.

I want to gather material for the Lives of the Obscure.
— Virginia Woolf (1882–1941)

CHAPTER ONE

Flowers

Mrs Dalloway said she would buy the flowers herself.
(Virginia Woolf)

Day One

April 7, 1924

Marie said she would buy some flowers, and the trams, the pigeons, and the motor cars all murmured "yes." She was light upon her feet; quick, careful, lest she should brush against another. None, she thought; there would be none who would know her, though some had smiled. *Odd affinities she had with people she had never spoken to.** She would buy the flowers on her way back, and as she walked her head was set low.

She paused to allow a file of children to pass in front of her. Nineteen in all. Two-by-two save one, who turned and looked. It was her hat. Johannes may have bought it in Russia. But she should quicken her step. *She ... never tired of walking, for all her delicacy.* On she walked. On. I love walking in London, she thought.

---

* In this chapter, all italicised quotations come from Woolf (most from *Mrs Dalloway*, some from her diaries and letters).

Did Johannes ever come this way? On foot, to his office. He did not like the omnibus and, besides, walking was even more natural than talking, he would say, quoting their friend, the eminent Linguist, Mr. X, as he had been introduced the night they had first met.

The Linguist was an elegant man with a fine moustache, the points of which seemed to quiver as if receiving messages from the air. Some said his name was Ferdinand de Saussure, Professor Ferdinand de Saussure. He certainly spoke with authority; though was inclined, Johannes would say, to mistake language for Switzerland. "A panorama of the Alps," the Linguist had said, "must be taken from just one point. The same is true of a language." The Linguist's great-grandfather, she had heard, was a mountaineer. Among the first to conquer Mont Blanc. But she must be getting on. Such traffic. Piccadilly. Such traffic.

"City of death." Yes, that was it. That was what he had said about Mont Blanc. Shelley, not the Linguist. Shelley, the poet. Strange thing to say, or write, whatever the light. Though he was an unbeliever, Shelley that is, even among the mountains. Especially among the mountains, Johannes had said, pointing out that the unbelieving poet had signed the guest book at Chamonix as "Percy Bysshe Shelley, **Atheist**." Ah, and here, right here was Somerset House. *Over the Strand … the clouds were of mountainous white.*

Perhaps, she thought, she should not read so much. After all, there were, these days, so many curious books and so many curious authors. Mrs. Woolf, for instance, or Mr. Eliot, Mr. Eliot-the-Clerk, as Johannes would say. Mr. Eliot, however, she rather liked, seeing that he had written about a woman called Marie. Moreover *his* Marie, Mr. Eliot's, was also inclined to read through the night. And then there was Miss Emily Dickinson, the hermit of Amherst, they said. "Our lives are Swiss," she had written, "So still — so cool." Yes. "Till some odd afternoon, the Alps neglect their Curtains." Yes. "And we look further on."

Marie paused, a little faint, and glimpsed a poster in the window of a shop. "The British Empire Exhibition, Wembley Stadium." Yes, many would come. Odd, though, that the poster should portray London as a woman in bronze, naked and slim. Marie tugged at her coat. April was indeed a cruel month, just as Mr. Eliot had thought. And, now, a shower was upon them. Rain, rain all over London, she should not wonder, even at the Exhibition. *It is nature that is the ruin of Wembley,* she thought. The problem of the sky remains, she thought. *Is it, one wonders, part of the Exhibition?* Marie put up her umbrella. How mountainous those clouds.

Was Johannes out in the rain? Perhaps, but then he was used to weather of all kinds. He travelled so much. What with his languages. French, German, even Russian. The rubber-trade took him to so many places.

❀

Metropolitan Police
— January 7, 1927 —
Johannes Schad has paid periodical visits to the Continent on business and pleasure and intends doing so in the future.

❀

She did not, herself, like to travel by train; it was not, she had heard, altogether safe. *Villains there must be … battering the brains of a girl out in a train.* The continental trains were, though, very different. She had once said so to the Linguist. He, though, had simply muttered something about trains in general, about how no two trains, whatever we think, are identical. "We [invariably] assign [the same] identity to two [quite different] trains," he had said. "For instance, 'the 8.45 from Geneva to Paris.' One [such train]… leaves twenty-four hours after the other, [and yet] we treat it as the 'same' train."

Trafalgar Square was stirring. People of all nations and none, she thought. She had not intended to come this way but paused to open her purse for a man without legs, his upturned cap begging on his behalf. He gazed for a moment. *Every man fell in love with her.* "The bride is beautiful," as Johannes would say.

It is true that he would sometimes add "but, she is married to another man." This, though, had been a jest of his. "The bride is beautiful, but she is married to another man" were, he would explain, the famous words of a famous telegram. Coded words. The cable, he would say, had been wired from Palestine by two Jewish zealots hot-foot from the world's first Zionist Congress, a gathering held, strange to say, in Basel. Yes, *his* Basel. The two zealots had, apparently, gone off in vainest search of Israel. Zion. The Promised Land. And they had found her indeed to be beautiful. But also to be another's.

The man without the legs smiled. Then touched his cap and smiled again. She must help him. Find a baker's. Ah, here. That smile, though. Yes that smile, it *lifted her up and up when — oh! a pistol shot in the street outside!*

"Dear, those motorcars," said Miss Pym, *going to the window to look, and coming back and smiling apologetically as if those motorcars, these tyres of motorcars, were all her fault.*

No, thought Marie, it was *her* fault. She had grown comfortable from the tyres that rubber made, and, in fact, from all that rubber made. Yes, the disturbance in the street was her fault. But she could not stop. She must give the man the sandwich. She could not stop. She was expected at noon. By another man.

Marie's shoes concerned her. The heels, though modest, were about to give way, and the points of her shoes were worn. Better not to look down; best look up, right up. And why not, seeing that *all down The Mall people were … looking up into the sky. See, an aeroplane! There it was coming over the trees, letting out white smoke behind, which curled and twisted, actually writing something!* The Linguist, how he would have loved these letters. *"C was it? And an E? Then an L?"* There was, she saw, no "A" in the sky. Don't tell the Linguist. He had loved the French letter-sound *a*, handling it like the most fragile shell. "In its consistency," he had once said, "it is something solid, but thin, that cracks easily if struck."

The aeroplane above breathed several more letters into the sky. But it was not a day to stand and watch. Not like that day in Palmers Green. The dazzling day. 1912 it was, before they had moved in. "Honeymoon Land," or so it was called. Newly-minted suburbia. Modern Houses for Modern Couples. This dazzling day, they said, was the day an airman, Italian, heading for Hendon, had found his engine faltering high over Honeymoon Land and, seeing Broomfield Park, had attempted to effect a landing. The aeroplane was, though, by now flying so low that its wings, they said, touched first one roof and then another before finally settling, with a murmur, upon the slates of 75 Derwent Road.

Fig. 3. Photograph of 75 Derwent Road, Palmers Green (1912). Enfield Local Studies Archive.

Mrs. Woolf, apparently, had said that *in or about December, 1910, human character changed.* In Palmers Green it had surely changed two years later, changed with an aeroplane upon a slated roof and a stranded aviator, a continental traveller emerging from a wounded butterfly. He had waved, they said, waved to the Honeymooners below, waved from his suburban Alp, waved as if he had something to communicate, just like, so like, the aeroplane even now assaulting *the ears of all the people … in Pic-*

cadilly. But what was it? What was it? What had he been trying to say? *What word was it?*

The traffic stammered an answer, and Marie strained to listen; but here, now, were *boys in uniform, carrying guns ... and the wreath ... to the empty tomb.* The Cenotaph, they are marching to the Cenotaph. Greek, it was, for *empty tomb.* Yes, but what might it mean *to be the mother whose sons have been killed*? What might it mean to be a wife?

Johannes, though, had not fought. He was thirty-four at the outbreak and, besides, he too was an Alien. He had still volunteered, saying he had languages and that he was ready to prosecute the War with words. To be an Interpreter. And he did get a letter, from the War Office. But he had merely been placed upon the Waiting List.

❧

Her own tomb, as it were, was an empty tomb — having no dead sons to mourn, nor buried husband. Empty, perfectly empty, she thought. And, as the boys in uniform disappeared toward Whitehall, she remembered the annual silence. November silence. It had been strange to hear it at home, all that silence, on the wireless. Just Johannes and her. In the front parlour. Throughout the whole two minutes she had sat and covered her ears. Johannes had stood, his arms stiff at his side. It was, she had said, at the end, as if he were still awaiting The Call. From the War Office. He had asked her not to make light of the silence.

❧

The Swiss Observer
— November 17, 1923 —
We Swiss are as deeply concerned in Armistice Day
as any other nation.
(Editor)

❧

The Swiss, Johannes had added, were always readied for war. He had then pointed to an old slip of paper he had drawn from inside his jacket. On it, he said, were lines once set down by the Linguist. Swiss, of course. See, said Johannes, war is even on his mind. "Victory all … along the line." "Advancing with all … big guns." Johannes ran his finger along the words. He then looked up. The War, he added, *had* reached the Alps. True, it was only the Dolomite Alps, but all the signs of the War (the bones, the wire, the shells, etc.) remained. Bloodless signs.

This perpendicular Flanders, vertical Somme, could still, apparently, be seen, seen in the snow. "Snow," Johannes had remarked, "is itself an engine of war." Yes, she had said. Yes, she knew, for *she had read late at night of the retreat from Moscow.* Poor Napoleon, she thought. Defeated by Russian snow. Repelled, by the cold. The snow.

Now, however, at last it was the Spring, and she must head for Regent Street, where the windows would surely be glorious. As she walked, she thought once more of the Alps, and the dead. Yes, there had been the young men, the soldiers, but there were also the others. The others who had died in the Alps. She had read of them in *The Swiss Observer,* a London weekly that Johannes used to take. The Organ of the Colony, he called it. Each and every week, it seemed, someone had fallen to their death whilst walking the Alps. Pleasure-seekers they were, such as Miss Lina Schwarz, a telephonist from Geneva who had ascended the Pointe Pelouse in Savoy when, suddenly seized with dizziness, she fell off. Apparently.

A man atop a passing omnibus nodded. But the bride, she thought, is married to another. She then paused to open her bag; an over-night bag, Johannes had called it. Yes, all she might need.

But why mourn just one victim of the Alps? In the Alps, she heard, you could not move for Calvaries. Over the years, so many had fallen and died that, at almost every turn, every climb, there was a cross, a Golgotha, yet another Saviour. It was absurd. *When a man … says he is Christ … you invoke proportion.*

Yes, the man on the omnibus might nod but people would continue to die falling. Such as, for example, that *Eton tutor, a nice young man … [who] now lies at the bottom of a crevasse in Switzerland … crushed beside his [fiancée] Mary … the two bodies for ever … frozen*. Both of them.

And what, she wondered, might it be like to fall with another? Miss Schwarz, the telephonist, had fallen, whirled, descended alone, but what would it be like to plummet hand-in-hand? And how would you be remembered, the two of you? Would it mean that not one cross but two might mark the place where you finally shatter? And, if the two of you were married, might a future passer-by interpret the crosses as witness to both a *Christ … and Christess*? Or even, dare she say it, a Mr. and Mrs. Christ? She liked the idea of married Saviours. A single cross had always puzzled her.

A seedy-looking nondescript man … stood on the steps of St Paul's Cathedral …. Why not enter in? he thought, [and] … put this leather bag stuffed with pamphlets before … a cross, the symbol of something.

Marie paused before St. James's Church. Why not enter in? Yes, why not? Because its cross would be empty, and today, just today, she did not want reminding of the Resurrection. Poor Mary being told not to touch her risen Lord, not to hold on tight. No, she would not enter in. It is true that she was reborn, that she was washed in the Blood, and that she had *seen the light … years … ago,* but today she might see the dark.

Marie looked behind. Was he following her, the Linguist? He had followed her before, or somebody had. Somebody like him. But she would not quicken her step. *He started after her. … Was she, he wondered, … respectable?* And *was* she? *Was* she respectable? There were, of course, all those nights spent apart. But then *he … insisted, after her illness, that she must sleep undisturbed* and, besides, Dr. Stopes, the famous Dr. Marie Stopes, had always advised that husband and wife should have separate bedrooms.

Her own bedroom, in the mornings, had the light. It would wake her early. Johannes's bedroom, though not communicating, was just across the landing. *The supreme mystery ... was simply this: here was one room; there another.* No, not a mystery, Johannes would say, merely an arrangement, an arrangement of souls. And, "no soul," said Dr. Stopes, "could grow ... without spells of solitude." Marie missed him nevertheless. Her soul, she said, missed his. But, he said, she could always ring him. It was his joke. Honeymoon Land, Johannes would say, was possessed of an excellent telephone exchange.

Once, as if to prove his point, he had added that *people were talking behind the bedroom walls.* Yes, she had said, people did talk. She had read in the *Recorder* that, in Palmers Green, "girls who went into service discussed their mistress's failings with freedom."

Marie suspected that Nelly spoke freely; and, more than once, had aired her suspicion. "Breathes there a woman with tongue so tied she never discusses the servant problem?" the *Recorder* had asked. No, she had murmured; her tongue was never so tied, least not her French tongue. If she and Johannes ever wished to keep words to themselves, to puzzle Nelly, they would simply talk in French.

She thought again of the Linguist. "Suppose," he once had said, "suppose someone pronounces the French word *nu*." Suppose indeed. And suppose, she thought, just suppose you were overheard by a girl who understood French, who knew that *nu* meant "naked," and who might also see someone naked, and with another? What then?

But just a word, just a word overheard, even such a word, what could that betray? What could that prove? Besides, she thought, what could spoken words ever prove? They come, they go. As the Linguist had once whispered, "It would be impossible to photograph the utterance of a word."

On and on she went ... up Regent Street, now thinking of all the teeth in Paris, and all the x-rays she had taken. The surgery had been so busy. And how much she had seen in the wide-open mouths, the *lips gaping wide.*

The other day she had read, in the *Recorder,* "Do you examine your children's teeth?" No. No, she did not. Besides, her qualifications were not recognised here. Not in England. So, no, she examined nobody's teeth, and did not desire to do so. What could be seen within the wide-open mouth was, at times, quite unbearable. *Pneumonia in* [*the*] *throat, for instance, the germs* [*forever*] *copulating.*

She walked on, as another shower whipped her cheek. And, through the rain, she saw a woman who wore a mackintosh, a green mackintosh. It was *Miss Kilman standing still in the street for a moment to mutter, "It is the flesh."* Marie nodded her assent. *This Christian … woman* was right, so very right. But not the green mackintosh, in that respect Miss Kilman erred. She, Marie, was also a Christian, married to Christ; but the bride was still to be beautiful, and so should never wear such a mackintosh. Miss Kilman, she had heard, was even given to *standing … upon the landing in her mackintosh.* A large dark motorcar crept by, its new tyres piano-black.

Yes, Miss Kilman stood on the landing, and yes she, Marie, had also lingered, some nights, upon the landing. At Johannes's door. And there, right there, *she would think what in the world she could do to give him pleasure (short always of the one thing).* Some nights she would even go into his room, *and he could see her with tears running down her cheeks going to her writing-table and dashing off that one line.* Strange, how it often ended that way. Sometimes she would write that same one line again and again.

In the morning, she would wonder at her writing. Page after page, and always *that one line.* The night of truth, she used to say. The Linguist, however, had always said of writing, "We must be aware of its defects." The Linguist had not liked writing, not liked to set things down. He had, in fact, never written her; instead, he would whisper. Through the traffic. Writing, he believed, was a wretched poison, and was now even infecting speech, pronunciation. "In Paris," he had sighed, "in Paris one already hears *sept femmes* with the 't' pronounced."

But, why *sept femmes*? she had asked. Why not *sept **hommes***? Or *sept **rues***? Why seven women? Were there only women in Paris? The Linguist had said nothing, and she had apologised.

She had been speaking like one of Mrs. Pankhurst's women. Such women were legion in Palmers Green. Some had even set fire to the letterbox at the corner of Fearnley Road. Its gaping mouth had smoked like a gun, and when the box was opened the Royal Mail was nothing but ash. It had been a kind of treason. England had trembled.

And on she walked. Dear England, she thought. Her father, he was English, but her mother was French, and she herself, Marie, had chosen France for her passport. A blow had been struck; a window broken; a brick dislodged. She had betrayed the Kingdom, connived against *this isle of men, this dear, dear land*. She had chosen to be not English. *To be not English even among the dead.*

As she walked, Marie thought how long she had continued her betrayal, it becoming a secret treason, a secret un-weaving, a nightly work of nothing and tears, a nightly not-thinking of England. And it almost made her smile at the policeman who, just now, had arrested the traffic.

How little the policeman knew. How little he could have guessed. For instance, that she was a friend of the eminent Linguist. Or that he, the Linguist, had a wife who was also called Marie. How little, too, could the policeman have guessed that within but half an hour she, Marie, Johannes's Marie, as it were, would undress. *Women must put off their rich apparel. At midday they must disrobe.* Her finest underclothes would be laid on a chair, her body cast in Russian perfume, and she would be alone in a room with a man who was not her husband.

Marie quickened her step, *crossed Oxford Street … and turned down one of the little streets … Now, and now, the great moment was approaching.* Yes, here was Queen Anne Street, and here was number 20. She stood before the door and rang. An ambulance passed by. The door was soon opened by a girl who led her along a corridor and into a faded room. A waiting room. She declined the invitation to remove her coat and stared at a door that led to another room. *She made to hide her dress, like a virgin protecting her chastity … Now the door opened, and … for a single second she could not remember what he was called.*

The man in the doorway was known to both her and Johannes; known, though not well. He smiled. All would be fine, he said. They would not be alone; there would be a witness. It was the only way and would be for the best. He then withdrew.

There were, she now noticed, two others in the waiting room. A man and a woman. They looked up as if she were a guest and this their drawing room. The man stood up and introduced himself as Hugh Whitbread, the woman beside him being Mrs. Whitbread. *They had just come up, he said, to see doctors. Other people came to see pictures, go to the opera ...; the[y] ... came "to see doctors."* Marie nodded, sat down, and drew from her bag a book. Mr. Whitbread coughed, desiring to speak. *His wife,* he explained, *had some internal ailment.* How openly the stranger spoke. Johannes never spoke of ailments, or complaints, but then *Dr. Holmes [had] said there was nothing the matter with him.*

❋

The High Court of Justice

I do order that Inspectors be appointed to examine the parts and organs of generation of Johannes Schad to report whether he is capable of performing the act of generation; and also to examine the parts and organs of generation of Marie Schad and to report whether she is, or is not, a Virgin, and hath or hath not any impediment on her part to prevent the consummation of Marriage.

(W. Inderwick, Registrar)

❋

Something had changed. It was the Whitbreads. They had gone. And in their place stood an older woman, a nurse, a kind of angel, grey. Would Mrs. Schad care to follow her? The seraph was beckoning her back toward the hall and, once there, led her to a staircase. *Like a nun withdrawing, or a child exploring a tower, she went upstairs.* At the third turn or break in the staircase, Marie stopped. It was a little larger than the landing at home. She looked out. Our lives, she thought, are Swiss. At last, she could see forever. And flinched.

But what could *he* see? Johannes. He had always said that from Basel one could see Israel. Or, so said the Zionists. Milk and honey, etc. From Basel, he would say, the Promised Land could at least be seen, if not entered. Like Paradise, she thought. The nurse coughed. Marie had heard much about Paradise, but knew it was not for all. Dr. Stopes had written about a newly married couple who thought they were "entering Paradise" but were, apparently, mistaken.

A horn sounded in the street, and Marie followed the nurse up another flight of stairs, then through an open door. She paused once more. Here, at last, she would be seen. Dr. Stevens looked up from his desk, rose to his feet, and moved toward a basin of water. He washed his hands in silence. The nurse motioned Marie toward a curtain. *Women … at midday … must disrobe.* The policeman would once again stop the traffic, and she would now undress. The bride, she thought, is beautiful. The Linguist had smiled when first she had said this, as if he too were about to talk of beauty. But no. "To speak of a linguistic law," he had remarked, "is like trying to lay hands on a ghost." The doctor washed his hands a second time. She closed her eyes. Tight.

❀

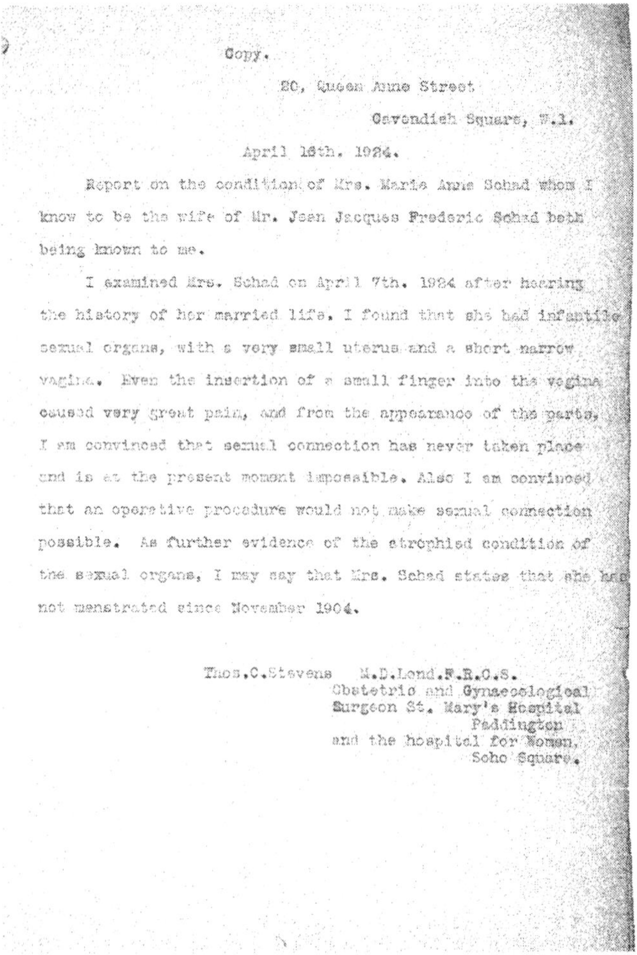

Copy.

20, Queen Anne Street

Cavendish Square, W.1.

April 16th. 1924.

Report on the condition of Mrs. Marie Anne Schad whom I know to be the wife of Mr. Jean Jacques Frederic Schad both being known to me.

I examined Mrs. Schad on April 7th. 1924 after hearing the history of her married life. I found that she had infantile sexual organs, with a very small uterus and a short narrow vagina. Even the insertion of a small finger into the vagina caused very great pain, and from the appearance of the parts, I am convinced that sexual connection has never taken place and is at the present moment impossible. Also I am convinced that an operative procedure would not make sexual connection possible. As further evidence of the atrophied condition of the sexual organs, I may say that Mrs. Schad states that she has not menstrated since November 1904.

Thos.C.Stevens   M.D.Lond.F.R.C.S.
Obstetric and Gynaecological
Surgeon St. Mary's Hospital
Paddington
and the hospital for Women,
Soho Square.

Fig. 4. Report of Gynaecological Examination, April 7, 1924.
The National Archives.

After it all, and once outside, Marie stood in the doorway. She closed her eyes again. Tight shut again. And here she might have stayed. In very great pain. But, there were still the flowers to buy, and so she began to walk. Very slowly.

She *must* buy the flowers, she thought, as two men passed by. *"I have come over,"* said one, *"to see lawyers about the divorce."* She knew there was a flower-stall nearby; she had passed it on her way. Ah, there it was, vivid with every possible colour. Red? Yes. And she would have them wrapped. Thank you. Behind her, two smart women waited, one laughing and the other talking of *"men … who sent their wives to Court."*

Marie, though, would *not* be sent. She would go of her own volition. And she would take flowers. "Are flowers," she asked, "allowed in Court?"

※

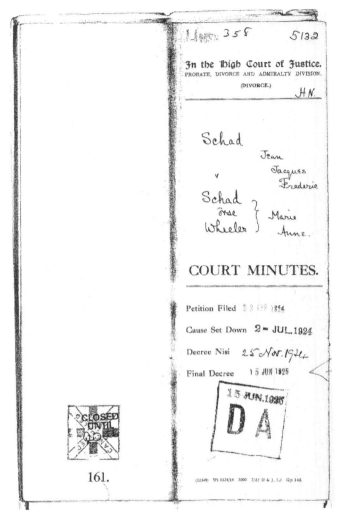

Fig. 5. Court Minutes of Schad v Schad, née Wheeler.
The National Archives.

Day Two

November 25, 1924

Marie had brought some flowers with her and held them tight. Her coat matched the dark of the vast, stone-built, entrance hall. She did not particularly like the echoes or footfalls. Nor the whispers. Another cathedral, she thought, and sat down. The bench was cold.

Beside her was a tall, angular woman. "It is to be an annulment," whispered the woman. She paused, then began again: "Dr. Stopes herself has had an annulment." Marie lay the flowers at her feet. "It happens, you know," whispered the woman. "Dr. Stopes has written, I believe, about a nullity case that took place after twenty years of supposed marriage."

Marie did not care for the word "supposed." It was true that she and Johannes had rarely made a show of their affection; true they had not always spoken over dinner, unless Johannes had invited guests. But a couple need not make an exhibition of love; need not speak, nor even touch. Two can, sometimes, simply lie together, hearing the same sounds, feeling the same air press upon their limbs. And two can, surely, sleep apart. As Dr. Stopes herself recommended. *A little independence there must be between people living together.*

Yes, she thought, yes, a little independence; *a room of one's own,* a bedroom of one's own and, above all, a bed in which one could inhale fresh, un-breathed air. She sighed but would not cry. Not now. Not here. Her shoes, she thought, were worse than ever. She then looked up. Across the hall stood Johannes wearing the same black suit he had worn in that wondrous summer of theirs, in Paris, on the very day they had stood side-by-side, before God and Man. A miracle it had been. Then.

A clear, light voice was now heard above the whispers, and echoes of whispers. It was his name and hers. His first, that of the Petitioner. Then hers, that of the Respondent. Should they enter together? No, they should not. She would enter alone. But first, and with the flowers. Violet.

The Courtroom was dark and, once within, the Usher, a pale man, showed her to a seat. The judge, it would be Sir Thomas Horridge, should soon appear. Marie caught Johannes's eye. He looked down. *The business of copulation was filth to him before the end. But this may not be the end.* The world might turn. Sir Thomas could surely see to that. He was a Knight. And here he came. She straightened her hat. Had the Usher noticed her hat? Or, *was it that she had taken off her wedding ring?*

"Marriage," began Sir Thomas, "is founded on words of Divine authority." To dissolve a marriage would, then, be to dissolve God. She looked around. *Perhaps, after all, there is no God?*

Sir Thomas now called upon the evidence of Dr. Stevens, to be read by Johannes's barrister, a thin man. The first testimony concerned herself, but she would not lower her eyes. The thin man's voice rose and fell; at times loud, at others quiet. Some words she heard, some she did not. "Very great pain," she heard. "Not since November 1904," she heard. "Both being known to me," she heard. Was it not strange, she thought, to be seen by one to whom they were already known?

"Not since November 1904" — she heard the words again. "Not since November 1904." She closed her eyes tight shut. Paris, Johannes, and their courtship froze beneath her eyelids. Bloodless. No trace of blood, none at all. She had known what this could mean, but it could not have been the case. And she had bled no more, thereafter. No more the Curse.

She wished to say something, but the thin man had begun to read again, informing the Court that the Petitioner had successfully demonstrated himself capable of the act of generation. But *how,* was not said; or under what conditions, or before whom.

She must now speak, address the Court, the Crown as it were, and risk contempt. The assembled would doubtless turnabout, and all behold the bride, the still un-ravished bride. And, though she might suffer a rush of November blood, she would speak. She rose to her feet, still holding her flowers, and lifted her head. But Sir Thomas had gone, and the courtroom was already beginning, in silence, to empty. She looked across at Johannes, who mouthed, she thought, "I am sorry." His lips brushed the air. *He has left me; I am alone for ever.*

She had been, apparently, nobody's wife; there had been, apparently, no marriage to cancel. And she wondered by what English magic the Court had erased something which had never existed in the first place. Nothing. It was just as Mr. Eliot had written. Nothing again.

"But what," she said, aloud, quietly tearing at the silence, "what of the statement? Dr. Stevens's statement, it contains errors, the finest of errors." Her solicitor was already leaving. "Dr. Stevens," she continued, "meant to say 'menstruated,' but what the typist had set down is 'menstrated.' The *'u'* is not there." She waved a carbon copy of the statement. "Look. There is no letter 'u.' The assertion that she 'had not *menstrated* since November 1904' was, surely, inadmissible, illegitimate, a kind of bastard?"

Her solicitor had now gone. Marie would, though, continue to speak. "His name," she said, "the doctor's name, it's also wrong. It says 'Thomas C. Stevens' but it should say 'Thomas G. Stevens.' 'G' for George. Where there is a 'C' there should be a 'G.' Look. Look." Again she waved the statement.

Silence. There was silence. She looked around the Court. Only the Usher had remained. But he at least had listened; she felt sure he had listened.

And now, yes now, the Usher spoke. He wished to remind her of what the eminent Linguist had always said. Ah, the Usher too seemed to know him. The Linguist, he continued, had always said that words would change, and letters disappear. For example, the word "menstruated" might lose the letter "u," said the Usher, but such is merely the forgetfulness of language.

"Consider," he added, "the German word, *Bethaus,* meaning 'temple.'"

She looked puzzled.

"Recall," continued the Usher, "how the word had once been spelt Betahus."

Marie sat down, and the Usher concluded. "According to the Linguist, the change was but 'the result of an accident ... the fall of the "a" in *Betahus*.'"

No, she said. The Linguist had, for once, been mistaken; had been wrong to talk of the *fall* of the "a." No, the "a" had not *fallen* but merely moved, migrated. Whilst once the "a" came *before* the letter "h" (*Betahus*), now it came *after* the letter "h" (*Bethaus*). The "a" had passed through the "h" as if it were scarcely there. As the Linguist might surely have guessed, for he had also once said that the "aspirate 'h' … is an orthographic ghost." The "a," therefore, was *not* fallen, was *not* gone. No, it was simply elsewhere, in another room, as it were.

The Usher was perturbed; the woman, she was right. The Linguist had erred. Within the word *Betahus* there was no crevasse, no place to fall. It was as if the Linguist had somehow been thinking of an accident somewhere in the Alps. The Usher, deeply troubled, sat down; the woman would now develop her case.

"If," she said, "the letter 'a' had not disappeared, then perhaps she too, Marie Schad, would not simply disappear?" The Usher said nothing. "Instead, might I yet pass," she continued, "like the 'a,' through some door, some wall, and there, *like a nun who has left the world,* find asylum?"

She had risen to her feet but was possessed by a terrible dizziness. The Usher offered her his arm and inquired if she would like him to telephone for a cab. Yes, she said; to Victoria, for she would go South that night, toward Paris. And there she would meet the Linguist, who would arrive on the 8:45 from Geneva.

But did she not know, inquired the Usher, his face torn in two, did she not know that the Linguist was dead? That he had died in 1913? She did not move, her face as still as a doll.

Yes, she said. Yes, she had known, had always known. But the Linguist, she said, when last they met, had whispered, "Let us *begin* with death." Begin, she echoed, begin — not end.

There was, once more, the dizziness. The Usher again offered his arm and inquired if she were well enough to travel alone. He paused, then spoke again. Could he not (here he hesitated) — could he not *accompany* her? To the station.

Marie, for a moment, said nothing. Such kindness; she had never encountered such kindness. No, she said, gently. The man had not quite understood, had not quite understood this leaving like a nun, this leaving the world, this beginning with death. *This killing oneself.* She would, though, give to the man her flowers.

He thanked her.

Outside, the cries of the street welcomed Marie. *This killing oneself,* she thought, *does one set about it with a table knife?* She walked on. Or, she wondered, could one simply walk in front of a motor car? *In the midst of traffic there was the habitation of God.* And this killing oneself, she thought, should one set about it today, or next week? Or, exactly a year and a day after one's undressing, one's disrobing?

✺

— April 8, 1925 —

London … is shot with the accident I saw this morning … a woman crying "Oh oh oh," faintly, pinned against the railings with a motorcar on top of her. (Woolf)

Some diabolical official is playing about with our letters.
— Franz Kafka (1883–1924)

CHAPTER TWO

Trials

I/IV

Accused

No, dearly beloved, Marie did not walk under a motorcar. That was quite another woman, one who need not trouble us. Marie, you see, *did* make it through the traffic, and across the Channel, back here, to Paris. In fact, she first returned almost a year before. And, once here, she drew close again to her dearest friend, Madeleine.

She, Madeleine, is wife to one who was, as it happens, the Pastor of what is called the Tab, or Tabernacle. This is that most surprising Parisian thing, a temple or church of the Drowned. To clarify, it is a church of the *happily* Drowned, the fully-immersed people of God. Baptists, would you believe it. Yes, here, in Paris.

Marie herself once passed through the Tabernacle waters. This was when young and born again, some years before her English exile. Upon return, though, to the Drowned, she had news for the Drowned. Or at least for Madeleine.

> Marie's husband, smitten by a young woman seventeen years younger than himself, has turned her

> out. …. Marie … has agreed to facilitate a divorce
> by declaring that she has never had conjugal rela-
> tions with him. The divorce is on the pretext that
> Marie has infantile organs.
> (Madeleine Blocher-Saillens, May 1924)

❋

Hard words, are they not? But are they true? Well, it is certainly the case that Johannes is smitten by another woman. And,
yes, she is indeed younger by seventeen years. Born, 1897. As it
happens, she too is called Marie, Marie Haile; though Johannes
chooses always to call her "Marnie," gently insinuating an alien
"n." I can also testify that this second Marie marries Johannes.
This is in August 1925, in Sussex. Together they have three children, one of whom will become my father. Yes, my father.

What, then, am I now to think? What to make of all of this?
Here. Now. This evening. In this lecture. Above all, whom am I
to believe? Johannes, or Marie? The word of a doctor, or the diary of a friend? High Court, or Low Church? London, or Paris?
If Paris, Johannes becomes, in a heartbeat, suspected of both
perjury and bigamy. The view from the Tabernacle is, then, that
Johannes stands accused. My father's father, accused.

Being kin, blood-related, I should perhaps seek to defend Johannes; however, my only real thought, poor scholar that I am,
is this: that Johannes, as a man accused, may be likened to Herr
Joseph K. I think, of course, of the hero, if that is the word, of
Herr Kafka's fine and famous novel, *The Trial* (1925). Herr K., as
you know, is a man who stands accused. Indeed Herr K. is, as it
happens, a clerk, just like the young Johannes.

It is true, I accept, that Herr K. ends his life in a quarry and
in the company of theatrical executioners. Frock coats, top hats,
etc. Johannes, on the other hand, comes to an end in a suburban
bed, no killers in sight, with or without top hats. Johannes, however, is not wholly unfamiliar with execution. You see, he is, or
claims to be, the son of the son of the son of the son of the son
of the son of one Uli Schad. Poor Uli, a Basel weaver, was done

away with in 1653 for his part in leading, or attempting to lead, a disaster. A peasant rebellion, that is. The six other leaders were beheaded, like kings. Uli alone was sent, for still greater shame, to the gallows. And, with no Priest. No holy comfort, none.

Fig. 6. Etching of Uli Schad. Historisches Museum Basel.
Photo: Peter Portner.

II/IV

Arrested

Kindly allow me, dearly beloved, to start again. To recommence my lecture. And to do so by returning to *The Trial,* Herr Kafka's, and to the sentence with which it all begins. "Someone must have been telling lies about Joseph K." Astonishing. You see, Marie, or possibly Madeleine, *may* have been telling lies about Johannes. Here, in Paris. But, then again, perhaps not.

I will, therefore, now look into his case, and do so with the tools of my own clerkly trade. Books. Modern books. Such as *The Trial.* It is, please note, a book that many scholars, even real ones, believe to be born of the guilt that Herr Kafka once felt upon terminating an engagement to be married.

> I ... didn't visit her parents. Merely sent a messenger with a letter of farewell. Letter dishonest and coquettish. [It said], "Don't think badly [*schlechtem*] of me." Speech from the gallows.
> (Kafka, July 27, 1914)

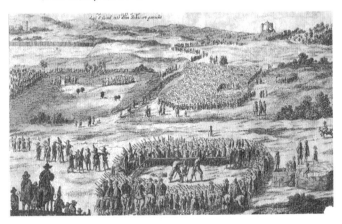

Fig. 7. Drawing of the execution of Uli Schad (ca. 1653).
Zentral & Hochschulbibliothek Luzern.

❋

These last exquisite words I stole from Herr Kafka's diary. They mirror so daintily, I think, the whole of *The Trial*: a man is accused, a man is condemned. Beautiful. *The Trial* in domestic miniature.

By the way, dearly beloved, have you noticed how very domestic, even (dare I say it) how very intimate, is the world of Herr K.? The courts, I mean. Wherever he turns, or looks, within the House of Law, he finds himself touch-close to a young woman. And every time it is a different young woman. Never the same. One, I find, in every room. And then there are all those beds. All warm, I think, with bodies. Like the bed in which Herr K. is arrested. Or in which the Advocate works. Or over which, upon re-entering the Court, Herr K. must clamber. Climb. Bed, bed, bed. Beds everywhere. Ah, how telling. How suggestive of the flesh and all its desires.

"No," you may say, a little disgusted. Beds, you may say, exist not merely to stage our sexual encounters. Far from it, you may say. A bed, you may say, also provides for falling to sleep. Or being ill. Or even giving birth. And all this I do accept. However, in the House of Law, the bed, I say, is finally and essentially, the conjugal bed. The scene of marital union. Conjugal union, you see, is the Law's great and secret preoccupation. Obsession, even.

Ah, you smile. Perhaps you don't quite believe me? Well then, watch, with me, the woman in the Interrogation Chamber. Herr K's. Come close, close up, and watch how the woman sleeps so beautifully alongside her darling husband, and then, all of a sudden, she gently stirs, wakes, and looks up only to see, looking down upon her, none other than the Examining Magistrate. With, no doubt, a kind of grin upon his face.

Again, take a closer look at Herr K. himself. Peer discretely over his shoulder, as he leafs through the books upon the shelves of the Interrogation Chamber. Now, what very particular book does he find secreted there? Any idea? Suggestion? No? Well, let me then enlighten you. It is, I am afraid, a work of pornography.

Conjugal pornography. Shameless, nevertheless. Its title, *How Grete was Plagued by her Husband.*

It is not, I know, the case that each and every husband is capable of plaguing his wife. Or at least not the husband (if husband he is) whom Herr K. comes across within another of the Court's many ancient volumes. It is, I fear, another book of doubtful character. This time with pictures.

> A man and a woman were siting naked on a sofa; the obscene intention of the artist was evident enough, yet his skill was so limited that nothing emerged from the picture save the all-too-solid figures of a man and a woman sitting rigidly upright and, because of the bad perspective, apparently finding the utmost difficulty even in turning towards each other.
>
> (*The Trial*)

The artist, I feel, very much hopes that these two lovers of his, naked as they are, should come together. He yearns for it, indeed. As do I. Sadly, though, this Adam and Eve, as it were, are so badly drawn, the perspective so very poor, that it would appear they will never be as one. Under the laws of classical perspective, they are doomed to remain apart. Forever.

How sad. How very sad.

But wait. These times of ours are, I gather, modern times. On the whole. And the world, I hear, is now full of art with no regard whatsoever for the iron laws of perspective. Think of such as the lawless Signor Picasso, or Monsieur Matisse. Think of them. No, don't just think of them — call them, telephone them if need be, and quick. Summon them here, now, this evening, to this very lecture hall, and ask them to view, all aslant and askew, our naked couple. And the outcome? The upshot? Why, it is that our Adam and Eve might yet be seen, thank God, to be about to come together. Paradise thus made possible, their relationship saved, redeemed. Hallelujah.

Hallelujah, indeed. Especially if, by the miracle of analogy, we might also come to witness the redemption of the marriage of Marie and Johannes. For they are also, you see, an all-too-solid Adam and Eve sitting naked together, rigidly upright, finding forever the utmost difficulty even in turning toward each other. Or so it is said back in London. And yet, what if Marie and Johannes are also only being kept apart by bad perspective? By distances that can yet be overcome? Overcome by something so ready-to-hand as a cool disregard for classical perspective? If so, if the case, then they too would yet find no difficulty in finally turning toward each other. They too might yet melt, at last, together. In union. Passionate union. Think of it.

❋

You have, perhaps, by now ceased to think of it. Had your fill, dearly beloved. If so, you may have spotted a flaw, or lacuna, in my argument, in your dear professor's thesis. Yes, you might say, it is true that the laws of perspective hardly obtain in the case of coitus; true that in the confusion of union, its rough and tumble, all such laws are suspended or broken. Nevertheless, you might add, Johannes and Marie's fate is sealed, fixed — there is no possibility whatsoever that they might yet come together. Not now. The past is forever the past, and simply cannot be changed. And to suggest anything other is absurd.

Fair point, fair point indeed. Were it not that Herr Kafka sees things otherwise. "I pray for the past," he says. Pray that it might yet change.

And why not? If God is God, then could He not choose to change the past? Rot, you may say. Change the past? The very idea. But it is, in fact, a not unfamiliar notion. Even among scholars of Theology, once Queen of the Sciences. So, let us pray. Yes, you and I, let us pray for Marie and Johannes. Just as the Drowned doubtless did. Indeed, let us pray so fervently that the past *is* eventually changed, and Marie and Johannes *do* yet somehow become one flesh. One. Amen.

I see you smile again. But I am most serious and will certainly pray, and upon my knees. And will do so in full awareness that *if* my supplication is answered, *if* Johannes and Marie do in fact come together, and *if* therefore Johannes never marries his second Marie, then *I would not be here.* I would, I realise, have prayed myself out of existence. As you can see, however, this is not, as yet, the case. Perhaps I am too solid.

Not so the pages of *The Trial.* They are, in fact, so thin, so translucent, so diaphanous that I can, as I say, glimpse through them the accusable figure of Johannes. Yes, Johannes. And I glimpse him most clearly when sweet Miss Leni puts to Herr K. two questions that I myself should like to ask poor Johannes.

Question one: Do you have a sweetheart?

Question two: Has she any physical defect?

※

Well, as you know, Johannes does have a sweetheart, even before the annulment. Or, so the Drowned say. She, this sweetheart, is to become Marie the Second, as if a queen. But does she, this second Queen Marie, have a physical defect? Well, does she? What do you think? No idea? Well, sadly, I must report that she does have a defect. You see, when Johannes first meets Queen Marie II, she is a consumptive. Or at least, she is a convalescent consumptive. At Bognor Regis, England, far in the royal south, far in the summer. A frail thing.

And what of Marie the First? Is it really the case that she has a defect? That, of course, is the overwhelming question, the question to which the appointed examiner, good Dr. Stevens, must speak. But, what does *Miss Leni* think? What is her view, or take, on Marie's possible physical imperfection? Or blemish? Her unfitness for marriage?

I see Miss Leni "raise her hand," right hand, pause for a second, and then stretch out two middle fingers, between which she displays "a connecting web of skin."

How curious that web of skin. Is it indeed her answer? Coded? Just for me? If so, Miss Leni, I think, concurs with Dr. Stevens. But Madeleine, in Paris, shakes her well-drowned head. "No," says her head. The good doctor is not to be trusted.

And neither, perhaps, is Miss Leni. She is, you see, no disinterested party. Offers no neutral, Alpine view. Her interrogation of Joseph K. is, in fact, pure seduction. Pure. Lower your head, dearly beloved, bend your ear, and hear how her questioning ends with her whispering, so sweetly, "You belong to me now." Me.

Beware, then, Miss Leni. Her voice so soft. As is her body, albeit out of joint. Just look at her. See how her advances are ever-so-slightly at odds with lovemaking's classical laws. The laws we know so well, you and I. "She clasped his head, bent over him, and bit … him on the neck." "She … scrambled up until she was kneeling open-mouthed upon his knees." "A final aimless kiss landed on his shoulder." Miss Leni, I fear, is in truth the pornographer's badly-drawn woman. Or rather, she is that woman just beginning to come to life. Making her first-ever amatory moves in the world. First-ever.

Clumsy?

Why yes, she would indeed be clumsy. As clumsy as a clerk on a bicycle, you might say. Or so Herr K. might say, seeing he is himself a bit of a cyclist. Oh, did you not know? Herr K. is in possession of a "bicycle licence." And thus also, I presume, a bicycle. All of which should warm Johannes's heart, presuming its tyres (the bicycle that is) are made of rubber.

Ah, rubber. Dear rubber. It everywhere encompasses us. And yet, the full extent of its ministry is still something of a secret. So secret, in fact, it is known only to a strange cove called "J.W.L." Full name withheld. A furtive fellow, as well he might be, possessed of this the very secret of our modern world. The secret that is the ubiquity of rubber. King Rubber, as it were. It is a secret that came to J.W.L. in a vision, a vision of a city. 1913 the year. It was a gleaming city that he envisioned at first, but one that, in a twinkling of an eye, was somehow denuded of all rubber. Of a sudden, he says, every office in the city was a ruin, every desk a wreck, as erasers resolved into dust, papers fell apart in confusion, and telephones, now without receivers, hung, limp, from tangles of naked wires. It was as if the end had come, the end of our world. Yours and mine. Rubber, you see, is our only defence. Against catastrophe.

You look uncertain. Unconvinced. Well, consider once more Herr K. He, who, in the moment of his arrest, the moment of his need to identify himself, to establish who on earth he is, reaches for (of all things) a bicycle license. Yes, bicycle license. In short, poor Joseph K. depends upon a document that in turn depends upon a bicycle that in turn depends upon the rubber of its tyres. Rubber, yes, rubber. Dear rubber.

And it is again rubber, again a case of rubber, when Herr K. comes to the Great Realisation that his arrest could not possibly have taken place at work, at the office. At home, yes; at the office, no, never. And why not? Well, because in the office he has upon his desk not only "the general telephone" but also "the office telephone," and each, he says, daily "stand[s] before me." Herr K., you see, knows he is protected by the telephones. They are, as it were, his guardian angels, angels that are made of rubber, yes rubber, albeit in part. Think, dearly beloved, of the receiver, or the casing for the wires, etc. etc. If only Herr K. had remained at his desk, enjoying forever the faithful protection of its rubber-edged seraphim. His error, his fatal error, was to leave the office. To go home. It was at home that he fell foul of the Law. It was there he was arrested.

❋

Ah, how strangely vulnerable we are, all of us, in our homes. Vulnerable to the Law, that is. It is a lesson I myself have learnt from not only the long-closed case of Herr K. but also the as-yet-open case of Johannes. You see, one moment Johannes is merely a man in a marriage; the next he is a petitioner in court; yet another (here in Paris) he stands accused of having a sweetheart.

Herr K.'s Uncle: What case is this?
Herr K.: A criminal case.

Indeed, a case of perjury. Not to mention bigamy; for, you see, if Johannes's marriage to Marie was only annulled on false evidence, then Johannes is still (or already) married when he marries again. Marries a second wife. Which is, I gather, against the Law. Bigamy.

But you, dearly beloved, may wonder by what authority is this case brought? Who am I to be interrogating my father's father? In whose name do I speak? Well, I would have thought that was obvious. Behold my gown, my lectern, this august auditorium. Yes, my authority is granted to me by scholarship itself. There is, you see, no more inquisitorial institution than this mystical body we fondly call the Academy.

In fact, on occasion, at night, I do discern something of the Academy's dark shadow in the case of poor Herr K.

"The real *question*," he cries, "is, who accuses me? What authority is conducting these proceedings?"

The real *answer*, I cry, is, the bloody Academy!

Herr K. nods at this. "This arrest," he whispers, "gives me the feeling of something very learned."

Quite, I say. And it is a feeling, Herr K., that must surely grow greater with every book that lines the courtroom walls. The walls that now surround you.

However, dearly beloved, we should not be surprised at this. Not surprised to find the Academy lurking about this particular House of Law. Herr K.'s, that is. After all, the man who first notifies Herr K. of his arrest is a man who is "reading a book." Yes, a book. Of some kind or other. Indeed, dearly beloved, if you open the door, the door to the office lumber room, the one wherein the whipping is going on, you will find not only "empty … ink-bottles," a "candle" and "a bookcase" but also a pile of "useless papers." Useless, please note. Behold, I say, the scholar's cell. Whipping notwithstanding.

You look a little doubtful. Well, to persuade you, allow me to offer you a citation. One of my very best bits of useless paper, as it were. It is a quotation from Herr K., as quotable as he is killable.

"There can be no doubt," he says, "that behind all the actions of this court of justice … there is a great organisation at work [which] … has at its disposal … an indispensable … retinue of servants, clerks, … and other assistants."

It would be hard, I suggest, to find a more telling description of the modern university. Not least our own.

Herr K. does, I confess, go on to claim that this great organisation "employs corrupt warders, stupid Inspectors, … police, and … perhaps even hangmen." Here, you might say, the resemblance to a university begins to falter somewhat. You might accept, with a shrug, that the world of scholarship succumbs to occasional stupidity and perhaps, just perhaps, some policing of a sort, a higher and necessary sort; however, I suspect you would draw the line at hangmen. Arguing, perhaps, that no university actually marches people out and hangs them, that there are no gallows in the quad, no gibbet in the examination hall, no lectures given from the scaffold. Or at least not here. Well, we shall see.

But what can already be seen is this: that insofar as Herr K.'s courtrooms do shadow-forth a university then it is, alas, that saddest species of university, a student-less one.

"There was a time," says the Advocate, "when several young students … worked for me, but today I work alone."

Rest assured, dearly beloved, I am not about to suggest that the Advocate's students have been marched out and hanged. However, do not forget the War. Do not forget how many of the students of Europe's finest universities were marched out and left in the trenches. Indeed, given our modern tubercular plague, those students not marched to the trenches are, instead, being put on trains to sanatoria where equally high death-rates are achieved.

Once there, however, once settled in their airy dormitories, some are busy, even now, creating universities of a wholly new kind. A sickening kind. The most famous is at Davos, the ski resort high in the Alps. It is a dazzling place. A dazzling place which, each and every year, thanks to a certain Herr Doktor Muller, hosts a dazzling philosophical knees-up. A symposium, if you must. Its purpose: to occupy the dying minds of the resort's more book-bound inmates. Poor souls. Or perhaps I now think of Herr Thomas Mann's intoxicating novel *The Magic Mountain* (1924), set, as it is, in an imaginary Davos sanatorium. Berghof, it is called, this sanatorium, and it is itself already a shadow-university, what with its meandering lectures and doomed romances. It is no miracle that Doktor Muller's annual symposium is known, to the knowing, as "the University on the Magic Mountain."

By the way, should you be wondering, Herr Kafka himself, although tubercular, does not go to Davos. True, it had once been on the cards. That was in 1920. August. And he was then already so ill as to be what we term, after Berghof, "a horizontaller." "You try to send me to Davos," he wrote. Indeed, in 1924, March, he declared, "I *am* ... going to Davos." Now, though, Herr Kafka is too ill, too horizontal, even to travel, even to seek the cure. Far too ill.

❃

III/IV

Frozen

It is, I accept, unfortunate that Herr Kafka never makes it to Davos, to the snow-capped roof of Europe. It is, however, a fate he always anticipated. "I [have] watched you," he says, "as I would watch mountain climbers from my deck chair." Herr Kafka, you see, is doomed to stay below. One could not, after all, be further from the summit of a mountain than when confined to a deck chair.

But, why on earth pass one's time watching mountaineers? "To see," he says, "whether I could recognise them up there in the snow." Well, good luck to him. From a distance, it is nigh impossible to recognise any mountaineer. Though that, perhaps, is Herr Kafka's point. That he cannot really see anyone in the snow. On the mountain.

"But wait," you cry.

Pardon?

"By seeing no-one in the snow does Herr Kafka not thereby see, or foresee, a very particular *someone* in the snow?"

Who?

"Herr Heidegger. Martin Heidegger. Philosopher. And occasional skier."

Continue.

"In 1929, Herr Professor Heidegger is in Davos, at one of the symposia."

Indeed. Albeit as thinker rather than skier.

"A fine distinction."

True. Especially since he is there to think about Nothing, or to be precise —

"*The* Nothing."

Excellent. Congratulations. It would indeed be perfectly legitimate to suggest that the No-One, or Nothing, which Herr Kafka sees in the snow is Herr Heidegger. Dear Herr Heidegger, up there with his goggles, baggy pants, and ageing skis. Ah, you smile. I am gratified.

❋

By the way, I do believe that Herr Kafka somehow always had Herr Heidegger in his sights. Herr Heidegger the *Nothing*-man, that is. You see, way back in 1913, Herr Kafka declares that "our task," the task of modernity, is "to accomplish *the negative.*"

With regard to this noble task, I am myself, as you know, doing my utmost. And will continue to do so by here observing that Herr Heidegger, our philosophical magician, accomplishes a "negative" that is, *mirabile dictu,* even more negative than "the negative." But how? By what rough magic? Well, Herr Heidegger himself says this, that "The 'Nothing' is more original than the Not and Negation." For Herr Heidegger, you see, it is not Negation which produces Nothing but the other way about. In the beginning, as it were, is "Nothing." That, you see, is the law that Herr Heidegger hands down from the Magic Mountain. Or rather, almost. For our magician wants no-one to run away, hot-foot, with what he calls the "nonsensical idea of a Nothing that 'is.'" And so I won't — run away, that is. Not at my age. Or at least not with such a foolish idea. Clearly, Nothing cannot *be.* Not as such.

And what is more, dearly beloved, Nothing cannot, apparently, be *thought.* Seek not, says Herr Heidegger, an *idea* of Nothing but an "*experience* of Nothing." A hard saying, is it not? Indeed, if true, Nothing would cease to be the business of the scholar. The man of ideas. Not, then, my business, and not even Herr Heidegger's. Or, at least, not the one on the mountain.

Though there is another one. Yes, another Herr Heidegger. His twin, if you will. This other Herr Heidegger, first name unknown, was the German master at some English preparatory school. Somewhere in the North, I think. Sadly, though, he was brutally killed. In 1904, or thereabouts. He was, in fact, riding a bike just before he was killed. A very nasty affair. You may perhaps recall it, for the crime, in the end, was solved by none other than the famous Mr. Holmes, Mr. Sherlock Holmes. The detective. By the way, in solving the crime, Mr. Holmes made much of Herr Heidegger's bicycle tyre, its precise type and design. Its tread, indeed. However, my particular point, or thought, is that this other Herr Heidegger might be said to have had, in fact, an "*experience* of Nothing." Of Nothing on wheels, as it were.

No. Sorry. Correction. Not even *this* Herr Heidegger will really do, seeing that the nothing of his death was merely a negation of his life, his vivid, cycling life. That is all.

And much the same may be said of even Herr K. Another dead cyclist. Also killed. Or executed, perhaps. In his case "like a dog"; and even dogs live before they die.

As do all of us, I gather. Mind you, there is or was (or perhaps was not) that still-born child who, in January 1916, "was found," at a post-mortem inquest, "never to have lived at all." I saw this in the Palmers Green *Reporter*. Marie's local newspaper, in London. As you may know.

But I stray, decline, fall off. So must return, to my point, my Alpine point, or question. Which, now, is this, that: *If,* in 1929, up there in his snowclad tower, Herr Heidegger is really scanning the horizon for not just negation but rather Nothing itself, and indeed the Nothing which must be experienced, or felt, *then* does he not somehow glimpse poor Marie?

After all, it is Marie, apparently, who knows, really knows, not the mere negation of a thing-that-once-was but rather Nothing itself, full-blown and pure. It is, indeed, a Nothing that has been the case, they say, for nineteen years. There having been, they say, *no* marriage. None at all. She and Johannes have been, they say, merely two people who happened to be, for the most part, within the same lonely house, the same lonely bedroom, even the same lonely bed, at least on occasion. That is all, they say. At worst, it is, I fear, faintly indecent, an almost living-in-sin. At best, it is, I suppose, all rather modern, even avant-garde.

Either way, they say, it has not been a marriage. Or at least not as defined by the Law, flesh-minded as it is. Flesh-minded since, for the Law, it seems, it is either coitus or nothing, penetration or nothing. This is also the founding principle of pornography. So I am told. I now know why a courtroom library might include some books of filth.

Mind you, Herr Kafka always knew. Being a knowing fellow. And what he knows all too well is just how peculiar is this entanglement of Law and Flesh that we (you and I) call marriage. Such a strange entanglement. Deadly entanglement. "Through marriage," says Herr Kafka, "I shall perish." In short, marriage, for Herr Kafka, is a kind of Nothing.

Correction. Nothing is, in fact, what he is as an unmarried man. He believes, you see, that "marriage [would be] the dissolution of the nothingness" that he is *already,* as Bachelor Kafka, Herr Kafka the single-man. Marriage, then, would serve to Nothing the Nothing that Herr Kafka already is. It would render him doubly Nothing.

To view all this another way: were Herr Kafka ever fool enough to marry, he would finally become something or someone (a married man, that is) which would in turn make possible, if not inevitable, his immediate annihilation.

You follow me? If not, try this: "The smile on your mouth was the deadest thing alive enough to have strength to die." Thomas Hardy.

By the way, being alive enough to die is not an error that Herr Kafka cares to make. Or at least not alongside Felice Bauer, the woman with whom, as his bride, he would be doing (or sharing) the dying. Herr Kafka, you see, considers marriage to be an elaborate suicide pact. A case of till-death-do-us-*not*-part. "As a child," he tells Felice, "I used to … look … at a bad colour-print depicting the suicide of two lovers. [It was] a winter's night, [and] … the couple stood at the end of a … landing-stage, about to take the decisive step." Once again, two badly-drawn and frozen lovers. Poor Felice. Dear Felice.

Dear Felice, indeed. If not, Dearest Felice, as in "Dearest [Felice], of the four men I consider … my true blood-relations, Grillparzer, Dostoyevsky, Kleist and Flaubert, [only] Dostoyevsky … got married; and … Kleist, when compelled to shoot himself on the Wannsee, was the only one to find the right way out."

What Herr Kafka, by the way, fails to mention is that Herr Kleist blasts himself to Kingdom-come on the clear understanding that his bride, Henriette Vogel, will do likewise, that she too will suicide on the Wannsee. As indeed she does, obliging to the last.

Dear Felice, though, will have known all this, known that the Wannsee is where lovers agree to vanish. Hand in hand, as it were. It is, then, no wonder that when Herr Kafka has a dream about, of all places, the Wannsee she, Felice, is hardly amused. "We were ... in the Wannsee," he writes, "which you didn't like."

As the dream continues, our two sorry lovers "pass ... into ... a cemetery." In Herr Kafka's dreamy head, the Wannsee means, for lovers, quite simply, death. Once upon a time, it was Kleist and Henriette with their smoking guns. Now, it is himself and sweet Felice dream-waltzing through graves. "We passed through a wrought-iron gate as into ... a cemetery, and had many experiences, for the telling of which it is now too late."

❀

I should, perhaps, here offer two pale observations. Each drawn from useless papers, scribbles, notes-to-self, found somewhere toward the broken back of a broken drawer. In that broken desk of mine. They, my notes, are as follows:

1. Both Herr Kafka and Felice are, undoubtedly, Jews.
2. Wannsee signals the end for many a Jew. Some lovers, some not.

In this latter connection, I think of a certain meeting or gathering held at a snow-bound Wannsee mansion in 1942. January. It is a meeting of minds and views. Perspectives, as it were. Not to mention, the very best wine and food. A symposium, if you will. And the disputants are there to ponder a question, a very particular question, the Jewish Question. They are there, in fact, to find an Answer to the Question. This they do, over their food, the bread, the wine, etc. And, in the end, the Answer to the Question, they say, is what they call The End. The End of Them All. You may have heard of It. Heard of the ditches, the busy little gas-vans, the showers that are not showers, and all the other masked houses of execution, the houses that house six million cemetery experiences for the telling of which it is now too late.

Yes, too late. Too late for telling. But not too late (not, at least, by my watch) for arguing. Arguing that Herr Kafka somehow sees, or foresees, something of all this, all this dying, in the shape, or form of *marriage*. Odd, very odd, I know — so near as this is to saying that Herr Kafka feels unable to marry Felice because thirty years later millions of fellow Jews will be married to everlasting night, each marriage a shot-gun marriage, as it were. Yes, odd. Except for this: that both the institution of marriage and the organized murder of millions entail the careful administration of flesh. To put this a better way: both, in their respective ways, oversee the throwing together of naked bodies. I am sorry to say this, dearly beloved. So sorry. You know how, on occasion, I grow dark. But remember, please, that dear Herr Kafka sees within marriage not only "dissolution" but also "that I shall perish." Perish. Remember too that Milena Jesenská, another sweetheart of Herr Kafka's, a later sweetheart, will die in a camp. Ravensbrück. The concentration camp.

So, to take this further, allow me to ask you a question. A difficult one, as if this were one of our little examinations. Concentrate please. The question concerns Felicia and Milena, lover one and lover two, respectively. The question is as follows:

How far and in what ways is it possible to argue that the disquiet felt by Felice from within Herr Kafka's Wannsee dream ("you didn't like it") anticipates what Milena will later endure within one of the very camps that serve to realise Herr Hitler's Wannsee dream?

You look confused. Allow me to simplify the question:

Is it possible that Herr Kafka's *first* beloved might glimpse the death of his second beloved? In short, might we say that the two Wannsee dreams are woven together? Herr Kafka's dream and Herr Hitler's. The lover's dream and the executioner's. Might we say that? Might we? Might we? Answer me. Answer.

Well, I think, myself, that, yes, we might say that. Might well say that. And, indeed, I *will* say that. If only because Herr Kafka believes, above all, that those who love and those who are dead prove the closest of neighbors. "Kisses," he says, "don't reach their destination, rather they are drunk on their way by the ghosts."

Again, I am sorry. I have, just now, misled you. Quoted a little out of context. An old scholar's trick, crime. Sin, even. I shall, therefore, seek redemption. Confess, right now, in the relative dark. Confess that, in truth, Herr Kafka has in mind not just any kisses, not just any old kisses, but "*written* kisses." Yes, written.

Mind you, some would say that, in a sense, *all* kisses are written. That all kisses are cold kisses. Kisses that fail. That fail to unite, to join. That, however passionately we embrace, however intensely we kiss, we somehow remain apart. Unfed, as it were. Doomed. "The ghosts won't starve, but we will perish," says Herr K..

The work of perishing, of dying, is not, you see, something undertaken only Out There, or Elsewhere. In, say, the ditch or the van or the shower. In fact, forget ditch, van, and shower. The dying is here, right here. As close as our breath, as our lips. Yours and mine, were we to kiss. All lovers, you see, however close, do somehow freeze. Somehow die in the snow. Believe me.

❋

IV/IV

Posted

By the way, talking of snow, do not forget how very difficult it is to be recognised in the snow. Both literal and metaphorical snow. I am thinking now, in particular, of Herr Kafka's unfortunate sisters, all three: Gabriela, Valeria, and Ottla. All three, you see, disappear into the Wannsee snow, without record or trace, no-one knowing exactly where or when. No-one.

The case of K.'s beloved, his second beloved, Milena, is very different. For scholars, even bad ones, *can* establish, and with exquisite clerical precision, the where, when, and why of her passing. *Place*: Ravensbrück. *Date*: May 17, 1944. *Cause*: kidney infection.

There. Perfect. Milena, you see, is not a Jew but a Catholic. She is deported not for her blood or breeding or (if you must) who she is, but simply and purely (yes purely) for what she does, does for the Czech Resistance. And that is why we have place, date, and cause. Why she stands out in the Wannsee snow. Why she leaves there, out there, a perfect Christian print. Perfect.

Like Marie, in fact. For her too we have place, date, cause, where, when, why. All carefully filed. Tucked away. Somewhere or other in that windowless cell of mine. I also have, here and there, the annulment papers. On the floor, I think. Beyond that, however, all I have are a few pages from Madeleine's diary, a tearful Tabernacle obituary and, from Marie herself, in her own poor hand, just one stray letter, from 1909, along with a single postcard. That is all. That is it. Nothing more. Nothing.

The postcard, by the way, is sent from a village in Brittany, up North. Frozen North in fact, the card being stamped (boot on face, as it were) January 5th 1942. Just 15 days before the snow began to fall forever at Wannsee.

So, then, what we have, apropos Marie, is next to nothing, and then, of a sudden, out of all this next-to-nothing, a postcard from January 1942. A postcard from Wannsee, if you will.

Fig. 8. Letter from Marie to Madeleine (January 5, 1942).
Blocher Saillens Archive.

❀

There are, I suppose, precious few postcards from Wannsee. Most of those who might have sent them now lie, face-down, in the Wannsee snow. Being Jews. That Marie manages to get a message out is a Tabernacle trick, a sleight of Christian hand. Those with whom she is staying, her Northern hosts, are, you see, also the happily-Drowned. What is more, Madeleine, to whom she writes, is now, by roundabout miracle, Pastor of the Drowned. Their Shepherdess, as it were. This postcard is, then, a second Christian print in the ice. A frozen cross, as it were.

But there is, believe me, still more, to this, to this icy sign. It being also, or nearly, an Hebraic scar, a Jewish wound. An ice-cold Star of David, if you will. You see, here in France, by 1942, the rumour, the murmur, among the Protestant few is that they will soon be pursued just as the Jews are already pursued. "After the Jews, without a doubt, it is our turn," says Madeleine.

And this is in November of 1942, that is to say several months *after* the Great Round Up, the *Rafle du Vel' d'Hiv.* Here in Paris. You recall? The city-wide Midnight Rehousing Scheme. July

16th. Dead of summer night. Thousands of sleepless Jews all swept away on silent buses. All off, they say, to the *Vélodrome d'Hiver.* To where, in less exceptional times, hibernating bicycles go around and around in circles. But not now.

No, not now, for things here are different now; there is, alas, no time now for going around and around. There are more pressing tasks. Like proving you are Christian. Always difficult, I find. But one way is to wave, like a handkerchief, your Certificate of Baptism. If you have one, dearly beloved. I refer, of course, to a Certificate of *Infant* Baptism, *Catholic* Baptism. Proper baptism. Which, naturally, only a few of the Protestant few possess. They are, you see, in peril, more than they have been for centuries. Or so they murmur, behind their pulpits, exchanging sorry stories of their fathers' fathers' fathers, persecuted ancients called Huguenots.

"The Germans," says Madeleine, "have allowed only children under seven to stay with their mothers." She thinks of the Jews. But adds, "exactly as they did to the Huguenots."

This last may or may not be true. I do not know, to be honest; but the darkest Huguenot day, so dark as to be more of a night, is, doubtless, St Bartholomew's Day, 1572. August 23rd. A famous massacre, it was. At a famous Paris wedding. One that went wrong. Not the first. Nor the last. This wedding, though, went so very wrong that it ended with thousands of stiffening Huguenots. It all began, they say, with good King Charles IX taking pot-shots at his fleeing Protestant guests from an upper-floor window of the Louvre. The window was open.

In Paris of old, you see, one use of an open window was to kill Protestants. In modern Paris, open windows are, I fear, being occasionally used for the killing of Jews. Although they jump from the windows, they are in fact pushed.

But what, you may wonder, is my point? At this late stage in my discourse. Well, it is that here in France, Catholic France, it is so easy to mistake the children of Abraham for the children of Luther. In fact, the mistake is most often made by Luther's tribe itself. They are, I find, the most confusable of children. In particular, the drowned ones, the Baptists, such as they are. As but a few of the few, remnant of a remnant, they, the Drowned, fall time-and-again for that most faded Christian dream. The dream that the Church is, in the End, at the Last, to be God's new Israel, the latter-day children of Abraham.

Yes, a dog-eared dream, is it not? But it is most passionately dreamed by whoever they are that dream at the Tab, as they call it. Tabernacle, that is. And what name could be more Jewish? Indeed, what thing, or object, could be more Jewish than the first-ever Tabernacle? You know, Jahweh's tent-for-the-Wilderness. His wigwam, big-top, marquee. Where He sees you, face-to-face, if you are Moses and all-at-sea in the sands, the desert, the Wilderness. And (again) my point? What is it? Well, that Marie, as one of the Tab, is that queerest of fish, a dream-Jew, a Jew by force-of-desert-mind, desert-dream.

But, perhaps, you do not quite believe me? Well, then, examine that postcard from the North. Marie's. It is, I suggest, a card not only from the Wannsee but the Wilderness.

> Dear Madeleine,
> After a good period, Sara has had a sudden turn for the worse. This morning her temperature was 38 degrees, and this afternoon 39. There is nothing we can do to control the infection. Naturally, she is very weak and scarcely able to eat. Mme Matthews, however, always so kind, has prepared some woodcock and quail. These Sara has managed to eat. Please pray that she be delivered.
> Yours,
> Marie

"Yours, Marie, *The Wilderness*," as it were. The Wilderness of the Jews. Her sister, you see, Sara, you see, is an invalid, you see, nigh-unto-death, you see, and yet both, you see, are daily sustained by providential kindness. And this kindness, you see, includes gifts of poultry, which, in turn, includes, you see, of all possible fowl, all possible species, the quail. Yes, quail. Of all the birds in all the sky, you see, quail was, you see, the very bird, you see, sent from Heaven, to feed the Jews. In the Wilderness. Yes, the Wilderness.

I can myself, even now, hear the howling Sinai wind. Not to mention the cry of Israel. Her cry for deliverance. And can you? Here, this evening, in our darkening auditorium.

No?

Well then, listen. Listen, I say. Listen, as, with Sara on the very verge of desert-death, Marie begs Madeleine to "Pray that she [Sara] be delivered." Yes, delivered.

Fig. 9. Portrait of Sara Wheeler, Paris (1897). Blocher Saillens Archive.

✻

No, wait, please. Don't go. Not yet. I have had a thought, of a sort. A question. It is this: does Marie ask Madeleine to pray for Sara's deliverance from *death* or from *life*? Quick. What think you? Come on. Death. Life. Which is it? Always a hard one, I know. Well, the fact is, Sara does not die. Not yet, at least. So, *is* she delivered or not? Has a miracle happened or not?

No, I don't know either.

Indeed, come to think of it, I don't even know if Marie's prayer is heard, received. After all, if written kisses may not reach their destination, then what chance written *prayers*? In particular, prayers written on a post-card, and thus so easily drunk along the way to Heaven by not only ghosts but postmen. Curious postmen. Perhaps, though, Marie's postman heeds her call to pray. Perhaps he falls to his postman-knees in the street. And perhaps his postman-prayers are answered. Indeed, perhaps Jehovah listens best to men in the street. Or at least, better than he listens to men at lecterns. Perhaps. It is difficult to say. As we say. You and I.

✻

Things, though, are not always difficult-to-say. Certainly not in the case of poor Milena, or indeed the unfortunate Kafka sisters. Alas, no ambiguity there. No twisting hermeneutic agony. No riddling postcard over which to do a-song-and-bloody-dance. These women, these Wannsee women as it were, are most certainly *not* delivered. They are lost, without question, without shadow of doubt. No ambiguity, none. None. Indeed, with respect to these particular women, I am, I fear, left with nothing to puzzle over, nothing to examine, nothing to interrogate. I am in short, redundant. Pointless, even, you might say.

"The enquiry into Nothing puts us, the enquirers, ourselves into question." So says Herr Heidegger. And, I fear, the bastard might be right. Right with respect to the almighty Wannsee

Nothing that does for Milena, et al. Not to mention the nothing that is annulment, the nothing that does for Marie.

Am I, then, in the end, at the last, to be put so far into question that I too become as nothing? Am I? And, if so, will anyone ever attend to me again? Will you? You, my beloved students. My fellow enquirers. Or will you too disappear, like the others, the other students, those long-ago departed to the trenches? Or sanatoria. Leaving me alone, with no-one to speak to, face-to-face.

You may smile, but it happens, and to the very best of scholars. Even, for instance, to the eminent Linguist himself, Professor de Saussure. When giving his towering lectures on Sanskrit, at Geneva, he would, most years, behold an ever-diminishing audience. As one fine and loyal student recalls, although the first lecture was full, "at the second, there were only twenty of us; at the third, three; [and] at the fourth, I found myself alone with a Bulgarian woman." Alone, think of that. All alone. Albeit with a woman. And who is young, no doubt.

It is easy, you see, to find that one's course is a vanishing course, that one labours within a university, which is, if you will, a university of the disappearing kind. So easy. Please, then, dear students, do not abandon me. When, one night, I reach the very end of the very last of my lectures, do not rise and go with a cheer, or hoorah.

Do not, that is, be like the Genevan student, Herr Albert Riedlanger. On July 3rd 1907, "when the final bell rings" at the very end of the last of the lectures given that year by Professor de Saussure, the treacherous Herr Riedlanger closes his notes with: "Finis, D. G." Being translated, "It is finished, by the Grace of God [*Deo Gratia*]."

※

Now. Listen carefully. Read my falling lips. One final coda. And it is this: that I will not have the eventual cessation of *my* intellectual labours attributed to the Grace of God. I will not, that is, have Jehovah invoked when I finally end my great enquiry, and the theatre empties, and I am, once more, null and void, and hanging out of an open window.

Do not be thanking God then. No, do not ever be thanking God. Not hereabouts. Within the university. For what on earth has the Almighty to do with the labours of the modern scholar? I accept that I may, this evening, have invoked his name once or twice, but for this I apologize. I was foolish. Weak. Please be assured that I have not, in any substantive manner, allowed God to dull my thinking. Scholarly thought, if professional, must be finally independent of religion. And certainly cleansed of all pietistic phrases or terms. Such as, for instance, *Le Seigneur,* as Marie or Sara would say. Enthusiasts both.

Beautiful they may be (I am not blind) but their holy rumours are intolerable. To be prevented. In the end, at the end, and in the Final Analysis, those who speak of God will simply be silenced. Or at least that is my intent, my avowed intent.

And it is, dear students, with this avowal, this promise, that I come to the end of my lecture. Right upon the bell. Please, then, allow me, ladies, to be the first to exit the theatre. Ladies, I must make haste. Make way.

❋

> It is reported ... that when men are in danger ... they have no consideration even for beautiful strange women ... [not even] if these women happen to be in the way of their flight from the burning theatre.
> (Kafka, 1910)

❋

Fig. 10. Marie or Sara Wheeler, c. 1905.

We … have decided … to reply … to the riff-raff
who make a profession of thinking.
— The Surrealists (1930)

CHAPTER THREE

Coffins

The year of Marie's return to Paris, 1924, is also the year that saw, in that same city of light, the birth of Surrealism.

1924 ... that year when catastrophes were the day's small change.
(Louis Aragon, *Paris Peasant*)

❋

I/V

Fairground

Marie was not familiar with the fine men and women who emerged from a building that looked like a church. It seemed as if a funeral service had just ended. One of the women, who stood at the door, was in full mourning, whilst some were weeping and stopping to speak with her as they left. And all the while an almighty hot wind blew wild, threatening to lift heavenwards the long dresses of the women, not least the dress of the woman in mourning, the seeming widow.

Fig. 11. Still from *Entr'Acte* (Paris, 1924), directed by René Clair.
Les Ballets Suedois.

Fig. 12. Still from *Entr'Acte* (Paris, 1924), directed by René Clair.
Les Ballets Suedois.

Before the apartment, in the road, stood a hearse. It was, though, a peculiar hearse, decorated with stars, and festooned with paper chains and the strangest wreaths one could imagine, being made of bread and ham. The fine men and women, each one a mourner, she presumed, fell into order behind the hearse in rows of three. All were formally dressed, and some indeed wore huge garlands of flowers. Among them she saw several top-hatted men who were, she presumed, the pall-bearers, though there was no coffin in view. None. Marie watched as one of the top-hatted men picked regally at a wreath of bread, and ate a little. Of the bread.

The coffin-less hearse was not motorized, but horse-drawn. Or rather, it was designed to be drawn by a horse, though where one might expect to see a horse there stood a camel. A solemn-faced beast. And beside the camel stood a man dressed in frock-coat and cocked hat. Like a man of the theatre, she thought.

Once the mourners had assembled behind the hearse, the cortège, led by the camel, began to move off. The hearse, however, proceeded at a pace that caused the mourners to pursue

Fig. 13. Still from *Entr'Acte* (Paris, 1924), directed by René Clair.
Les Ballets Suedois.

rather than follow, and to leap and bound. This they did as if grief had become, for them, an everyday ballet and their feet knew nothing of gravity. Gone now were all tears and, as the cortège departed, Marie could see it was headed not for a cemetery but a fairground, Luna Park. As if, she thought, they knew that death were overcome, and the camel would lead all through the eye of the needle.

Marie had intended, that morning, to walk to the Gare de Lyon to meet the eminent Linguist. She had imagined she would meet him alighting, descending, from his train, the 8:45 from Geneva. She had, though, somehow gone astray, been blown west across the city, and now found herself here, amongst these leaping mourners. But who exactly were they?

She would ask a passer-by, a pale and upright man, an Englishman newly arrived, it so happened. He stood upright, as if a soldier, and clutched, as if a rifle, a bouquet of now-dead flowers. She thought, indeed, that he had a somewhat familiar face; but could not quite place him until he remarked that he was, he thought, the Usher, from the High Court, in the Strand. London. He then explained that the leaping mourners, not to mention the camel, were agents of the Revolution.

"Which Revolution?" she inquired.

"The Surrealist Revolution," he replied, before adding that it had but recently begun, here in Paris. He did not entirely approve, but did appreciate the absence of bullets.

The Usher, she thought, seemed to know much about the Revolution, so asked if he could please say a little more. What, for instance, was its dearest tenet?

"An absolute commitment," he murmured, "to chance, accident, hazard. If such truly exists."

The Usher appeared to be a little troubled by talk of chance, but to find comfort in recalling that Professor Saussure had once declared that "everything … in language is … completely accidental." The Usher hastily added that this had nothing to do with the eminent Professor's proclivity for gambling. This he whispered, clearly desirous that neither mourners nor camel should know that the Father of Modern Linguistics was a man half-in-love with hazard.

The Usher now affected a cough, or rather a clearing of throat, as if to reprimand himself. He had been found guilty of digression and would return to the matter arising, the Revolution. In the first instance this seemed to mean pressing into Marie's unadorned hand a book called *Liberty or Love!* Date of composition, "December 13, 1924," he chimed. It was, he said, a loving disaster of a novel. A surrealist disaster, a hymn to chance. Newly born. But written, he felt, just for her. "Take, read," he said. Marie thanked the Usher, who went upon his way, a-marching. She herself would follow the cortège. And as she did so she opened the book, quite at random, just as some of the saints had done.

"Strange destiny," she read, "by which … the Mermaid and the Chanteuse pass … each other in a … Paris suburb." She looked up. Then read again. "Strange destiny, by which you or I … take a seat … in front of the very person who is able to unite us with the man or woman who has been lost." But did she wish to be united, or re-united, with such a one? A lost one? Perhaps she had no choice. Perhaps this city, this now Surrealist city, was so condemned to chance, to hazard, that any and every encounter were possible.

She opened the book again, once more at random. This time she read that a man called Corsair Sanglot and woman called Louise Lame, along with some polar explorers and madmen, all "inadvertently united on the arid plain of a manuscript." She looked up and considered the arid plain of Paris, this manuscript of a city. She could see no madmen or polar explorers, unless the mourners counted as such, but perhaps there, over there, she espied Mademoiselle Lame, or rather her reflection in that window, shop-window. Ah, yes, how beautiful she was.

Marie once more broke open the book; this time, speedily, as if she were a thief. "Take off your clothes," she read. "The fisherwoman's dress falls to the ground," she read. "The naked woman knocks hard upon every door," she read. And paused. Yes, she had knocked upon doors, many a door, often with Madeleine. They had the Gospel to proclaim, and so had gone knocking,

Fig. 14. Photograph of Machlis "Bebe Cadum" Posters, Paris.
Roger Viollet / TopFoto.

seeking to save the lost, those lost within their homes. She had
not, though, been naked. Not when knocking upon each door.
Not gone without clothes.

She thought now of London, the clinic, and Johannes, and
of how he too, like her, had been subject to examination. Once
more she turned to the book.

"On reaching the second floor," she read, "the young man
knocked at the door of an apartment. A tall foot-man in gold-
rimmed livery opened the door and showed [the young man]
into a vast reception room [where] ... flunkies gathered about
him. The ... Club [was] an immense organization ... employ[ing]
women the world over to pleasure the most handsome men."

Johannes, she thought, was a handsome man, and indeed she
had herself, on occasion, attended to him. As it were. But that,
perhaps, was not the act of a wife, more the labor of a woman
who simply happened to aid in the spilling of seed. Seed sufficient to conceive, she had heard, half a world. She paused and
thought, for a moment, of half a world. Half a world unborn.

Hundreds of millions of lives not lived. Again and again. Unborn again and again.

Marie returned to the book.

"The wind," she read, "buffeted the city [and] … Bébé Cadum beckoned." Ah yes, she thought, the laughing billboard child, the quite impossible child. "From the top of the buildings," she read, "Bébé Cadum watches." "Beneath the Bridge at Passy," she read, "Bébé Cadum was waiting."

But was the infant waiting for *her*? If so, then she must find him, embrace him, comfort him. This child of hers. Hers? Impossible. Inconceivable. But not absolutely. After all, she had read that even spilt seed can, on occasion, be effectual. The still unravished bride, even though not quite a wife, may yet prove a mother. Miracle children existed. Impossible children were possible. "Bébé Cadum," she read, "was born without the aid of his parents." She looked about the fairground. Where was this child? This holy child? Where? Where? Had no-one seen him?

She read on. The child, Bébé Cadum, she learnt, was newly imperiled, endangered, the victim of "an army," an army as impossible as the child himself, for it was, she read, "an army of pneumatic tyres." How she feared for the child. "The tyres," she read, "coiled around him." Yes, feared. "Bébé Cadum, or rather Christ," she read, "was thirty-three years old." Feared most terribly. "GOLGOTHA," she read. "Weep, you virgins," she read. "Weep."

But Marie did not weep. Not a single tear. She knew that pneumatic tyres could do terrible things, serve appalling ends, not least the wheeling of thousands of men to the Front. And yet that word "pneumatic" she cherished. For she had once, at the Tabernacle, heard faraway talk of "Pneumatology," a rumoured theology of the Holy Ghost, they had said. God, the Holy Ghost. He who had once burst upon Jerusalem in the form of an almighty wind to inaugurate an age of signs and wonders. And such, she knew, could still be looked for. Madeleine called it "Revival." In America and Wales, they spoke of "The Awakening."

Marie thought again of the skipping mourners and, as even as she did so, someone behind her announced "The Great Awakening of the Universe." She turned to find it was another passerby, this time a Poet, apparently. Beneath a bowler-hat. The Poet welcomed her to Luna Park, Paris's finest fairground. He then added that, unlike the pale Englishman, he was unequivocally *for* the Surrealist Revolution, the Revolution of Mourners, as it were. "The Great Awakening," he cried again, gesturing toward the mourners.

Hallelujah? Should Marie whisper "Hallelujah"? Perhaps. She would ask the Poet, ask him if now, today, at Luna Park, the Kingdom had come. The Poet looked around, at the water chute, the vibrating bridge, and the scenic railway with its miniature trains that climbed a miniature mountain range. "Salvation is nowhere," he replied, adding that this was his favourite Surrealist outrage. He also remarked, in passing, that he only ever spoke in quotations — words that had fallen through the holes in the trouser pockets of his Surrealist colleagues. At this point he cheerily threw his bowler hat into the air, as if saying "Salvation is nowhere" were much the same as saying "Salvation is everywhere."

No, she thought, broad was the path to Destruction, and narrow the way to Salvation. The Poet must understand this, must see that Salvation was not everywhere but somewhere, of a very local habitation and address, a very particular street, as it were. And all this she explained, to which the Poet responded by whispering, "Let us go [then]. Let us go down the Good News Boulevard and make a show of it." Ah, she thought, Rue Belliard. He thinks of Rue Belliard, where the Tab was soon to perch, high up in Montmartre, among the cinema-theatres, there to communicate the Good News of Christ. Praise God for Rue Belliard, 163 Rue Belliard. It was a light in the cinematic dark, she said.

"Bravo for darkened rooms," replied the Poet.

"But why 'bravo'?" asked Marie. "Why 'bravo' for the dark? Why speak like that? With such disregard for custom? Throwing words so heedlessly to the wind."

"It was the bait I set for the unknown," he said.

"The unknown?" she said

"*L'inconnu*," he said, "the chaste and audacious nude [*nu*]."

The Poet, greatly moved by his word-play, now stooped to bow low before Marie, as if in solemn recognition. He was quickly joined by five of the mourners; each somewhat damp, washed clean by the water chute. Together they greeted the Poet, who at once introduced them to Marie as "lyrical misfits." The mourners doffed their hats, top-hats, and whispered, as one, "We are the [very] last kings." Then, without speaking, each last king took out a tiny piece of paper and huge royal pencil, and proceeded to set down a single word or phrase. "The new," wrote the first; "the exquisite," wrote the second; "shall drink," wrote the third; "wine," wrote the fourth; and "corpse," wrote the fifth. They immediately allowed their pieces of paper, as if divine litter, to fall gently to the fairground asphalt. Upon reaching the ground, the litter somehow fell into a miracle of syntactical order. Marie looked down and read. "The exquisite" "corpse" "shall drink" "the new" "wine." Ah, she thought, Scripture. Found Scripture. Holy Scripture. For was not Christ himself the exquisite corpse who, no more a corpse, now drinks forever the new wine? The new wine of the new Dispensation?

Yes, she thought, and she thanked the royal mourners. It was, she said, a sign, if not also a wonder. The mourners, in response, and as one, took a step toward Marie, as if to consider who exactly she was. The Poet would assist them by making three suggestions:

1. "[A] waxwork that fashion has stripped of their clothes."
2. "[A] film heroine who, in search of a lost ring, [is now] encase[d] … in a diving suit."
3. "A … girl abducted by a sultan [who] endures dreadful boredom in [his] seraglio until a bit of fun arrives in the shape of an aviator who has made a forced landing."

The mourners were unsure, divided. They were, though, unanimous in believing that here, before them, stood their long-sought-for muse, *l'Inconnue,* the Unknown herself, she of whom they had only ever known the "vanished perfume." As if to confirm this, the Poet confessed that she was the "sweet woman of the winds." He then added, "This woman … I followed her around the walls of a convent. She was in full mourning." He paused, before resuming: "I was getting set, however, to catch up with her when she suddenly turned about, half-opened her coat and showed me her nakedness."

Marie, alarmed, turned to the Poet and asked upon what authority he spoke? In whose name, as it were?

"I get all my information straight from heaven," he replied. He added, however, that "I have never been a Christian. I do not understand the laws." He looked away, then concluded, wistfully, "I am an animal."

The Poet, thought Marie, is mistaken. Twice over. First, salvation defied the law. Second, salvation would surely not exclude the beasts of the field. It was true that, at the Tab, Pastor Saillens had once asked "Would Christ have died for mere animals?" implying the answer was "No." But, perhaps Christ would. Perhaps, indeed, He had. After all, God cared greatly for animals. It was clear. In the Scriptures. Had there not been room for animals in the Ark? Two of every species. Man and wife, as it were. What is more, when in the wilderness, "Jesus," it is written, "was with the beasts." *Among* the beasts, she thought, *there* for them, even, perhaps, as *one* of them. All this she now explained, to the Poet. She then paused.

Did the Poet understand?

He nodded, before grandly saying, "The doe … I carry wounded on my shoulders."

She could not see a doe or indeed any beast, wounded or otherwise, upon his shoulders, but the Poet continued, declaring, "Th[is] doe transfigures the world."

Yes, she thought. Yes, this poor man is not far from the Lamb, the world-transforming Lamb of God. Was, then, a conversion in the offing? Before she could ask, though, the Poet drew from under his hat a tiny crucifix.

"This cross," he said.

"Yes," she said.

"This cross," he continued, "commemorate[s] … an accident."

"An accident?"

"An accident that [had] happened to thought."

No, she thought. It was not an accident. Accidents were terrible things. Motor-cars the worst. She must, however, press on. Eternity was in the balance. Indeed, if this were Gospel Hour at Rue Meslay there would follow, right now, an invitation to respond, a call to the front, or to sign a Decision Card, or lift your hand or rise to your feet, a soul redeemed, in full view of all, before vanishing, newly reborn, into the Paris dark. She looked around, at the Poet and the mourners, her fairground congregation.

"Does anyone," she whispered, "wish to be saved?"

Silence.

"Today," she added.

Silence again, save for the roar of the water-chute. She then enquired once more, at which point the Poet stepped forward, albeit only half a pace.

"Salvation?" she inquired.

He shook his head, explaining that he was urgently required to "lead ... a lobster on a leash [to] ... the Palais-Royal."

"But what of salvation?"

"No theologian's argument will transform a Surrealist."

"Then what can?"

"Only the love of [a] ... female saint."

No, she thought. And flinched. No. Not love. Not that. Though there was death. Yes, death. A consummation devoutly to be wished, praise God. She turned toward the tiny mountain railway, thinking once more of the train from Geneva. What if, she wondered, she were to die, right now? Might that perhaps be sufficient to transform the Poet? If, say, she were to throw herself from a miniature train, to vanish down a tiny ravine, might that make him think again? Think of God?

Self-slaughter had never really crossed her mind before, certainly not in London, not even in the last days. Back there, in Palmers Green, it would have seemed a strange thing to do, an alien act. Here in Paris, it seemed a kind of commonplace, like a telegram. Here, almost every day, there was, in the papers, a report of suicide.

This she mentioned to the Usher, who had, somehow, reappeared. Dead flowers in hand. For a moment he stood to attention, then, with a sigh, he observed, as they boarded their miniature carriage, that the Surrealists were, in his view, excessively concerned with suicide reports. Indeed, they had made it their catastrophic business to reprint them under the quizzical headline "Is Suicide a Solution?" Two of these reprinted notices, however, had caught his own eye, he confessed. The Usher now drew a cutting from a pocket, and read it aloud.

> In Margny-les-Cerises, Madame … Marie Thiroux, … had got up during the … night, gathered her lantern and umbrella, and then threw herself down her neighbour's well.

The Usher took out a pen and slowly encircled the name "Marie." He paused as the miniature train reached the peak of the miniature mountain. He admired the miniature view. Switzerland, he sighed. He then drew forth a second cutting, from another pocket, and proceeded to read this aloud as well.

> Toward 4 o'clock in the morning, a tall, slender woman, walking … along the Quai des Celestins, suitcase in hand, suddenly … threw herself into the water.… The only things found in the suitcase were a few items of lingerie marked with the initial "W."

The Usher fell silent, leaving Marie to inwardly ponder this initial "W" for herself. And this she did. What, she wondered, if the "W" had stood for "Wheeler"? What then? Not that she had ever initialled her own clothes, let alone her under-garments, not even when she once had owned so many clothes. In the year of her marriage, when preparing her trousseau, she had, it is true, bought for herself no less than eighteen embroidered blouses and six petticoats, not to mention several girdles and ostrich feathers.

Marie thought again of that poor woman with the suitcase, and then of what the Poet, that revelatory man, had quoted or recited in the final seconds before she had hastened to board the miniature train.

"The corpse puts on its makeup," he had cried.

"The elegant gesture of the drowned," he had cried.

"She is the laundress of fish," he had cried.

And there had been more, still more, from the Poet's wild lips, even as her train had departed, still more prophetic fragments, fierce rags and tatters that plagued her, beset her, spoke to her.

"Your heart is a charade that the whole world has guessed," was one such tatter.

"Darling, ... I hasten to you. Here are my lips. Me ... damned, damned," was another.

"Perhaps, all she ever did was wake up at my side," was still another.

But the fiercest rag of all was his last.

"Marie's marriage was consummated — amid an overflow of sighs."

II/V

Lecture Hall

> Marie's marriage was consummated — amid an overflow of sighs.
> (André Breton and Paul Éluard, *The Immaculate Conception,* 1930)

Good evening, dearly beloved, I am delighted once more to address you and to argue, if I may, that this last surrealist rag, this *sigh*-blown rag from Messieurs Breton and Éluard, does somehow relate to my Marie, Marie Wheeler. To do so is, I accept, likely to lead to condemnation. To my being accused of forsaking scholarship's straitened gate, its narrow way. So: am I guilty? Guilty of misreading? Of confusing my Marie with another's, a surreal Marie. Marie and "Marie," as it were. Do I cross lives as others cross wires?

Perhaps. If so, forgive me. Please. But you see, I think only as these Surrealists do — they who discern, within the walls of Paris, millions of souls who, though oblivious to each other, live in the greatest possible proximity to each other.

Listen to just one of the surrealist crowd, M. Robert Desnos. Listen, hand to your ear, as he whispers this: that in Paris "remarkable people ... continually miss each other [but only] by a minute." And so they do. For just as the Mermaid and the Chanteuse cross in a dark Paris suburb, or Corsair Sanglot and Mlle Lame almost touch as they pass in the Place de la Concorde, so, I say, Marie and "Marie," real and surreal, come within but a sigh of each other. At the point of consummation. If that it is.

But perhaps you find it all too hard to credit that *my* Marie, my Tabernacle Marie, should ever stray into surrealist Paris, lobster Paris, as it were. This incredulity I do understand. However, observe, with me, just how closely, on one occasion, Marie, mine, comes to the Mermaid and Corsair Sanglot. It is when both Corsair and Mermaid are overlooking the Gare Saint-Lazare, and do so from the Boulevard des Batignolles. Yes, Boulevard des

Batignolles. As intersects, of course, with the Rue de Rome, the very road on which, at number 107, Marie, as a girl, lived and blossomed. Yes, the very road. What is more, still more, it is the road to which she returns in 1924, the very year in which both Corsair and Mermaid are imagined into very existence.

Here, let me show you, show you how the two roads cross, here on this skeletal map of mine, this one, the one scratched upon the blackboard.

Which blackboard?

Are you blind? Allow me, or rather M. Desnos, to give you a clue. Here goes.

"On the blackboard of a ruinous ... lecture-hall, lost in the lair of stray cats, Circumstance's black genius traces itineraries that cross but do not meet."

This is, you see, my ruinous lecture-hall. Welcome. Don't mind the cats. It is, alas, the best a black genius can manage. My previous lecture-hall burnt down. Remember? Besides, these are difficult times for the Academy. The Lobsters, you see, consider all scholars to be "false ... scholars." Moreover, they have been known, the bastards, to sabotage our lectures, rudely hurling themselves beneath the speeding wheels of our elegant discourse. They seek, you see, to "combat ... scholarly research," "want[ing] nothing whatever to do with those ... who use their minds as they would a savings bank." Well, sadly, we scholars have little choice. These days thought is our only wealth.

But this, I feel, the Lobsters forget. Take M. Aragon, for example, a ragged habitué of the Passage de l'Opéra. You perhaps know him? He, the clown, has nothing better to do than hang around lamenting that scholars do not stop at the Passage shoe-shine parlors and spend a while in the parlors' elevated arm-chairs, their "thrones of chance."

"Alas," he sighs, "professors tend to keep their shoes dirty."

Well, alas, we simply do not possess the money to have them shined. Nor do we share M. Aragon's high estimation of "thrones of chance." We scholars, philosopher-kings as we are, occupy thrones of quite another kind — namely, professorial chairs. These chairs of ours, our university chairs, may now be somewhat battered or fragile, but at least they have nothing to do with chance. Nothing. Besides, why clean one's shoes if only then returning to a lecture hall overrun with incontinent cats? Why?

By the way, forgive my prejudice, but I would not myself trust any man who wears well-polished shoes. As M Aragon himself remarks, "these days [it is] ... Don Juan [who] need[s] ... clean shoes." M. Aragon thinks, in particular, of "brogues with heels of laminated rubber," these being, apparently, "the shoes for adultery and seaside resorts." They are *not,* please note, the shoes for the Library or Common Room. Not, that is, the kind of shoes a scholar would wear. As I heard, just the other day, "rubber heels ... [are] for sport, not the office."

Or at least not the academic office. Rubber heels might, I accept, befit the commercial office. Unlike scholars, you see, commercial men are famously inclined to both adultery and the seaside. Consider, for example, Johannes. As you may recall, he first met Marie-the-Second while on vacation at Bognor Regis. She, a consumptive, being there to take the air, the seaside air. And, of course, if Johannes's marriage to Marie-the-First were *falsely* annulled, what the world takes to be a marriage to Marie-the-Second might, perhaps, be called adultery. At the seaside.

But does Johannes wear rubber-heeled shoes? Is he really guilty of an elaborate form of adultery? With Marie-the-Second, the Consumptive? Well, if he is, please do not overlook the sheer, post-card pathos of our seaside scene, a scene that M. Desnos has, I think, somehow spied upon. As if the butler.

"Happy is the consumptive," he murmurs. "Her breath ... [is] supported by a ... pillow of ... air," he murmurs. "[And] her fiancé [is] attentive to the tremor of her lips."

Ah yes, her lips. Yes, look. Examine her lips, those of poor, consumptive Marie, for there you might well discern a tremor. A sadness. Johannes, you see, is not her first fiancé. Before him there was, I must reveal, another beloved. An unknown soldier. Or at least unknown to me. But he was Lost. In France. Where so many fiancés are lost. Marched off and lost.

"Birds … have ghosts," says M. Desnos. And so too, these days, do fiancés. Johannes is certainly a kind of ghost, of the lost fiancé. But is he a rubber-heeled ghost? An accusable ghost? If so, he is, I say, very much on the mind of the Lobsters.

"I think," says M. Breton, "of all the men lost in [our] echoing courts of justice [who] … believe that they must answer — here for an affair of the heart, there for a crime."

Johannes?

Perhaps. But then, there are so many such men hereabouts. Paris at this hour is full of interrogated men, so many being, as M. Aragon says, "suspected of Surrealism." Indeed, some of the suspects are condemned, he says, to "be broken on the wheel and hanged." Amidst such a sorry mob, Johannes is difficult to spot.

The task may not, though, be impossible. There may yet be hope. Consider one very particular figure that M. Aragon observes, as ever, from and within the Passage de l'Opéra. Which, by the way, is itself condemned, soon to be knocked down, to make way for a road, a broad road, one fit for that coming king of the asphalt, the Automobile. Make way. Clear the streets.

I am sorry, I digressed. Albeit briefly. My point was, and is, that the figure to be noted in the Passage de l'Opéra is a "surly … man … playing with a hoop … and … magic wand," who is, we learn, "a regular customer … name of Sch—."

Yes, "Sch—." Might, perhaps, that be "Schad"? "*Johannes* Schad"? Is he the surly man? I do wonder. It is a possibility. There is a chance. Chance.

❋

I know, by the way, what you are thinking, dearly beloved. Namely, that if "Sch—" really is an elision or castration, as it were, of "Schad" then our man in the Passage de l'Opéra might just, theoretically, be myself, *Scholar* Schad. After all, our man does call his hoop the "wheel of becoming," a peculiarly learned allusion — to Buddhism, to be precise. So, *might* this man with wand and hoop be me? Is it I who have been spotted bowling my way through the newly-condemned arcade?

No. Impossible. Absurd. Although it is the case, I must confess, that I do sometimes escape this crumbling auditorium, out through the window, and off into the Paris streets, there pursuant of an academy *sans murs*. At such wondrous times, the arcade becomes my library, the cinema is my study, and the statues are my students, yes my students, with whom I speak, face to face. What is more, at night, I dream that somewhere within this wondrous extra-mural university I may yet come across some trace or rag, or rag of a rag, of Marie. Marie the First.

Allow me, dearly beloved, to explain. It won't take long. Believe me. You see, dear Professor Saussure once taught at the École des Hautes Études. This was back in the 1880s. At the time, he had one particularly fine student, a young man called M. Passy. He too is now a distinguished scholar, but he is also, as it happens, *mirabile dictu,* one of the happily-Drowned. Yes, a bookish Baptist. Indeed, a man of the Tab. Quite a coincidence. Remarkable, in fact, is it not? Moreover, and here is the thing, Professor Passy forsakes the four-walled academy to establish a free-to-all summer school. *L'Université Populaire,* it is called. A university *sans murs* that is open to every beast of the field. Doe, lamb, poor man, etc. And so, you see, whenever I clamber through the window of this here lecture hall, I dream of effecting what chess men might call the "Passy Maneuver," an extra-mural migration that will, thereby, somehow bring me nearer, however imperceptibly, to Marie, Professor Passy's co-religionist. His Tabernacle sister.

Yes, yes, it is, I accept, a desperate stratagem, a chasing of breeze. Pursuit of dearest nothing. But then, how else can I pursue one who does not exist? Not before the Law, that is. Or at least not as Marie Schad. And, by the way, please note that, even after the High Court judgement, my runaway calls herself not "Marie *Wheeler*" but rather "Marie Schad-Wheeler." Still a no-one. Or, at least, half a no-one.

And how do I know? Know that she signs herself "Schad-Wheeler"? Well, I have seen it for myself, this hyphenation, this

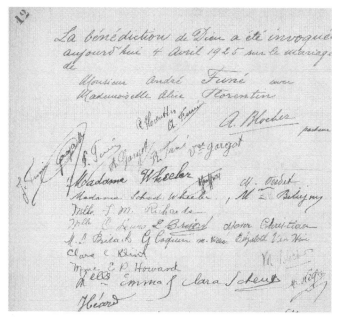

Fig. 15. Page from Tabernacle Marriage Blessing (April 4, 1925).
Blocher Saillens Archive.

coupling. Seen it upon a tiny piece of paper. Would you like me
to show you? It's somewhere here. Under a cat. Ah, here we are.
Be careful with it. Not the cat, the piece of paper. Look, see, it is
to do with a blessing, a blessing of some new-born Tabernacle
marriage. A kind of solemnization. And here, look, among the
solemnizing signatures, is "Madame Schad-Wheeler." Can you
see it? It's half-hidden. Among the crowd. Of solemn hands.

Quite something, is it not? How she signs herself? How, even
now, months beyond the annulment, she still bears the scar of
her marriage. A marriage that, according to the Law, never was.
Madame Schad-Wheeler has, of course, no legal existence. She
is just a juridical ghost. But, then, who better to counter-sign
this Tabernacle blessing? For it too has no legal substance, being
not the marriage itself — that was a pantomime of a civic kind,
an office panto, as it were. This Tabernacle blessing, in the eye

99

of the State, is a kind of nothing. If it is anything, it is a trick of faith.

As might now be said of Marie herself. Now that she is back in Paris, her life become a parable.

> There is one thing I should like to set down; it is the story of Marie Wheeler … [who] for 19 years never once gave any money to the church. … All I ever heard from her was to do with her house, her motor-car and her profusion of furs.
>
> Her husband had lost his faith and she maintained only an outward form of piety. One month ago she returned to her mother's and relayed to me her sad story.
> (Madeleine, May 21, 1924)

Behold the Prodigal Daughter. Marie, the Prodigal. Back from the far country — England, marriage, a house, and a profusion of furs. Not to mention a motorcar, one in which she might tour the far country. Waving as she goes.

A woman with a car is, I suppose, a rare and dazzling thing. A thing yet to come, as it were. Marie is thus, if you will, a migrant from that farthest country of all, the Future. But, then, she always was. Even in the days of her courtship.

> Marie wants, once more, to defer her marriage on the grounds that she is not sufficiently sure of the future. She'd like Johannes to earn 4,500 or 5,000 francs a year [but he] … currently earns 4,200, [so] … they each save 12 francs a year. Everything is calculated. They live only for the future.
> (Madeleine, January 25, 1905)

The future, alas, did not come — as you know. Or at least not the future for which Johannes and Marie had lived. Marriage. But, then, might it not be argued, painfully, abstrusely, theologically, that every Christian marriage is marked, nay wounded, by a future that does not come? I think here, now, even among all these stinking cats, of the Early Church. First century. The Primitives. You see, these earliest of Christians, it is rumored, only sought to marry once it had first become clear that their Lord might not return. Or at least, not within their lifetime. Remember mad Saint Paul.

> Brethren, the time is short, … [and] I would have you without carefulness … [while] he that is married careth for the things … of the world.
> (St Paul, Letter to the Church at Corinth)

In short, dearly beloved, do not marry. Sleep alone. Walk alone. Live alone. And think only of that Eventual Day. Last Day. Judgement Day. The day that shall see the return of Christ. The immortal Groom. He whose arrival will be a consummation to be *most* devoutly wished. For it shall be the consummation of His marriage to the Church. The *ekklēsia* herself. His bride. Her. The spotless one.

❋

I am sorry. Forgive me. I have fallen, head-first, into the mire of a sermon. Not to mention, another damned parable. Just as familiar and just as biblical. It is the one that exhorts us to look forward to the greatest wedding of all. At the end of time. You see, we, all of us, are, even now, to be busy, busy preparing the ecclesial Bride, beautifying the ecclesial Bride. Work, work. Wait, wait. Expect. And ensure that everything is ready, everything calculated. Tick-tock. Tick-tock.

But still, it seems, He has not come. Look about you. No end is in sight. Not to this present world. Still, it seems, the great Groom tarries. Still, it seems, the beloved Bride awaits. Still, it seems, the Marriage is deferred. Tick-tick, tick-tock. Yawn. Tick-tock.

So. Then. What shall we do? What shall we do meantime? While we wait. Well, allow me to suggest, or, rather, propose,

Fig. 16. Marcel Duchamp, *The Bride Stripped Bare by Her Bachelors, Even* (1915–23). Philadelphia Museum of Art: Bequest of Katherine S. Dreier, 1952-98-1. © Association Marcel Duchamp / ADAGP, Paris and DACS, London, 2018.

that in the meantime, in our boredom, we, I and you — yes you, in the front row, you — be married. He, Christ, has not as yet returned. Or so it very much seems, hereabouts. Therefore, let us marry. Let us marry notwithstanding the fact that our marriage will be made of disappointment, of the still-not-yet, the still-not-yet of the Marriage of our Lord.

Sad? Yes. In a way. But it is simply the slow, sad truth of Christian marriage. And not only Christian marriage in the days of the early Church. It is the sad truth of *every* Christian marriage. Ever since. For each such marriage is so thoroughly stained by the not-yet of *the* Marriage, the Marriage-to-Come, as to be a marriage half crossed-out, rubbed-away, erased. Like a face in the sand. At the seaside.

Poor Marie and Johannes are, then, you see, every Christian bride and groom, every Christian man and wife. Their disaster is ours. Yours and mine. Should we be Christians.

※

A little bewildered? Do not fear. I will scribble, or scratch, my proposal, my thesis, upon the board. My notes, my workings. By which everything is calculated, enumerated.

My work, I know, is rather controversial. Some do, indeed, denounce my work. Behind my back. Accuse me of a certain opportunism. For instance, M. Breton.

"Mathematicians," he says, "attracted by this blackboard, have taken advantage of the women's disappearance."

But what care I for Lobster Breton? Besides, my workings are just as careful, as taking of pains, as are the calculations of fellow Lobster, M. Marcel Duchamp. I think now of a dream-of-a-machine of his. He calls it "The Bride [*Mariée*] Stripped Bare by Her Bachelors, Even."

Odd, is it not? This machine. Where, you might wonder, is the bride? Where indeed? Well, she, apparently, is the figure at the top. M. Duchamp calls her the "motor-bride." But where, then, you say, are her heartless bachelors? Well, they, I gather, are represented by the machine at the bottom, what M. Duchamp calls the "bachelor-machine." Yes. Quite. I share your puzzlement.

Whatever, my greatest concern is that our two machines are, alas, far from united. Far from one flesh, as it were. M. Duchamp claims that what we here behold is a "*desire*-motor." Maybe, but it is hardly, I say, a marriage. Not in my book. This here, I say, is a work of eternal non-consummation. However devoutly it is wished for. Or desired, even.

And yes, machines do have it in them to desire. As do these two unfortunate machines, which together surely desire above all *not* to be what M. Duchamp says they are. Or amount to. Namely, a "celibate machine." What could be worse? I ask you. What?

What indeed. However, be assured that M. Duchamp's celibate machine is, by no means, *any* celibate machine. No. It is, I say, that most wonderful machine, the Automobile. This here "desire-motor" is, you see, "the internal combustion engine." In short, make way. Clear the streets. Here comes a glorious motor-car. In fact, here comes "a motor car [that is] climbing a slope, … as if exhausted, … [but that] turns over faster and faster until it roars triumphantly." Astonishing is it not? That this car, though so nearly exhausted, finally makes it. All the way. All the way to the top, the crown, of the hill. Ah, sublime. Sublime.

"But what," you say — painfully, cruelly, and pointing your elegant fingers — "what manner of hill is this?"

What? Well, I am not altogether sure. We are not told. Duchamp's notations are unclear. To say the least. We have, though, perhaps, three sorry clues. Yes, three. Three crippled clues. Here, see, look. Scratched. On the board.

Clue the First: The Bride is also known as the "Hung Woman."
Clue the Second: The machine is "a shiny metal gallows."
Clue the Third: A gallows is, invariably, to be found upon a hill.

So, what think? What infer? Deduce? No idea? None? Well then, I shall enlighten you. The hill in question, Monsieur Duchamp's surrealist hill, is a bloody execution hill. Where the State goes to kill. Quick march. Be gone, filth, be gone.

No, not you! Don't you go. Please. Not you. I'm not finished. Not yet. And besides, this hill, it is the sweetest possible execution hill — Christ's. Sweet Golgotha.

You look puzzled. But is it not clear? Clear as day? Crucifixion day. Monsieur Duchamp's clanking and naked bride is Christ, you see. Christ crucified. "Christ," he says, "was also stripped bare." So too *my* Marie. Bare.

Bare. Yes, as bare as Christ. Marie, my very own Christ. She who went, departed, lifted her skirts and ran, vanished, took her leave of history — and all for me. Had she not done so, I simply would not be. Not be at all.

Some, like Monsieur Breton, might in fact say I have taken advantage of a woman's disappearance. Shamelessly seized the opportunity to be born. But no. She, this woman, I say, somehow laid down her life for me. Greater love hath no-one. No-one. Not even you, dearly beloved.

✻

III/V

Office

"Ah, splendid — show in the infinite," said the Poet.

Marie entered, along with the Usher, and the cold of the street. She had visited two days before, on the Saturday, but had been told by two garlanded mourners that the Office was closing. Yes, this is 15 Rue de Grenelle, they had said. And yes, this is indeed, they had said, the recently established Office for Surrealist Research, as announced upon the door. However, it was 6:30 p.m. precisely, and Surrealists, they had explained, were most particular in their attention to clocks. Moreover, tomorrow, being Sunday, was to be a day of rest from surrealist labor. Even the Revolution had its Sabbath. Alas, she would have to return on Monday.

Marie had, for a moment, wondered what Surrealists did when not being surrealist, or at least when not conducting Surrealist Research. She had not enquired at the time, but did now raise the question of Sunday closure as she and the Usher sat down. The Poet, seated like half-a-king at his desk, considered her question. Her Monday question.

"The God within," he finally replied, "does not … rest on the seventh day"; however, the Poet, not being God (neither within nor without), most certainly did. Hurrah, as it were, for the Sabbath! "Lovemaking chapels," he murmured. "Glowing with Sunday happiness," he murmured.

The Poet now stared at a box of well-drilled index cards as if he had not quite seen their like before. "Lodging-House," it said on one the side of the box. "Ideas, Unclassifiable," it said on the other. There was also both a telephone and a Bible, three volumes thereof, upon his desk. He carefully rearranged the four objects, first in one constellation then another, before taking out his handkerchief and dusting all three volumes. "Secular dust," he muttered.

The Usher coughed a polite cough to draw forth the Poet's attention. The latter looked up post-haste but only to address

Marie. He asked, with scientific air, if she had anything to report in the way of dreams, coincidences, secrets, inventions, or indeed (and this he bellowed) "the intimacies of your bedroom." He added, in a whisper, that anonymity was, in her case, a given. He produced a snow-white index card, picked up a huge pencil, and appeared ready to set down whatever she might say. She said nothing.

It was, she thought, a peculiar place. On the one hand, it was an office, in the sense that everything here was calculated — there being a huge "15" on the door and a sign to boast not only opening and closing times but a telephone number. On the other hand, it was not like any office she had ever seen before. In one corner, stood a headless statue; while, upon the wall, was a book pinioned there by forks; and, from the ceiling, was suspended a plaster-cast woman — stripped bare, once more. Her again. The poet glanced toward her, this hanging woman. "The overwhelming law," he commented, "of [our] … invented country."

Marie now noticed that there were two others in the office, two men, attendants who were also ready, they said, to take down whatever she cared to say or confess. Or, did she have not so much *something* to report but rather someone to report? An enemy of the Revolution, perhaps? Someone with, say, a "passion for reduction … [Or, a] terror of the … Plural?" Did she, by any chance, know anyone like that? On the streets of Paris? There were a few around — in particular, "a sinister joker who, one evening near Châtelet, [had] stopped the passers-by along the quay … and … asked [each one]… 'What is your name?'" Had she come across this fellow? This desperate-to-know man, murderer of mystery, killer of the Unknown, the beautiful Unknown, *l'Inconnue*? Did she, by any chance, know this man? Did she? Had he perhaps pursued even her? Had he? This sinister fellow. Marie looked around, as did the Usher. They said nothing.

The Poet, as if defeated, slumped back into his seat. He paused, before beginning to tug a large logbook from one of the drawers in his desk. The book, it seemed, was reluctant to emerge, almost as if it were shy; but the Poet continued to tug, explaining all the while that the book was there to record the business of the Office. Its Research. He seemed not to like the word Research, or at least not altogether.

With a final tug, the logbook was dragged into the open. It appeared to be largely unused, almost virginal. The Poet flicked through the pages, a casual aviator passing high over many a blank, or empty space, each a pure white hole in Office time, Research time. Tick-Tock. He finally flew over a small crowd of names, as if huddled together. They were the names of those who had visited the Office on Tuesday, November 25th 1924. A busy day it had been, with visits from no less than five, quite perfect strangers. Two of the names intrigued the Poet — one being a Mademoiselle Terpsé and the other a Mr. Harold Tetley. A wondrous coupling, he thought. Terpsichore and Tea, as it were.

He stared hard at the man and woman seated before him, and wondered if they themselves were, perhaps, Tetley and Terpsé, now returned as lovers, or even to be wed. It was unlikely, he felt, but it was theoretically possible; there was a chance. Chance.

The Poet put this to one of the two attendants who declared no interest whatsoever in the identity of the man and woman. Instead, he wished to highlight the despotic fact that, for the most part, the Office for Surrealist Research would appear not to have been overly successful. Indeed, was it not the case that their logbook might best be described as The Golden Book of Our Inaction?

This contention prompted a violent Office colloquy. It focused, in particular, on what exactly constituted a book. Was there not something rather moribund about the seeming wholeness of a book? Indeed, was it not significant that the book per se, the codex, had been invented by that most moribund race, the Christians? And Christians, were they not, alas, lovers of the End? Those for whom God, in terms of revelation, was all but done and dusted? Yes, the Office for Surrealist Research was, it is true, indisputably the shop for *writing*, but it was of the Automatic kind: write, write, write, and whatever you do *dontstop-*

dontthinkgoodnessmenowhateveryoudodontthinkjustdontstop-tothinkjustdont. So, what had they, the Surrealists, to do with books as such?

The Usher felt moved to join the colloquy and thus enquired, very politely, if either of the attendants or indeed the Poet had any interest in the Classics? The Poet, though, was ready for this and, picking up a pen, *wrotewrotewrotewrotelikemadlikemad-likemadasmadinfactasamadmachineyesthatmadbloodymad.* He then turned the sheet of paper toward the Usher. "We have nothing to do with Literature[,]" it said. The attendants applauded, as if to say this was indeed the way to Change the World.

The Usher, though, was alarmed, and inquired what the Office did "have to do with" if it were not Literature? Was it not a place for research? Or was it, perhaps, a place in which research took the form of, say, mere judgment? Mere, naked examination? In other words, was this place of theirs, the Office, in truth, alas, a species of university?

The Poet appeared alarmed to be interrogated in this way, but was again ready. He gently explained that the Office was a "machine for killing."

The Usher asked for clarification.

The Poet replied that the Office was a "machine for killing what *is* in order to fulfil what is *not.*"

"Does that explain the headless statue?" asked the Usher.

The Poet said nothing, though pointed to a badly-typed document which carefully enumerated several points of order, house rules, the rules of Revolution. Break them, and one would be "liable to sanctions."

"Sanctions?'" said the Usher.

The Poet made as if to chop off his own head at the grimy nape of his neck, his ink-stained hand the blade of Madame Guillotine. "The Widow" herself. Marie flinched, and pulled from a bag the now dead-fish-of-a-book that the Usher had given her. As before, she opened it at random, and read.

> At the moment Corsair Sanglot emerged ... into the
> Place de la Concorde, noting with approval ... [the]

> adorable guillotine …, the crowd gathered around
> the engine of retribution watching Louis XVI climb
> the steps.

Marie lifted her head from the book. She felt for dear Louis XVI. How cruel a machine for killing. She now closed the book. How cruel a machine. She felt for all kings condemned to die. Not only poor King Louis but also poor King Charles — England's very own. No head to place his crown upon, not in the end. Back in the far country, she and Johannes had daily cause to think of Charles — their house, in Palmers Green, having borne the name "Carisbrooke." Though only three-bedroomed. One more room than needed.

Strange, she thought, to name such a house after a castle, let alone a castle that had once been the prison of a king, one all-but-doomed to die, even. Poor King, she thought. Poor Charles. At least his execution was not followed by that of his Queen. She thought now of Louis XVI and Marie Antoinette. It was said that the latter, poor Queen Marie, when changing into her execution clothes, was afforded no privacy. The guards watched on. "Poor Marie," she whispered. Out loud.

The Poet was alarmed, "The Hundred Headless Woman!" he cried.

"And what of her?" inquired the Usher. "What of the Headless Woman?"

"She keeps her secret," said the Poet.

❀

IV/V

Crowd

It behooves me, dearly beloved, at this point in my discourse, to disclose that Johannes once wrote a poem, so-called, a still-born rhyming thing. Its final dead-end couplet is this: the wooden declaration that, "I doubt not the secret lies / In dainty Marie's shining eyes."

This corpse of a poem is written long after the annulment and is, in fact, one of several that Johannes wrestles cold to the page in later life. Some of these metrical stiffs make it, indeed, as far as the *Swiss Observer,* to publication therein. These are the patriotic dead, word-corpses dedicated to what Johannes once called "the perfect State." Switzerland, naturally. This particular corpse, however, the one with "Marie's shining eyes," is dedicated to that perfect *woman,* Marie-the-Second, Marie-the-once-Consumptive, now Marie-the-Mother. Here it is, the complete corpse. On the blackboard.

Wimbledon

As I sat in the centre court
And watched the experts at their sport
I wished I could award a prize
To Marie with the shining eyes.

She's the one whom people seldom see,
Is neither star nor referee
She's there to plan and organize,
Is Marie with the shining eyes.

There's little fun that comes her way,
Hers is the spadework, day by day.
She solves the problems that arise,
That's Marie with the shining eyes.

How to account for her success?
(Small wonder she got in the press).
I doubt not that the secret lies
In dainty Marie's shining eyes.

As I say, a corpse. Albeit a twitching one, given this final couplet, the one about "the secret." Evidence, I believe, that the poem is haunted. Haunted, that is, by the Marie whom Johannes has not seen for years. Marie-the-First.

And is there a secret that lies in the shining eyes of this earlier Marie? This original Marie? My Marie. My own. My very own. I am not sure. I have never looked her in the eye. Or at least not for real, not in the flesh, not in such a way as she could ever return my dusty gaze. It is true that I have a portrait photograph of her and have often, at night, stared at her shining eyes therein. But it dates from 1897. Which is from before her marriage — if there *was* a before, a before nothing, as it were. I would not, then, expect to see any secret in those eyes. Not those eyes in the photograph, those nineteenth-century eyes. No.

Her eyes, however, they will grow older, grow modern – will see planes, cars, wars, etc.. And it is, I suppose, within those *twentieth-century* eyes, eyes I have never seen, not even in a photograph, that the secret might just lie. In this connection, this *secret* connection, I should perhaps now mention this: that Marie, according to Madeleine, only agrees to facilitate the annulment for "fear that her husband would otherwise kill himself."

Whether that would be by means of drowning, or hanging, or rubber, I'm afraid I simply do not know. I am, in this regard, as clueless as these bloody cats. But, if there is a secret in Marie's twentieth-century eyes, it might, I think, have something to do not only with marriage but death. Violent death. And that, I confess, is why I am drawn to the Lobster Office — it being, apparently, "the machine for killing," the Killing Office, so to speak.

You may, perhaps, be surprised by this, having hitherto thought that the Lobsters labor at a machine for living. For life.

Fig. 17. Eugène Atget, "The Eclipse, April 1912,"
from *Les dernières conversions.*

No, not at all. They are, above all, mourners. Do not be fooled by
their garlands. These men are for death. And say so.

"The simplest surrealist act," says M. Breton, "consists of
dashing down into the street, pistol in hand, and firing random-
ly [*au hasard*] … into the crowd."

Be warned. Keep off the streets.

❋

By the way, dearly beloved, M. Breton's crowd is not just any
crowd. No, it is a *cretinous* crowd. You see, those who shoot at
the crowd are those "who [have] … dreamed of … putting an
end to cretinization." Thus, shoot at the crowd, and you shoot
at cretins.

Indeed, even as you shoot, and even as the cretins drop,
screaming and bleeding, do bear in mind that "cretin," the word,

Fig. 18. Photograph of L'Église Chrétienne Primitive (1898).

comes to us from the Alps. It is how, up there, they pronounce *Chretien.* "Christian," if you will. In sum, in short, M. Breton's lobster-gun fires at one very particular crowd—namely, the Christian crowd. All believers take cover. Look out for M. Breton.

Look out as well for M. Peret, another local Lobster, this one wild with a passion for taking to the streets and, once there, "insulting a priest," any priest. And why not shoot him too? The priest. The prayerful bastard.

After all, these Christians, they simply clog the streets of Lobster Paris, as if just waiting to be shot, the clowns. Remember the front-cover of *La Revolution Surréaliste.* Issue the seventh. The one with the photograph of a mob of curious Parisians all scanning the sky and, beneath them, the legend which spells out their fate. They are, it says, "The Last Conversions." Voila! Yet more imperiled Christians. That most endangered of species.

It is said, I gather, by those who know such things, that this crowd, the one in the photograph, gestures toward a very particular sainted crowd. That they are, in truth, "The *Latest* Conversions." That is to say, those several men-of-very-modern-thought who fall famously for Jesus. Or at least, for his bride, the Church. The *painted* one, that is. The one in Rome. I think here of such glittering Catholic converts as M. Cocteau *et al.*

Whatever, my point is this: that, once again, the Lobsters' mad and random fire targets the Christian crowd. And, thank God, I say. As this, for me, poor Scholar Schad, means hope — hope that random Lobster-fire might yet, might still, assist me in my sorry search to find and save sweet, lost Marie. Our lady of the Christian herd.

Speaking of which, I have, in fact, within my briefcase, a well-worn photograph of Marie's very particular Christian herd. The Tabernacle herd. It is from 1898. Back then, by the way, they were invariably known as *L'Eglise Chrétienne Primitive* — primitive in the sense of being alike in creed to the earliest, first-century Christians, those wild and killable enemies of the State. Them. The "*First* Conversions," as it were. Here, here is the photograph. Just look, don't touch.

Marie, they say, is second from the left, far left. Toward the upper middle. There. Her hat, it's disappearing into the dark be-hind her. Pulled down hard, as if to eclipse her eyes. Her shining eyes. Yes, she's the one to the left of the skyward-looking seraph. The one with, I think, an Almighty White Feather in her hat. Her. Yes. Marie's the one beside her. Or so they say.

To be honest, though, I am not convinced. This woman looks just so different from the one in the other photograph, the por-trait photograph. The one from just a year before, 1897. Indeed, I believe that this here woman in the hat, her jaw so set, eyes unseen, is *not* Marie. Not her at all. This woman is, to be frank, too plain. Too Christian, if you will. Too primitive. Too killable.

❋

Forgive my frankness, my black genius, perhaps; but as a scholar I was taught to see the world with a knowing eye. Which is to say, with the eye of power, the eye of the sovereign, as it were — he who has the authority to kill. Yes, him. Remember Charles

IX? At his palace window? Firing at the scurrying Huguenots? Well, consider this: since good King Charles could not possibly have shot *all* the Huguenots he must somehow, or in some sense, have selected whom to shoot. And what, if he were, in the split second of casual slaughter, to have, on the whole, inclined toward murdering those who did not happen particularly to please his sovereign eye? It is a thought. Not impossible. And if it were the case then, once again, Christians, or at least Protestants, could be described as the especial prey of near-random bullets. Almost arbitrary killing.

❧

I think now, as so often is the case, of the Occupation. Of our jackbooted guests. And the Jews. Who die. Die purely because they are Jews. Without discrimination, as it were. None. All of them, it seems, must die. Not just a few or some, but all. Like the Gypsies, and the Homosexuals. For those Christians among us, however, it is different. They are killed more by chance. Insofar as they die with the assistance of our Nazi friends, they do so rather haphazardly. One is hung here, another is shot there, etc. — but not *because* they are Christians.

One of these is M. Hubert Caldecott. He was shot along with forty-seven others. Shot at Fort Mont-Valérien. As part of a reprisal execution. He just happened, as it were, to be killed. The memorial for M. Caldecott was held at the Tabernacle. October 24th 1941, 163 Rue Belliard. Madeleine preached Gospel. Primitive mourners gathered. Though not, perhaps, with garlands.

You might now wish, dearly beloved, to ring loud the protest bell. Or at least, the lecture bell, were it not cracked. You might wish to denounce what would appear to be my emergent thesis — namely, that within the history of Paris, and indeed Western modernity in general, the killing of Christians is distinguished, if not ennobled, by a certain contingency, by something, on occasion, approaching chance. Pure chance. Rot, you think. Cat's shit, you think. Or so I suspect. From the way you look.

Well, what about the twenty-sixth? Of August. Remember? One of the End days. Last days. The one with the bombs. Our German guests are waving a fond farewell to Paris and, from above, the dear Luftwaffe are tearfully bombing us, their eagle-eyes so full of tears they have no idea what they hit. Just a few bombs. Here and there. But one place that is hit, smashed, kissed-to-smithereens by these pure, pure bombs of chance is 163 Rue Belliard. Yes, the Tab.

"What," asks Madeleine, "has happened to the Tabernacle?"

Why, Nothing. What has happened is Nothing. Nothing has dropped from the sky, and the church is itself now Nothing. Or at least no more than "four walls, ... a staircase," and a "baptistry full of ... broken glass."

Ah, the symmetry. The Surrealism of the accidental bomb perfectly mirrored by the Surrealism of the ruined church. Walls without a roof. A staircase going nowhere. A holy bathtub ready to cut the bathing believer to a thousand pieces. Blood bath. Astonishing.

Cue M. Desnos.

"In cities where strength is deployed," he says, "wonderfully is your church destroyed."

That, by the way, was way back in 1924. These bastard Lobsters, you see, speak better than they know. Better than they know of the ruinous future of Paris.

Cue M. Breton.

Years ago, he says, "I know what the year 1939 has in store for me."

He did not say *what* he had in mind; however, if it were the fall of Paris to Herr Hitler, he would have been but one year out. But one bloody year.

✸

V/V

Motor-Car

Dearly beloved, you perhaps recall how the Office for Surrealist Research is, by its own admission, a "killing machine." It will, then, have come as no surprise that those who work in the Office, its Lobster-clerks, anticipate the very worst that is to come to Paris, the blackest genius, as it were. Herr Hitler, yes. But Satan too. Yes, dear Beelzebub himself. Indeed, even now, right now, one particular ink-stained Lobster sounds the alarum.

"Satan," he says, "Satan sets off again by motor-car, for Paris!"

Quick! Quick, I say. Leave every possible office. Take to every possible street. And, once there, scan the traffic for Satan's motor-car. Not, though, in order to avoid the damned thing, but rather to stop and to search it.

And why?

Well, that is simple. For I have heard that "in the back of the car," "wrapped in her coat," is none other than, yes, "the Unknown Woman." *L'Inconnue* herself.

And is this sweet Marie? Is she this Unknown Woman? The one in the back of Satan's motor-car? Unlikely, I know. But there is a chance. It is a possibility, however remote. Here in Paris, you see, if you chase Satanic cars you also chase Marie. Or at least her shadow, her Tabernacle shadow.

And why is that? Why?

Well, simply because these cars owe their demonization to none other than that Baptist brother of hers, Professor Passy.

"The motor-car," he says, is "truly diabolic."

Professor Passy, you see, thinks that every car is Satan's. And thus to be shunned, avoided. Like the plague. Even by those invited to his funeral.

"Please do not come," he says, "by motor-car."

And he is right. Never drive to a cemetery. It is, I think, no place to go in a motor car. Not even with a corpse. Ask the Lobsters. Or at least the Convulsionaries, so-called. I gather they regularly take a "decomposed corpse … in a car to the Place de la Concorde."

The moral, I think, is clear. If you are going to drive anywhere, even with a stiff in the back, don't, for heaven's sake, head for the cemetery. The Place de la Concorde, for all its convulsive traffic, would be better. Or even Luna Park, whence our garlanded mourners go. The ones led by the solemn-faced camel.

Ah yes, the camel. You have heard, perhaps, of the solemn-faced camel? If not, you know, at least, of the camel-faced M. Desnos. Well, he has left us a note. Final. Defiant. Here. Here it is. On the blackboard. Fingered in the dust.

> To hell with Louise Lame's hearse; … [although it] may wend its way through Paris, … I shall not raise my hat to it.

And why not? Why does M. Desnos not raise his hat to the passing hearse?

Well, it is because he has, apparently, "a rendezvous with Louise *tomorrow*." Yes, tomorrow. The day *after* her funeral. Bizarre is it not? Lobster Desnos, it would seem, believes in some kind of life after death; or, at least, believes that *l'Inconnue,* our Woman of the Winds, is still to be pursued even after dying. In short, that we who pursue her, whoever she is, should never, not ever, be duped by a hearse that is heading merely to the cemetery.

Should we not then, you and I, follow, instead, the hearse that is drawn by the camel? The one that goes to the fairground? After all, you see, that way also lies the Tabernacle, happy home to the happily-Drowned, a tribe who will have, in the end, with respect to death, no truck with sorrow, no truck with anything but all the fun of the fair. The resurrection fair.

But is that so? Truly? Really?

Well, what says Professor Passy? Regarding death. Funerals. His own, for example.

Thou shalt not drive.

Pardon?

It's what he says. Or thereabouts. About his funeral.
I know. But is that all?
All?
All he says about the funeral?
No.
What else, then, does he say?
"We wait … for the Lord … who shall change our vile body … unto His glorious body."
Resurrection?
Of the body.
What?
There will be a changing.
Of our bodies?
Vile to glorious.
Excellent.
Ours for His.
At last.
(*Pause.*)
And Marie, what says she to this?
Amen.
How do you know?
Because of what she says.
When?
When dying.
And what is it? What is it she says? When dying.
"I am ready."
Are you sure?
It's recorded.
What is?
"I am ready."
Ready for what?
She doesn't say.
But she is ready?
Yes.
The *bride* is ready?
Yes.

I am bringing you … by sovereign science, a Woman of the past.
— Stéphane Mallarmé (1842–1898)

CHAPTER FOUR

Letters

Part One

Armistice Eve

❁

I/II

Powys Lane, Palmers Green, London, N13

❁

"… that disagreeable post-man …"
(Edith Wensley, *"Lucholm,"* 22 Powys Lane, November 10, 1918)

Disagreeable I may be. Or may have become. But then, Sir, I bear a heavy load. Even now, with the End so near. It is the black-edged letters, Sir. They keep on coming. "We deeply regret etc." I swear they grow still heavier. And the heaviest are when it is the King and Queen who deeply regret. First one son and then another. Like no. 22, Sir. "Lucholm." The Wensleys. They've *no* sons now. None.

No sons at "Carisbrooke," either. Just down the road, Sir. I forget the number. House number. Home to the Schads, or Schadows, as I call them. Mind you, Sir, they had no sons to lose. So, no letters from the Palace. Not for them. Letters from abroad, though. Get plenty of those. Basel. Paris.

Ever been to Paris, Sir? I have. Lived there, in fact. Worked there, Sir. In a postal capacity. Senior. Clerical. At least, to begin with.

Ah, how I loved old-time Paris, Sir. *La Belle Époque.* All those boulevards, Sir. Such fine roads. Later, once deployed out-with the office, I must have walked hundreds of Parisian roads. Beautiful, some. Though not Rue de Rome. Nothing very special, Rue de Rome. Not in itself. But I always think of it, Sir. Along here. When I reach the Schadows.

Why, Sir?

Well, because Sir, Rue de Rome is where Mrs. Schad once lived. Number 107, Sir. 107 Rue de Rome. It's where she lived when young. Intriguing, is it not?

But wait, Sir. Please. Just for a minute. There is more, much more. You see, Sir, the most intriguing thing is that only a few doors away lived none other, believe it or not, than Monsieur Mallarmé. Yes, Monsieur Stéphane Mallarmé.

Who, Sir? Who *is* he?

Well, he is the Magician, Sir. The Magician of Rue de Rome. It's what they call him. He's a poet, Sir. Works magic. They say it is the words. His way with them. And that is doubtless true; but Monsieur Mallarmé also finds magic in the humble business of collecting, sorting, and delivering of letters. The magic of the Post.

No, truly, Sir. Monsieur Mallarme calls it "the *glory* of the Post." Quite a tribute, I feel. To my work, my calling.

Vocation, Sir?

Indeed, Sir. As Monsieur Mallarmé well knew. You see, he addressed one or two poems to *me*. Yes, me! His humble *facteur*. "Halt, postman" etc.

No, Sir. I would not lie. Not with regard to said poems. Even if they are perhaps a little imperious in tone. "Take your stick … and run!" "Skip, run and dance" etc.

Hence, by the way, my attempt, even now, to skip and run from door to door. Notwithstanding my burdensome bag. I realise that this represents a departure from regular Royal Mail procedure. But what else can I do? Monsieur Mallarmé is, as I say, a Magician.

Weary, Sir? I shall, then, be brief. Just leave you with this. An anecdote. Of a postal kind. Namely, that in Monsieur Mallarmé's London days, when still young, it was only "the postman's double-knock" which, each dawn, would "bring … [him back] to life." Knock, knock. Who's there? Postman Christ, as it were. Young Monsieur Mallarmé's diurnal Resurrection Man. The Magician's Magician, indeed.

But I go too far, and too fast. I run and skip, as it were, at the double. Halt, Postman, halt.

To resume, then. And promptly. The wind growing cold. One last postal revelation. It is this, Sir, the revelation. That the house within which Monsieur Mallarmé lived, though initially number 87 was, in the year of 1884, altered to number 89.

Yes, really. And all at once. In the twinkling of a bureaucratic eye. The whole road renumbered. Outcome: postal hiatus of a most devilish kind, believe me. Wrong house, wrong door, wrong reader. Letters opened in error. Letters read in error. Disaster. Disaster. Not least for the unfortunate man who had ordered the re-numbering. Disaster. Damnation. Demotion.

I am sorry. I will recover myself. Sort myself. After all, letters, Sir, have a genius for failing. Failing to reach their destination. Whether Monsieur Mallarmé wholly appreciated this, I am not certain. But for sure he knew the risk in sending a telegram. A lesson he learnt, Sir, the hardest of ways. "I dare not," he once said, "use the telegram system because of old memories."

By the way, Sir, I must confess that Monsieur Mallarmé did not *say* this as such. No, he *wrote* it. In a letter, in fact. One I came across myself, as it happens. Letters, Sir. No safer than telegrams.

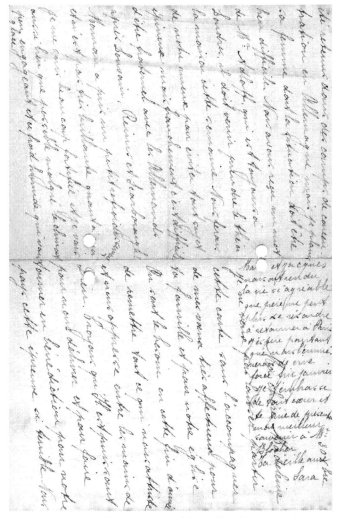

Fig. 19. Letter from Sara to Madeleine (October 30, 1914).
Blocher Saillens Archive.

✲

Ah, looks like rain. Better not dawdle. Though, perhaps, Sir, you are wondering, even now, how I ever came to read one of Monsieur Mallarmé's letters? Well, Sir, someone has to keep an eye on the mail. Maintain a certain oversight. Was true enough back then, Sir, in Paris. Still more the case in time of war. Even hereabouts. Not least in the case of the Schads. Aliens both.

Yes, rain, Sir.

Neither, I realise, is an *enemy* Alien. Indeed, Mrs. Schad, or Madame Schad, being French, is of the allied, or friendly variety. Mr. Schad, however, is of the neutral kind and only just. Swiss, you see. Basel. True, he may not be *against* us, as such; but he cannot be *for* us either. In Basel, I gather, they speak, pray, plot, etc. in German.

But don't fret, Sir. All letters destined for non-belligerent nations are subject to examination. This might, I know, seem a little under-hand, but the case of Mr. Schad, or rather Herr Schad, would suggest the measure justified.

Why? Well allow me to refer you, Sir, notwithstanding the rain, to the day that Herr Schad received a visit from an enemy Alien. Herr Alfred Adloff. A German. His visit is mentioned in a letter. This one, Sir. Don't drop it. Not in the rain.

It's from the Schads, Sir. Or at least from within their walls. "Carisbrooke." Mind you, it's written, in point of fact, by Madame Schad's sister, Mademoiselle Wheeler. Mademoiselle Sara Wheeler. See? Top right. Beside the date, Sir. October 30, 1914. See? Dark times, Sir. Which is why she was here, Mademoiselle Wheeler. Staying here. With the Schads. Paris, you see. Too dangerous, Sir. Enemy at the door, as it were. Anyway, Herr Adloff's name is on the left. North-west, as it were. Ten o'clock. See? That's the bit you need to read.

> My dear Madeleine,
> We have received a note from Herr Adloff who is still in London. He would like to take tea here this week. We will do our best to avoid all testing topics;

Fig. 20. Photograph of Inspector Frederick Wensley, 22 Powys Lane.
National Portrait Gallery, London. Photo: Howard Coster.

but, naturally, it is difficult now to be brotherly with
the Germans. …
Your dear friend,
Sara

Herr Adloff, Sir, is a co-religionist. A brother in Christ. They are
all Baptists, you see. All of them, Baptists. Dissenters, Sir. Non-
Conformists. And all from the same hole-in-the-wall chapel.
Paris hole-in-the-wall. Rue Meslay. Number 61, if I am not mistaken.

As for how thing went when Brother Adloff took tea with the
Schads, well, I do not rightly know. The letter, though, is dated
October 30th, see? So, the day he came would have been, most
likely, a November day. Dark, no doubt. Like today.

So, did they turn up the gaslight, Sir? To greet Herr Adloff?
To welcome him, both brother and foe? Did they smile? Shake

his hand? Look him in the eye? Even exchange a holy kiss? And was the best china used? And did they speak? Speak at all? If so, did they avoid all "testing topics"? A late-afternoon armistice brokered. Brokered at the breaking, Sir, of Baptist biscuits.

Well, Sir, what say you?

Well, nor have I. Or at least not yet. I have, though, for some years now, kept a vigilant eye on "Carisbrooke." And, indeed, continue to do so. My investigations, if you will, are ongoing. As Mr. Wensley would say. You know, number 22, the one who's lost both sons. Mr. Wensley. *Inspector* Wensley, beg his pardon. Of the Yard. "Detective of the Future." So says the *Daily Mail*.

Mr. Wensley, Sir, is the man for murder. He catches killers, that is. Not spies. So, not quite the man to keep an eye on our Carisbrooke Aliens. Besides, he cannot keep an eye on every inch of London. Not even with the Flying Squad. Those magnificent men of his may speed across our beleaguered capital in their shining new motor-cars, but they cannot look down every street, into every house. Not the whole directory, A to Z.

I do, though, Sir, know a man who can. *Can* see all of London.

Why, yes, Sir, it is indeed Monsieur Mallarmé. In fact, it is his most especial gift, or trick. Even when in Paris. One pull at his pipe, a pipe last used in England, and the "whole of London," he says, "became visible." Quite a trick. All of London. As if from an air-ship. Rubber, Sir. What will they think of next?

Am sure He does, Sir.

❋

Oh, Sir. Before you go, one last thing: when in London, Monsieur Mallarmé once lamented its "grey sky." Yes, really. It was, in fact, yet another November day. So grey that even "God," he said, "cannot see you." "His spy, the sun," being blinded.

Arresting words, don't you think? Mind you, still more arresting, Sir, is that upon his return to Paris, Monsieur Mallarmé does himself become God's London spy.

Yes, Sir, exactly — his pipe! One pull at that pipe of his and, hey presto, the Magician of Rue de Rome is also the Magician of, let us say, Leicester Square, Piccadilly, or even Holland Park Avenue, heaven help us. Not to mention, Sir, every other London haunt or walk.

Yes, even Powys Lane, Sir. In fact, *especially* Powys Lane. Madame Schad being, of course, an erstwhile neighbour of Monsieur Mallarmé's.

Indeed, come to think of it, he might well have once chanced to pass her upon the street. Rue de Rome, that is. Picture the scene, Sir. A young woman is just strolling along, a youthful Madame Schad. Or Mademoiselle Wheeler, as was. Marie Wheeler. And also walking along, perhaps in the other direction, is the ancient Magician himself, turning his magical head, but-ever-so-slightly, to regard the young woman.

Why, Sir?

Well, Sir she was young. Reason enough, they say, to turn a man's head. Or, it may simply be, Sir, that he overheard her name. The Magician's mother, you see, was also called Marie. Not to mention his wife, sister, and, indeed, his fancy woman. Marie times four. Or, corruptions thereof.

Yes, curious. Very. But please, Sir, don't worry. I'm not out here to preach to the November winds that Monsieur Mallarmé necessarily knew the young Madame Schad. Not as such. Besides, by the time she is just seventeen he is quite perfectly dead. Asphyxiated. His face, at the last, a violent red. Fitting, they say. Of the coughing kind.

No, don't go, Sir.

Yes, it *is* damned unlikely that the bloody Magician ever knew the girl. But it may, Sir, still have been within his curious power, his curious art, somehow to write about her. His poetry being "a throw of the dice." Chance meanings, yes. But, also chance *meetings,* Sir. Meetings. And of this he is well aware, my Monsieur Mallarmé.

"Why," he says, "do I get the feeling that I've come … about a … subject … unknown … to me?"

Why, indeed.

"Does … the poet," he says, "not listen for the future echo?"

Why, yes, he does. He listens, ear-to-the-wall, as it were, for that echo-to-come which is, I say, the life-to-come of a girl just down the road. Her *married* life-to-come.

But does she realise this? Madame Schad. Does she? Or even Herr Schad? Do they *realize* they have been listened to? Overheard, as it were. Are they aware? The Schads?

Well, Sir, they are now.

How?

Well, you see, Sir, for some time, I have taken the liberty of pressing through their letterbox not merely whatever His Majesty's Mail has for them but also sundry carefully selected Mallarméan fragments. Some poems, some letters. Don't worry, Sir, only a few at a time. So as not to cause alarm. The letters I simply re-address. Reusing, you see, the old envelopes. There *is* a War on, Sir. For the poems, mind, I have to use new envelopes. Hard to find, but where there's a will. Anyway, the letters I direct to Herr Schad, and the poems to Madame Schad. I then pop them through their letter box. Sometimes, first post of the day. Other times, last. Just enough to reveal, with each delivery, a soupcon more of how the magical Monsieur Mallarmé somehow foreknew their lives. Foreknew them well, in fact. Very well.

I beg your pardon, Sir? Do I think I bloody-well own the writings of Monsieur Mallarmé? Well, yes I do, Sir. In a manner. Monsieur Mallarmé's writing, his corpus, it is, you see, "a bequest to someone ambiguous." That is to say, to the poor bloody someone who *reads* the ever-ambiguous Monsieur Mallarmé. And that someone, here, now, today, c'est moi. C'est bloody moi. Boots, bag, and all.

Sir, I see, is rather alarmed. Surprised perhaps to learn of such a passion for Monsieur Mallarmé out here, in N13. But does Sir not know that Palmers Green has its very own *Société Littéraire Française*? A monthly gathering. True, I am not myself a member. It being a decidedly *un*ambiguous body. Indeed, its members have made it all too clear that they do not approve of my diurnal Mallarméan deliveries. It was, they intimated, no way for anyone to first encounter Mallarme's work, or indeed French letters of any kind. Just shoved through the door, dropped wil-ly-nilly to the floor. Might it not, they said, risk impromptu or hasty reading? Even, someone reading upon all fours? Might that not lead, they said, to a certain desperation?

Well, Sir, to this last I replied, as I made for the exit, that Monsieur Mallarmé himself considered "reading ... a desperate practice." Moreover, I added, one was simply conducting one of his "modern experiments in reading."

But such experiments, they cried, are dangerous. May lead, they cried, to the most disastrous misreading.

Why yes, I bellowed, in reply, but is that not the exquisite risk upon which all great writing depends? To quote, I bellowed, Monsieur Mallarmé himself, "a book ... is ... *rewritten* by the one who reads."

And with that, Sir, I departed, sack on my back. Good day, Sir.

II/II

"Carisbrooke"

The study, thought Johannes. It was cold. Even for November. And these letters, these second-hand letters. How odd. Very odd. Yes, cold. All of them sent before. And each, save one, written and signed in the same hand. Cold. "M. Mallarmé." 87 Rue de Rome. 89 Rue de Rome. Yes, so cold.

Mail from Rue de Rome was to be expected. Only to be expected. But these, these letters, had first been sent twenty, thirty years ago. What is more they had been written, it was clear, to people quite other than themselves, Marie and he. Who exactly they were, these other people, it was difficult to say. Someone had erased their names. "Not Known at this Address," each envelope now said, in official hand. And each re-directed to Powys Lane. "Carisbrooke." Better put on his coat.

"Carisbrooke." His three-bedroomed castle. Ha. Hardly. Not now. Not now that he was so like that first poor king of Carisbrooke. The real Carisbrooke. On the Isle of Wight. He too, poor Charles I, had trouble with the postman, it seems. Letters opened, intercepted, diverted. Poor soul. "Betrayed by a devil," he had cried. "A rogue is at the post-house," he had cried. Poor prisoner King, islanded King. Solitary, wifeless. Even the secret letters, the cryptic ones, "K" for King, etc., had failed. Even those smuggled out by the King's own laundress. Mary Wheeler her name. Coincidence? They too had gone wrong.

But not as wrong as these. These letters from this so-called Mallarmé fellow. Johannes tugged at the band that bound them together. Elastic. It was bad enough, he thought, that the letters had ended up here, but they had also, like the envelopes, been defaced. Doctored. A sentence here, a phrase there, each one carefully circled. Still worse, much worse, these encircled words seemed, somehow, to be about him. Johannes. About his life.

At first, these words had been kindly enough. Almost singsong, in love, like him, with Switzerland. And Marie. And her eyes.

"Switzerland. There is so much blue in that country, quite apart from the sky — and Marie's eyes which … follow me."

Yes, he had thought, it *was* all so blue in Switzerland. Its warless skies. No Zeppelin clouds. And the lakes beneath them. Blue again. And, as for Marie's eyes, her shining eyes: yes, they did, at times, follow him; or so he felt whenever he left her.

Not so kindly, so sing-song, were the later letters. Or rather, the circled words therein.

"Marie is a foreigner … be careful."

"Poor Marie has no tears left."

"The isolation is killing Marie."

Isolation was, he thought, a little too strong. There was Nelly. And, besides, Sara had been with them. Sister Sara, or St. Catherine, as Marie had once called her. St. Catherine the Virgin. He tugged a little at the band. Elastic. Tight. Well made.

He had, at first, wondered if he should mention the letters to Marie. He had not been sure. Or at least not until he received one particular letter. It was in quite another hand. And not, for once, a letter *from* M. Mallarmé but *to* M. Mallarmé. This time the encircled words were, "Do not read this sentence to Marie." He had not done so. In fact, he had read none of them to her.

Then, one day, Dammit, he had thought. Dammit. Enough. Enough of these bloody letters. This bombardment. Time for retaliatory action. And in kind. From here on selected letters would be Returned to Sender, fired back across the Channel. Each letter with certain very particular words encircled by Johannes.

Shell one: "Marie says you are a wretch …. Your last letter… spoke of our marriage [as] … a mere figment of the imagination."

Shell two: "You'll tell me there are two of us. No, there's only one of us. Marie weeps when I weep."

Shell three: "Marie was vexed with … the remarks [you] made … about her position which is … one of utter suffering."

This return of fire, Carisbrooke had hoped, would see the end of the siege. And it did. Or almost. Just one more letter arrived. With one last message. The final shot of a retreating army.

"Why … not consider … [marriage as] a way of having … peace?"

No, thought Johannes. He needed no lessons in peace. He was Swiss. A man of peace. Neutral. However bad the fighting. Neutral. However many nuns were raped. Neutral. However many infants were lost. Neutral. He had no choice. Switzerland was his country, still his country, his only country, and Switzerland had not declared war upon anyone. And neither had "Carisbrooke," his "Carisbrooke." Nor its King, King Johannes, a King who hated no one. Who only sought, indeed, to love. To love his Queen. His poor French Queen.

That, though, had not been easy. There being no royal issue. They had tried. Yes, tried everything. And Marie had sought help. Even in Paris, before the War. She had been seen by the celebrated Dr. Pinard. At considerable cost. She had, therefore, travelled alone. Besides, at the time, things had been difficult at work, in the company. At the office. *Dans la maison,* as Marie would say.

And now, now, there were all these bloody letters. An outrage, they were. Affront to good sense. Absurd. Quite absurd. Apart from one. One, he had welcomed. Even cherished. Harbored, in his desk. It was, he had hoped, a sign. Or word, prophetic word, as they would have said at the Tabernacle. He had kept the letter for the day, a day yet-to-come, when he might finally be able to send it, as it were, to Marie, slipping it, perhaps, beneath her bedroom door. He had often reread it.

"Do you remember our walks … when it rained … [and] you ran pushing … our astonished young queen, in her pram?"

✺

Part Two

Armistice Day

❀

I/III

"Carisbrooke" Still

> A good deal of anxiety has been caused of late by
> irregularities in the Postal Service. Many letters dis-
> patched from Church House and others addressed
> to the Baptist Union have not been delivered, and
> no trace of them can be found.
> (*The Baptist Times and Freeman,* July 23, 1915)

It was all over, thought Marie. At last, praise God. But the blankets, she thought. There was cheering outside. The blankets, had
they been lost? Such cheering. Had the blankets never arrived?
At HQ. Baptist HQ. There had been thirteen. Some women, at
church, had sent them off. Such had been the clamour for blankets. In Flanders. Sleep, they had said, was desperately called
for. Even blankets worn in the middle would do. They would be
transformed. Cut up and remade. For the men.

And for children as well. After all, the Home Front must not
be overlooked. Here too blankets were needed. Here too sleep
was needed. And cold could kill, she knew. One bad night, and a
poorly child could be lost. True, very true. But she and Johannes
had had no blankets worn in the middle. Had none to send.
None to parcel up and put in the post. At least it was one less risk
to be taken with the mail. One less chance. More cheers outside.

Not, she thought, that everything Baptists had entrusted to
the post had been lost. Not everything. That would be ridicu-
lous. There was, for instance, that telegram from the Touring
Club, the Baptist Touring Club. 1914, it was, in the summer. Just
after the Arch-Duke had been shot. And his wife. The Club had

been trapped in Switzerland. In Lucerne. But they had managed to send a telegram. From Hotel Engel. "All well," it had said. "All well, Engel," she had read. "All well, *Angel,*" Johannes had said, translating. War had broken out, but all was well with the Touring Club. And, indeed, the Postal Service. At that point.

Not for long, though. For soon there had been reports of problems. Difficulties. Anxiety in Baptist House. Concern at the Baptist Union. So, could she be sure of the socks? Certain of the gloves? Or of the handkerchiefs? Had they ever made it to the Front? And what of the Open Letter? To the Baptists of Germany. Had it ever got through? The one signed, "We remain your beloved Brethren." Had that arrived? If letters had not made it from Baptist House to Baptist Union, from, as it were, the left hand to the right, how could anyone be sure the Open Letter had made it through all that barbed wire to Berlin? To the beloved Enemy. And if not, what had happened to their greetings? Their love? Ah, now they were singing outside.

Yes, she thought. And what had happened to that child? The one put up for adoption. That was yet another letter. "Dear *Baptist Times,* etc." Poor mite. Just five months old, the letter had said. In need of a home. A Baptist home. Had any readers responded? Perhaps a reader without a child. But with an empty room. Well, had they? She had asked Johannes. But he, like her, was not aware that a home had ever been found. But what, she had said, if a letter that was offering a home had not reached Baptist House? What then?

Or, what if the offer had come from, say, "The Wilderness, London"? How could anyone reply to such an address? And yet one of the blankets sent to Baptist House had come from a lady who had indeed given as her address simply, "The Wilderness, London." To think that somewhere in London was a woman in a wilderness. Marie thought, for a moment, of John the Baptist. Perhaps she was not alone. The room needed dusting. How they sang.

❀

The post, she thought. So much depended upon it. Even, say, proclaiming the Gospel. With tracts. What if, for instance, she had subscribed to *The Monthly Visitor*? For its excellent tracts. What if she had subscribed, but it had not arrived? *The Monthly Visitor*. What then? Just think of it. She would speak to Nelly about the dust.

And then, she thought, there had been all those letters sent from Church. To the Front. In France. One hundred of the men of the Church had responded to the Call. But had the letters reached them? And what of all the prayers? The prayers for the men. Had they got through? She thought for a moment. Yes. Yes, they had. Praise God. In the first two years just one of the hundred had been killed. Poor Mr. Pearce. A miracle, it was.

Yes, miracle. Indeed, she had heard talk, news, of a Revival at the Front. Reports, even, of baptisms. One in a freezing bath-house. Private Phillip Boase, the candidate. The *Baptist Times* had said, "Readers, please pray for Private Boase." She had done so. Every night.

So, no, Christ's Kingdom had by no means fallen. The King had remained on the Throne. Daily had been the evidence of Grace. Of a Pentecost, even. "A great effusion of the Holy Ghost," they had said. Hallelujah. A season of signs and wonders.

Like Revival Week. At the Church. There had been, she knew, some "meetings with signs following." She had read this in the *Baptist Times*. Nothing more was said. About the meetings. Not a word. No more was needed. Many a reader would know what was meant. Healing, falling, tongues, visions. Manifestations. Signs. Of the Spirit. These things were not easily spoken of. But she had thanked God and waited on such signs herself. On news of Jesus. Like manna from heaven, it would be. Ah, the dust, you could write in it.

❈

Just like manna, in fact, had been those peculiar envelopes that had recently tumbled through their door. So many addressed to her. All stuffed with the strangest writing. Word-rags, most peculiar word-rags. But each one a blessing, each one seeming to know her so well. Her life.

"We are witnessing ..., far from the public square, a trembling of the veil."

Yes, just as it had been. In Revival Week. Their meetings had indeed been far from the public square, very far. And yet they had surely witnessed a trembling of the veil. As in baptism, she thought. Ask Private Boase, in the bathhouse. Ask *him*.

If still alive.

No. A careless thought. Her mind had wandered. Distracted. Such was the bustle outside. The flags and the bells. And laughter. It's all over, she thought. And paused. For a moment. Looked down at the carpet.

She would start again. Return to those rags in the envelopes.

"Meanwhile, not far away [was] the thorough washing of the Temple, [with] its floods of glory... [and] ... still invisible Dancer [*danseuse*]."

Baptism, thought Marie, again. The washing, the floods of glory, and, in the midst, yes, the Dancer. She who dances, as it were, through the waters. Dances with Christ. As she had once done. Yes, danced. Through the waters. Ah, how she had danced.

No, she thought again. No. That way lay vanity, self-regard.

"Your Venetian mirror, deep as a ... spring of water, ... who has [not] gazed at herself in it? ... More than one woman has bathed the sin of her beauty in these waters."

Yes, who has not, in the instant of baptism, caught her own reflection in the water? Her beauty thereby becoming her sin. There were, she knew, many who felt that the immersion of a young woman risked modesty — her figure, as she rises, so far from invisible.

"Perhaps, if I looked for a long time, I might see a naked ghost."

Yes, some men *had* looked a long time. Too long. Some still did. She moved from the window seat to the chair in the far corner of the room, the furthest from the road. And the laughter.

❋

The house, it had at first, in the beginning, been so very quiet. Quite unlike the Tab. Its dazzling sermons, fire-cracker prayers, ecstatic utterances. The house, in the beginning, had been another world. Still and empty. In the beginning. But then, but then, one brilliant day, the rags through the door had begun.

"It will be as if the [ballet] were happening, Sir or Madam, in your [very own] house."

And so it proved. For, as rag followed rag, their life together, Johannes and her, had become an enchanted dance; so delicate, so chaste, almost without embrace. A private kind of flight. Parlour, hallway, staircase, and landing.

"The floor avoided by her leap acquire[d] a ... virginity undreamt of."

"She dance[d] as though unclothed ... [and] called into the air."

Yes, called by Johannes. Each dark night. Month after month. Year after year. Called to a performance of love altogether undreamt of, unheard of. And meanwhile, yes, meanwhile, Kings and Queens in faraway motorcars were all being shot. Barbed wire was tearing at all the faces of Europe. And yards of mud were being both won and lost. *These* things were heard of. Not her. She was *un*heard of. Altogether unheard of. But she was most certainly *seen*. By Johannes. And, as though unclothed. Indeed, on occasion, as unclothed. Yes, for Johannes. She had danced. For Johannes.

Silence.

Silence.

The house was silent. So too the street.

For a moment. A while.

And then, "Step up! Step up!" A raucous cry from the street. It was like the cry of a passing mountebank, and as if she were his sorry exhibit. But who was this man? This uniformed showman?

"A Man of Letters," he bellowed. "Her Daily Visitor," he bellowed. "The Disagreeable Man," he bellowed. And shook his heavy burden-bag.

But on whose authority did he speak? Or bellow?

"Monsieur Mallarmé," he bellowed. "Monsieur Stéphane Mallarmé. From number 89," he bellowed. "Rue de Rome," he bellowed. "Did she not recall? The Magician?" It was on *his* authority that the Disagreeable Man spoke. Monsieur Mallarmé's. "After all," he bellowed, "it was Monsieur Mallarmé who had first cried 'Step up! Step Up!'"

"And what did he cry next?"

"'It's only a penny!'"

"What is?"

"The show. Performance."

The Disagreeable Man then doffed his cap to a gathering crowd and, gesturing toward Marie, cried aloud, again in the words (he said) of Monsieur Mallarmé, "'Ladies and Gentleman, … she [*la personne*] who has had the honour of submitting herself to your judgment needs no costume to impress you!'"

Marie considered the crowd. Was she really without costume? Completely? For all to see. To judge her, examine her. The crowd, stood below, far below, in the road, just in front of their house. But where now was she? Where exactly? Ah yes, the roof. She was on the roof. Of "Carisbrooke." The battlements, as it were. But was this really so? What said the Disagreeable Man?

"Why yes," he replied, "Monsieur Mallarmé did indeed see 'naked, [and] framed by the roof up above, someone waving wildly.'"

And was *she* that someone?

Why yes, said the Man. Again.

How strange, she thought. To be upon the roof, waving, wild and naked. Waving, like an airman. Wild, like those who still look for God. And naked. Naked. But naked like whom?

"Like Salome," cried the Man, "naked like Salome. She who danced 'to seduce a king.'"

But which king? She knew no kings. How, then, could he compare her to Salome? Marie knew not a single king.

"But is there no king in 'Carisbrooke?'" asked the Man. "No king to dance for? Not even in the royal bedchamber?"

The Man then pointed to one who had, he said, appeared at an upper window. She, being upon the roof, would not be able to see, but the figure at the window, he said, appeared to be climbing to the window's ledge. It was, said the Man, "Carisbrooke"'s very own shadow-king. But what was he about to do? Shoot at the assembled? Threaten to leap to his death? Or, like the real King of Carisbrooke, attempt a coward's escape to the continent?

The Man suddenly stopped. As if he had seen a ghost, or rather had not. "Ah!" he said, "I have been mistaken." He apologized. There was, he now could see, no king at the window. Indeed, there was, he had heard, no king in the house. No king of the castle, as it were. Only a jester, court jester, called Johannes. Or John, as sometimes known. John the Baptist, as it were. He who had lost his head. At her request.

"Whose request?"

"Salome's."

"But I am *not* Salome. Yes, I may have danced, danced for Johannes. Never, though, have I danced for his head."

"But is Johannes not a guilty man?"

"Guilty?"

"Yes. Of losing his faith."

She said nothing.

"And should not he who loses his faith also, like a king, lose his head?"

Again she said nothing.

"It could be arranged," he said. "Each day Johannes takes the train to Tower Hill, does he not?

She nodded.

"Well, where better to remove an unwanted head?"

"No," she said.

"Why not?" said the Man. "Many have questioned the point or purpose of a head. Monsieur Mallarmé, for instance. The 'useless head,' he called it."

"This harsh epithet," added the Man, "does, though, somewhat misrepresent Monsieur Mallarmé's views vis-a-vis the value of having a head. Indeed, Monsieur Mallarmé held, on the whole, that a head is of very considerable use. Not least, with respect to the art of love. Hence," said the Man, "Monsieur Mallarmé's fascination with dear sweet Salome. And the head of John the Baptist."

"Explain," she said.

"Well," he said, "does the beheaded Baptist not demonstrate that one might, after a fashion, love with only one's head?"

"I do not understand," she said.

"Then listen," said the Man, "to Salome. Monsieur Mallarme's Salome. Listen as she whispers to the Baptist's bleeding head: 'If you wish,' she whispers, 'we shall make love with your lips and without a word.'"

The Man paused. Did she, the woman on the roof, recognise this sentiment at all? Did she?

Silence.

Might, indeed, she ever have spoken thus herself? To Johannes?

Silence.

The Man is wrong, thought Marie. A wrong man. Bad. Truly disagreeable. She would pray for him.

And this she told him. At which the Man paused, frozen. And looked at her. Then, of a sudden, he fell upon his knees. There in the street. A kind of scandal, it was.

Silence again. Silence. And then the Man lifted his sorry head. He would himself, he said, now attempt to pray. To pray a prayer. A prayer of Monsieur Mallarmé's, he said. It was the only prayer he knew, he said. And was, he confessed, a hopeless prayer. Disastrous. He bent his head. His lips, they were moving.

❋

II/III

London EC3, then "Carisbrooke" Once More

The flesh is sad, alas, and I have read all the books.
(Mallarmé)

All. All of them. Johannes had read all of them. All the books.
Of every imaginable kind. And though the people in the streets
were cheering, cheering the End, the End of It All, the flesh, his
flesh, alas, was sad. True it was that some books had, at times,
provided relief. Gladdened his flesh. But not today.

Today he would read *The Rubber World*. The office Bible, as it
were. And, as bells clanged and strangers danced, he hurried to
the station, Tower Hill, and there found the train, the train for
home, and an empty carriage. As he sat down he pulled the book
from his case. He now gazed at the opened book. Page the first.
Contents. Here, before him, the World of Rubber, alphabetical
in organisation, each entry a sentence marching backwards.

"Army, French, rubber clothing for."

"Ball, suicide, caused by."

"Calendar Rolls, lubricating box for."

And so on. And on. Until, at last, "War, the opening door."

Johannes paused. Looked up. The people, he could see, were
waving. But yes, the War had been good for trade; an opening
door, indeed.

His office, all offices, had closed as soon as they had heard.
An armistice, they said. In a railway carriage, they said. In a sid-
ing. In a forest. War, the closing door. Eleven o'clock. On the
stroke. Slam. And Big Ben had sounded. His four-year silence
broken. Eleven o'clock. Exactly. The train now halted. Moor-
gate. He looked around his motionless carriage. It was over, he
thought. All over. Even here, so far from any visible forest.

"We want the King! We want the King!" they had been shout-
ing, in the Mall. Outside the Palace. But Johannes looked down
and read on. A — B — C — **D**. D for "Dancing Pump, 'Castle.'"
Odd. Footwear? Rubber sole? Perhaps. He did not claim to

know of every possible application. There being so many. "Raincoats, for Dolls," for example. Or, "Slide Rules for Rubber Men." Besides, rubber was not always rubber.

"Definition, Direct, of Rubber, Impossible," he read.

Like God, he supposed. Or war. Or marriage, come to think of it. He thought of the famous Mrs. Stopes. She had said that a Christian marriage was sealed not by the State or the Law, or even by vows made before God, but rather by the act of coitus. Coitus, he thought. Definition, Direct, of Coitus, Impossible, he thought. And closed *The Rubber World*.

"Palmers Green," cried the guard, who would soon, he thought, be home. Johannes descended from the train and headed, as ever, westward. For "Carisbrooke." Once there, at the door, he halted. It had begun to rain, even as he stood there, at the door. He held the key up to the lock. And paused. "Umbrella, for tapping in rainy weather," he had read. But why for tapping? Why the tapping? Odd, he thought, as he entered, removing his raincoat. He set down his briefcase. It felt empty. Like the parlour. Front parlour.

It was here that, each evening, he sat to read. Here that he had read all the books. Here that the flesh had, alas, grown so sad. Today, though, there was a book that he had not seen before. It had been left on his chair. And, with it, a note in a half-familiar hand informing the reader that it was not just any book but rather "*the* Book." It was, apparently, the Book of which its author, Stéphane Mallarmé (him again) had always dreamt. Just as the War had been the War-to-end-all-wars this was the Book-to-end-all-books. By M. Mallarmé. It contained all that M. Mallarmé had ever written, apparently.

Johannes reached for a knife, a paper knife. And began, with both considerable art and skill, to uncut the pages of the book. Soon, long before his patient work was done, he came across words that, somehow, someone had encircled.

"The virgin folds of a new book lend themselves to a sacrifice whose blood [had] stained … ancient volumes red."

He looked around.

"They await the introduction of a weapon."

Johannes put down his knife. He was not accustomed to blood. To bleeding. Other men had bled. At the Front. He was, in this regard, unusual. As was Marie. Other women bled once a month. Blood, the Monthly Visitor, as it were. Not Marie. Or at least not for some years. It had stopped one November, apparently. He wondered if that too had been on the eleventh day and at the eleventh hour. On the dot. It was unlikely. Marie did not get along with clocks. With hours and minutes. Neither did he. In that respect, he thought, they were most unlike the War.

And then there was, of course, the blood they had not shed. That too set them apart from the War. Marooned. Far from action. Perhaps, though, far also from Salvation. He thought of Pastor Saillens, back in Paris. Ruben Saillens. "The Apostle of France," he had been hailed. That was in the middle of the war, when he came to London to preach blood. In Bloomsbury. "No Salvation without the Shedding of Blood," he had preached.

Johannes surveyed the parlour. The chairs, the piano, the table. No sight of blood. None. Not in this room or any other. Was it, then, a house also without Salvation? It was true that the Apostle himself had baptised Johannes back in Paris. But that was so long ago. Before marriage, before hostilities, before his sailing the world. On business, mainly. Holland. Scandinavia. Russia. America. That had been 1912. September. Just four months late for the Titanic. Now, *there* was a baptism gone wrong.

Like his own?

Hard to say. He was always at church. New Southgate, Baptist. But perhaps he struggled, these days, to find words at the door for Rev. Joynes.

Just as he had struggled to find words for Apostle Ruben a few years back. Again November. Yes, *five* Novembers ago. If Novembers could be counted. Back in 1913 it was. It had been twenty-five years since Pastor Saillens had founded the Cause in Paris, and so would Marie and he kindly add their memories to a book to mark this anniversary? Yes, said Marie, writing several lines that recalled the time before her baptism, when still but an *auditrice*. A listener, if you will. Still hearing her way to full assurance of faith. Johannes himself had managed no more than four words. *Affecteux message de reconnaissance.*

Fig. 21. Inscription in Livre de mémoire d'anniversaire (1913). Blocher Saillens Archive.

That had been it. Barely a doffed hat. No mention of the Lord. Or Marie. But then neither had she mentioned him, Johannes. Not in her response. Almost as if they were not really married. And she did seem a little unsure. "Marie Schad-Wheeler," she had signed. As if but half-married. Or even, as they would say in the office, still a maid.

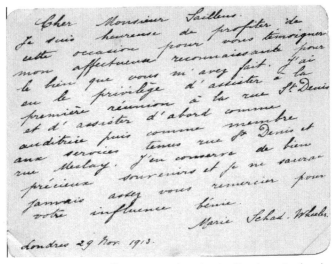

Fig. 22. Note to M. Saillens in Livre de mémoire d'anniversaire (1913).
Blocher Saillens Archive.

❋

Johannes yawned and read again, "the virgin folds await the introduction of a weapon." Virgin, he thought. Dammit, he thought. Someone was playing a game with him. Someone well-read. A scholar, not a gentleman. He would, though, cut a few more pages. He then found, again encircled, "an uncut page contains a secret." Yes, someone was most definitely playing a game. He cut again. And again. And again. Until he read, "It's only in the family that you find the monastery." He paused. Listened to the clock. Then cut yet again and read, "He leaves the room and is lost on the stairs."

Johannes looked down. He had left the parlour. He looked down again. At the hall, below. The uncarpeted staircase felt hard beneath his feet. He had reached the half-landing, the point at which you could either continue straight on toward the bedroom at the rear, or follow the staircase in making an about-turn and then head for the master bedroom. At the front. And there he stood. Upon the half-landing. Dumb, like a beast. In no-man's land. Outside, the bells. "We want the King! We want the King!" But the King, this King, of Carisbrooke, his flesh was sad, alas. And he wept. And as he wept he cut, cut open the Book, and as he cut he found a poem encircled. Obscene it was.

> Because the paper reported a rape,
> Because the maid had forgotten to button her
> > blouse,
> …
> Or because he lay awake with his leg
> Shamelessly brushing another leg beneath the
> > sheets,
> Some simpleton plants his cold dry wife beneath
> > him,
> …
> And because those two creatures coupled in their
> > sleep
> O Shakespeare, and Dante, a poet may be born!

No, it had not been like that. Yes, he had read of rapes in the papers. Yes, the girl had forgotten, at times, to button her blouse. And yes, he had laid awake. Often he had laid awake. In his castle. Such was the conscience of the King. But no, no — two creatures had *not* coupled in their sleep. Besides, that was not possible. Not in their sleep. Surely not. No, there had not been any coupling. None. He insisted on that. And would do so under oath, before a court. Yes. And would do so even though there was bound, one day, to be someone who would not believe him. Some smart bastard hymning the inexorable logic of what it was to live, as a hot-blooded man, in a world full of newspapers, maids, and insomnia. Yes, this future accuser, skilled in reasoning, might well invoke some such because-because-because. But no, there had been no coupling, none. None, none. Awake or asleep. And, therefore, *no* poet born. No Shakespeare, no Dante. Not even a scholar. Thank God.

❋

III/III

"Carisbrooke" Still

Within a stately palace, once the scene
Of royal splendour,
Today is gathered a distinguished host
Come here to treat with nations in defeat
And set a shattered world upon its feet.
…
One day a stranger sought to penetrate:
"This is my realm, my name is Peace."
They looked at him, the angel no one knew,
Then said: "Begone, there is no seat for you."
(Johannes, "The Angel of Peace" — upon the Treaty
of Versailles, 1919)

There was a knock at the door. Johannes waited. But Nelly did not answer. Knock, knock. She too, like Marie, must have gone out. Gone off. Enlisted, as it were. By a dancing crowd. Knock, knock. Johannes descended and opened the door. Peace. Peace had come to the world, but there, at the door, stood no angel. No annunciating angel. Least not a straight-backed one.

He was, said the one-at-the-door, the Disagreeable Man of Powys Lane. He would, though, also answer to the name of Monsieur Mallarmé or, if Sir preferred, the Magician of Rue de Rome. He, the man-at-the-door, had now read so much of the Magician's writing as to have grown, he explained, quite confused as to his own identity. Postman or poet, he was no longer sure. Notwithstanding his boots and crookèd back. And so it was (with apologies) that he now found himself occasionally speaking as if he were Monsieur Mallarmé and, indeed, in the Magician's very own words. This begged, he realized, the question of quite how Herr Schad was to discern exactly when this was the case. But Sir could rest assured that it would be clear. Or clear enough.

Whatever, with respect to the question of identity, or who-was-who, it was the-man-at-the-door's duty to observe, for the record, that the number on Sir's Passport, 12976, consisted in exactly the same five digits as the number on his Identity Book, 16792. A pleasing economy, this reusing of digits, but curious nonetheless. Quite a coincidence. Or accident, of a sort. The man-at-the-door paused before adding that "for some time," however, his "thought [had] abstained from ... accidents" and so he, the man-at-the-door, would say no more about it, this coincidence.

Besides, he felt he should, here and now, apologise to Herr Schad for his very particular rat-a-tat-tat at the door. It was, he knew, rather eccentric; not unlike, say, "a call at the door that [was] like the sound of an hour missing from the clock." A once-peculiar thought, Sir, this losing or mislaying of an hour. Though of late, of course, the nation had, for the sake of Daylight Saving, grown accustomed to the thought — now willingly foregoing one hour of the clock each and every Spring. He thanked God, however, that they had not let slip the hour beginning eleven of the clock this particular morning.

How terrible, Sir, it would be to lose an hour that one had actually wanted to live. Or, still worse, to have lived an hour that was subsequently ruled not to have existed, to have been "a moment not marked on any clock." One must be careful, Sir, not to erase one's time on earth — not "to annul [say] a day of your life." Or a year, come to think of it. Or several years. Did Sir understand? Did Madam? Did anyone, indeed? Perhaps not. With the nation's biannual doctoring of clocks, perhaps "no one can tell the hour any more."

But enough of time. Herr Schad must be wondering why he, the man-at-the-door, was now the man-halfway-down-the-hallway. And though Sir might be charmed to have "heaven's beggars tread our roads" he doubtless did not wish to have them tread his hall. So, why? Why was he, heaven's beggar, now in Herr Schad's hallway? Rough as he was. Well, that was simple — he was driven by "fondness for an abandoned house." He would concede that "Carisbrooke" was not altogether abandoned, but there was something about Sir that suggested abandonment. Such as the way Sir lingered in the hallway in a manner reminiscent of a man he once knew who "was obliged to sit across from [a] … mirror in order not to doubt … [him]self."

This, though, was understandable. Things, it seemed, did not go well with Sir. He could tell, by the "alien tear" in his eye. For Sir, he sensed, the dancing in the street, the cheers of the soldiers, "the song of the sailors," etc. were no more than "sad festivals on distant dying shores." He was sorry to labour the point, to continue "to plough … a sad storm," as it were, but it really did seem that, for Herr Schad, "the Sky is dead" and even "the trees are bored."

Perhaps, then, he could offer Sir some help — a little advice, or even a coin. Yes. Perhaps he would say to Sir something like "Dear Christian, down on your knees!" and then fling a coin in Sir's direction and add, "It will — if you're not afraid — buy you a cutlass!"

Sir might well protest, saying that all fighting is finally over now, and indeed that a cutlass is of negligible use within modern warfare. Or, even that he, Herr Schad, is an Alien, and thus a non-combatant. And this would be true, all true, but it did put him in mind of a very particular and recent editorial in *The Baptist Times*. Sir took it, perhaps? Whatever, the editorial had declared, *vis-à-vis* "The Alien in Our Midst," that "the foreigner should be naturalised and made to fight in the King's Army." Sir might argue that the King in question here is, in fact, King Jesus, and that "the foreigner" in question is but a poetic personification of all those fleshy passions to which unredeemed men give succour, or asylum. And yes, this might well be argued. Nevertheless, he, the man-in-the-hallway, would still, even with respect to this metaphoric Alien, be put in mind of Herr Schad.

But he must yet again apologise. This time, for not having ceased to prate since crossing the threshold. He really should give Sir a chance to speak. And, indeed, would do so. Yes, he would ask him how life was here in childless "Carisbrooke," this "castle of purity," "this tomb for two." Did Sir like it so quiet? Or, would he prefer to avoid the subject? Perhaps Sir was perturbed by talk of a tomb? Perhaps he felt it bad form to speak of such when so many at the Front had died without tombs. Or burial of any kind. Or, indeed, bodies to be buried.

Or, perhaps it was, quite simply, that so very many had lately lost their sons? Like the unfortunate Wensleys. At number 22. If so, if this were indeed the cause of Sir's reticence upon the subject of tombs, he should explain that Monsieur Mallarmé himself had lost his one and only son. Anatole, his name. True, Anatole had died of rheumatic fever rather than shrapnel, and had only ever encountered Germans when, as a child, playing in the street; nevertheless, there had been an occasion, in one particular game, when "the Germans came back to attack him." Ah, Anatole, poor Anatole.

Monsieur Mallarmé, by the way, did "not know what they ha[d] ... done with him." With young Anatole. Just, Sir, as many now would say of their fallen soldier-sons. There was, though, at least the comfort that "he [Anatole] does not *know* ... he is dead." In contrast, Monsieur Mallarmé himself seemed to be very much aware of being no more. He would often remark, "I am perfectly dead."

Come to think of it, was not Sir also perfectly dead? Albeit "dead ... less in the ordinary way" — that is to say, less in the humdrum or non-breathing way and more in the fantastical way of being dead in spirit. Dead *in one's sins,* that is. Not to put too fine a point upon it.

So, what says Sir? In his defence, as it were. Is Sir about to say, for instance, "my pockets are ... empty and I don't sleep with the maid"? Perhaps. But even if true, even if he had lived a monk's life, Sir must understand this, that: "One day you *will* commit a crime." A future crime, that is. A case, if you will, for Inspector Wensley, our very own "*Detective* of the Future." Herr Schad would doubtless be relieved to know that this crime of his would not be anything like that committed by Monsieur Mallarmé's favourite, the pantomimic Pierrot. Sir, thank God, was not about to tickle his wife to death. No, his crime would be merely a matter of perjury-cum-bigamy. Or, so his learned accusers would say.

Sir's crime would not, then, be that of a giant but rather of, say, a "little man." To invoke the game of chess, it would be the crime of a pawn. Think, Sir, of one who cries out, in confession, "I hold the Queen! O certain punishment!" Certain indeed. Particularly, Sir, if one continues to have and hold another Queen. An old Queen. A Queen who would, then, need to disappear. Vanish. Into thinnest London air.

Ah, Herr Schad, it seems, is somewhat puzzled. To clarify, the Queen who might one day need to disappear is, sadly, the current Mrs. Schad. Madame Schad herself.

But what might *she* say? Madame Schad. Right now. Today. Wherever she is. What might she enquire? What question might she put to Herr Schad? To her beloved King? Would it be, for instance, something tender, like,

"Am I beautiful?"

Or,

"Were you not about to touch me?"

Or, would it be something a little darker, like, say,

"What cunning demon stirs in you this sinister emotion?"

Yes, perhaps it would be this last. This last question. The one about the demon. Yes. For if this present Queen is unable to provide His Highness with a child, as appears to be the case, then Sir might well be stirred by a demon from within, within himself. A demon who wishes to be born. An as-yet unborn demon. Perhaps, indeed, a demon not yet conceived but who thinks, even now, "I love being born."

And *does* such a demon stir Herr Schad? Cause his flesh to grow sad? If so, Sir himself is not, strictly speaking, to blame. Or to be cursed. Condemned. No, rather, it would be the yet-to-be-born demon who stood condemned. Him. That "future ghost." The bastard.

So, what, then, says Herr Schad to all of this?

Nothing?

Not a word?

Silence?

Well, perhaps he, the man-in-the-hallway, could make a suggestion. Did Herr Schad wish, in fact, to say this: that, "I [am]

afraid of dying when I sleep alone"? Is that what Sir really wished to say? Here. In the hallway. Is that what it would all be about? The fear of dying in a lonely bed? In short, is that why he would seek a new queen? A younger queen? A queen that would out-live him, out-sleep him? A queen that would always be there to lie beside him. Until the very end. Is that it?

Ah, still nothing?

Sir, still holds his peace?

Well, what Herr Schad must realise is that if, in the end, this whole affair were simply to do with fear of dying alone in a bed-made-for-two, then he, the man-in-the-hallway, would have to point out that, recently, around ten million men had died in mud, rain, and trench; and that each and every one of them would have rejoiced to die in any damned bed, with or without an ageing queen. Indeed, had Sir not realised that today, outside, all ten million, all ten million dead, were gathered? In Powys Lane. At his door, right now. All ten million. All the dead. Had Sir not realised this?

No?

Well, now that Sir *had* been made aware of the ten million, what would he say to them?

What?

No idea?

Well, would Sir not say something like, "Let us forget!" Yes, that would be typical of Sir. Well, how wrong Sir would be. How very wrong. Herr Schad must understand that the ten million would never allow themselves to be forgotten. That the dead just never go away. Sir might imagine that there is such a thing as the "supreme adieu," a final and absolute "waving adieu" with some "terrible handkerchief." But there is not. No. There is no handkerchief sufficiently terrible for such a Great Goodbye, Al-mighty Farewell.

So, silence is it?

Herr Schad says nothing, does he? Has he, like the guns of Flanders, finally lost his voice? Is there really nothing more Sir would like to say?

No?

Well, how about, "Please forget me"? As if to say, forget my sins. Both present and future. Is that what Sir might desire finally to say? Is it? Is it? For if so, he, the man-of-the-hallway, would cry No! No, he would not forget the sinful Herr Schad. And neither would Madame Schad.

Yes, her. Madame Schad. Queen Marie herself. Remember her? Now, at the End. Sir might think, or dream, that soon she, "the shadow lady-magician, … [would] wander" off, and away. But, yet again, no, no. She would never just wander off. Never simply go. Disappear. Not Queen Marie. Not one who looks as she does. For what Herr Schad must understand is this, that, "No one can die with such eyes." No one. No one. Herr Schad would never, then, be forgotten. Never. Or at least not by dear Queen Marie. She of the shining eyes.

❉

...to see the object as in itself it really is not.
— Oscar Wilde (1854–1900)

CHAPTER FIVE

Revelations

I/V

L'Exposition Universelle, Paris
— Autumn, 1900 —

LADY BRACKNELL: To be born, or at any rate bred, in a handbag ... seems to me to display a contempt for the ordinary decencies of family life that reminds one of the worst excesses of the French Revolution. (Oscar Wilde, *The Importance of Being Earnest,* 1895)

As ever, dear Lady Bracknell, is right. However, I regret to say that at hand is the revelation of a still greater disregard for the ordinary decencies of life. Not to mention death. I gather, that is, from the Reverend Chasuble, that Messrs Moncrieff and Worthing, though gentlemen both, "have expressed a desire for immediate baptism."

LADY BRACKNELL: The idea is grotesque — irreligious!

Quite. And no less grotesque is that here in Paris, but five years on, two more gentlemen, if that is the word, express this same morbid desire. One is a somewhat modern young man called Herr Johannes Schad. From Basel. He is a clerk. In trade. Rubber, I believe. The other is Mr. Oscar Wilde.

OSCAR WILDE: *Mr. Melmoth* is my name. It is my new name.

So it is. But the tyrannous fact remains that you request the sacrament of baptism. A desire expressed from, appropriately enough, your death-bed. Whether in a semi or fully recumbent posture is not known. You are, though, undoubtedly resident at the Hotel d'Alsace. 13 Rue des Beaux Arts. Hardly a place in which to be seen, still less to die. The date in question is November 30th, and the Church to which you seek entry is that of Rome. It is, I gather, a matter of sundry oils applied, in extravagant manner, to bodily extremities. Not only hands but even feet.

OSCAR WILDE: The feet of joy.

If you insist. To proceed, however, to the case of Herr Schad, his sacramental indiscretion occurs just across the Seine. Within an obscure establishment known, to its inmates, as the Paris Tabernacle. 61 Rue Meslay. The unfashionable side. The date, in this instance, is September 30th, with baptism here taking the somewhat theatrical form of immersion.

JACK: Immersion!

Indeed, but —

DR. CHASUBLE: You need have no apprehension. Sprinkling is all that is necessary, or, I think, advisable. Our weather is so changeable.

Ah yes, the weather in England is certainly given to wilful changes of mind. However, it is no less mercurial here in Paris, and yet Herr Schad is still sufficiently abandoned to take to the waters of the Tabernacle. It is, I believe, a kind of Aquarium. Herr Schad, you see, is spiritually re-born in a water-tank. Or bath-tub. Of the overgrown variety. Such are the wonders of modern plumbing.

OSCAR WILDE: It is absurd to say the age of miracles is past.

Quite. As you yourself, Mr. Melmoth, heroically attempted to demonstrate, even at the risk of a severe chill. I have in mind the occasion, but three years ago, a week before Whitsun, I believe, on which you sought Regeneration in the distinctly murky sea-water off the Normandy coast.

OSCAR WILDE: [Ah yes,] I attended Mass ... and afterwards bathed. I [thus] went into the water *without* being a Pagan. The consequence was that I was not tempted by Sirens or other Mer-maidens. ... I really think that this is a remarkable thing.

Ah, you pose, Sir, as a Baptist. No wonder your friends, such as they are, have termed you a Dissenter.

JACK: Good heavens!

Quite. But even before his reckless Normandy plunge, Mr. Melmoth has displayed a remarkable enthusiasm for baptism. He was, I gather, sprinkled not only as a babe in arms but also as an infant — the first time as a Protestant and the second a Catholic.

JACK: Good heavens!

Good heavens, indeed. Baptism is not usually deemed to be, as dear Basil Hallward might say, "a thing that one can do now and then." Nevertheless, if we are to take Mr. Melmoth as our spiritual pattern, perhaps it is.

DR. CHASUBLE: I am grieved to hear such sentiments. ... They savour [I fear] of the heretical views of the Anabaptists.

I do apologise. Anabaptists are, indeed, most heretical. Not least in their morbid inclination to redistribute wealth. In this regard, I am guided by the Church of England's Articles of Religion. Number 38, as if an omnibus. Which advises that "The Riches and Goods of Christians are not common ... as certain Anabaptists do *falsely* boast." Falsely, please note.

HERR WINCKELKOPF: I had no idea that you felt so strongly about religion.

Only where property is concerned. Hence my admiration for Reverend Chasuble, who has, I gather, "refuted the views of Anabaptism" in no less than "four ... unpublished sermons." To be baptised more than the once may, he fears, have disastrous social consequences.

ALGERNON: But I have not been christened for years.

JACK: Yes, but you have been christened. That is the important thing.

ALGERNON: Quite so. So I know my constitution can stand it.

Granted; however, can *the* constitution stand it? The *political* constitution? After all, this way, the way of Second Baptism, lies what the Radical papers call, I believe, Socialism. Is that not so, Lady Bracknell?

LADY BRACKNELL: Algernon, I forbid you to be baptized. I will not hear of such excesses.

Quite. To be baptized, or at any rate re-baptized, displays a contempt for the ordinary decencies of political life that reminds one, or at least myself, of the worst excesses of the Swiss Peasant Rebellion of 1653.

LADY BRACKNELL: I beg your pardon?

Forgive me, but I think, as so often, of Herr Schad's excitable ancestor, Uli Schad, Chief Clerk of said Peasant Rebellion. The Basel branch. All of which prompts one to wonder whether young Herr Schad also thinks of his misguided forefather even as he descends into the Aquarium bath-tub.

LORD HENRY: Explain.

Well you see, the excesses of 1653 do rather savour of the Anabaptists. The Swiss variety. A sorry tribe who, to a man, felt sure that the New Jerusalem was to be found somewhere up one Alp, or another. For this belief, naturally, they were executed. Hung, burnt, etc. On occasion, simply drowned. The *Third* Baptism, as it was darkly known. To the Authorities. Such is the Law.

IVAN THE CZAR: The fearful law.

Indeed.

Pause.

I am sorry. I have digressed. Though from what I am not altogether sure. Whatever it *was*, my point most certainly now is this: that, here in Paris, at this particular hour, Herr Schad could hardly avoid his Fatherland's proclivity for revolutionary outrage.

DUCHESS OF PAISLEY: Pray go on.

Why, look about you. As you will see, the *Exposition Universelle* rejoices in a host of delightful pavilions, one for every nation, except, that is, for dear little Switzerland. A nation which, being endowed with far more Nature than is advisable, is represented by an entire mountain village: cowbells, dancing peasants, alpine horns, cardboard mountains, etc. All regrettable enough; but, still worse, its chapel is dedicated to none other than Mr. William Tell. A man inclined not only to wear an apple upon his head (or was that his son?) but to foment revolution.

MRS. ALLONBY: I am sorry to hear it.

Indeed. And, as if this were not enough, the name of Mr. Tell was, I gather, frequently invoked by such as the combustible Uli. So, you see, young Herr Schad, in his Tabernacle tub, must surely be mindful of the very particular sin of revolution. The sin of his fathers, as it were. And if not, then he most certainly should be. Given the myriad opportunities that the *Exposition* kindly affords to part with one's money, what could be more contemptuous of the ordinary decencies of economic life than to pass one's time in a water-tank?

MRS. ARBUTHNOT: Nothing.

Exactly. And what, in fact, could be more contemptuous of the ordinary decencies of *philosophical* life than to receive a form of baptism that is known, to its devotees, as Conditional Baptism.

JACK: What on earth do you mean?

Why, I mean a baptism in which the officiating priest is in that most unphilosophical of all predicaments, namely that of *not* knowing. To be precise, not knowing whether or not the candidate has already been baptized. At the last, you see, the unfortunate Mr. Melmoth loses the power of both reason and speech, and so is quite unable to advise the Reverend Dunne, his hastily summoned ecclesiastic. Indeed, Mr. Melmoth's final attempt at verbal communication is, frankly, a rather disappointing aphorism.

OSCAR WILDE: One steamboat is very much like another.

A perfectly reasonable proposition, I grant, but not exactly hilarious, and hardly, I feel, apropos. It certainly leaves poor Father Dunne none the wiser as to whether or not Mr. Melmoth has already succumbed to the Sirens of baptism. Let alone as to whether or not he desires Regeneration.

It is, I suspect, somewhat difficult to express such a desire without words, even if possessed of a rare talent for mime. Or charades. Indeed, can it be done at all? Can wordless hands, fingers or even one's face, ever communicate a desire for salvation? Is it possible? Given, say, a face like Mr. Melmoth's.

CECILY: [It certainly] looks like repentance.

But *does* it, dear Cecily? Can anything *look* like repentance? You refer, I believe, to the eating of muffins, which makes, I think, my point. And, even if not, we who are concerned with the fate of Mr. Melmoth's soul have more than enough uncertainty to endure.

LORD HENRY: Explain.

Well, you see, in Conditional Baptism the conventional "I baptize you, et cetera." is immediately followed by the aside, "*If* you are not already baptized." Which, I feel, is hardly the way to effect divine sacrament. Indeed, it could be likened to solemnly announcing, "I declare you man and wife" but then casually remarking, "*If* you are not already married."

DORIAN GRAY: I shudder at the thought.

Quite. Though I myself would call it a species of *un*-thought. The *opposite* of thought. Of *respectable* thought — the thought, that is, of *certainty*. In brief, thought as it should be. As laid down for our guidance by the admirably dull Herr Professor Hegel.

LORD GORING: [But] it is love and not German philosophy that is the true explanation of the world.

Ah, a delightful axiom, but I speak of *this* particular world. This one, in dear Paris. Here in the midst of the *Exposition Universelle*. It is, I accept, invariably said that the *Exposition* "constitute[s] the [very] synthesis of nineteenth-century philosophy"; however, if true, it is a most peculiar synthesis. One looks about and what does one see but "palpable shams"? All about us, the most disquieting improbabilities. Air Sports, for instance.

JACK: Good heavens!

Good heavens, indeed, Jack. And then there are what they call, I believe, Theatre-Phones. Not to mention Hypnotists, Wireless Telegraphy, Talking Films, and indeed (God help us)

Fig. 23. Photograph of the Manoir à l'Envers (Paris, 1900). Alamy
Banque D'Images .

La Maison de Rire. This last, needless to say, is by no means as
comical as the Allegorical Tableaux or at least those intended for
our moral improvement. I think, for instance, of "Nature Disrobing before Science." All of Paris, it would seem, is off to the
bath-tub.

DUCHESS OF PAISLEY: Pray go on.

I shall. For my fear is this: that the *Exposition* seeks to turn
the world Upside Down. In short, that its secret emblem is the
altogether alarming *Manoir à l'Envers*, an edifice that is, of
course, head-over-arse. As they say in Synod. Or is that the Music Hall? Whatever, within said *Manoir,* the tables and chairs etc.
stand not upon the floor, as is customary, I believe. Instead, they
are suspended above one's very head. As if, I imagine, the very
blade of the guillotine.

OSCAR WILDE: To conclude?

Why, my conclusion is this: that if the *Exposition* really is the
philosophical terminus of the nineteenth century, may Heaven
preserve us. I need hardly remind you who it is that claimed to

Fig. 24. Photograph of the Église Baptiste de la Rue Meslay (Paris, 1899). Blocher Saillens Archive.

up-turn Professor Hegel's noble synthesis, to rudely turn dear Herr Hegel upside down.

MICHAEL, THE PEASANT: And who is that?

I would rather not say. Suffice it to observe that this way, lies, I fear, the excesses of yet another revolution. Here in Paris, you see, the ground itself now shifts beneath one's feet. Quite literally so, in fact. I am thinking of those who imperil what may remain of their sanity upon the *Trottoir Roulant.*

THE SWALLOW: I cannot do that.

No, neither can I. Perish the thought. It is sufficiently alarming merely to *observe* the pavement move, let alone be moved along upon it, as if one were luggage. Paris, you see, is a city that moves, that *goes,* if you will. Indeed, by November, all these pavilions and palaces will go, be gone. In short, this is a fugitive city. Mr. Melmoth's, as it were. Made in his ephemeral likeness. Would you not agree, dear Ernest?

ERNEST LA JEUNESSE: Nature [has here] … gathered together all her glories for Oscar …. In every palace … he [has] built again his … palace of fame.

Exactly. Though these passing palaces speak, I fear, not only of fame but also of a yet greater vulgarity — namely, one's unfortunate need of God. I have in mind the Scriptural advice that "Here we have no continuing city." In short, that we are not to overly invest in this present world, but rather to look unto the next. God's, that is. This world, apparently, is but a passing show.

A precept, I suspect, dear to the habitués of that dear little Tabernacle building, the Aquarium. 61 Rue Meslay is, you see, itself but a temporary arrangement. For in truth, in fact, it is merely, in origin, what is called, I gather, a warehouse. It is merely dressed up as a church: some drapery here, a curtain there, et cetera.

LADY BRACKNELL: A thoroughly experienced French maid [can] produce … a really marvellous result.

Indeed. And how appropriate it is that a tabernacle is, literally speaking, a tent. Or, at least, species thereof. With, then, its myriad fleeting castles, Paris is, these days, a whole city of tabernacles. Or, if you will, a Tabernacle City. Which is to say, a Holy City. One is, then, hardly surprised that the two who are so desirous of baptism, Messrs Melmoth and Schad, are themselves both visitors, migrants of a kind.

JACK: Is that clever?

I think so. It might even be true. Albeit, less so if Herr Schad harbours ulterior motives.

LADY BRACKNELL: I beg your pardon?

Well, what if, like both Jack and Algernon, he desires baptism merely to secure the favour of a particular young woman? One of those young women at the Aquarium. One who has herself already passed through its tap-waters. One of its most alluring naiads, sirens, mermaidens. As Mr. Melmoth reminds us, the medium of water is not without its temptations, its crimes. To speak frankly, our two baptists, both Melmoth and Schad, may yet require investigation.

MABEL CHILTERN: The police should interfere.

Precisely. And if not at the Aquarium then at least at the Hotel d'Alsace. Which will, no doubt, be already familiar to the police. Here, in Paris, I find, detectives keep an alarmingly close

Fig. 25. Photograph of a British "Bobby" (Paris, 1900), from *Burton Holmes Travelogues: Round about Paris, Paris Exposition* (1901).

eye upon hotels. One can, in fact, barely move for loitering policemen.

LORD GORING: It is what the police are for.

Quite. And how ably they do it. Ever devoted to their calling, as it were. Consider, as evidence, this photograph. Here. This one.

Yes, it is indeed of *Le Pavillon de la Grande-Bretagne* and, in particular, one of our very own brave constables. He does not, I admit, cut a particularly imposing figure; however, what he may lack in juridical air he more than compensates for in style. His left hand raised so elegantly toward, I think, his very splendid hat. Or should that be helmet?

Regardless, I am somewhat perplexed by this lifted hand. It might almost be the beginning of a salute, were it not the left. Or, perhaps, the wiping of a tear from an eye, were it not that policemen do not cry. Unlike other men. Other men I know. Could it, in fact, be that, like the unhappy Mr. Melmoth, our nonchalant constable attempts a gesture intended to express a desire for baptism?

JACK: Oh, that is nonsense!

Ah, but not if it were a desire for the baptism of *another*. That is to say, a child. Or infant. Living as we do in an age of carelessness, our policemen, I gather, are not infrequently left holding mislaid infants, many of whom are felt to be in want of baptism. Indeed, according to Lady Bracknell, our London constables were once left holding, or nearly holding, an infant who would, one day, *himself* desire baptism.

CECILY: Jack?

The very same.

LADY BRACKNELL: Twenty-eight years ago, … a perambulator that contained a baby of the male sex [was], … through the … Metropolitan Police, … discovered standing by itself in … Bayswater. … But, the baby was not there!

Ah, such a scene! A veritable tableau, if you will. For, herein one may discern, to one's edification, both a Coming and a Going, Entrance and Departure. That is to say, first the Entrance, as it were, of the Law — if we may so speak of the Metropolitan Police. And then the Departure, as it were, of he-who-one-day-would-seek-to-be-baptized, the baby, the infant Jack. He, the latter, is now simply "not there!" The Law is after him, but he is gone. It is, I believe, a perfect miniature of Grace. Or, so some might say. At the Aquarium.

❋

II/V

The High Court, London
— May 1924 —

In 1897, one of the legal figures involved in initial preparations to divorce Oscar and Constance Wilde was the solicitor Frederick Inderwick KC. In 1924, when Johannes petitioned to annul his marriage to Marie the Registrar was, as it happens, Inderwick's son, William.

❀

PROBATE, DIVORCE, AND ADMIRALTY DIVISION
May 27, 1924

UPON HEARING the Solicitors for both parties I do order that Edwin Francis White FRCS of 388 Upper Richmond Road, Putney and Lennard Stokes, MRCS LRCP of Upton Cottage, Upton near Andover, Hants be appointed as Inspectors to examine the parts and organs of generation of Jean Jacques Frederic Schad the Petitioner in this Cause to report in writing whether he is capable of performing the act of generation, and if incapable whether such his Impotency can or cannot be relieved or removed by art or skill; and also to examine the parts and organs of generation of Marie Anne Schad otherwise Wheeler the Respondent in this Cause and to report in writing whether she is, or is not, a Virgin, and hath or hath not any impediment on her part to prevent the consummation of Marriage, and whether such impediment (if any) can or cannot be removed by art or skill.
W. Inderwick
Registrar

Ah, impotence, "The Importance of *Impotence*." As we say, hereabouts. Not especially witty, I know. So, how about "The *Impotence* of Being Earnest"? Or should that be "The Impotence of Being Learned"? Of being one who merely spends his days writing, scribbling away, with little art or skill. In the far corner of the Court.

No. On the contrary, in fact. My office, though modest, *is* endowed with a certain authority. I *do* wear a crown of sorts. Albeit borrowed. So, no, I am not quite condemned to Impotency. I can instruct. Can command. As in this present Cause. Wherein, I do order and do further order etc. etc. Indeed, if necessary, I can compel. If resistance is met, if my writ does not run, my orders can always be enforced.

MR. GRISBY: I do not [myself] employ personal violence of any kind. The Officer of the Court, [however], whose function it is to seize the [accused], ... is waiting ... outside.

It is, you see, wise to do as I order. Even if it is to undertake the examination of a perfect stranger. Or, if one *is* that perfect stranger, to submit to such. Whether that is for the first or, in fact, the second time. Again, as in this present Cause. The Respondent, she has, I note, already been examined. Last month. The seventh. Indeed, a damning report it was. Damning. Quite conclusive, I would have thought. Further examinations, however, have been called for. And no one, it seems, is completely sure why. Such is the Law. Regrettable. Very. But the Court must know. Must clarify. The Crown having a perfectly legitimate interest in marriage. Every marriage. Every marriage-bed, indeed. Or bedroom. Such is the prerogative of the Crown. The State. The Polis.

OSCAR WILDE: The ... "city of the sun" [is marred by] ... injudicious marriages.

Exactly. And there are so many. Injudicious marriages, that is. Which is why they must, I am afraid, be identified. Made visible. Brought to the light. As must any marriage that proves, in truth, not really to be a marriage. Even if, as in the present Cause, the pale shadow thereof has lasted almost twenty years.

LORD ILLINGWORTH: Twenty years of romance make a woman look like a ruin.

And twenty years of *marriage*?

LORD ILLINGWORTH: Twenty years of marriage make her something like a public building.

That, sir, is absurd!

OSCAR WILDE: I hope marriage has not made you too serious.

Only *this* one, *this* marriage. If marriage it is. Which is why, on behalf of the Crown, the State, your City of the Sun, I have ordered that it be examined. Gone into.

ALGERNON: In married life three is company, and two is none.

What, sir, do you imply? That I or anyone else in this Court is, in some way, involved in this marriage? We, the Court, simply seek to determine, and with medical exactitude, whether or not it really is a marriage.

OSCAR WILDE: The Sultan —

I beg your pardon?

OSCAR WILDE: The Sultan does not know how much he is married.

You speak, Mr. Wilde, as if marriage were a matter of degree, or extent. The Court cannot allow such sophistry. To quote yourself, "This is not the moment for German scepticism."

OSCAR WILDE: Keep your own words to yourself. Leave me mine.

But words, Mr. Wilde, may not be owned, are not faithful. They are not, as it were, the marrying kind. Not inclined to have and to hold. In short, Mr. Wilde, I believe you mistake words for persons. And it is only persons, persons made in the image of God, the One, the One-and-Only-and-Forever, who marry.

LADY MARKBY: [But] nowadays people marry as often as they can.

And how often is that?

MABEL CHILTERN: Once a week.

I beg your pardon?

MABEL CHILTEN: Once a week is quite often enough.

To marry?

MABEL CHILTEN: To propose.

But what do *you* say, Mr. Wilde?

OSCAR WILDE: Would you repeat that question?

CECIL GRAHAM: Have you been twice married and once divorced, or twice divorced and once married?

LORD AUGUSTUS: I really don't remember.

Neither, I think, does Mr. Schad. Our Petitioner. It is rumoured that he already plans to marry again.

METROPOLITAN POLICE: Schad … appears to be a respectable man.

So he does. But what is known of his present domestic circumstances?

METROPOLITAN POLICE: His … sister is now keeping house for him.

Ah, a lonely house.

Pause.

SIR ROBERT CHILTERN: God has given us a lonely house.

You too?

SIR ROBERT CHILTERN: God.

But what has God to do with a lonely house? You speak as if the Almighty were opposed to marriage.

DR. CHASUBLE: The Primitive Church —

Yes?

DR. CHASUBLE: The Primitive Church was distinctly against marriage.

But not anymore. Both Petitioner and Respondent, when resident in Paris, belonged to what is sometimes called, I understand, the *Église Chrétienne Primitive,* and its adherents, it is clear, most certainly marry. Or at least attempt to. Their God, it seems, has no desire for a lonely house. Besides, what kind of God could ever desire such?

OSCAR WILDE: Christ.

I am sorry?

OSCAR WILDE: Christ, … [He who] … now … sits in his lone dishonoured House.

Ah, and what, Mr. Wilde, does he do, this lonely Christ of yours?

OSCAR WILDE: Weeps, perchance for me.

Weeps? For you? Why should Christ weep for you? You who, with regard to holy matrimony, have led a whole nation into confusion. Or, at very least, misunderstanding.

Pause.

LADY WINDERMERE: The proper basis for marriage is … misunderstanding.

Of what kind?

LADY WINDERMERE: Mutual.

And what if the misunderstanding is not mutual? What if only one of the two misunderstand?

LANE: Yes, sir.

What do you mean, "Yes, sir"? Tell the Court, Mr. Lane, what you really think of marriage.

LANE: I believe it is a very pleasant state, sir.

Is that it? Have you nothing more to say?

LANE: I have had very little experience of it myself. … I have only been married once. [And] that was in consequence of a misunderstanding between myself and a young person.

A young person? Which young person?

OSCAR WILDE: You read it … badly.

Read what badly?

OSCAR WILDE: My … work.

I do not care. Who is this person? This unfortunate person?

OSCAR WILDE: You read … badly[!]

I said, who is she? This person. She whose whole marriage was but a misunderstanding. Who on earth is she?

MISS PRISM: I admit with shame that I do not know.

Might she, then, be the Respondent? The woman in this present Cause? Namely, Mrs. Schad, otherwise Wheeler. Speak, Mr. Wilde. Speak to the Court.

SIR EDWARD CLARKE: My lord, … hidden meanings have been most unjustly read into the … works of my client.

Well, what else did you expect? If Mr. Wilde writes of a young person married as a result of a misunderstanding and then says nothing more of her, not a single sorry word, we are bound to ask after this poor, bewildered person. Even if she is no longer young. Even if "a woman of no importance."

OSCAR WILDE: You read … badly.

Silence! Silence in Court.

OSCAR WILDE: May I say nothing, my lord?

No. You shall, for once, be silent. And remain so until the Crown has proceeded to put to Mrs. Schad a number of questions. Upon the answers to which much shall depend.

> *Did you ever embrace him?*
> *Never.*
> *Did you ever kiss him?*
> *Never.*
> *Did you ever put your hand on his person?*
> *Never.*
> *And then bring him into your bedroom?*
> *Never.*
> *Sleep in the same bed with him all night?*
> *Never.*
> *Each of you having taken off all your clothes, did you take his person in your hand?*
> (Edward Carson interrogating Oscar Wilde, The Old Bailey, Wednesday, April 3, 1895)

❋

III/V

Paris, Once More
— Undated —

JACK: I have carefully preserved the Court Guides
of the period.
LADY BRACKNELL: I have known strange errors in
that publication.
(*The Importance of Being Earnest*)

Once again, dear Lady Bracknell is to be heeded. The courts do
indeed, on occasion, fall into error. And not only in their Guides
but also, I gather, in what they admit as evidence. One here
thinks, as always, in fact, or most nights, of the letter submitted
to the High Court, in London, in 1924, from a certain, or possibly uncertain, Dr. Thomas G. Stevens. It is a letter detailing his
examination of the unfortunate wife, or supposed wife, of Herr
Schad, our man of rubber. Whatever, one's concern is that the
letter to the Court includes one or two strange orthographical
errors. It would seem as if Dr. Stevens cannot spell. Or at least,
cannot spell that unfortunate word, "menstruated." Or indeed
his own name. Middle name. Or initial thereof.

Is it, then, a false letter? Unlikely, one accepts, but false letters
are written. In particular, they are written, it would seem, by
those in Authority. This is certainly the view from Switzerland;
or rather the view of the rubber gentleman's inflammable ancestor, Uli Schad. Our rebellious man. The one on the scaffold. On
a hill, Gellert Hill, just beyond the walls of old Basel. It is said
that he accused the authorities of *falsche Briefe*. And for this, of
course, he died.

Pause.

So much, however, for the view *from* Switzerland. Which is,
naturally, of far less interest than the view *of* Switzerland. One
thinks now of young Lady Agatha.

DUCHESS OF BERWICK: Dear girl, she is so fond of photographs of Switzerland. Such a pure taste, I think.

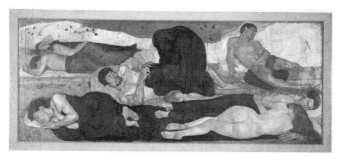

Fig. 26. Ferdinand Hodler, *Die Nacht* [*The Night*] (1889–90). Oil on canvas. 116 × 299 cm. Kunstmuseum Bern Staat, Bern.

Pure indeed; but not, I fear, a taste altogether shared by Mr. Melmoth.

OSCAR WILDE: I don't like Switzerland: it has produced nothing, save theologians and waiters.

But is there a difference? Perhaps there is, with regard to kissing. You are, Mr. Melmoth, an enthusiast, I hear, for kissing waiters. Less so theologians. Or at least those of the Alpine variety.

OSCAR WILDE: The Swiss are … ugly … carved out of wood, most of them; the others are carved out of turnips.

And who among us would wish to kiss a man carved out of wood? Or turnips, for that matter. Indeed, is a man made of wood even capable of being kissed?

OSCAR WILDE: The chastity of Switzerland has got on my nerves.

Quite. Though there is the painting, *Night,* by that Swiss fellow, Herr Hodler. I first saw it, as perhaps did Johannes, at the *Exposition.* Here there are, one feels, precious few signs of chastity. Still less of turnips. I think of the two couples, to the right and the left, respectively. How close they lie, the Swiss. *Herr und Frau, Monsieur et Madame*; even, I presume, the unfortunate Uli and Wife. Herr Uli was, you see, a married man. So had a wife to watch him slowly ascend the steps to the gallows. And swing.

DR. CHASUBLE: Dead?

Quite dead.

MISS PRISM: What a lesson for him!

Indeed. And what a view. What a view he commanded even as he died. From the scaffold, up on Gellert Hill. From whence there is no doubting the quality of the prospect. Particularly at that time of the year. July. The seventh, to be precise.

LORD ILLINGWORTH: Are you sure?

On the whole. I seldom err with respect to dates.

LORD HENRY: My wife … never gets confused over … dates.

Excellent. And tonight, neither do I. Which, in this connection, is most fortunate. July seventh is, you see, also the day on which, in 1897, Mr. Charles Wooldridge, Trooper, wife-murderer, and fellow inmate of Mr. Melmoth, is executed at Reading Gaol. Berkshire. Such a rural county. The woods, the fields, the glades.

DUCHESS OF BERWICK: There is nothing like Nature, is there?

No. Thank God.

Pause.

To return, however, to this coincidence of dates, this —

OSCAR WILDE: Awful calendar of crime.

If you insist, Mr. Melmoth. I myself, in my present and confined situation, prefer to talk of the thoughtfulness of the Law. To which we have so much to be grateful. Not least with regard to the timing of our deaths.

OSCAR WILDE: I will take care not to die on the wrong date.

I am glad to hear it, Mr. Melmoth. Very glad. I must, though, point out that you carelessly allow yourself to pass away on November 30th. Now, I have no objection to dying in November, per se. It is, indeed, an eminently suitable month in which to die, what with all its failing light. Falling dark. It is just that there is no special romance, no particular vibration, attached to the 30th of November. Whilst there is to, say, the seventh, that being the death-date, on the whole, of poor Basil Hayward, dear friend of Dorian Gray. Then again, there is the thirteenth, the day on which you yourself, Mr. Melmoth, upon your way to Reading Gaol, were left exposed to comment at Clapham Junction. For one half of an hour. As long as is the silence in Heaven, I gather. Before the Throne, of the Lamb. Once all have been judged.

I am sorry. I have digressed, grown biblical.

However, to resume my audit of November's days of vibration, there is, I suggest, the twelfth, the very last day of the *Exposition Universelle,* a day of exemplary finality — cannons, drums, lights going out, and all just before midnight. What better November day on which to die? But no, you, sir, insist on living until the thirtieth, a most prosaic end for one otherwise so devoted to vibration.

Pause.

Some may, perhaps, deem it nit-picking to judge a man by his chosen day of death. But nothing, I believe, tells one more about a man. In particular, a man who dies on July seventh. Herr Uli, of course. Not to mention poor Trooper Woolridge.

DR. CHASUBLE: Were you with him at the end?

Trooper Woolridge?

DR. CHASUBLE: Yes.

I do not think so, Reverend Father. But, then, who really is with a man as he hangs? As he faces the noose. Some might claim they are, such as a priest, a doctor, an executioner.

OSCAR WILDE: The Hanging Committee.

No. They hang *paintings*. In galleries. I am thinking, here, tonight, of the hanging of *men*. In particular, I am thinking that, though a fellow may say he is with the hanging man, in truth he is not. After all, such a fellow —

OSCAR WILDE: [D]oes not [himself] die a death of shame
   On a day of dark disgrace,
   Nor have a noose about his neck,
   Nor a cloth upon his face

   …

   He does not [himself] wake at dawn …
   To put on convict-clothes,
   While some coarse-mouthed Doctor gloats, and
   notes
   Each new and nerve-twitched pose.

   …

> He does not [himself] bend his head to hear
> The Burial Office read,
> Nor, while the terror of his soul
> Tells him he is not dead,
> Cross his own coffin, as he moves
> Into the hideous shed.
> [Nor, at last, does he] … stare upon the air
> Through a little roof of glass.

Quite. Who among us really knows, as yet at least, what it is to be roughly woken at dawn? And then examined by a course-mouthed doctor. One's final view of the world glimpsed through a filthy skylight.

OSCAR WILDE: [Here] the shed in which people are hanged … [has] a glass roof, like a photographer's studio on the sands at Margate. [Indeed,] … for eighteen months, I thought it was the studio for photographing prisoners.

An understandable error. Having one's photograph taken in Margate would be bound to end badly. The Kentish skyline is, I gather, decidedly morbid. Certainly, if compared to that view enjoyed by Herr Uli, from his scaffold. Basel Land in all its mid-summer glory.

CECILY: The weather … continues charming.

Indeed, thus ensuring poor Uli a quite invigorating prospect. Sufficient, I dare say, to make even a condemned man feel glad to be alive. Full, as it were, of vital force, the force of the blood which even as, even *because,* the noose is tightening, rushes at last to enliven him, stiffen him, enlarge him.

GWENDOLEN: Whenever people talk … about the weather … I always feel quite certain they mean something else.

I am sorry. Forgive me. Please forgive me. I am just a man. Of flesh. And blood. I am not, I confess, made in the neutral and neutered image of Switzerland. Expect, then, no impartiality from me. Not with respect to death. Nor with respect to marriage. I am, you see, no celibate scholar. Not dead from waist down. Indeed, I am barely a scholar in any regard. My university, if I still have one, is —

OSCAR WILDE: The University of Matrimony?

No. My studies, such as they are, relate to —

OSCAR WILDE: A dissertation on widows, as … the matrimonially fittest?

No. Again, no. If I could make any academic claim it would be to the title of —

ANTONIO MIGGE: Professor of Massage?

Emeritus, alas. But I keep my hand in. A quotation here, a fragment there — it is astonishing what, with a little manipulation, can be achieved. Created.

OSCAR WILDE: Criticism can recreate the past for us from the very smallest fragment of language or art, just as surely as the man of science can, from some tiny bone, call Behemoth out of his cave, and make Leviathan swim once more across the startled sea.

Indeed. And how adept one may become at recovering the lost or disappeared. Not least those who, like the Behemoth or Leviathan, never actually existed at all. But then —

OSCAR WILDE: The only real people are the people who never existed.

Such as Mr. Melmoth, of course. Or, indeed, possibly, Mrs. Johannes Schad. Our rubber gentleman's wife. Or supposed wife.

MADELAINE: Johannes … turned her out.

Yes. So you say. As if he were all but a wife-murderer. To which, indeed, there is perhaps some elaborate calendrical clue. After all, as you know, his ancestor Uli shares his execution day with no other than poor Trooper Wooldridge.

Pause.

By the way, it seems to me that murdering one's wife may, in fact, be more common than often supposed. Where else do you think that that blood on the carpet came from?

MRS. OTIS: How horrid. I don't at all care for bloodstains in a sitting room.

But could one not make an exception for the blood of one's wife?

LADY BRACKNELL: I beg your pardon?

MRS. UMNEY: It is the blood of Lady Eleanore, … [she] who was murdered on that very spot by her … husband.

Exactly and, try as one might, the stain will simply not go away.

WASHINGTON OTIS: Nonsense … Pinkerton's Champion Stain Remover … will clean it up in no time.

But alas its cleansing effect is merely temporary. The stain may go for a while, and yet in the morning, at dawn, one wakes to find the stain has returned. Every morning, again and again and again. It is a sorry state of affairs, indicative, I fear, of —

WASHINGTON OTIS: The Permanence of Sanguineous Stains.

Or at least of those stains left by the blood of one's wife.

Pause.

THOMAS STEVENS: Mrs. Schad states that she has not menstrated since November 1904.

Does she not give a particular date? Say which November day?

THOMAS STEVENS: The female mind does not lend itself readily to accurate remembrance.

But did you not ask her, probe her, enquire after the precise date and circumstances of this final issue, letting, bleeding?

THOMAS STEVENS: The female mind … will omit, from shyness or sentimentality, the important symptoms and … lead the attention away from one trouble to another.

So what does one do? How does one ever coax a woman to speak precisely, to tell the truth, to —

THOMAS STEVENS: Speak of her real trouble?

Exactly. How on earth is it done? Tell me, please.

THOMAS STEVENS: It is … necessary to lead the patient through devious channels.

Curtain.

❖

To make disappear the stain left by the blood of one's victim may well prove beyond the means of even the most modern detergents. However, to make the victim themselves disappear is,

I gather, not wholly impossible. Or at least not if one knows the right man, a man who might be persuaded to do what he should not. To use his expertise in ways he should not.

I think of my dear friend, Mr. Alan Campbell. 152 Hertford Street, Mayfair. He is a scientific man who, as it happens, makes an appearance in Mr. Melmoth's peculiar novel, *Dorian Gray.* Herein, dear Campbell quite literally does away with a corpse. A fanciful episode involving the dissolution of the body by means of various "chemicals," in particular "nitric acid." The body in question proves, it turns out, "an admirable subject" for this "curious experiment." One moment it is "the thing … seated … [at] the table" upstairs, "with bowed head and humped back," and the next, by means of a little science, it is simply not there at all. "Upstairs … the thing that had been sitting at the table was gone."

As I say, a fanciful episode, within, indeed, a fanciful novel. The episode is, however, susceptible to fine interpretation — as, indeed, a dark Allegory of Divorce. You see, *Dorian Gray* is initially published, within *Lippincott's Magazine,* alongside a two-essay debate upon (of all things) divorce. Moreover, the debate is entitled, "The In*dissolubility* of Marriage." The first essay contends that a marriage may never be dissolved; the second that, on the contrary, it may. We are thus reminded that, in this our modern age, dissolution is a possibility that haunts every man's marriage.

Or, to be precise, every man's *wife.* In *Dorian Gray,* you see, the dissolving of the body runs parallel to a subplot to which most scholars turn a blind eye: namely, Lord Henry Wotton's divorce, his ridding himself of his wife. Once again, the thing, as it were, formerly seated at the table, disappears. The thing upstairs. Her. Lord Henry's wife.

People may yet wonder where "the thing" has gone, but reasons can be imagined. Rumours can be started. Rumours like, let us say, she —

LORD HENRY: Fell into the Seine off an omnibus.

Indeed. As if, perhaps, seized by a desire for immediate baptism. Besides, the stairs on Paris omnibuses are so very treacher-

Fig. 27. Edward Hopper, *Stairway at 48, Rue de Lille, Paris,* 1906. Oil on wood, 12 7/8 × 9 5/16 in. [32.7 × 23.7 cm]. Whitney Museum of American Art, New York; Josephine N. Hopper Bequest 70.1295. © Heirs of Josephine N. Hopper, licensed by the Whitney Museum of American Art.

ous. But then, come to think of it, are not all stairs treacherous? How very steep, for example, are the stairs to the scaffold? Or baptistery? Or even the marriage bed?

I have myself, as a once-married man, seen the latter stairs. Indeed, I can now reveal that I have also seen the very stairs that led young Herr Schad and his bride to *their* marriage bed. Or at least, I have seen the stairs that *led* to those stairs. Remarkable is it not? They are, you see, stairs that have been painted, depicted that is. By Mr. Edward Hopper. In 1906.

He was, Mr. Hopper, at the time, lodging within, of all places, the *Église du Tabernacle,* 48 Rue de Lille, the very church in which, it is said, Marie and Johannes had their marriage blessed just a year before.

GILBERT: How steep are the stairs.

Quite.

❋

IV/V

A Crowded House
— Undated —

Uli Schad is currently ill in bed.
(Urs Hostettler, 1653)

Every room has five or six doors, and the characters
rush in and out, … chase each other, … misunderstand each other, … make scenes and tableaux, and
distribute a gentle air of lunacy.
(Oscar Wilde, 1887)

There are, I think, too many doors. Tonight. And so many come
and go. Tonight. God, you see, has given me a far from lonely
house. Mine, indeed, is a crowded house, madhouse, sick house,
Maison de Rire, Manoir à l'Envers. It may even be thought a
house of ill repute.

OSCAR WILDE: Suddenly the police entered and —

Yes?

OSCAR WILDE: Arrested everybody.

Quite. This house is so easily mistaken for something else.
Just like the Hanging House. The one at Reading. The one you,
Mr. Melmoth, mistook for a photographer's shed. At Margate.

I wonder, by the way, if Trooper Wooldridge made the same
mistake? Did he think, for a moment, even as he faced the
noose, that he was in Margate? His last thought, was it: where is
the damned photographer?

Poor soul.

Well, it was, I suppose, bound to happen to someone. Being executed, that is. Seeing that they arrested everybody. Not
everybody in Margate, thank God. I mean Basel. Or rather, to
be precise, Liestal, where Uli et al revolted. The leaders there,
they all got it in the neck. Chop. Save Uli, the one that swung,
the chief rouser of rabble. The rebel king. Used to jump onto the
table and weep, he did. I read that. Somewhere.

By the way, he owned, they say, "half-a-house." I read that too. "Half-a-house." Just like rubber-man when he moved, once married, to London. A dreary suburb called Palmers Green. His half-a-house, he called it semi-detached. Same thing. Thin walls. Be careful what you say. Another far-from-lonely house. What with the neighbours. Not to mention the girl. And there *was* one, I gather. Nelly.

OSCAR WLDE: It was a horrible thing to have a spy in one's house.

Particularly if given to talk. As well she might have been, Nelly. Seeing, it turns out, that Herr and Madame Schad were not, perhaps, really man and wife. Not really.

LADY MARKBY: Families are so mixed nowadays. Indeed, as a rule, everybody turns out to be somebody else.

Pause.

GWENDOLEN: [So,] what is your … name?

I beg your pardon?

GWENDOLEN: What is your … name, now that you have become someone else?

I am not quite sure, but —

OSCAR WLDE: Most people are other people.

Indeed. And I am no exception. Not even here, within these far-from-thin-walls. And bent, as I am, over this book. This tome. A kind of life, or diary, I suppose. Though not my own.

OSCAR WLDE: Everyone should keep someone else's diary. I sometimes suspect you of keeping mine.

Well, we all make mistakes, Mr. Melmoth. Grow confused. Besides, as you say, one steamboat is very much like another. Unless, of course, it is not. That is to say, unless it changes. Is transformed. Re-christened, as it were. Converted.

Pause.

ROBERT ROSS: I told [Oscar] … I should never attempt his conversion until … he was serious.

And what did he say?

OSCAR WILDE: The growth of common sense in the English Church is a thing very much to be regretted.

Then try the Aquarium, in Paris. Everybody there is sufficiently free of common sense to swear that formerly they were someone else. Someone bad.

MISS PRISM: I am not in favour of this modern mania for turning bad people into good at a moment's notice.

Bravo.

DORIAN GRAY: [But] *I* should like to be somebody else.

No, dear Dorian, you'd be a liability. You would —

LORD HENRY: Go ... about like ... [a] revivalist.

Exactly. Or a Baptist. At the Aquarium, I hear, they hold a hundred prayer meetings a month. So much praying is surely not good for you. Say too many prayers and you might alter the world. Might even alter England.

Indeed, England, I fear, may already have been changed.

LORD ILLINGWORTH: You do?

Why, yes. Do you not recall the London Revival? 1905. July 1905. Exeter Hall. The Baptists, apparently, declared it a "veritable Pentecost." Babblings, faintings, dramas. Meetings with sighs, as it were. Frightful stuff. Swift upon the heels of the wedding, it was. The wedding in Paris. Rubber-man's wedding. If it was a wedding. If, indeed, it was a Pentecost. A visitation of the Spirit. Of God's deposit, guarantee, earnest.

SAINT PAUL: God hath ... given [us] the earnest of the Spirit.

Earnest? Earnest, you say? Earnest of the Spirit? *Holy* Spirit? How very alarming. I shall, henceforth, beware any man called Earnest.

Pause.

Or should that be, any man called Johannes? John, to you and I.

GWENDOLEN: Is *your* name ... John?

JACK: I could deny it if I liked.

I too, but it would be fruitless. It produces, I accept, very few vibrations. No more, in fact, than its notorious domesticity "Jack." Moreover, I hear that —

OSCAR WILDE: Anything may happen to a person called John.

Or, indeed, to —

GWENDOLEN: Any woman who is *married* to a man called John.

Though quite *what* might happen I am really not sure.

GWENDOLEN: Any woman married to a man called John ... would ... never be allowed ... a single moment's solitude.

Pause.

Or, should that be, I wonder, any woman married to a man called *Jesus*?

LADY BRACKNELL: I beg your pardon?

OSCAR WILDE: One always thinks of [Jesus] ... as —

Yes?

OSCAR WILDE: A young bridegroom.

Precisely.

Pause.

One question, if I may: what kind of bridegroom does one imagine Christ to be? What kind of *husband,* if you will?

LORD CAVERSHAM: Ideal.

I'm sorry?

LORD CAVERSHAM: An ideal husband.

MABEL CHILTERN: I don't think I should like that.

Why ever not?

MABEL CHILTERN: It sounds like something in the next world.

Which next world? Heaven? Or the other one?

MAN: In Hell I have always lived.

And Heaven?

MAN: Never have I been able to imagine it.

Let us try, then, at least to imagine Hell. Come on. Someone. In what way might we describe it?

Silence.

How about, as —

LORD CAVERSHAM: A lot of damned nobodies.

Excellent. And, what do they do, these nobodies?

LORD CAVERSHAM: Talk ... about nothing.

How dreadful. As bad as Heaven. Which, by the way, I gather is also afflicted by the absence of marriage.

LADY BRACKNELL: I beg your pardon?

Why, it is said that in Heaven they neither marry nor are given in marriage but are as the angels. The angels in Palmers Green. In which case, if true, I fear that —

JACK: A passionate celibacy is all that any of us can look forward to.

In short, all we have yet-to-come are —

OSCAR WILDE: Un-kissed kisses.

Indeed. Un-loved love, you might say. Love that is lost. For eternity.

Pause.

OSCAR WILDE: Love is never lost.

I beg your pardon?

OSCAR WILDE: Love is never lost.

Unlike parents, then. They can be lost.

LADY BRACKNELL: To lose one parent —

And people, people in general, they too, I fear, can be lost. For example, —

URS HOSTETTLER: We hear nothing of Uli Schad these days.

Ah, him. Well, he is sick. You said so yourself. Sick even unto death. Execution. Swinging in the midsummer Basel breeze. But, you see, others too are lost. And not just by means of the noose, the drop, all of a sudden, and at but a moment's notice. Others are lost by degrees, gradations, increments.

MADELEINE: The Schads have begun a system of not eating.

It may take years but, in the end, they vanish.

MADELEINE: Johannes sometimes goes from eight in the morning to seven at evening without eating.

It may be painful. But it can be done.

MADELEINE: Marie has only an egg at midday.

It happens more often than you think.

MRS. CHEVELEY: Not a year passes in England without somebody disappearing.

Or a Church. Baptist, that is.

LADY BRACKNELL: I beg your pardon?

Attend. Listen. A recitation, from *The Baptist Churches of London, 1612–1928.*

Clears throat.

"Southwark, 1887: vanished. Finsbury, 1912: vanished. Greenwich, no date: seems to have vanished."

MRS. ARBUTHNOT: Stop!

"Islington, 1813: dissolved. Islington, 1867: announced extinct. St Pancras, c.1903: expired."

MRS. CHEVELEY: Stop! Stop!

"Croydon, 1797: heard of no longer. Bermondsey, 1918: closed. Stoke Newington, 1922: disbanded."

Pause. A certain sadness is in the air. So many having disappeared.

LADY MARKBY: Someone should arrange a proper system of assisted emigration.

Good idea.

MRS. JOYCE: The Women's Emigration Association.

That'll do. Just pack them off. All the unwanted ones.

LADY MARKBY: Mrs. Jekyll —

For instance.

LADY MARKBY: So broken-hearted that she went into a convent. Or on to the operatic stage, I forget which.

Easily done, the forgetting. Indeed, when someone disappears it is often hard enough just to *know* where they have gone, let alone remember. A church goes missing. A wife disappears. It is always bewildering. So easy to grow confused. One minute they are with you; the next, hey presto, they are gone. Much like that enigmatic Lord of yours. Jesus, Christ, the Bridegroom.

SECOND NAZARENE: He is in every place ... but it is hard to find Him.

As on the road. To Emmaus. When he vanished. Just like that. On the road.

> Did you kiss him on the road?
> (Edward Carson interrogating Oscar Wilde, The Old Bailey, Wednesday April 3, 1895)

❋

V/V

A Postscript, from Paris.
From Marie to Johannes.
— 1924 —

Did *we* kiss, Johannes? It is difficult to say. Now that —

MISS PRISM: I am unmarried.

Now that —

DR. CHASUBLE: I am a celibate.

Now that —

LADY WINDERMERE: My life is separate from yours.

But then —

MRS. ERLYNNE: I prefer living in the south. London is too full of fogs.

And, besides, Johannes, you now have *her*. Your new Marie.

Pause.

Please remember, however, that —

OSCAR WILDE: I am still looking for you in Paris.

And that —

OSCAR WILDE: I am not sorry that I loved you.

Since —

OSCAR WILDE: Love is never lost.

She had become quite expert at sitting in [on] other people's lives.
— Katherine Mansfield (1888–1923)

CHAPTER SIX

Houses

I/V

God's House
— Paris, September 1925 —

I want also to mention Monsieur Wheeler. … He
planned to go to England to rewrite his will, desiring to leave almost nothing to his wife [and two
daughters]. He had taken out his passport, [but]
two or three days before his departure he was hit by
a motor-lorry near to his house and died immediately. God is a consuming fire.
(Madeleine, September 2, 1925)

— Beggars.
— Where?
— They might have been beggars.
— Who?
— The sisters. Ours. In Christ. Had he not died.
— Christ?
— No, their father.
— They're fatherless?
— Many are. Now. After the War.

— Name two.
— *The Daughters of the Late Colonel.**
— Married?
— No.
— *Father would never forgive them.*
— But he's dead. How *could* he now forgive them?
— *That was [nevertheless] what they felt.*
— When?
— *When they went into his room.*
— Why?
— *His watch still ticks.*
　[Pause.]
— *There had been nobody for them to marry.*
— No men?
— None. Least none who were not wholly blown away. Ask Miss Mansfield.
— Who?
— She knows the Colonel's daughters. Moreover —
— Yes?
— Her brother was also blown away.
— *There was a hole in the air where he was. She looked through and through him.*

❀

Katherine Mansfield, celebrated modernist and author of "The Daughters of the Late Colonel," lost her brother in the War. He was killed, in France, in 1915, by a hand-grenade. It was an accident.

❀

— The sisters …
— Which ones?

---

* In this chapter, all italicised quotations come from Katherine Mansfield — her fiction, diaries, letters, and notebooks.

— The Wheelers. They had no-one to lose.

— *To the trenches.*

— No brothers?

— None.

— No husbands?

— Not quite.

— No-one, then, to miss? No hole through which to look?

— Until now.

— I'm sorry?

— These monsters. The lorries.

— Where?

— On our roads. After the War, so many were left behind.

— And the men who drive them?

— The same. Also left behind. Soldiers. Veterans.

— Accustomed, then, to seeing the dead?

— Not beneath their tyres.

    [Pause.]

— Pneumatic?

— Sorry?

— The tyres, the lorries' tyres. Pneumatic are they?

— How else could they bear such heavy loads?

— Giant tyres, I hear.

— You think of the rubber?

— Herr Schad, to be precise. Johannes Schad. He was a brother once.

— Tabernacle?

— Naturally.

— And does Marie?

— What?

— Think of him? Johannes.

— Think what?

— [That] *Father would never forgive.*

— For having married into rubber?

— Not now. Not after this.

    [Pause.]

— *Father would never forgive.*

— Not even before.

— I'm sorry?

— Well he was off, was he not?

— Who?

— The old man. Off to London. Solicitors.

— Solicitors?

— To change his last will and testament.

— Or, so it is thought.

— But his passport, they found it. In his jacket.

— When?

— When he was dead.

   [Pause.]

— *One gets mortally tired of speedometers.*

— Not in Paris, Miss Mansfield.

— *I would love to be somewhere where the taxis ran one over.*

— Welcome to Paris.

— *Run into by a … wagon.*

— Welcome to Paris.

— *People do bang into me.*

❀

"A new way of killing is born: one can now kill with a car."

(*Machines de Mort,* Paris, 1934)

❀

— *If she …*

— If she what?

— *If she'd been a driver, she couldn't have stopped smiling … at the absurd way he was urged to hurry.*

— Yes, but *who* urged the driver to hurry?

— Which driver?

— The lorry driver. The own who knocked the old man down.

— Ah, yes.

— Well, who urged *him* to hurry?

— God.

— I'm sorry?

— God. They say it was God who urged the lorry driver to hurry, who whispered in his ear. Being, as He is, an all-consuming fire. Even upon the roads.

— Who?

— God.

[Pause.]

— I will, I think, be more careful henceforth.

— When crossing the street?

— More reverend.

— Might you kneel?

— More prayerful.

— At the kerb?

— Indeed.

[Pause.]

— *"Will you marry me?"* [*he asked*]. *Br-r-r-r … whoo-hoo … bz-z-z … bang, bump! … Three trams were passing. Constantia nodded.*

— Why? Why did she nod?

— Who?

— Constantia.

— I'm sorry?

— Why did Constantia nod when asked to marry? Why did she not simply say "Yes"?

— "Yes" to being married?

— Yes.

— As if in church?

— Yes.

— On her wedding day?

— Yes.

— Before God, instead of trams?

— Yes.

— Because her voice, it could not be heard. Above the traffic.

Minutes of an Act of Marriage
— 17th Arrondissement, Paris, 1905 —

They were asked if they wished to take one another for husband & wife, and [after] each of them
… [had]   replied affirmatively and separately in a
loud voice it was pronounced in the name of the law
that Johann Jakob Friedrich Schad and Marie Anne
Wheeler were united in marriage.

— But they were *not.*
— Not what?
— Married.
— Who?
— Johannes and Marie.
— So it now seems.
— *They **sounded** married.*
— But that's not enough.
— As you should know, Miss Mansfield.

On March 2, 1909, in London, Mansfield married
George Bowden, a teacher of elocution, or Voice
Professor, as sometimes known. The next morning,
she left him even before the marriage was consummated.

❀

— Miss Mansfield, I presume you understand that voices, even
if raised, work no final magic. Not with respect to marriage.
— *You can't advise me.*
— Pardon?
— *You can't advise me, Mr. Absurdity.*
— I don't *advise,* Miss Mansfield, I *lament.*
— Lament what?
— That, however, clearly one speaks, however loud one's voice,
however one might holla or shout, one is still not thereby
married. Not quite.

— Not even if the groom is a Professor of Speech?

— Ah, but a Professor of Speech would know only too well the limits of the voice.

— I'm sorry?

— I have in mind another.

— Another what?

— Professor of Speech.

— The eminent Linguist?

— Mr. X himself.

— And what of him?

— I'm sorry?

— How did he view the voice? The eminent Linguist.

— Man's vocal apparatus might *not,* he said, have been made for speaking.

— Not for speaking?

— No.

— Then for what?

— What?

— For what else could one's vocal apparatus possibly be made?

— *Half-words.*

— Pardon?

— *Words that have never really been born.*
  [Pause.]

— Here's a thought.

— Where?

— Do you think speech might be an accident?

— A terrible mistake?

— Misuse of apparatus.

— I fear it is all too obvious.
  [Pause.]

— Might it, then, do you think, it's just a thought, be better if marriage vows were made by, say, semaphore? Or a general waving of arms. An extravagant mime, if you will.

— As in the motion pictures?

— Quite.

— Ask Miss Mansfield. She's been in a movie.

— *Walking about a big bare studio.*

— You may have spied her.
— *In slap-up evening dress.*
— Out of the corner of your eye.
— *A cinematograph[ic] figure.*
— Name of the picture?
— *"Love in False Teeth."*
— Really?
— Not really.
— Not really false?
— Not really love.

> In London, around 1917, Mansfield worked as an extra in a number of films. It is not known which films they are.

❀

— Let us resume.
— Our lives?
— Our thread. Our question.
— Which is?
— What if all couples were to marry without a word?
— In silence?
— Yes.
— Simply by means of gesture?
— Yes.
— Outcome?
— Fewer disastrous weddings.
— Or, would there, in fact, be fewer who even complete the ceremony?
— Pardon?
— What if, I mean to say, our bodies, unlike our words, told the truth?
— *"I feel … that our marriage would be a mistake," she beat [with her arms].*
— But was she understood?
— Who?

— The bride. Or, did she beat her arms in vain? Her wings? Did she wave them in vain?
[Pause.]

— Or were her gestures somehow ill-conceived, or simply wrong?

— It's the way of the world.

— *Wrong house ... wrong doors.*

— Quite.

— *False coins ... false move[s].*

— And then there's the teeth.

— Teeth?

— *False Teeth.*

— Ah yes.

— And the accident.

— What accident?

— *[The] old man* —

— Ah, yes, in the street.

— *Humbly waiting for someone to attend to him.*

— Wrong man.

— Wrong street.

— Wrong truck.

— Wrong driver.

— Wrong God.

— Wrong fire.
[Pause.]

— *A fly ... walked bang into [a] ... fire — rushed in, committed suicide.*

— Yes, but that was a fly, not a man.

— Not even an old man.

— Men simply don't walk bang into fire.

— Suicide can, then, be ruled out?

— I can't speak for the fly.

— But the man? The old man?

— What about him?

— Did he, perhaps, *choose* God's consuming fire? Did he seek out the onrushing truck?

— But he had his passport. He was off, I say. On his way to London.

— So it is said.

[Pause.]

— Besides, the old man knew only too well the terrible force of fire.

— Pardon?

— He had encountered fire before.

— He had?

— Do you not recall?

— Recall what?

— *An old man drowned in tears?*

— No, the conflagration, Miss Mansfield. I speak of the conflagration.

— Which one?

— The one in the tunnel, train tunnel, at Gare Saint-Lazare, just across the road from chez Wheeler.

— *Gare Saint-Lazare ... [was] cold.*

— No, hot. It was hot as hell.

Fig. 28. Photograph of the Gare Saint-Lazare (October 16, 1921). Bibliothèque Nationale de France.

On October 16, 1921, at Gare Saint-Lazare, a colli-
sion between two locomotives in the tunnel caused
an inferno that killed 28 people. It proved impossible to identify some of the dead.

❈

— *If … a fire had broken out, and … only our charred bodies
found, it would have been … natural to suppose we were to-
gether. We [would] have looked exactly like the other couples.*
— But, pray, Miss Mansfield, what do you think incinerated
couples look like?
— Do you imagine, Miss Mansfield, that every such couple cling
together in a passionate and perpetual embrace?
— Well, I myself do.
— Sorry?
— That is precisely how I envisage the afterlife.
— You do?
— Naturally.
— *In Heaven … conjugal rights [are] a "specialité de la maison."*
— Exactly.
— Pardon?
— "My Father's House has many rooms."
— One for each couple?
— *It [is] … a law of marriage.*
— And thus of Heaven.
 [Pause.]
— But what if either husband or wife is …
— Yes?
— Not admitted. Damned. Apostate.
— I'm sorry?
— I think of the Schads.
— But why?
— Because they are, by all accounts, eventually to go very sepa-
rate ways.
— Eventually?

— Come eternity.

[Pause.]

— *I saw myself driving through Eternity.*

— Good heavens.

— [*It was*] *in a timeless taxi* …. [*And*] *the taxi man … was most sinister. I could not get him to stop. The more I knocked the faster he went … in the moonlight.*

— I fear, Miss Mansfield, that you spend too long in automobiles.

— Or in the moonlight.

— Or picture-house.

— Ah yes.

— Whatever, Miss Mansfield, you must understand that automobiles, whether upon the silver screen or not, have little or nothing to do with eternity.

— But what of old Monsieur Wheeler?

— Pardon?

— Was he not driven, as it were, to eternity? And in an instant?

— It was a truck.

— Yes, but it had four wheels.

— It was a truck. Not a taxi.

— Yes, but, perhaps, in the truck, at the wheel, it was, once again, that taxi-man. That sinister man. The one too much in love with eternity. That man who, though told to stop, goes faster and faster until —

— Stop there! Eternity is no lawless road.

— It's not?

— By no means. Eternity *is* the Law. Law itself.

— It is?

— Indeed. Try, for example, leaving one's daughters penniless —

— Like Monsieur Wheeler?

— Exactly. Just try doing what he sought to do and —

— Yes?

— Eternity will descend.

— Like the guillotine?

— Or a truck.

[Pause].

— Hurrah for the Law?

— Exactly.

— And what say you, Miss Mansfield?

— *Damnation take the Law!*

— No, damnation *is* the Law, Miss Mansfield. Read your Bible.
  [Pause.]

— By the way, this good, this particular good —

— Which good?

— This saving of the daughters from beggary.

— I'm sorry?

— I mean the good that is the prevention of their father rewriting the will. That is the good I have in mind.

— Ah, yes. And what of it?

— It can't be denied, can it? Can't be gainsaid?

— No. Not at all.

— Notwithstanding their father's violent death.

— No.

— Nor the pain he may have endured.

— No.

— Nor the consequent sadness?

— No.

— Excellent. So, this good, this particular good, it remains?

— Yes.

— However stubbornly?

— Yes.

— A bad that is good?

— Yes.

— A wrong that is right.

— Yes.

— A heavenly trick?

— Yes.

— A heavenly ruse?

— Quite.
  [Pause.]

— *The frightening thing about this house —*

— Yes, Miss Mansfield?

— *The frightening thing about this ... house is its smugness — an eternal Jesus-Christ ... smugness. ... [It] is most sinister ... a perfect setting for a ... murder.*

❋

II/V

House Without
— Paris, September 1925 —

If [only] Marie had sought first the Kingdom of
God and its justice.
(Madeleine, May 21, 1924)

Marie sat at the window. The traffic was moving, but the voices
were still in her head. *Something had happened. ... "What's the
matter?" ... "There's been a horrible accident." ... "A man killed."*
Ah, what fuss had been made. A scene. *Father would never forgive.* Not all the fuss. Perspective was needed. Thank God for the
Tab. Thank God. She had returned to the fold.

Father would never forgive. Perhaps not. Of late he himself
had missed so many services, meetings. Not clear why. She
looked across to the hall-way. And imagined *Father [was] ...
there, among his overcoats.* As if standing by the door. The door
he used to answer.

Now, it was they who had to answer. Whoever it was.

And there had been so many, with their *Knockings at the
Door.* And their sayings. *Every man ... has his murderer,* said
one, a stranger. Fancy *coming into an honest woman's house,* she
had thought, *at this hour of the night,* she had thought, *making a
scene — getting the police after you.* Unpleasant man. Much *like
the horrid creature in his nightshirt who [had] began mumbling
about the wrong door.*

Or was the other man worse? The one that came so late,
made scenes and mumbled about the police. Not to mention
names and papers and Father. Yes, Marie had said, he had tak-
en his passport with him. Yes, she had said, it was British. Yes,
she had said, she herself was French. Odd? No, her mother was
French. Had she, therefore, renounced England? In a manner
of speaking. Father would never forgive. He had been English.
Yes, an Alien.

❄

In 1924, right across Paris, inspectors were sent door
to door to verify the identity of every foreigner who
had registered with the police.

❄

The man had asked just a few more questions. How long had her
father lived here? Where born? Did he not have a Certificate of
Baptism? No, he was Protestant. Baptist. Pardon? And on and
on. On and on until, *You're not married, are you?*

No, that was a nun. It was a nun who had asked that, might
have been talking to herself. There had been *a knock at the door.
Two sisters of Nazareth. Two shabby old nuns wheeling a perambulator.*

Ah, another empty perambulator, Marie had thought. So
many there were here. "Madame does *not* want a child," as they
said these days in Paris. Though not in London.

No, not in London. When Marie had lived in Palmers Green
she had once gone *down to the City … and found Baby Week in
the fullest of full blasts. Indeed, she had been the only woman with
her quiver empty between Charing X and Victoria Station.* But
what did she expect? What had she ever expected? She hadn't
really been married, had she? No, apparently not. Nevertheless,
she had tried. To have children. Madame *did* want a child.

Yes, she had tried. Had not just given up. Not at first, not in
the early years. She had been aware of a problem. Of one kind
or another. Had seen so many a doctor. *I am sick of a sore dis-
ease,* she had thought, *and not all the wise men who dwell in the
valley of the shadow of Harley Street can cure me of my ill.* No,
none, not even Dr. Stevens. *Harley Street, Wimpole Street, Wel-
beck Street, Queen Anne.* Ah yes, *Queen Anne Street.* Number 20,
to be precise. *One of those white tiled rooms, with … too many
wash basins.*

Not that Dr. Stevens saw her with a view to a cure. Not in the
white tiled room. He had asked for "the history of her married

life." And so she had told him. First, she had said, there was one doctor, then another and another and another. And sometimes she had been *told to undress*. But, all the wise men in the valley of the shadow of Harley Street could not cure her of her ill, and thus it was that she had arisen, and gone forth, saying *I [shall] go to Paris in the Spring and ask [yet another] … to treat me.*

> I hope to go to Paris this Spring, though Johannes
> will not travel this time. I am going in particular to
> see Dr. Pinard. If, though, he cannot offer me hope,
> I will adopt a little girl as soon as possible.
> (Marie, letter to Madeleine, [January?] 1909)

❀

It had not been altogether easy. The train to Paris. There was, for instance, *that … thing which … was bound to happen … to every woman on earth who travelled alone.* And then there were all those other things that might happen. *Supposing,* for instance, *you lost your purse at midnight in a snowbound train in North Russia.* But, she wondered, would that be much worse than losing your purse at any other time on a snowbound train in North Russia?

Or, was it the case that certain times really are worse than others? For a woman, that is. *Frau Lehman's bad time, she had heard, was approaching. [She] … referred to it as her "journey to Rome."* Strange name for it. As if a pilgrimage. Or migration. Mind you, some called it The Curse. Or even *Aunt Martha.*

She looked out of the window. Across the road, toward Gare Saint-Lazare. *A train is passing,* she thought. Not quite a snowbound train. The kind that Johannes liked. *My husband,* she used to say, *is never so happy as when he is travelling.*

Marie herself might like to go to Rome. *Try for a winter in the South … wherever it is, she thought. Or, perhaps Switzerland will do the trick. The Swiss Cure,* she thought. So many women went there now, and alone. It had its hazards, mind. She knew that.

Like Snakes and Ladders, it was.

Charing X
Travelling 1st [class but] with 2nd class ticket. **Pay 3d.**
…
Folkestone. Rough sea. …
Seasick. **Stay at YWCA one turn.**
Hit sailor with your umbrella. **Pay 1d**
Boulogne. …
   Passport out of order. …
   Miss a turn.
Alas, more snakes than ladders, she thought.
Frasne: Kissed in tunnel. **Miss 2 turns.**
Vallorbe: Carrying gold out of France. **Pay 3d.**
…
Wearing False Nose. **Back to Vallorbe.**
Sion. *[Switzerland]*
…
Step on Passenger's dog.
…
Cow puts its head in Window. …
Madman enters carriage.

Ah, the Madman. Him again. As always. When you travel alone. Or live alone. Always the Madman, with his books, making a scene.
   I am, he always says, *making a special study of literature.*
   I've never yet, he always says, *made advances to any woman.*
   Without my clothes, he always says, *I am rather charming.*
   And he always wants to know all about you. Wants to know every turn, every throw of the dice. How often have you been sick? How often have you kissed? How often have you missed? Missed a turn. Or the train to Rome. Or to Sion. Or, should that be Zion? It is enough to make you hit the man, hit him with your umbrella or jump on his dog or wear a False Nose and tell him he's come in through the Wrong Door and found the Wrong Woman and that she, you, myself, is, are, am, of no real interest and know no-one of any real interest. No-one, for instance, carrying gold out of France and with a passport out of

order. Or, indeed, lying in court. Or drafting false medical reports. Her life, he must know, was not a film nor she an extra or
some kind of stunt-woman. *Can you aviate — high-dive — drive
a car — buck jump — shoot?* No, she most certainly could not.
He really had got the Wrong Woman. He must understand that.
Her train to Paris, to see Dr. Pinard, the train she had caught in
1909, had not pulled into a city of high drama and intrigue — let
alone, or so it turned out, of hope, hope of ever finally having a
child, a beautiful child, a beautiful child of her own. No, there
had, in the end, been no such hope. No such child. None.

※

III/V

Shadow House
— Paris, September 1932 —

Mansfield had no children. She did, though, have
a miscarriage and, after marrying John Middleton
Murry in 1918, had hoped to adopt, sometimes re-
ferring to an imaginary child called "Dicky." However, in 1917, she was diagnosed with tuberculosis.
Thereafter, she criss-crossed Europe seeing many
different doctors and attempting many kinds of
treatment as she sought, in vain, to make a cure. She
died in 1923, aged 34.

No. No such child, thought Marie. Or at least, no child as might
appear in records, or papers. Though there were her *Shadow
Children*. Or, were they another woman's? Perhaps they held
them in common. *The Shadow Children … crept out of their
little places and … came … and smiled at her.* Exactly why the
children smiled she was not sure, but she always returned their
smiles. One by one. At times she even embraced them or attempted to embrace them. *Shadow children … I kiss you.*

But saying I kiss you is not the same as really kissing you. In
fact, thought Marie, if I say I kiss you, is it not clear that, for at
least that moment, I do *not* kiss you? My lips being otherwise
engaged, as it were. "I kiss you" must, then, always be a false-
hood, a hole in the air. But at least she could peer through the
hole, at the shadow children, each and every one of them. And
there were so many here, *in the valley of the shadow,* this *shadowy country that we exiles from health inhabit.* She paused, grew
fine in distinction and, this time, *thought of the shadow of the
border of* [the] *… shadowy country.*

We exiles, she thought, *exiles from health.* Compelled to flee,
and, once at the border, as it were, clutch, as if passports, these
letters from our doctors. *I see you with your passport … explaining that your wife is ill.*

But was her passport out of order? Was it false? The letter from Dr. Stevens? There was that misspelling, not to mention the wrong initial, in his name, the doctor's. So, was she *really*, as he had reported, only a shadow of a woman? Capable only of bearing shadow children? She was not sure. Had never been sure. Never sure if it really was herself that was the problem, the source of all the shadows.

It was true, however, that Johannes had now proved beyond all doubt that he was no shadow of a man. Or at least, not when with another woman. Another Marie. With her, this other Marie, Johannes had fathered, she heard, two children. Real children. Not shadow children but those made of flesh and bone, of all that can be broken. And, as if to prove it, Johannes, she heard, had lately put both children in the back of his motor-car and driven slap bang into another.

> In the summer of 1932, Johannes and Marie II undertook a driving holiday through France with their two young sons. Their motor-car, though, was involved in a crash; and it was bad enough to cause Johannes never again to drive. Both boys were hurt, with the driver of the other car having to pay compensation. One boy had a broken jaw and the other, a two-year old, the father of the present author, suffered concussion. His name was "Dicky."

❋

How dreadful, thought Marie, when she had heard. Heard of the crash. The accident. The injured. More shadows, as it were. New shadows. New shadows for shadow land. This land so full of *strange places that illness carries me into.* And in each and every strange place there were all these *strange people ... the succession of black-coated gentleman, the men to whom she'd whispered 99, 44, 1-2-3.*

99, 44, 1-2-3. All these numbers, she thought. All this count-ing. But she did not like to count. Not years. Not months or weeks. Or even days.

*Friday 2nd March: **A.M.*** ("A.M." for "Aunt Martha").

*Tuesday 6th March: **E.A.M.*** ("E.A.M." for "Exit Aunt Mar-tha").

So, yes, 1-2-3-**4** days. Four days. About average. For a visit from Aunt Martha. Even though "A.M." had not visited for a while.

So, when did she last visit? I beg your pardon? When did A.M. make her last visit? Ah, she thought, being *asked ... inde-cent questions [is] ... one [more] horror of being ill.* Or, of being *said* to be ill. Or at least, said to be the problem.

In this connection, by the way, had the black-coated gentle-men not considered the possibility that, *as a rule, he [her hus-band had] merely kissed her*? Kept his distance. But *no-one lis-tens to a patient.* Least of all her husband. Doctors do talk, was all that Johannes had said. *Not that I care ... who ... knows,* he had added. *Not that I wouldn't ... take the front page of the Daily Mirror and have our two names on it.*

Yes, they do talk, the doctors. They talk about shocking things. Sometimes they even wrote them down, for anyone to see. Like Dr. Stevens. He had in fact written a whole book. A *book for a rubber shop?* No, it wasn't like that. Was it, then, *about ... bedroom talk?* Well, yes, in a way. Full of women's complaints, it was.

One particular complaint she could not forget. Apparently, this complaint "is only seen in monsters." Or so Dr. Stevens had written. "It is only seen in monsters with other abnormalities," he had written. Marie herself did not know any monsters. She certainly hadn't yet seen one in any of the clinics or waiting rooms in which she had sat. She wondered if they too, the mon-sters, were asked indecent questions.

She herself had been asked many such questions. Once, in fact, she had replied, *"Oh doctor ... isn't there anything I can keep to myself?"* She had found some pleasure in answering his ques-tion with a question, loving as she did the shape of a question, its twist, its bend, its beautiful abnormality. Indeed, she thought, perhaps *the beauty of life* [*itself was*] *... the haunting beauty of "the question."*

Marie looked in the mirror. The beauty of the question, she thought. Or should that be the question of beauty? That, after all, had been the *first* question, *her* first question. She recalled *the afternoon of* [*her*] *... wedding day, when* [*they*] *sat in the ... botanical gardens and listened to the band ... and she ... said, ... "Do you think physical beauty is so very important?" ... and ...* [*he*] *answered ... "I didn't hear what you said."* The question was left, hanging, in the park, drowned, by the band. Over the years, she had asked it again and again until it had long lost all the beauty of a question. Had grown plain, in fact.

❀

So, *why had he married her?* Johannes had *asked this question on ... average about three times a day.* But, did that not just make him *an average British husband?* Well, no, seeing he was not actually British. And, alas, was not exactly average. But then neither was she. And he had said so.

Yes, he had said so. Said that she might not be exactly average. And, in response, she had simply pointed to a *corset box that she'd kept by her for a long time ...* [*and to*] *the lettering on it: Medium Women's 28.* Medium. Average. Yes, but had she, he wondered, ever worn the corset? Or was it, in fact, an empty box? Indeed, had it only ever been empty? He had then thought of an advertisement he had seen *for the enlargement of Beautiful Breasts.*

❀

Marie wants to add to her trousseau, and so has just bought five or six petticoats and some girdles.
(Madeleine, January 25, 1905)

Really — her underclothes! Were they, she wondered, quite right? I *wish,* she had once said, *I wish I was more of a stoic about un-*

der-linen. Johannes had replied to this. If her under-linen were to be identified with any particular worldview then he would suggest not so much Stoicism as Christianity. Or was that absurd? Perhaps not. There was, after all, that day when she had *knelt on [her] ... petticoat all through church.* Besides, she did, on occasion, *wear a crucifix under [her] ... clothes.* He knew, he had said, that *every wife has her cross,* but not that it was kept warm, the cross, not in such a manner.

He had said this one night, as they were preparing for bed. And she had reddened, perhaps, in the dark. *Our bedrooms,* she had whispered, *they communicate.*

"With each other?" he had said.

"With *God,*" she had said.

"As in Eden?" he had said.

There had then been silence before they spoke again.

Were they going to get undressed? he had said. As if Adam.

Don't forget to say your prayers, she had said. As if Eve. And he did not forget, at least not whenever she reminded him.

Did you kneel?

Yes, he would say.

And did those rubber [soles] ... show on your shoes?

Yes, he would say.

But prayers and the rubber soles of his shoes: how could such different things, he had wondered, belong together? Be in the same room? Even the same Creation? Perhaps they could not.

And, perhaps, neither could he and Marie. *She was [though] his wife — that girl.* Yes, but what if she herself did not quite belong in the world? The real world. Of rubber and shoes et cetera. *She never undressed in front of anyone.* Save Jesus, he had thought.

❀

The Lord Jesus Christ ... has opened His clinic. His consulting-room is open to all.
(Reverend Rubens Saillens, July 22, 1925)

❋

If Jesus, thought Johannes, were a kind of doctor, would He, being God, have any questions to ask? If so, what one question might Jesus ask? Of, say, a woman? Would it be an unimaginable question? *The Question of Questions,* as it were.

Johannes had often wondered what he himself might have asked Marie. Might it have been, *How much do you love me*? Or, perhaps, *I suppose you love Jesus*? An indecent question, he knew. Not one to be asked in polite circles. Nor in the office. But he did need to know, if he may, how her love for Jesus compared to her love for him? And she was not to reply, *I hold you ... like God.* Like Jesus. That would be no answer, and he would simply ask the question again, even though he knew it was a trap. In which he was caught. Or, perhaps, just perhaps, in which he was held.

Held safe? Was that possible? Was it, he had wondered, a *Christian trap,* this question? The question of love. Hold me, he had thought. Like God. Please. Someone.

❋

Fig. 29. Edgar Brandt, *Porte da Ascensore* (1926).
Museu Calouste Gulbenkian.

IV/V

House of the Unknown
— Paris, 1933 —

In 1928, the Tabernacle moved to Rue Belliard, in Montmartre. There the church finally had purpose-built premises, a modern chapel featuring an ornamented wrought-iron gate designed by the celebrated Art Deco designer, Edgar Brandt, whose other work included the torch for the eternal flame at the Tomb of the Unknown Soldier in the Arc de Triomphe. The Montmartre site had been chosen because "it was that part of Paris where there were the most cinemas and the fewest places of worship."

❋

— Do you think it's a trap?
— What is?
— The fretwork.
— More like a veil.
— What is?
— The gate. The Tabernacle gate.
— It does, though, help to hide us.
— From whom?
— Those who are after us.
— *One [does] read of people being followed.*
— But by whom?
— The curious.
— *There had been, one year, … a mysterious man who put a note on the jug of water outside their bedroom.*
— Whose bedroom?
— Don't ask. Tabernacle names should not be disclosed.

❋

The Lord has so marvellously blessed us of late. …
The first evening, N. was here, [and] was crying. …
Some of the converts concern us, however; such
as F., a young student of philosophy. … Another
young Christian man, Monsieur P., has asked me to
find him a young Christian wife.
(Madeleine, 1931)

— A word, if I may, regarding our sister, N.
— What of her?
— Could she be a wife for Monsieur P.?
— Not if she is married.
— What if widowed? Or —
— *Neither married nor unmarried.*
— Or, indeed, living a life that is —
— Yes?
— *Not what I mean by a married life.*
— Ask Madame Blocher-Saillens.
— Who?
— Pastor Madeleine.
— Ask her what?
— Ask her: when is one married and when is one not?
— But which is *she*?
— Pardon?
— Which is *she*?
— I'm not altogether certain.

※

It was in 1930 that Madeleine became Pastor of the
Tabernacle; this was following the sudden death
of her husband, Arthur Blocher, the then Pastor.
When Madeleine was elected to succeed him, thus
becoming the first female pastor in France, there
was much debate concerning her appointment. One
argument in favour, however, was that "in a good

marriage two become one flesh, therefore Monsieur Blocher is not entirely dead."

❋

— *I do not believe* —
— We know, Miss Mansfield.
— *I do not believe in the conjugal "We."*
— But what of the flesh, Miss Mansfield?
— The *one* flesh, Miss Mansfield.
— A union so powerful.
— So especial.
— As to survive.
— Endure.
— Forever.
  [Silence.]
— Question:
— What are *you* here for, Miss Mansfield?
— Answer:
— Nerves.
— Question:
— *What are **you** here for?*
— Answer:
— *To forget.*
— Forget what?
— *Someone ... said "Forget, forget that you've been wed."*
— But can one?
  [Silence.]
— I said, can one forget that one is wed?
— Speak, Miss Mansfield.
— *You* —
— Me?
  [Miss Mansfield nods.]
— *You ... will marry some woman who will* [then] *show me the door.*
— Ah, I am sorry. So sorry.
  [Miss Mansfield draws closer.]

— *I [will though] come and sing in the street you live in.*
— Wearing what, Miss Mansfield?
— *My beautiful Russian dress.*
— Borrowed, Miss Mansfield?
— *Given.*
— By whom, Miss Mansfield?
— *My anonymous friend.*
— Ah, Monsieur P.?
  [Silence.]
— I said, Miss Mansfield, might your anonymous friend be the
  amorous Monsieur P.?
— Or is it, perhaps, one who has travelled to Russia?
— The beautiful Russian dress being his returning gift?
— No, his *parting* gift.
— Ah, you mean to say it's all over? For Miss Mansfield?
— Who?
— You know, the woman in the street. In the Russian dress.
  [Pause.]
— *He heard her cry "Au revoir!"*
— Not "Adieu," Miss Mansfield?
  [Silence.]
— Perhaps Miss Mansfield thought she would return.
— But is shown the door.
— Exactly. Which is why she stands outside. Stands in the street,
  in the Russian dress, and sings.
— Alone? Or accompanied?
— Can't you hear it?
— Hear what?
— *A barrel organ grinding out a Catholic chant.*
  [Pause.]
— You know, Miss Mansfield —
— Yes?
— She reminds me of someone.
— Who?
— A sister. In Christ.
— But there are so many.
— Name one.

— Marie Wheeler.
— Name two.
— *The … nuns … at her door.*
— Ah, them.
  [Pause.]
— The nuns.
— Yes?
— Why are they at the door?
— They are not quite sure.
— It's often the way with virgins.
— *On the doorstep stood an elderly virgin … who had this habit of turning up … and then saying, … "My dear, send me away!"*
— But wherever can she go? This virgin.
— The streets.
— *As the night waxed … [I] went … to search for a church.*
— You did, Miss Mansfield?
— *But, not finding one open, I had to offer up prayers in the open street.*
— Did you kneel?
  [Silence.]
— Miss Mansfield, did you kneel?
— Answer, Miss Mansfield!
— *Salvation Army women [were] doling [out] tracts.*
— In the dark?
— *They gave me one.*
— What did it say, Miss Mansfield?
— *"Are you corrupted?"*
— An indecent question, Miss Mansfield.
— For a modern woman.
— Such as yourself.
— *I am not as modern as I ought to be.*
— Turn to Christ, then, Miss Mansfield.
— *I … do … desire to be saved.*
— Really?
— *I believe, help Thou my unbelief.*
— Quick!
— Quick what?

— Find a sister.
— Why?
— To help save Miss Mansfield.
— She believes?
— Indeed.
— Are you sure?
— *I feel ... like a preacher.*
— See!
— *I really have a gospel.*
— See again!
— Ah, but is it merely modernist?
— I beg your pardon?
— Her gospel, is it modernist?

> These modernist pastors, what bad they do.
> (Madeleine, 1931)

❀

— *If —*
— Yes, Miss Mansfield?
— *If you were a man —*
— Me?
— *You would be a ... Revivalist.*
— Quite. But I am not. Not a man, real man. Nor Revivalist.
— It's Madame Blocher-Saillens you need. Our pastor. She seeks
  Revival. Conversion of the many.

❀

> Madeleine often recalled one particular Revival
> story. It concerned "an unknown woman [*incon-
> nue*]" who, one evening, having missed her train
> out of Paris, thought she would see a film; however,
> thinking she was entering a cinema, chanced upon
> a meeting hall in which the Tabernacle was holding

a mission. Hearing a sermon on the Titanic, she was soundly converted.

✺

— *I ... [once] met a woman who'd been in the cinema.*
— Was she also unknown, Miss Mansfield?
— *I ... [once] met a woman who'd been in the cinema.*
— But it wasn't a cinema, Miss Mansfield.
— It was a mission hall, Miss Mansfield.
— Did the woman not notice, Miss Mansfield?
— The hymns?
— The sermon?
— The Titanic? The fear. The cries for deliverance. As the band played on. And the hymns were sung. And many were rescued, though not all.
— *What Ultimate Cinema!*
— If you insist, Miss Mansfield.
— She does. She thinks film-cameras are everywhere.
— Even the mission hall?
— Even the mission hall.
— But why? Why ever does she think this?
— The War.
— *The soldiers['] ... eyes [were] fixed on a train as though they expected at least one camera at every window.*
— Perhaps there was.
— Was what?
— A camera at every window.
— But why?
— The soldiers might have been extras.
— *Walking about a bare studio.*
— In a manner, Miss Mansfield.
— *In slap-up evening dress.*
— At a stretch, Miss Mansfield.
  [Pause.]
— Do you think the soldiers were thereby saved?
— Saved?

— By the cameras.

— Saved from what?

— Oblivion.

— In a way.

[Pause.]

— *She had her camera. She had just returned from ... Communion.*

[Pause.]

— What if ...

— Yes?

— What if a camera, film-camera, were an instrument of Grace?

— Like Communion?

— Indeed.

— Unlikely.

— But do not cameras, film-cameras, pursue us? Glimpse us? Capture us?

— And what has such to do with Grace?

— Just think of someone. Imagine. Mind's eye

[Nothing.]

— I said, imagine!

— Imagine who?

— *A creature.*

— Yes, a distant, fleeting creature.

— *Rac[ing] along a platform, dodging the passengers.*

— Pursued?

— By a camera.

— Glimpsed?

— In the crowd.

— Captured?

— On screen, the silver screen.

[Pause.]

— Well, what do you see? Imagine? Mind's eye.

— I see —

— Yes?

— I see someone blessed.

— Blessed? With what?

— With —

— Yes?
— *Security.*
— What kind?
— *The security of a cinematograph[ic] figure.*
— Exactly.
— Ah, praise God.
  [Pause.]
— *I … [once] met a woman who'd been in the cinema, … lovely eyes & battered hair. I shall not forget her.*
— Not forget who?
— Marie. Marie Wheeler.
— Who?
— Our sister. In Christ. The one with the shining eyes.
— But Miss Mansfield said that the woman in question had been in the cinema.
— No, it merely looked like a cinema. It was, in truth, a mission hall. Remember? One of ours. One no doubt attended by Marie.
— But Miss Mansfield said the woman in question had *lovely* eyes — not shining, like Marie's.
— Shining eyes *are* lovely eyes, I find. In the dark.

❋

V/V

House of Steps
— Paris, May 1934 —

Marie's sister, Sara, was diagnosed with tuberculosis in 1911. Her health was made still worse when she developed uraemia. After many years of being an invalid she was, by 1934, on the verge of death. On April 20 of that year, she was, as Sara herself records, visited by "a friend from the country"; the friend, who remains anonymous, told Sara she would be healed. Sara was, by this point, completely unable to walk or even stand without the most acute vertigo; she thus dismissed talk of healing as "an absurdity." On April 24, however, after reading in Genesis of how "God visited Sara," she began, she writes, "in the arms of my sister," to walk again, "gliding from one chair to another ... without touching the ground." No-one else saw these scenes, the sisters having "locked the door" since "it seemed to us too beautiful, too sacred to be seen by men." Over the next few weeks Sara continued to improve dramatically, and on May 20, 1934, Pentecost Sunday, she "was able to go by motor-car to church, and there witness to what God had done."

This, thought Marie, *is the way to travel.* The motor-car was Sara's idea. What better way to get to the Tab. After all this time. And ah, how quiet were the streets, and how quickly they moved. Half an hour? No, much less. *The driver had been told how fast he had to drive.* Strange the way the buildings swam. Marie *sat in the front of the car, the cold air blew upon* [*her*] *face.* With the window down, it fair battered her hair, the air. *She leaned out of the window. A-ah,* she thought, *I am baptised.*

Marie was glad she had remembered her hat. *I'll ... come,* she had said, *with a sailor hat tied on with a motor-veil.* You could hardly see her face, said Sara. Not beneath that hat. And then, my goodness, there was the veil. Like a bride's. But it kept her hat on, the sailor hat. She had feared it might blow off in the car.

And in church? Sorry. Was everyone there? At the Tab? Oh yes, everyone. Father. Son. And Holy Ghost. It being Pentecost. Yes, Pentecost. Signs, wonders, and *monster big prayer[s]*. Even tongues. *Half-words,* thought Marie. Language reborn. Such is Grace. Such is revival, hallelujah. Like *drowned men building a raft.* Yes, the impossible is here. And *I am only surprised at God.*

Though there was the alarming wind, as they returned. Not to mention that alarming cyclist ahead, wandering all over the road. A bookish figure. Is he, perhaps, shaking his head? Questioning things? *"Oh,"* said Sara, *"people [do] question miracles. ... [Just] fly along, dear."*

Yes, like flying, it was, in the car. Though not everyone, thought Marie, questioned miracles. She wasn't sure, for instance, that Johannes questioned miracles. He simply hadn't talked about miracles, or at least not used the word. Though others did. Here and there. Marie had heard them. *Over-*heard, that is. *"Nobody is going to ... take her in his arms,"* they had said, *"and yet ... she ... expect[s] the miracle to happen."*

Yes, but it *did* happen. At least in Sara's case. God had indeed visited Sara. As in Genesis. Knock, knock, and behold, *at the door, ... [was one] who would treat her like a queen.* Hallelujah.

As Herr Adloff had said, "miracles have not ceased." He said that in a letter, when he was in a camp, of all places. Prison camp. In the war. And Marie had taken his words to heart. His prison words. Had believed them. Though not *always,* as she had once told Johannes. Not always, not every time.

"It is," he had said, *"no use expecting miracles."*

But believing, she had said, was *not* expecting, or at least not insisting. You can't simply insist. Can't simply *say one must have a miracle.*

And Sara hadn't insisted. Not even when, as she said, "night descended" or when she felt like "a drowned person" all "soaking and frozen" or had to close her eyes "to stop everything dancing" or had, for company, only "a demon at her side," who told her, with "a diabolical laugh," that "ahead was only nothingness." Such a demon. Terrible demon.

Marie looked out of the car. It had been a long day. The Tab, then lunch and tea with friends. *We came back ... in the twilight. I sat in the front of the car.* Yes, the light had been in her eyes. But now they were home. Rue de Rome. Several motorcars were parked. And a truck. An old man was crossing. And a gendarme looked on. He looked worried, she thought. As if he remembered the accident. Remembered that day on which *"the miracle" didn't happen.* No, it didn't always happen. Sometimes people just died. She knew that. The gendarme frowned.

But then, seeing her, he smiled. As if to say, *one must have a miracle. ... Have you any suggestions?* No, Marie had not. Though many had, over the years, made suggestions to *her.* Doctors and other men. *The miracle,* they would say, *is but postponed.* And it had been. Postponed until the day that Sara needed it. Hallelujah.

Standing at the door, she reached into her bag. She had the key in her bag. Here we are. Home again. And the door flew open — *whoosh* — with the wind. The hallway. Full of flowers.

❋

On January 9, 1923, Mansfield died at the Le Prieuré des Basses-Loges in Fontainebleau-Avon, near Paris. It was once a monastery but was now the Institute for the Harmonious Development of Mankind. Mansfield had gone to stay there in the hope of a cure. The evening of her death she spent in the salon. At around 10 p.m. she said she would retire to her room on the first floor; but as she went up the stairs she began to cough, blood pouring from her mouth. A few minutes later she was dead.

❋

Marie *went upstairs but that was fatal. Have I a home?* she thought, *Am I any man's wife? Is it all over?* Marie was always thinking on the stairs. Or dreaming. Perhaps it was the exertion. *Every house ought to have ... an electric staircase.* It would be very modern. Anyway, *Have I a home? Am I any man's wife? Is it all over?* It was hard to say, from here. On the stairs. Where she did tend to dream. To drift. *John is downstairs.* Yes, John. Sometimes she had called him John, dear Johannes. Yes, *John is downstairs discussing the theory of relativity.* With whom, Marie was no longer sure. Now that there was *another woman around. Now that another woman ... comes & goes on the stairs.* Comes and goes. Up and down. As if in two places at once. Ah, she thought, there's relativity for you. But then, she thought, some *people [do] come out of themselves on the stairs.*

It is not hard to discern an oversize monk's cell, to which intellectu-als … retreat … to weave a … sermon, undaunted by the thought that it will be given to rows of empty seats, if … given at all.
—Walter Benjamin (1892–1940)

CHAPTER SEVEN

Rooms

I/IV

Glass

25 Rue Jasmin, Paris
April 9, 1934

Dear Herr Wiesengrund,
I have been offered the prospect of delivering a lecture on the German literature of the last decade. [It was to be] at the home of a gynaecologist [Dr. Jean Dalsace] who is rather well known here. But one week before the appointed date — [after] the invitation cards had already been sent out — the doctor fell ill with serious pulmonary inflammation. ... It now seems ... unlikely that I shall ... present the lecture this season.
Yours,
Walter Benjamin

Yes, unlikely. Indeed, most unlikely. In fact, quite impossible, my dearly beloved. This season or any other. Herr Dr. Benjamin, German, Jewish, and half-homeless, had thought the lecture

Fig. 30. Photograph of La Maison de Verre, 31 Rue Saint-Guillaume
(ca. 1931). Musée des Arts Décoratifs
© Jean Collas / Fonds photographique Pierre Chareau.

might be the first of a number, a sequence. Those attending were
to purchase a ticket for all the lectures. Or so the poor beggar
dreamt. Mistakenly, it turns out.

A pity, I suppose. For him. Dr. Dalsace's home, you see, is a
modernist triumph. Architecturally. *La Maison de Verre,* they
call it. House of Glass. 31 Rue Saint-Guillaume. You may know
it? Glass all over. Walls, doors, panels. An avant-garde palace of
mirrors. Not, as I say, that Dr. Benjamin's fumbling frame was
ever reflected therein. Ever repeated again and again in its cool,
Art Deco glass.

"But, the *many lecterns!*"*

I beg your pardon.

"The many lecterns!"

I'm sorry?

---

* In this chapter, all italicised quotations come from Walter Benjamin; as
and when these quotations are modified, this is indicated by reversion to
regular font, without any square brackets to otherwise highlight the shift.

"The *lecterns, they stood all over the place!*"

No, Dr. Benjamin. There were no lecterns. Not one. There was no lecture. Not in the end.

[Pause. Turn to face auditorium again.]

Ladies and Gentlemen, this lecture of Dr. Benjamin's, this never-given lecture, is, in part, the subject of *my* lecture. This evening's. On behalf of the extra-mural wing of —

"The *department of demonology*?"

Quite. A valedictory, in fact. It being my final hurrah. Hence the admission tickets. No flowers, though, by request. Not even dead ones, tell the Usher. Yes, the pale fellow. From London.

[Clear throat. Resume discourse.]

Now, why is it, you wonder, that Dr. Benjamin's hopeless un-lecture should so catch my closing eye? Here, at the last. Why indeed? Well, it is not, I confess, because of any interest in Dr. Benjamin himself. On the contrary. It is purely because of his connection to Dr. Dalsace's House of Glass.

And what, you wonder, is the appeal of the house? Well, you see, it accommodates not only a first-floor salon large enough for literary soirees but also the good doctor's office, clinic, and consultation room. The latter are all below, upon the ground floor. With easy and discrete access. And it is here that the women, yes, the women, come and go talking of — well, not, perhaps, of Michelangelo. What they talk of is, though, hard to tell, from a distance, merely from their expressions, their faces.

"*In Paris even the most refined women wear make-up.*"

Quite, Dr. Benjamin.

"They appear, indeed, to be *mass-produced.*"

Seen one, seen them all, Dr. Benjamin.

[Pause. Turn to auditorium once more.]

I'm sorry. Where am I? Ah yes, why so drawn to the House of Glass? Well, it is, of course, that I hope for a glimpse of one particular woman coming and going — namely, my long-sought-for Marie. She is, you see, no stranger to clinics of the Dalsace kind. Whether in London or Paris.

What is more, she is no stranger to houses made of glass. Or at least, houses made partly of glass. The Tabernacle, you see,

Fig. 31. Photograph of the Église Baptiste de la Rue Meslay (Paris, 1899). Blocher Saillens Archive.

once boasted a roof of glass. Back in *La Belle Époque.* When housed at 61 Rue Meslay. It is evident, this roof, from the photograph. This one. On the screen. As projected, albeit not well. Bloody Usher.

By the way, in addition to the pointed roof of glass, please note, high on either side, the fine-looking galleries. What we here then discern, I suggest, is the spectre of one of Paris's myriad erstwhile arcades. Later converted, as it were. As, perhaps, was meant to be.

Dr. Benjamin, what say you?

"The *arcade* was always a *nave with side chapels.*"

Amen, Dr. Benjamin. If not Hallelujah. As they doubtless chorused at 61 Rue Meslay the day that Marie herself took to its baptismal waters. 1891 it was. The year she was drowned with Jesus, her back to the water, slowly reclining, held all the while. And, as she leant, she would surely have glanced up to see the arcadian glass, yes, even as she inclined, dead, as it were, to the world. The glass above, the last thing she saw; as well as the first, once raised again, soaking, gasping. Glass. Glass.

[Pause. Recover composure, perspective.]

I am sorry. My point? You may perhaps now wonder what on earth was my point? My particular point. Well, it remains simply this: that the house of God, or at least this one, this Tabernacle house, is itself a house of glass.

"Glass … is the enemy of secrecy."

Indeed, Dr. Benjamin. Tell no one.

[Pause.]

Whatever, I must now, dearly beloved, return you to chez Dalsace. Rue Saint-Guillaume. Just a few elegant minutes away, as it happens, from 48 Rue de Lille.

So, who among you knows 48 Rue de Lille? And, indeed, its significance. Just wave to me if you do. Please wave. Someone. Please.

[Silence. Nothing.]

Well, then, I shall tell you. 48 Rue de Lille is where the Drowned of Paris built their one and only Gothic raft, *L'Église Baptiste.* 1873. A proper church, this one. Ornate, arched. It was not where Marie herself went to drown or indeed Johannes. Nor was it where they weekly bowed their heads and mumbled to Jesus, but it is where their marriage, if marriage it was, was blessed. If blessed it was. In 1905.

But why point this out? This proximity. Of Rue de Lille. Well, if one heads south from there toward Rue Saint-Guillaume one walks through streets upon which Marie herself might still wander, even now, as she seeks, perhaps, to recall that day of Questionable Blessing. Back in 1905. And if so, if she really does walk these streets, then perhaps she may yet encounter poor Dr. Benjamin on his way to the House of Glass. Indeed, perhaps she has already done so. Albeit fleetingly. This chance, this possibility, it cannot be denied me. It being in the very nature of this dear city of ours. Its milling boulevards.

"In Paris … the crowd is … an asylum … for the abandoned."

Thank God, Dr. Benjamin.

[Pause.]

Fig. 32. Photograph of the Église Baptiste, 48 Rue de Lille.
Wikimedia Commons.

By the way, dear faithful, I should perhaps mention that, sadly, Dr. Benjamin here is himself divorced. Separated. Abandoned, as it were. And, as is so often the case, he has since become a man rather inclined to linger upon the asphalt.

"I have been alone in Paris for some time."

Several years, Dr. Benjamin. More than enough to grow adept at observing —

"The 'femme passante.'"

Quite. And thus to become —

"The eroticist in the crowd."

Exactly. And is it, Dr. Benjamin, love at first sight?

"No, *love at last sight.*"

[Dr. Benjamin straightens his tie, clearly preparing to speak again, to develop his wandering theme.]

"Taking a stroll in ... Montmartre —"

Ah, Rue Belliard, the Tab.

"On Sundays —"

Before or after Gospel Hour?

"I walk up to the woman closest to me."

Then why not speak to her, Dr. Benjamin? You never know what might ensue or follow. For instance —

"The triumphant encounter of the abandoned couple?"

Why, yes, if the woman in question were poor, abandoned Marie.

[Dr. Benjamin does not respond, though taps at a loaded briefcase. Then, as if now possessed of a riddle, or most terrible hypothesis, he speaks again.]

"What if two married couples become acquainted?"

Why, nothing.

"But what if, in the first instance, two, one from each couple, *are mutually attracted*?"

Oh dear.

"And then *very soon* afterwards *the other two also enter into the most intimate relationship.*"

Good heavens. A veritable chiasmus. A sorry exchange.

[Dr. Benjamin signals disagreement.]

"A situation ... overwhelmingly ... beautiful."

Are you sure?

[Dr. Benjamin nods, then resumes.]

"It is, though, a situation that speaks not of love."

None?

"None."

Then of what does it speak, Dr. Benjamin?

"The continuing *sacramental powers of the two collapsing marriages.*"

In short?

"The remains of marriage, its ruins."

To conclude?

"*Love,* in this case, *is … an illusion.*"

Meaning?

"The Black Mass lives here."

Really? Where?

"Here."

[Pause, then peer into half-full auditorium.]

Dearly beloved, allow me to clarify things. There is no material evidence whatsoever, none, to suggest, even for a moment, that Dr. Benjamin and Marie have exchanged spouses. It is true that Dr. Benjamin's erstwhile wife has escaped to England.

"Dora has opened up a boarding house in London."

Quite. But were I to stand here, dear friends, and suggest that Johannes, yes Johannes, now frequents this London boarding house —

"I have just written to my former wife."

Please don't interrupt, Dr. Benjamin. I was explaining to my audience here that were I to suggest that back in London, in said boarding house, Johannes falls head-over-arse in love with the former Frau Benjamin, you might well declare that —

"The Black Mass lives here again."

Do not interrupt!

"Satan is a dialectician —"

Shut it, pig!

"Who *holds the mirror up to marriage.*"

Enough! One more interruption, pig, and our Usher here will remove you. And then beat you. Beat you with his long-dead flowers. Understand?

[Pause. Then smile into the dark.]

To resume, dear friends. Where are we? Ah yes, the House of Glass. In which connection I must again confess to a little sophistry. A little bending of the world. There is, you see, no evidence, none in fact, that Marie has ever entered the House of Glass, ever trod its rubber-tiled entrance floor, the weight of her foot gently triggering the electric lighting, to then be welcomed by Dr. Dalsace, welcomed into his elegant office and its fine and private telephone-booth, there for the exclusive use of his fine and private clients. Or, should I say patients. Or —

"*The women we court?*"

Pardon?

"*The ... women who could have given themselves to us?*"

Hardly. These women are only there to be seen. By Dalsace.

"*In ... Paris ... before any man catches sight of her,* a woman *already sees herself ten times reflected.*"

[Pause. Turn to auditorium.]

So, yes, I confess that weak is my case, thin my thread, cold the trail. I am, in fact, and to be frank, fast declining, falling. Not the angel I was. I have, you see, pursued Marie for hundreds of years now. Have searched a universe of books for a trace of her face. But she, I think, avoids me.

"*The only person I find of interest finds me less so.*"

Exactly. Which is why, Dr. Benjamin, as I search these books, I so often resort to what you might call —

"*Magical reading?*"

Perhaps.

"*Magical criticism?*"

Well, if you insist.

"*Magical criticism is —*"

Yes?

"*Magical criticism is the highest stage of criticism.*"

Really? Or is it, simply, the final stage? Terminal? Valedictory?

[Pause. Relish awed silence. Then abandon lecture. Exit stage-left. Head for House of Glass. Upon arrival, find Dr. Benjamin somehow already there, standing outside the House of Glass.]

Ah, Dr. Benjamin. Waiting?

"*I was* once *sitting in the Café des Deux Magots* and *waiting* — but *I forget for whom.*"

I see your problem. Why, then, linger so?

"It is extremely difficult for me to walk."

Ah.

"I am forced to stop every three or four minutes."

Why, then, venture out at all? It being so cold.

"My apartment is [not] heated … enough … to write."

But here, out here, whatever do you do to pass the time?

"I *weave*."

Weave what?

"A professorial gown."

Really?

[Dr. Benjamin nods.]

Well, in that case I shall depart post-haste for —

"The *republic of professors*?"

Indeed. And, with them I shall share your revelation, professorial revelation, that reading, criticism, may yet be magical.

[Depart for Sorbonne. Return despised and rejected. Find
Dr. Benjamin still upon the pavement, outside the House of
Glass. Dr. Benjamin looks up and speaks.]

*"I must express my gratitude to you for having contacted the
professors."*

Do not mention it, Dr. Benjamin. It would appear, however,
that the republic of professors is not as yet ready for criticism of
a magical kind.

*"It is less and less likely that I will enter upon a university ca-
reer."*

Quite. No need, alas, for the professorial gown.

[Dr. Benjamin straightens his tie as before, then speaks once
more.]

"The *conventional scholarly attitude* —"

"Yes?"

"I … distinguish it *from the genuine."*

And, pray, what might constitute genuine scholarship?

[Dr. Benjamin reaches into his briefcase, pulls out a book,
and waves it aloft.]

"This."

And what is that?

"Nearly *the saddest thing in the world.*"

Really?

"I wrote it myself."

Whoever for?

"My wife."

Where?

"In the Princess Café ... close to a jazz band."

But why?

"Why what?"

Why write the nearly saddest thing in the world?

"Because —"

Yes?

"Because, *Sleeping Beauty sleeps behind the thorn hedge of [its] pages.*"

Ah, Sleeping Beauty.

[Dr. Benjamin stares at his book. Is now ready to speak once more.]

"*Sleeping Beauty* will, though, never be woken by *a prince of* merely conventional *scholarship.*"

How, then, can she ever be woken?

"By a *blow.*"

A blow?

"A *blow that* ... would *echo shrilly throughout the halls of academia.*"

Ah and, pray, who is to deliver this blow?

"A professor philosophiae extraordinariae."

Yourself?

[Dr. Benjamin nods.]

In that case, you must help me lay siege to this here House of Glass.

[Point to *la Maison de Verre.* Dr. Benjamin is still, however, bewildered.]

Is the connection not obvious? The connection with Sleeping Beauty? Surely you know that Sleeping Beauty sleeps not behind a hedge, but in a coffin made of *glass*? A house of glass, as it were.

[Dr. Benjamin says nothing.]

And, what if, what if this Sleeping Beauty of yours turns out, in fact, to be mine? My very own glass-house beauty?

[Dr. Benjamin says nothing.]

That is to say, sweet Marie. My beautiful Marie.

[Dr. Benjamin says nothing.]

Don't you see? Marie needs to be awoken.

[Dr. Benjamin says nothing.]

And are we not men enough, you and I? Men enough to awake her?

[Dr. Benjamin says nothing.]

Speak, bastard! Speak.

"In the universities —"

Yes?

"The erotic —"

Yes?

"Has been neutralised."

Neutralised?

[Dr. Benjamin nods.]

What on earth do you mean?

"Male impotence —"

Yes?

"It may be *socially ordained.*"

❀

Dalsace, on the basis of his work as a gynaecologist, famously argued that marital sterility is often due not to the wife but to the impotence of the husband, and that this might, in some cases, have psychic origins.

❀

Is there, then, Dr. Benjamin, no hope, for us? You and I? The impotent? The neutralised? The dead-from-the-waist-on-down?

[Dr. Benjamin says nothing.]

Nowhere we can go for, as it were, assistance? Something to stir us? Arouse us?

[Nothing.]

What about, say —

"The enfer."

I'm sorry?

"The enfer."

Hell?

[Dr. Benjamin nods.]

But which hell? Which *enfer*?

"The enfer of the Library."

Library?

[Dr. Benjamin gestures south-west. He then replies, with a most knowing look.]

"La Bibliothèque Nationale."

Ah. L'Enfer. L'Enfer de la BN. I follow you now.

[Dr. Benjamin smirks.]

You devil.

[Dr. Benjamin smirks again.]

Its darkest collection?

[Dr. Benjamin taps his nose.]

Of books that might excite?

[Dr. Benjamin winks.]

Quicken the circulation?

[Dr. Benjamin winks again.]

Lead one to perform? Hit the mark? Prove oneself to those that might —

"Pornography."

I knew it!

"More or less proscribed."

More, I suspect. Which, by the way, begs the question of how on earth they allowed you in?

"Obtaining official permission to use the 'enfer' is one of my few successes."

[Dr. Benjamin smiles, then turns. He is off back to hell. And its books.]

But what of dear Marie? What of her?

[Dr. Benjamin is now a few steps nearer to hell.]

Is there really no chance that you might, if only fleetingly, have come across dear, sweet Marie? Not even as, say, a reflection? In a pane of glass?

[Dr. Benjamin walks on.]

Or as one who stops to help you in the street?

[Dr. Benjamin walks further on.]

Or for whom you have waited? At, say, a café?

[On walks Dr. Benjamin.]

Or even as merely a voice half-heard?

[On, on.]

Or over-heard? On, say, the telephone?

"I have no telephone."

But you have had one.

"Danton 9073?"

Exactly.

[Dr. Benjamin continues to walk away.]

But there is, you know, more than one Paris. There is another. Another Paris.

[Dr. Benjamin continues to walk away.]

Might you have come across her *there*?

[Dr. Benjamin continues to walk away.]

In another Paris? An ever-so-slightly-different Paris?

[Dr. Benjamin continues to walk away, but now, finally, speaks.]

"A dream Paris?"

Yes.

"False Paris?"

Yes

"The Paris that doesn't exist?"

Yes.

"The Paris that *is an aggregate of all the … plans …that were never actually developed?"*

Yes.

[Dr. Benjamin stops, turns around. Then whispers.]

"This dream Paris, false Paris, this Paris that does not exist is in fact —"

Yes?

"The purer Paris, … the truer Paris."

※

II/IV

Fall

In July 1940, when Paris fell to the Germans, many buildings, both public and private, were plundered or requisitioned. La Maison de Verre, however, suffered neither fate. Dalsace and wife, being Jews, had fled before the Nazis even entered the city, and had already emptied the house of all valuables. The Nazis did consider requisitioning the house but, in the end, concluded that it was too expensive to heat and light. For four years, therefore, the House of Glass stood empty. It did not exist, as it were. Neither, it might be said, did the rest of Paris.

Paris, thought Marie, *has donned an unfamiliar appearance. All is dark in the evening, cars drive slowly, people stay at home.* It was, though, strange how some things seemed much the same. The world had changed, the Germans had seen to that, but not the sunlight, the statues, or the way men stared. And the theatres too. Or at least the *Théâtre des Ambassadeurs.* Under new management, she heard. It had formerly been Jewish. But a show was already up and running, just within days. And, as ever, it was a farce, the show. *We Are Not Married,* it was called. Three hours of laughter, the poster said. "Side-splitting laughter," it said.

She had wanted to tell Madeleine, about the laughter, but she had gone. As had so many, in the beginning. Especially the Jews. They had been the first to think of escape, and by whatever means.

One of them had said, *"If* I can't *build a bridge … I will have to … achieve salvation by swimming."* Yes, the Jews had always seemed to know that flight was their one and only salvation. Salvation, though, was a giant of a word. A skyscraper. Yes, big. Too big? Perhaps. Seeing a man might escape the Nazis, and yet not be Saved. If a man were not right with God, still his soul would, sadly, perish. It was difficult. Very difficult. Especially for the Jews, she thought. But they seemed to know they had to fly.

❀

> Benjamin did not leave Paris until May 1940. He left it so late because he needed the Bibliothèque Nationale. Here he worked daily toward completing a huge book on Paris and its arcades. "Nothing in the world could replace the Bibliothèque Nationale," he wrote. When Benjamin did finally attempt his escape he headed over the Pyrenees, bound for neutral Spain; however, he died on the way, in September 1940. It should, perhaps, be noted that Benjamin's library card did not expire until several months later, January 11, 1941. Moreover, he left the manuscript of his arcades book with a friend who worked at the Bibliothèque Nationale, and there the manuscript was safely kept throughout the War, even though two million other books were lost.

❀

Others too had departed. Like Madeleine and her family. That had been later, in June. They had headed South, for the Ardèche, by car. Almost as if off on holiday. Such, *at this time of year,* is the *centrifugal force that Paris communicates.* Some said that Madeleine's going had troubled her flock, the congregation. Perhaps. It is true that someone had pinned a horrid notice on the Tabernacle door. "They were afraid," it said.

But Marie had known that Madeleine would never forsake them. Never forget them. And, once returned, Madeleine was welcomed back. The congregation had been more relieved than anything. No side-splitting laughter. Not a case of *clowns making a comeback.* Not the hour, Marie thought, for clowns.

No. Things were certainly somber. And strange. What with the Germans everywhere. Bewildering it was. All this coming and going. Then and now. Before and after. On occasion, she had not even been sure which was which, or quite what o'clock it was, as it were. *In what time does man live?* She was not altogether sure. After all, death, she knew, was not the end.

This was not to say that *we … are resurrected in what happens to us.* No, it was not like that. Jesus alone was the Resurrection. Though there are your children. You can, perhaps, live on through them. Even if they are brought up by others. Like that little Jewish girl, just five years old. The one Madeleine had taken in. They had had to hide her, turn her into a kind of shadow.

※

Yesterday, I went for the first time to see the Place de la Concorde; it is frightening to see swastikas flying everywhere.
(Madeleine, December 31, 1940)

※

Yes, everywhere, thought Marie. Even the Tabernacle. One Sunday, old Herr Stutzel had walked in, just like that, wearing a magnificent buttonhole, a breath-taking rose, and in the centre was a swastika. Yes, he is German, but he is not a soldier. Indeed, he is meant to be a believer, a brother. In Christ. *You look first at people's lapels, and after that usually do not want to look them in the face.*

Like Herr Adloff. She did not want to look him in the face. Not now. It had been hard enough the last time, in England, even with Johannes there. And now it was, once more, so hard to bear, to suffer. His face. Once again, this brother was also her enemy.

※

Herr Adloff was in church on Sunday… He was defending his people [and] … accusing the Jews. He

dared to say that he was protecting the French from the English, since his factories produced the camouflage paint used by the German artillery.
(Madeleine, June 14, 1942)

❀

Herr Adloff had certainly worked hard, over the years. Had been, in fact, most successful. A first-rate businessman, Johannes would have said. And it was true that Herr Adloff's paint helped to protect them. From English bombs. It hid the guns, his camouflage paint. The guns could hardly be seen. Not in the countryside. Vanished, just like that, they did, among the trees and the leaves and the shadows. Hidden. Safe. As safe as if you were huddled at a desk in the Bibliothèque Nationale.

I flee there ... *every morning.*

Safe among the books. Safe beneath the foliage painted on the ceiling.

As one leafs through the pages down below, it rustles above.

[Pause.]

At least, she thought, Herr Adloff's factories did not make weapons.

To be found in the Passage de l'Opéra was the arms manufacturer.

Paint was, in that regard, she thought, a harmless line of business. But, could the same be said of rubber? The rubber trade? After all, bombers could not take off without tyres. Neither German nor English. You could see them sometimes. In the air. Not, though, made of rubber. No, tyres were not made of rubber now. You could not get rubber now. Not real rubber. Not rubber from India, or wherever else there are rubber trees. They made it from chemicals now. What was it called? The Germans made it by the ton. I.G. Farben, she had heard. They made it. The man-made rubber. Buna, they called it. I.G. Farben made it.

❀

I. G. Farben produced synthetic rubber at various factories. One was in Auschwitz, a factory in which Jews were worked to death. They also manufactured Zyklon-B, as used in the gas chambers.

✺

What *are the conditions for revolution*?
You tell me.
Unlimited trust in I.G. Farben and the peaceful perfecting of the air force.
A provocation?
Joke.

✺

But rubber, she thought, it has so many uses these days. A thousand-and-one. *The gas-mask in my room,* for example. Or just search the kitchen, or the bathroom. Even, she thought, the bedroom. Rubber could be found there as well, if you know where to look. In which particular drawer. The husband's friend, as it were. Garishly wrapped. *Green and violet, the colours of Fromms Akt.* Those horrid stripes. All over the packets. At least, she thought, they did not end any lives. Though they might, perhaps, have prevented lives. Millions, said Johannes. Millions of them had been sold. He had to be admired, Herr Fromm. The rubber-king of Germany. Lived in London, now, she heard. Being Jewish.
[Pause.]
On a rubber-rubber-mountain,
There lives a rubber-rubber-dwarf,
[Who] has a rubber-rubber-wife.
The rubber-rubber-wife
Has a rubber-rubber-child.
[And] the rubber-rubber-child
Has a rubber-rubber-ball.
[The rubber-rubber-child] threw it in the air
[And] the rubber-rubber-ball it broke.

And you are a Jew.

Like that young man, she thought, the candidate for baptism. There are three, Madeleine had said. Three to be baptized. And one is a Jew, she had said. Don't tell Herr Adloff, she had also said. But they didn't have to. He was wearing a yellow star, the Jewish young man. He had to wear it, even in church, even as he went into the water, even as he came up again. Out of the water. That horrid star. Still there. Poor soul. The young man knew it would never save him, baptism. Not from being taken away. But at least he would be with Jesus when he went. With Jesus in his heart. Like that poor Monsieur T. Or, so she hoped.

❀

> Madame T. has been rounded up, but her husband was not in when they came. … So, yesterday afternoon Monsieur T. came round asking if we could shelter him. I told him it … would compromise the work of the church. Monsieur T. grew desperate and wept. We tried to help him see the work [that] God had for him to do in the camps.
> (Madeleine, July 18, 1942)

❀

Had Monsieur T. abandoned his wife?

Yes, in a way.

And could the Tab not shelter him?

No, they could not. No. Madeleine was sorry. So very sorry. But they dare not. Not help, not hide him. How could they? It might, she said, harm the Cause. The Germans were watching.

Watching the work of God? In Paris?

Yes.

But *Hitler is doomed.*

Indeed. His eventual demise, however, seems some way off. In the meantime the Gospel must still be preached. And he, Monsieur T., must try to be calm. Try to see what work God would have for him to do in the camps. To which he would, no doubt, be sent. Once caught.

This work, thought Marie, Monsieur T. would have to undertake alone, without his wife. Wherever she was.

❀

Labouring for God, though, was always a joy. However hard. Or, so Marie now believed. Hallelujah. Once, when young, her faith had been largely formal. But that was when she first left for London. She had, since then, experienced Jesus. And now she longed to tell others about Him, dearest Him. Besides, all the signs were that His return was near. And all should be warned. All.

Marie thought once more of the Jews. Poor souls. Everything, she thought, must be done to help them. But the one thing most needful must not be forgotten. We must, said Madeleine, offer each and every Jew not only our sympathy but a New Testament. And so they, the Tab, had gone, as it were, into the highways and bye-ways.

And had spoken to as many a Jew as might stop and listen. And one, a man, had responded.

"I dreamed," he had said, "of women taking an interest in me."
He had then mimicked her.

"Allow me," he had said, "to direct your attention to the study of the Holy Scriptures."

Yes, her very words.

"As well as to the extremely moderate prices ... of my hosiery."

Ah! No. No. He had misheard. Misunderstood. She was by no means selling hosiery.

But it might just help, said the man, who added, by way of explanation, that scripture and hosiery were not wholly incompatible. The message of salvation and the things of the world surely lived cheek-to-cheek. Were nearest neighbours.

And how could he be sure?

"Consider," he said, "those bookshops on the mezzanine."

Which ones?

"Those that that sell not only *The Arts of Love* —"
(She grew concerned).
"But also The *Way to Heaven.*"
Ah, and did he himself know the way to Heaven?
"I have … grasped … justification through faith."
Praise God.
"But … as soon as I have mastered it …, it vanishes again."
She was saddened. Justification was precious, so precious.
Not least for a Jewish gentleman such as he. So soon to be
rounded up. And taken away. To the nearest station.
"Gare Saint-Lazare?"
Perhaps.
"*Where one* can then *head off for London*?"
Not quite, I'm afraid.
"The mountains?"
Not any more, I'm afraid.
"But *the final* train is leaving for the mountains."
The final train has already gone.

❋

The only trains that still carried Jews were, she knew, heading
for the camps. And why, thought Marie, why wave at those in
these terrible trains if one did not also share with them the Gospel? She could not bear *waving … to strangers passing by on a
moving train.* It was, she thought, like *waving to angels whenever
they waved to the unknown, never-returning people.*

Some there were, at the Tab, who did *not* just wave at the never-returning angels. They had actually joined the angels on the
trains. Pastor Feat, for instance. From Brittany. He had, it seems,
been accused of sabotage. *The denunciations originated from a
man in Paris.* A snake of a man. Talking snake. Pastor Feat had
now been deported to Dachau, she heard, and had died.

Marie thought once more of Monsieur T., and the work that
God had for him to do in the camps.

In my thoughts I am … in the camp.

She was not, however, altogether sure what work poor Monsieur T. would have to do. How exactly he would communicate the Gospel.

Could he do his *theology ... by whispers*?

No, that would not be sufficient. Would get him nowhere. [Pause.]

And what, she thought, if Monsieur T. were to die in a camp? Alone, still estranged, at the end, from his wife.

The ... night before death ... is ... the night of impotence.

She did not like to think of it. Not of being alone, at the end.

❋

In September 1940, having ascended the Pyrenees on foot, Benjamin reached a fishing village. This was at the Spanish border; and there, in a hotel, he committed suicide. His final night he spent alone, separated from the women with whom he had travelled. He was found in the morning, lying, half-naked, on the bed.

❋

Dying, thought Marie. Dying, and knowing you are dying, must be like standing on a cliff or precipice.

I live on the seventh floor.

And looking down.

The philosopher ... must be ... immune to vertigo.

She often had dreams like this. Her Alpine dream. As many did, she heard.

Last night, she thought, *I dreamed ... that I had come to a peak which offered a far-reaching view of all countries* and ... *spied other people standing on other peaks. One of them was suddenly seized by vertigo and plummeted down. This vertigo spread; other people were now plummeting ...* and *just as I myself was seized by this feeling, I woke up.*

But, what if she hadn't woken up? What if, instead, like all the others, she had also fallen, plummeted. Or even jumped? Having no better option. Jumped to her death. As was not now uncommon. Among the Jews.

It was like, she thought, in the movies. People standing on a ledge, or jumping from a bridge, or a window. All kinds of jumps or leaps she had seen. Some quite fantastic. Wonderful, in fact. Such was the magic of cinema. *A leap from a window ... can be shot in the studio ... while the ensuing fall may be filmed weeks later at an outdoor location.* One person jumps, quite another person falls. And lands, she thought. Hits the ground, the earth.

❋

Early on in the War, when Marie and Sara were staying in Brittany, they witnessed a number of German soldiers climbing sheer cliffs in preparation for the invasion of England. In March 1941, the sisters record that one of the soldiers had recently fallen to his death

❋

III/IV

Gate

On August 27, 1944, when the Nazis were being
forced out of Paris, a few German planes flew over
the city and, in a final act of defiance, dropped a
number of bombs. One of the bombs fell directly on
the Tabernacle, at 163 Rue Belliard. Madeleine first
knew of this when she tried to ring the Tabernacle
only to find that "the telephone [there] no longer
works."

It's not working, the telephone, at the Tab, it's not working. Hello? Tabernacle?

Danton 9037.

I'm sorry?

Danton 9037.

Is that the Tabernacle?

Danton 9037.

Sounds like a crossed wire.

You misunderstood me.

I'm sorry?

You misunderstood me … on the telephone.

Sorry?

Misunderstood me.

[Pause. Paris is about to be liberated.]

Perhaps, thought Marie, she had misunderstood Johannes. Misunderstood what he had meant. Or wanted. *You misunderstood me,* he would say. Though not at the end. She had understood then. It was very clear at the end. That she would have to leave. Move back to France. *I … informed* him *… of my change of address on the telephone.*

[Pause. Most of the Germans now leave Paris.]

Or, perhaps it was Johannes who had misunderstood. Or had misheard her change of address, on the telephone. Had got it wrong. It would not be surprising. It had been a difficult time.

She had certainly found things difficult, coming back to Paris, after all those years. She had lived in London long enough to feel almost English. Back in Paris she had felt, at first, like an Alien.
[Pause. A few last Germans destroy whatever they can.]

※

> I was told on the telephone ... that all that remains of the Tabernacle are the four walls and the stair-case. ... The doors and windows are gone, the baptistery is full of glass, [and] the pulpit has gone, but our beautiful gate is in-tact.
> (Madeleine, August 28, 1944)

Gone, thought Marie. Just like that. In a moment. Everything. All save the gate. The wrought-iron gate. She could hardly believe her eyes. How strange it now looked, the gate. All on its own. The beautiful gate, still beautiful. Marie stood by the gate, in front of it, and stared. *I am standing on the threshold about to enter. ... It is a complicated business.*

Yes, complicated, she thought, as she stared. And recalled the day she had returned to Paris. 1924. It had been a complicated day. Coming back. Getting off the boat-train. Taking the metro. Turning into Rue de Rome. Not knowing what to think. Or say. *The gates in Paris* are both *border gates and triumphal arches.* She had changed so much. And so much had happened. And she had felt like a perfect stranger by the time she had reached the house. *Thresholds ... are felt ... under the soles of* one's *feet.* And waited. 1924. To be ushered in. To the hallway. With the flowers, the ancient flowers. Yes, a stranger, she had been. Then. 1924. Or so she thought, as she stood at the gate, the beautiful Tabernacle gate. Now. 1944.

※

Every second is *the strait gate through which the Messiah might enter.*

❋

IV/IV

Storm

> We have just suffered a very sad and unexpected loss
> in the person of our dear … friend, Mme Wheeler.
> She had had influenza at the same time as her sister,
> … [and] on March 8, she suddenly suffered chronic
> uraemia, and nothing could arrest it. We had the
> privilege of seeing her the night before her death;
> she was perfectly lucid and said a fervent "Amen" to
> our prayer. She knew that she was dying and said …
> "I am ready."
> (Madeleine, April 1948)

Ah yes, Marie was ready for the end. As am I. Ready for the end
of my final lecture, at last resumed. After all these years. My last
gasp. The end of the end, if you will.

"The public —"

Ah, Dr. Benjamin, still with us?

*"The public has an ear only for the message that the author
would … utter … with his last breath."*

Quite.

[Turn once more toward auditorium.]

Dear public, dear friends, now, at my last, I see that you finally take an interest in my words. Hoping, no doubt, that this old
gowned fool of yours might have some rhetorical gold to share.
An obscene confession, perhaps. Or inflated promise. Or even a
simple curse. Well, I am afraid that these fallen lips of mine can
only muster this, that —

"The readiness is all."

Ah, Dr. Benjamin, you think of *Hamlet*. Or at least the end
thereof, the bitter end. The deaths. Elsinore condemned, and
the —

"Court reduced to a scaffold."

Indeed. Nothing to be seen but —

"Shadows of kings."

Philosopher-kings, to be precise; above all, His Highness Professor Hamlet. Who is, I think, not unlike you and I, Dr. Benjamin. Doomed scholar-princes, as we are.

[Pause.]

And is there anyone else, Dr. Benjamin?

[Silence.]

I say, Dr. Benjamin, is there anyone else? Anyone else at the end of *Hamlet* who might just be compared to folk hereabouts? Known to you and I, that is. And to those few still here assembled.

[Dr. Benjamin says nothing.]

Come, come, there must be others? Or are the shadows of kings left all alone?

[Dr. Benjamin shakes his head.]

Who, then, are with them? These shadow kings? Who comfort them? Stand with them? Upon the stage, at the end.

"There are *shadows of kings and*—"

Yes?

"*Shadows of kings and sad women.*"

Who?

"*Sad women.*"

Sad? By no means. No, Dr. Benjamin, the women are in no way sad. Least not the women hereabouts, Madeleine and Marie. Certainly not sweet, death-ward Marie. No, she was not sad. She was ready. Ready to die. Was that not obvious? Did you not see? See her at the last? Upon her death-bed.

"*I noticed that one of the women who was very beautiful*—"

Yes?

"*Was lying on a bed.*"

Indeed. And then what did you see?

[Silence.]

Speak, Dr. Benjamin.

"*She pushed aside a bit of the blanket.*"

Ah.

"*Not to let me see her body.*"

No?

"*But to see the pattern of her sheet.*"

Pattern?

"I was not at all able to distinguish it."

But, did you have no idea? None? Not a clue?

"I saw a piece of cloth covered with images."

And?

"The only ... element I was able to distinguish was —"

Yes?

"The top part of the letter 'd.'"

Ah, "d" for "divorce," perhaps. Not to mention that "d" which lingers languorously at the far end of "Schad." As in "Johannes Schad." Or plain "Monsieur Schad," as he is known, or cursed, hereabouts.

❋

The late Mme Wheeler ... left for London in 1906 after she married M. Schad, a member of our church; [however,] she suffered immense distress when, 18 years later, she was compelled to divorce.
(Madeleine, April 1948)

❋

I wonder, Dr. Benjamin, if you could tell me a little more about this very particular "d" of yours? The one that you saw with your very own eyes. On the sheet. The bed sheet. Could you describe, perhaps, its precise calligraphic form? How, for instance, would you interpret the top part of the letter "d"? The ascender.

"Its elongation?"

Indeed.

"It revealed —"

Yes?

"It revealed an ... aspiration to spirituality."

Ah, no, Dr. Benjamin. No. It reveals an aspiration for quite the opposite. This "d," you see, insofar as it is the "d" at the end of "Schad," is "d" for "damnation." Hell, in short. For, although it is almost twenty-five years since the divorce, and over 40 years since the wedding, the name of Monsieur Schad is still, even now, being dragged, corpse-like, through Tabernacle mire, and strung up from a-top its creaking pulpit.

And that, I say, is absurd. Bizarre. Do they not know, the clowns, that the marriage may never have been a marriage at all? That —

"It was ... for physiological reasons that the couple were unable to come together."

Exactly, Dr. Benjamin. And even if Johannes were to be blamed, condemned, damned, where upon earth is forgiveness? Where? Where, I say?

[Finally turn toward black auditorium. It is now empty. Pause. Clear throat for finale.]

Well, this is it, dearly departed, and once beloved. I must now bring my last lecture to an end. Bid adieu. Sign off. And I shall do so in quiet defiance. I shall sign, that is, as "Monsieur J. Schad."

[Turn to write upon the wall.]

"Please forgive the painfully complete signature."

What was that?

[Turn round to find that Dr. Benjamin now addresses the empty auditorium].

"Please forgive the painfully complete signature."

No, pig. Do not seek forgiveness for me. Nor for my signature. Nor for any of my sins. Written or not. No, do not seek forgiveness for me. Not from anyone. Here or elsewhere. I have no need for forgiveness. None. I want no —

"Storm of forgiveness."

No, no storm, thank you. Storms are perilous. One may not survive. May be blown away. Blasted. Become someone else.

Postscript

The reader may wish to know that Johannes's third child, my Aunt Jane, wrote as follows in relation to the history of his first marriage, or "marriage":

I did not know anything about a previous marriage until the day after my father died when my mother told me the story. … My mother used to say that the length of the non-consummated marriage was a tribute to my father's wonderful patience and dignity. I think my mother also said that the first wife's parents concealed her medical/personality problems and should never have let her marry.

— Email to author, August 10, 2011

Afterword
Or, Six Unnecessary Reflections

I

This book is my third desperate attempt at a life, an experimental life, that is. The other two focused on well-known philosophical figures, themselves both desperate, in their ways. The first, *Someone Called Derrida* (2007), is an ill-fated dream of memoir, Oxford, and murder. The second, *The Late Walter Benjamin* (2012), is a kind of after-life, a farce-of-a-novel mitigated only by some spectacular misreading.

II

This book takes modernism to the courts for its dubious claim to accommodate what Virginia Woolf once called "the lives of the obscure."

III

If this book has a theme, it is that of Negation. It is a theme which, arguably, lies at the very heart (if it has one) of modernism. As Franz Kafka writes, "What is laid upon us is to accomplish the negative." This poor book thinks, then, that it is a work of experimental literary criticism, seeking as it does to give a name and local habitation to modernism's great vision of Negation, or Nothing.

IV

In an attempt to do justice to all this Nothing, this book takes as its guide Oscar Wilde's declaration that "the primary aim of the critic is to see the object as in itself it really is *not*." In other words, this book seeks to ditch the positivist or realist assumptions of conventional literary criticism and instead have a drunken, post-critical way with its sources and texts. That is to say, whilst *Paris Bride* may suffer from many of the so-called virtues of conventional criticism (e.g. close reading, extensive citation, archival research, historical detail, and philosophical reach) it rarely, if ever, deploys formal argumentation. No chapter is confined, then, to the genre of the academic essay, but instead draws on a range of literary genres and devices that are, we think (the book and I), more in sympathy with the *non*-realist character of modernism itself. These are devices such as fragmentation, *flânerie,* textual collage, stream of consciousness, imagism, perspectivism, dream-text, the absurd, and so on.

V

In 1983, in his alarming essay "Post-Criticism," Gregory Ulmer claimed that literary criticism had finally woken up to the great modernist shift that had taken place within Western culture at the beginning of the twentieth century. "The break with … realism," he wrote, "which revolutionised the modernist arts, is now underway (belatedly) in criticism." Ulmer, though, jumped the gun. In the 1980s, the Yale School of deconstruction did indeed cock a snoop at the realist pretensions of most criticism and proposed, instead, the development of criticism *as* literature. However, in the intervening years, with the dominance of historicism, very few critical texts could be also described as literary. The times they are, though, a-rotting with an outbreak of outrageously *literary* literary criticism. Ulmer's modernist break?

VI

This book has a number of faults. More than I intended.

❀

Endnotes

Chapter One

On the Fourth — "Minutes of Acts of Marriage," Divorce Papers, The National Archives: J 77/ 2080. C450964. Hereafter National Archives (to whom I grateful for permission to quote from these papers) will be referred to as NA.

Mrs. Dalloway said — Virginia Woolf, *Mrs Dalloway,* ed. Stella McNichol (Harmondsworth: Penguin, 1992 [1925]), 3.

Odd affinities — Ibid., 167.

She ... never — Ibid., 169.

I love walking — Ibid., 6.

the eminent linguist — William James referred thus to Saussure in 1892. For further discussion on Saussure's visit to England in 1911, see John E. Joseph, "He Was an Englishman," *TLS* (November 16, 2007): 16.

"A panorama of — Ferdinand Saussure, *Course in General Linguistics,* trans. Roy Harris (La Salle: Open Court, 1983), 82. Originally published as *Cours de linguistique générale,* eds. Charles Bally and Albert Sechehaye (Paris: Payot, 1964 [1916]), 117.

Mont Blanc — Arnold Lunn, *The Swiss and Their Mountains* (London: George Allen, 1963), 68–69.

"City of— Percy Bysshe Shelley, "Mont Blanc" [1817], in *Poetical Works,* ed. Thomas Hutchinson (Oxford: Oxford University Press, 1970), 534.

the guest-book— G.R. de Beer, *Escape to Switzerland* (Harmondsworth: Penguin, 1945), 66–67.

Over the Strand — Woolf, *Mrs Dalloway,* 152.

woman called Marie— T.S. Eliot, "The Waste Land" [1922], in *The Complete Poems of T.S. Eliot* (London: Faber, 1969), ll. 15–18.

Our lives— Emily Dickinson, "Our Lives Are Swiss" [c.1896], in *The Complete Poems,* ed. Thomas H. Johnson (London: Faber, 1970), 41.

The British Empire— Cathy Ross, *Twenties London* (London: Philip Wilson Publishers, 2003), 8. The exhibition began on April 23, 1924.

April was indeed— See the opening of "The Waste Land."

It is nature— Virgina Woolf, *The Essays of Virginia Woolf,* ed. Andrew McNeillie, 6 vols. (London: Chatto and Windus, 1986–2012), 3.410–12.

Johannes Schad has— Metropolitan Police Special Report, January 7, 1925, Naturalisation Papers, NA: HO 144/ 6158. 230293.

Villains there must— Woolf, *Mrs Dalloway,* 190.

"We assign— Saussure, *Course in General Linguistics,* 107 / *Cours de linguistique générale,* 151.

Every man fell— Woolf, *Mrs Dalloway,* 148.

"This cable— Ghada Karmi, *Married to Another Man* (London: Pluto Press 2008). See also H. Haumann, ed., *The First Zionist Congress* (Basel: S Karger, 1997).

lifted her up— Woolf, *Mrs Dalloway,* 14.

that rubber made— Johannes worked in central London for Chautard, a Paris based rubber-trading company.

all down the— Woolf, *Mrs Dalloway,* 21–22.

"In its consistency— Joseph, "He Was an Englishman," 15.

"Honeymoon Land"— See *The Recorder, for Palmers Green, Winchmore Hill and Southgate,* December 7, 1914 (Consulted at Enfield Local Studies & Archive, to whom I am grateful for

permission to quote). Marie and Johannes moved to Powys Lane, Palmers Green in 1914.

an airman — *The Recorder,* December 19, 1912.

in or about — Virginia Woolf, *Collected Essays of Virginia Woolf,* ed. Leonard Woolf, 4 vols. (London: Hogarth, 1966–67), 3.332.

the ears of — Woolf, *Mrs Dalloway,* 22.

boys in uniform — Ibid., 23.

to be the — Ibid., 55–56.

The Waiting List — Letter from War Office to Johannes Schad, August 22, 1914, Naturalisation Papers, NA.

on the wireless — Remembrance Day's two-minute silence was first broadcast on BBC Radio in November 1923. For more discussion on this, see Emma Hanna, *The Great War on the Small Screen: Representing the First World War in Contemporary Britain* (Edinburgh: Edinburgh University Press, 2009), 8.

We Swiss are — *The Swiss Observer,* November 17, 1923.

"Victory all the — Jean Starobinski, *Words upon Words: The Anagrams of Ferdinand de Saussure,* trans. Olivia Emmet (New Haven: Yale University Press, 1979), 9.

she had read — Woolf, *Mrs Dalloway,* 34.

The Organ of — *The Swiss Observer* called itself "the official organ of the Swiss colony in Great Britain."

Miss Lina Schwarz — *The Swiss Observer,* July 16, 1921.

Calvaries — See Wilfred Noyce, *The Alps* (London: Thames and Hudson, 1963), 183–84.

When a man — Woolf, *Mrs Dalloway,* 108.

Eton tutor — Woolf, *The Diary of Virginia Woolf,* ed. Anne Olivier Bell, 5 vols. (London: Hogarth Press, 1979–85), 3.314.

Christ … and Christess — Woolf, *Mrs Dalloway,* 109.

A seedy-looking — Ibid., 31.

she had seen — Ibid., 136.

He started after — Ibid., 57–58.

he … insisted — Ibid., 34.

husband and wife — Marie Stopes, *Married Love,* ed. Ross McKibbin (Oxford: Oxford University Press, 2008 [1918]), 72.

The supreme mystery — Woolf, *Mrs Dalloway,* 140.

"No soul could — Stopes, *Married Love,* 72.

people were — Woolf, *Mrs Dalloway,* 72.

"girls who went — *Recorder,* November 10, 1907.

Nelly — According to the 1911 Census, Johannes and Marie had a live-in maid called Nelly Harding, aged 17.

"Suppose — Saussure, *Course in General Linguistics,* 8 / *Cours de linguistique générale,* 23.

"It would be — Ibid., 15 / ibid., 32.

On and on — Woolf, *Mrs Dalloway,* 58.

lips gaping wide — Ibid., 15.

"Do you — *Recorder,* November 17, 1907.

her qualifications — Marie had trained as a dentist in Paris, in those years this was a four-year course. Her name is to be found in *Odontologie: revue mensuelle,* 13–23 (1901), at which point she seems to have already undertaken two years of training. I am grateful, once again, to Jacques Blocher here.

Pneumonia in the — Woolf in a letter to Katherine Arnold-Fraser, August 23, 1922, in *Letters of Virginia Woolf,* eds. Nigel Nicolson and Joanne Trautmann, 6 vols. (London: Harcourt Brace Jovanovich, 1975–79), 2.549.

Miss Kilman standing — Woolf, *Mrs Dalloway,* 140.

This Christian — Ibid., 137.

standing … upon — Ibid., 136.

Yes, Miss Kilman — Ibid., 135.

she would think — Ibid., 170.

"We must be — Saussure, *Course in General Linguistics,* 24 / *Cours de linguistique générale,* 44.

"In Paris — Ibid., 31 / ibid., 54.

the letterbox — *Recorder,* November 5, 1912.

her mother was — See Police Report, Naturalisation Papers, NA.

this isle of — Woolf, *Mrs Dalloway,* 198.

also called Marie — Her maiden name was Faesch; she died in 1950.

Women must put — Woolf, *Mrs Dalloway,* 33.

crossed Oxford — Ibid., 59.

She made to — Ibid., 43.

They had just — Ibid., 6.

Dr. Holmes — Ibid., 73.

I do order — Appointment of Medical Inspectors, Divorce Papers. It should be pointed out that the date of this particular court order is May 27, 1924 and indeed that the medical inspectors appointed are Edwin Frances White of Putney and Leonard Stokes of Andover. It would appear, therefore, that the Court sought an additional examination of Marie, subsequent to that undertaken by Thomas George Stevens, almost as if it shared Marie's concerns regarding his statement. However, the *Schad v Schad* Divorce Papers in the National Archives do not include any reports from either White or Stokes.

Like a nun — Woolf, *Mrs Dalloway,* 33.

From Basel one — In 1897, Theodor Herzl declared: "In Basel, I have founded the Jewish state." Haumann, *The First Zionist Congress,* 134.

newly-married couple — Stopes, *Married Love,* 25.

Women … at — Woolf, *Mrs Dalloway,* 33.

"To speak of — Saussure, *Course in General Linguistics,* 90 / *Cours de linguistic générale,* 130. Here the word translated as "ghost" is *fantôme.*

Report on the — Medical Report, April 16, 1924, Divorce Papers, NA.

"I have come — Woolf, *Mrs Dalloway,* 49.

"men … who — Ibid., 162.

November 25, 1924 — This is the date of the decree nisi (*Schad v Schad née Wheeler*) hearing in the High Court. Divorce Papers, NA.

"Dr. Stopes herself — See Marie Stopes, *Marriage in My Time* (London: Rich and Cowan, 1935), 22–23.

a nullity case — Ibid., 23.

A little independence — Woolf, *Mrs Dalloway,* 8.

a room of — "A Room of One's Own" is an extended essay by Woolf based on lectures she gave at Cambridge in 1928.

Sir Thomas Horridge — Decree Nisi, November 25, 1924, Divorce Papers, NA. Sir Thomas Gardner Horridge (d. 1938) was married twice, with no children from either marriage.

The business of — Woolf, *Mrs Dalloway,* 97.

was it that — Ibid., 73.

"Marriage — These words were written by Lord Merrivale, *Marriage and Divorce* (London: George Allen, 1936), 15, who pronounced the Decree Absolute in the High Court on June 15, 1925. Divorce Papers, NA.

Perhaps, after all — Woolf, *Mrs Dalloway,* 111.

He has left me — Ibid., 51.

Nothing again — See Eliot's "The Waste Land," in *The Complete Poems of T.S. Eliot,* l. 120.

Thomas G. Stevens — Aleck Bourne, "Thomas George Stevens, Obituary," *Journal of Obstetrics and Gynaecology of the British Empire* 61 (1954): 123–25.

'the result of — Saussure, *Course in General Linguistics,* 226 / *Cours de linguistique générale,* 311. I should point out that where Roy Harris uses the word "fall" in his translation the original French has the word "suppression." Insofar as my reading hinges on the word "fall" then the "eminent linguist, Mr. X" (to quote William James, of course) is here not so much Saussure as Professor Harris; which is to say that the identity of Mr. X slips precisely as we might expect of Mr. X. In this connection we must never, of course, forget that even the "original" French text, *Cours de linguistique générale* (1916) was authored not by Saussure himself (he had died three years before), but by his students based on their notes from his lectures. In this sense Saussure, or at least the "author" of *The Course,* has always been Mr. X.

the letter h — Ibid., 30 / ibid., 53. I should point out that where Roy Harris uses the word "ghost" the original French has the phrase *un être fictif.* Here again, in this moment, the "eminent linguist" of my narrative is, you might say, as much Professor Harris as Professor de Saussure.

like a nun — Woolf, *Mrs Dalloway,* 33.

Let us begin — Ferdinand de Saussure, *Writings in General Linguistics* (Oxford: Oxford University Press, 2006), 101. Originally published as *Écrits de linguistique générale* (Paris: Editions Gallimard, 2002), 153.

This killing — Woolf, *Mrs Dalloway,* 101.

In the midst — Ibid., 146.

London … is — Woolf, *The Diary of Virginia Woolf,* 3.6.

Chapter Two

Some diabolical official — Kafka in a letter to Felice Bauer, November 28, 1912, in *Letters to Felice,* eds. Erich Heller and Jürgen Born, trans. James Stern and Elisabeth Duckworth (Harmondsworth: Penguin, 1973), 180. / *Schriften, Tagebücher, Briefe, Kritische Ausgabe,* 16 vols. (Frankfurt am Main: S. Fischer Verlag, 1982–99), 1.277. All subsequent references to Kafka are to this multi-volume edition, unless otherwise stated.

the Tabernacle — The Tabernacle name only came into use after 1922. Previously the church was known as *l'Eglise Baptiste de la Rue Meslay* or *Eglise Chrétienne Primitive*. For reasons of simplicity, though, I will, even when exploring these earlier days, usually refer to the church as the Tabernacle. For a detailed account of the church, see Sébastien Fath's wonderful *Une autre manière d'être chrétien en France. Socio-histoire de l'implantation Baptiste, 1810–1950* (Genève: Labor et Fides, 2001), 389–439.

Marie's husband — *Le Journal de Madeleine Blocher-Saillens* (unpublished), May 21, 1924, Archives Blocher-Saillens (hereafter abbreviated as Archives B-S). I am grateful to Jacques Blocher for permission to quote from these archives.

Uli Schad — This lineage is given as well-established fact in *The Swiss Observer,* December 16, 1955.

"Someone — Franz Kafka, *The Trial* [1925], trans. Willa and Edwin Muir (Harmondsworth: Penguin, 1953 [1937]), 7 / *Schriften,* 4.7.

I … didn't visit — Franz Kafka, July 27, 1914, *The Diaries of Franz Kafka, 1910–23,* ed. Max Brod (Harmondsworth: Penguin, 1972), 294 / *Schriften,* 3.660.

the bed in — *The Trial,* 7 / *Schriften,* 4.7.

the Advocate — Ibid., 209 / ibid., 4.258.

must clamber — Ibid., 181–82 / ibid., 4.221.

Examining Magistrate — Ibid., 64 / ibid., 4.81.

How Grete — Ibid., 61 / ibid., 4.77.

A man and — Ibid. / ibid.

"I pray for — Kafka in a letter to Felice Bauer, January 24, 1913, in *Letters to Felice,* 286 / *Schriften,* 9.58.

scholars of Theology — Consider, for example, *De divina omnipotentia* [1065] in Pierre Damien, *Lettre sur la toute-puissance divine. Introduction, texte critique, traduction et notes,* ed. and trans. André Cantin (Paris: Les Editions du Cerf, 1972).

Do you have — *The Trial,* 122–23 / *Schriften,* 4.144–45.

You belong — Ibid., 123 / ibid., 4.146.

"She clasped his — Ibid., 123 / ibid., 4.146.

"bicycle licence — Ibid., p. 11 / ibid., 4.12.

in a vision — J.W.L., *Slave Stories in Rubber-Seeking* (London: Walter Scott Publishing, 1913), 46.

"the general telephone — *The Trial,* 27 / *Schriften,* 4.34.

What case is — Ibid., 105 / ibid., 4.122.

"The real question — Ibid., 18 / ibid., 4.21.

"This arrest — Ibid., 27 / ibid., 4.33.

"reading a book — Ibid., 8 / ibid., 4.9.

"empty … ink-bottles — Ibid., 94 / ibid., 4.108.

"There can be — Ibid., 54 / ibid., 4.69.

"There was a — Ibid., 207 / ibid., 4.238.

Herr Doktor Muller — Peter E. Gordon, *Continental Divide: Heidegger, Cassirer, Davos* (Cambridge: Harvard University Press, 2010), 91.

"the University on — Ibid., 90.

"a horizontaller — Thomas Mann, *The Magic Mountain,* trans. H.T. Lowe-Porter (Harmondsworth: Penguin, 1960 [1924]), 73.

"You try to — Kafka in a letter to Milena Jesenská, Monday evening, in *Letters to Milena,* ed. Willy Hass, trans. Tania and James Stern (London: Vintage Books, 1999 [1935]), 110. Originally published as *Briefe an Milena,* eds. Jürgen Born and Michael Müller (Frankfurt am Main: Fischer Verlag, 1986), 277.

"I am … going — Sander Gilman, *Franz Kafka: The Jewish Patient* (London: Routledge, 1995), 282.

I [have] watched — Kafka in a letter to Milena Jesenská [June 3, 1920], in *Letters to Milena,* 33 / *Briefe an Milena,* 160.

occasional skier — Miguel de Beistegui, *The New Heidegger* (London: Continuum, 2005), 168.

"The Nothing — Gordon, *Continental Divide,* 176.

"our task" — Franz Kafka, *Aphorisms,* trans. Willa and Edwin Muir (New York: Schocken Books, 2015), 27.

"The 'Nothing' — Martin Heidegger, *Existence and Being,* trans. Werner Brock (Chicago: Gateway, 1949), 331. Originally published as *Gesamtausgabe,* ed. Friedrich-Wilhelm von Herrmann, 102 vols. (Frankfurt am Main: Vittorio Klostermann, 1975–), 9.108.

"nonsensical idea — Heidegger, *Existence and Being,* 333 / *Gesamtausgabe,* 9.109.

"experience of nothing — Ibid. / ibid.

another Herr Heidegger — Sherlock Holmes, *The Penguin Complete Sherlock Holmes* (Harmondsworth: Penguin, 1981), 547. For a stunning essay on both Heideggers, see Roger Ebbatson, *Heidegger's Bicycle: Interfering with Victorian Texts* (Brighton: Sussex Academic Press, 2006).

"like a dog" — Kafka, *The Trial,* 208 / *Schriften,* 4.312.

still-born child — *The Recorder,* January 3, 1916.

"Through marriage — Kafka in a letter to Felice Bauer, [July] 10, 1913, in *Letters to Felice,* 411 / *Schriften,* 9.236.

"marriage [would be] — Ibid. / ibid.

"The smile on — *The Complete Poetry of Thomas Hardy,* ed. James Gibson (London: Macmillan, 1976), 12.

"As a child — Kafka in a letter to Felice Bauer, February 26, 1913, in *Letters to Felice,* 318 / *Schriften,* 9.110.

"Dearest [Felice] — Ibid., 442 (translation modified) / Ibid., 9.275. It may be worth noting that the German word for "necessity," as here used by Kafka, is *Not*.

Kleist only blasts — Joachim Maass, *Kleist: A Biography,* trans. Ralph Manheim (London: Secker and Warburg, 1983), 280–81.

"We were ... in — Kafka in a letter to Felice Bauer, April 11, 1913, in *Letters to Felice,* 357 / *Schriften,* 9.165.

a certain meeting — I refer, of course, to the so-called Wannsee Conference at which senior Nazis met to approve the "Final Solution" to the "Jewish Question."

Milena Jesenská — Mary Hockaday, *Kafka, Love and Courage: The Life of Milena Jesenká* (London: André Deutsch, 1995), 219.

"Kisses don't — To Milena Jesenská [March 1922], in *Letters to Milena,* 183 / *Briefe an Milena,* 401.

some would say — For example, Jacques Derrida, who famously argues that all human attempts at communication (and thus even our kisses, one presumes) are haunted by the in-communication that, he argues, characterises writing: "our language, even if we speak it, has already lost life and warmth, it is already eaten by writing." Jacques Derrida, *Of Grammatology,* trans. Gayatri Chakravorty Spivak (Baltimore: John Hopkins University Press, 1976 [1967]), 226. Derrida might well have Kafka's kisses in mind when he elsewhere writes, "a letter can always not arrive at its destination." Jacques Derrida, *The Post Card,* trans. Alan Bass (Chicago: University of Chicago Press, 1987), 444.

All three — Frederick Karl, *Franz Kafka: Representative Man* (New York: International Publishing Corporation, 1993), 756.

kidney infection — Hockaday, *Kafka, Love and Courage,* 217.

"After the Jews — Madeleine Blocher-Saillens, *Témoin des années noires: Journal d'une femme pasteur, 1938–1945,* ed. Jacques E. Blocher (Paris: Les Éditions de Paris, 1998), 154. Madeleine's words were echoed by many others; see Michael R. Marrus and Robert O. Paxton, *Vichy France and the Jews* (Stanford: Stanford University Press, 1995), 204.

Rafle du Vel — For more on this, see, for example, Julian Jackson, *France: The Dark Years* (Oxford: Oxford University Press, 2001).

Certificate of Baptism — Michael R. Marrus, "French Protestant Churches and the Persecution of the Jews," in *The Holocaust and the Christian World: Reflections on the Past, Challenges for the Future,* eds. Carol Ritter, Stephen D. Smith, and Irena Steinfeldt (London: Continuum, 2000), 88.

"The Germans — Blocher-Saillens, *Témoin des années noires,* 138.

King Charles IX — Steven Lehrer, *Explorers of the Body* (New York: Doubleday, 2006), 152.

dog-eared dream — See Sébastien Fath, *Une autre manière d'être chrétien en France. Socio-histoire de l'implantation Baptiste, 1810–1950* (Geneva: Labor et Fides, 2001), 215.

first-ever Tabernacle — Numbers 4:15.

Dear Madeleine — Marie in a letter to Madeleine, January 5, 1942, Archives B-S. Marie and Sara's kind hosts in Brittany were Adolphe Huck (a former Tabernacle evangelist) and his wife. Blocher in an email to the author, April 27, 2015.

the very bird — Exodus 16:13.

"The enquiry into — Heidegger, *Existence and Being,* 348 / *Gesamtausgabe,* 9.121.

the first lecture — John E. Joseph, *Ferdinand de Saussure* (Oxford: Oxford University Press, 2012), 446.

"when the final — Ibid., 515.

It is reported — Kafka, Sunday July 19, 1910, in *Diaries,* 21 / *Schriften,* 3.28.

Chapter Three

We … have decided — André Breton, *Manifestoes of Surrealism,* trans. Richard Seaver and Helen R. Lane (Ann Arbor: University of Michigan Press, 1969), 193. Originally published as *Manifestes du surréalisme* (Paris: Jean-Jacques Pauvert, 1962 [1924–53]), 224.

1924 … that year — Louis Aragon, *Paris Peasant,* trans. Simon Watson Taylor (Boston: Exact Change, 1994 [1971]), 131.

Originally published as *Le paysan de Paris* [1926] (Paris: Gallimard, 1953), 160.

the fine men — The opening scene of this chapter is based closely upon a sequence from *Entr'acte,* the Surrealist film directed by René Clair, made and shown in Paris in 1924; see René Clair, *A Nous la Liberté and Entr'acte,* trans. Richard Jacques and Nicola Hayden (Simon and Schuster, New York, 1970), 129. For an excellent discussion of the film and mourning, see Christopher Townsend, "'The Art I Love Is the Art of Cowards': Francis Picabia and René Clair's *Entr'acte* and the Politics of Death and Remembrance in France after World War One," *Science as Culture* 18 (2009): 81–96.

"everything ... — Quoted in Joseph, "He Was an Englishman," 378.

"proclivity for gambling — Ibid., 339–40.

"December 13, 1924" — Robert Desnos, *Liberty or Love!,* trans. Terry Hale (London: Atlas Press, 1993), 37. Originally published as *La liberté ou l'amour!* (Paris: Gallimard, 1962 [1927]), 19.

"Strange destiny — Ibid., 109 / ibid., 97.

Corsair Sanglot — Ibid., 73 / ibid., 58.

"Take off — Ibid., 71 / ibid., 56.

"The naked woman — Ibid., 43 / ibid., 25.

she had knocked — The Tabernacle often did door-to-door evangelism, certainly in the late 1920s. Fath, *Une autre manière,* 393.

"On reaching the — Desnos, *Liberty or Love!,* 82 / *La liberté ou l'amour!* 67–68 (translation modified).

half a world — Marie Stopes writes, "By a single ejaculation, one man might fertilise nearly all the marriageable women in the world." Stopes, *Married Love,* 50.

"The wind — Desnos, *Liberty or Love!,* 40 / *La liberté ou l'amour!* 21.

"From the top — Ibid., 51 / ibid., 32.

"Beneath the Bridge — Ibid., 51/ ibid., 33.

even spilt seed — Marie Stopes writes, "A virgin woman who plays with a man and thinks she is safe from the consequences forgets that … the mesh of a flimsy piece of silk or cambric is, in proportion to the vital spermatozoa, as large as a railway tunnel to herself, and that when the drops of moisture come into external contact they may transmit the spermatozoa which make her a pregnant woman, though technically a virgin." Marie Stopes, *Marriage in My Time* (London: Rich and Cowen, 1935), 155.

"Bébé Cadum" — Desnos, *Liberty or Love!,* 52 / *La liberté ou l'amour!* 34. Bébe Cadum can also be seen in *Entr'acte,* in P. Sandro, "Parodic Narration in *Entr'acte,*" *Film Criticism* 1 (1979): 51.

"an army" — Desnos, *Liberty or Love!,* 54 / *La liberté ou l'amour!,* 35–36.

Verdun — Of the Battle of Verdun, in 1916, Harvey Samuel Firestone writes, "In two weeks more than 190 thousand men were transported on rubber into the inferno of No Man's Land." Firestone, *The Romance and Drama of the Rubber Industry* (Akron: The Firestone Tire and Rubber Co., 1932), 4.

"The Awakening" — North America experienced what was called its Third Great Awakening from the 1850s to the early 1900s, whilst Wales experienced its "Great Revival" in 1904–5. With its founding pastor, Ruben Saillens, travelling to both the US and Wales, the Tabernacle was very much influenced by these movements. Jacques E. Blocher, "Ruben Saillens: Prophète Camisard," *Théologie Évangélique* 4 (2005): 72–78.

"The Great Awakening — Breton, *Manifestoes of Surrealism,* 61 / *Manifestes du surréalisme,* 80.

"Salvation is nowhere" — This was a motto of Surrealism; cited in Gérard Durozoi, *History of the Surrealist Movement* (University of Chicago Press, 2002), 62.

"Let us go — André Breton and Paul Eluard, *The Immaculate Conception* (London: Atlas Press, 1990 [1930]), 31 / *L'immaculée conception* (Paris: Editions Seghers, 2011), 9.

Rue Belliard — The Tabernacle did not move to Rue Belliard until 1928, but had bought a plot there as early as 1921; this location was very deliberately chosen, Montmartre being "the part of Paris with the most cinemas and the fewest churches." Fath, *Une autre manière,* 391.

"Bravo for darkened — Breton, *Manifestoes of Surrealism,* 46 / *Manifestes du surréalisme,* 62.

"It was the bait — André Breton, *Break of Day,* trans. Mark Polizzotti and Mary Ann Caws (Lincoln: University of Nebraska Press, 1999), 7, 9 (translation modified). Originally published as *Le point du jour* (Paris: Gallimard, 1970 [1927]), 13, 15.

"lyrical misfits — Aragon, *Paris Peasant,* 59 / *Le paysan de Paris,* 72.

"We are the — Breton, *Manifestoes of Surrealism,* 63 / *Manifestes du surréalisme,* 82.

"The new — As Mark Polizzotti writes, "the [surrealist] game of 'Exquisite Corpse' [invented in 1926] was a variation on the traditional French game of "Petits Papiers"; it involved composing a sentence in collaboration with several others, no one having seen what was already written. The [surrealist version of the] game was based on the first sentence obtained: 'the exquisite / corpse / shall drink / the new / wine.'" Polizzotti, *Revolution of the Mind: The Life of André Breton* (London: Bloomsbury, 1995), 258.

"[A] waxwork — Aragon, *Paris Peasant,* 41 / *Le paysan de Paris,* 51.

"[A] film heroine — Ibid., 40 / ibid., 50.

"A ... girl — Ibid., 109 / ibid., 132.

"vanished perfume — This is attributed to André Breton. Jennifer Mundy, eds., *Surrealism: Desire Unbound* (Princeton: Princeton University Press, 2002), 161.

"sweet woman — Aragon, *Paris Peasant,* 127 / *Le paysan de Paris,* 155.

"This woman — Breton, *Manifestoes of Surrealism,* 83 / *Manifestes du surréalisme,* 107.

"I get all — Aragon, *Paris Peasant,* 86 / *Le paysan de Paris,* 104.

"I have never — This excerpt is from "With Your Permission," a collective Surrealist declaration made on October 23, 1927. Maurice Nadeau, *The History of Surrealism,* trans. Richard Howard (Harmondsworth: Penguin, 1968 [1964]), 284.

"*Would Christ have* — From a sermon given by Rubens Saillens, see *The Keswick Week, 1925* (London: Marshall Brothers, 1925), 110. Although he gave the sermon at the Keswick Convention in England, Saillens, who had founded the Tabernacle in 1888, was both an honorary pastor and father-in-law of the then Pastor, Arthur Saillens.

"*Jesus*" — Mark 1:13.

"*The doe* — André Breton, *Break of Day,* trans. Mark Polizzotti and Mary Ann Caws (Lincoln: University of Nebraska Press, 1999), 13. Originally published as *Le point du jour* (Paris: Gallimard, 1970 [1927]), 20.

"*This cross* — Aragon, *Paris Peasant,* 186 / *Le paysan de Paris,* 228.

Decision Card — For a description of the 1931 service, see Jacques E. Blocher, ed., *Madeleine Blocher-Saillens, Feministe et fondamentaliste* (Paris: Editions Excelsis, 2014), 104.

"*lead … a lobster* — Breton, *Break of Day,* 13 / *Le point du jour,* 20.

"*No theologian's argument* — Ernest Gengenbach, *Surréalisme et christianisme* (Rennes: Imprimerie Bretonne, 1938), 18.

suicide reports — For a fascinating discussion of the Surrealists' preoccupation with *faits divers,* in particular as reports of suicides, see Robin Walz, *Pulp Surrealism: Insolent Popular Culture in Early Twentieth-Century Paris* (Berkeley: University of California Press, 2000), 113–31.

"*Is Suicide a* — This question is posed in *La Révolution Surréaliste* 1 (December, 1924): 2.

In Margny-les-Cerises — Ibid., 13.

Toward 4 o'clock — Ibid., 20.

"*The corpse puts* — André Breton and Paul Éluard, *The Immaculate Conception* (London: Atlas Press, 1990 [1930]), 94. Originally published as Breton, *L'immaculée conception* (Paris: Editions Seghers, 2011), 60.

"*The elegant gesture* — Max Ernst, *The Hundred Headless Woman (La femme 100 têtes),* trans. Dorothea Tanning (New York: George Braziller, 1981 [1929]), 220–21.

"She is the — Breton, *Manifestoes of Surrealism,* 99 / *Manifestes du surréalisme,* 126.

"Your heart is — Aragon, *Paris Peasant,* 86 / *Le paysan de Paris,* 105.

"Darling … — Ibid., 174 / ibid., 212.

"Perhaps, all — Breton, *Manifestoes of Surrealism,* 107 / *Manifestes du surréalisme,* 137.

"Marie's marriage — Breton and Éluard, *The Immaculate Conception,* 56 / *L'immaculée conception,* 30 (emphasis mine).

"remarkable people — Desnos, *Liberty or Love!,* 109 / *La liberté ou l'amour!,* 97.

"On the blackboard — Ibid., 108 / ibid., 96.

"false … scholars — *La Révolution Surréaliste* 3 (April, 1925): 11.

sabotage our lectures — Note, for example, how "on May 29, [1924] they [the Surrealists] arrived at the Vieux-Colombier [Theatre] to protest a lecture by … professor Robert Aron." Polizzotti, *Revolution of the Mind,* 235.

"combat — Breton, *Manifestoes of Surrealism,* 129 / *Manifestes du surréalisme,* 159.

"thrones of chance — Aragon, *Paris Peasant,* 70 / *Le paysan de Paris,* 86.

"these days — Desnos, *Liberty or Love!,* 70 / *La liberté ou l'amour!,* 86.

"rubber heels — This advice from the early 1920s is cited in Austin Coates, *The Commerce in Rubber: The First 250 Years* (Oxford: Oxford University Press, 1987), 260.

"Happy is the — Desnos, *Liberty or Love!,* 57 / *La liberté ou l'amour!,* 39.

her first fiancé — I understand that he was called Carlton, though whether that was his first name or surname I do not know.

"Birds … have — Desnos, *Liberty or Love!,* 57 / *La liberté ou l'amour!,* 39.

"I think" — Breton, *Manifestoes of Surrealism,* 197 / *Manifestes du surréalisme,* 230.

"suspected of Surrealism" — Aragon, *Paris Peasant,* 66 / *Le paysan de Paris,* 81.

"surly … man — Ibid., 93–94 / ibid., 112–13.

"wheel of becoming"—Ibid., 94 / ibid., 114 (translation modified).

the statues—The Surrealists were fascinated by the myriad statues in Paris. For an excellent discussion of this fascination, see Simon Baker, *Surrealism, History and Revolution* (Oxford: Peter Lang, 2007), 147–230.

M. Passy—For Passy's relationship to Saussure, see Joseph, *Ferdinand de Saussure*, 330–31. For Passy's account of his baptism, in 1892, at the hands of Saillens, see Paul Passy, *Souvenirs d'un socialiste chrétien*, 2 vols. (Issy-les-Moulineaux: Editions "Je sers," 1930), 1.82.

beast of the field—Ibid., 2.76–80. In this scene, Passy describes his attempt, from around 1926 and in the village of Fontette (180 kilometers southeast of Paris), to make real the Danish idea of a "rural university [*université paysanne*]." He did this each summer for three to four months, establishing a co-operative community that mixed learning, farming, gymnastics, music, and worship. This he called *Liéfra*: *Li* from *Liberté*, *é* from *égalité*, *fra* from *fraternité*.

There is one—*Le journal de Madeleine,* May 21, 1924.

Marie wants—Ibid., January 25, 1905.

Brethren—1 Corinthians 7:29–33.

another damned parable—For the full parable, see the Parable of the Wedding Banquet, Matthew 22:1–14 and the Parable of the Ten Virgins, Matthew 25:1–13.

"Mathematicians"—Breton, *Break of Day,* 11 / *Le point du jour,* 17–18.

"The Bride—John Golding, *Duchamp: The Bride Stripped Bare by her Bachelors, Even* (Allen Lane: Penguin, 1973).

"motor-bride"—Michel Sanouillet and Elmer Peterson, eds., *The Writings of Marcel Duchamp* (Oxford: Oxford University Press, 1973), 95. Originally published as Michel Sanouillet, ed., *Marchand du sel, écrits de Marcel Duchamp* (Paris: Le Terrain Vague, 1959), 110.

desire-motor—Ibid., 39 / ibid., 53.

celibate machine—Ibid., 51 / ibid., 69.

"a motor car—Ibid., 43 / ibid., 57.

"Hung Woman" — Ibid., 45 / ibid., 63.

"a shiny metal — Ibid., 39 / ibid., 54.

"Ah, splendid — Louis Aragon, *A Wave of Dreams,* trans. Susan de Muth (London: Thin Man Press, 2010 [1924]), 45. Originally published as *Une vague de rêves* (Paris: Seghers, 1990), 35.

the Office — The Office for Surrealist Research was opened in October 1924 and closed in April 1925. Paul Thévenin, ed., *Bureau de recherches surréalistes. Cahier de la permanence* (Paris: Gallimard, 1988).

being Sunday — The Office was indeed closed on Sundays. Sven Spieker, *The Big Archive: Art From Bureaucracy* (Cambridge: MIT Press, 2008), 93.

"The God within" — Breton, *Break of Day,* 17 (translation modified) / *Le point du jour,* 25.

"Lovemaking chapels" — Aragon, *Paris Peasant,* 145 / *Le paysan de Paris,* 177.

"Glowing with Sunday — Ibid., 159 / ibid., 195.

index cards — On the importance of the card index to the work of the Surrealist Office, see Spieker, *The Big Archive,* 85–103.

"Lodging-House" — This was Louis Aragon's account of the purpose of the Surrealist Office, see ibid., 96.

a Bible — For the Office inventory, including a three-volume Bible, see Thévenin, *Bureau de recherches surréalistes,* 17.

"Secular dust" — Desnos, *Liberty or Love!,* 87 / *La liberté ou l'amour!,* 73.

"the intimacies of — Aragon, *Paris Peasant,* 86 / *Le paysan de Paris,* 104.

a headless statue — Thévenin, *Bureau de recherches surréalistes,* 27.

a book pinioned — For a first-hand account of the pinioned book and suspended woman, see Aragon, *A Wave of Dreams,* 41 / *Une vague du rêves,* 32.

"The overwhelming law" — Aragon, *Paris Peasant,* 144 / *Le paysan de Paris,* 177.

"passion for reduction" — Breton, *Break of Day,* 12 (translation modified) / *Le point du jour,* 19.

"a sinister jester" — Ibid., 12 / ibid., 19.

Mademoiselle Terpsé — Thévenin, *Bureau de recherches surréalistes,* 62.

The Golden Book — Ibid., 39.

codex — The development of the codex is often linked to the growth of early Christianity. Colin H. Roberts and T.C. Skeat, *The Birth of the Codex* (London: Oxford University Press, 1983), 38–67.

"We have nothing — This is from the Office for Surrealist Research's joint "Declaration of 27 January 1925." Reprinted in Maurice Nadeau, *The History of Surrealism,* trans. Richard Howard (Harmondsworth: Penguin, 1968), 262.

"machine for — Aragon, *A Wave of Dreams,* 41 (translation modified) / *Une vague de rêves,* 32.

"liable to sanctions" — Thévenin, *Bureau de recherches surréalistes,* 39.

At the moment — Desnos, *Liberty or Love!,* 121 / *La liberté ou l'amour!,* 110.

"Carisbrooke" — Petition for Nullity, April 22, 1924, Divorce Papers, NA.

Queen Marie — Antonia Fraser, *Marie Antoinette* (London: Wiedenfeld and Nicolson, 2001), 524.

"She keeps her — Ernst, *The Hundred Headless Woman,* 299, 309.

Wimbledon — This is one of around twenty poems by Johannes that we have. It is in fact dated 1946. Despite what "Scholar Schad" may say, I myself love Johannes' poems.

"fear that her — Le journal de Madeleine Blocher-Saillens, May 21, 1924.

"The simplest surrealist — Breton, *Manifestoes of Surrealism,* 125 / *Manifestes du surréalisme,* 155.

"who [have] … — Ibid., 125 / ibid., 155 (translation modified).

"insulting a priest" — This is part of a caption beneath a photograph of Peret appearing to accost a passing Priest. *La Révolution Surréaliste* 8 (December 1926): 12.

"The Last Conversions" — La Révolution Surréaliste 7 (June 1926): 7. The photograph is actually by Eugène Atget and called "The Eclipse," from April 1912. The crowd is, in fact, looking up at

an eclipse of the sun. Ian Walker, *City Gorged with Dreams: Surrealism and Documentary Photography in Interwar Paris* (Manchester: Manchester University Press, 2002), 90.

falling for Jesus — Georges Ribemont-Dessaignes writes, in the following issue of the journal, that "Conversions are in fashion." *La Révolution Surréaliste* 8: 23.

l'Eglise Chrétienne — At this time, "although the church knew itself as *l'Eglise Baptiste de la Rue Meslay,* it often used the name *Eglise Chrétienne Primitive* for the general public, and this was the name used on Paris street maps." Jacques Blocher in an email to the author, March 2016.

Or so they — The Tabernacle records would indicate that this is Marie.

M. Hubert Caldecott — Blocher-Saillens, *Témoin des années noires,* 108. For a transcript of the sermon preached at the memorial service, stressing Hubert's Christian faith, see Blocher, ed., *Madeleine Blocher-Saillens. Féministe et fondamentalise* (Paris: Edition Excelsis, 2014), 166–70.

the 26th? — See Blocher-Saillens, *Témoin des années noires,* 236.

"four walls — Ibid.

"In cities where — Desnos, *Liberty or Love!,* 33 / *La liberté ou l'amour!,* 15 (translation modified). Desnos generously attributes the poem to Arthur Rimbaud, but since he had died in 1891, this is believed to be a surrealist joke.

"I know what — Breton, *Manifestoes of Surrealism,* 202 / *Manifestes du surréalisme,* 235.

"Satan" — Jean Genbach (a.k.a, Ernest Gengenbach), *Satan à Paris* (Albi: Passage du Nord/Ouest, 2003 [1927]), 107.

"The motor car" — Paul Passy, *Souvenirs d'un socialiste chrétien,* 2 vols. (Issy-les-Moulineaux: Editions "Je sers," 1930), 2.70–71.

"Please do not — Ibid., 2.83.

"decomposed corpse — Aragon, *Paris Peasant,* 153 / *Le Paysan de Paris,* 188.

To hell with — Desnos, *Liberty or Love!,* 77–78 / *La Liberté ou l'amour!,* 61–63.

"a rendezvous — Ibid., 78 / ibid., 63.

"We wait — Passy requested Philippians 3:20 be cited on the invitations to his funeral. Passy, *Souvenirs d'un socialiste chrétien,* 2.83.

"I am ready" — *Le Bon Combat* (April 1948): 4, Archives B-S.

Chapter Four

I am bringing — Stéphane Mallarmé, *Collected Poems and Other Verse,* trans. and eds. E.H. and A.M. Blackmore (Oxford: Oxford University Press, 2006), 82, 83. The first page reference is to the French original and the second to the Blackmores's translation; in subsequent citations I do occasionally modify the translation. I should here acknowledge my debt to Henry Weinfeld's wonderful edition, *Collected Poems of Stéphane Mallarmé* (Berkeley: University of California Press, 1994). It is unusual, I realise, to read Mallarmé through or via World War One as I am doing in the chapter, but it is, in this connection, worth noting that his most famous poem, *A Throw of the Dice,* was not published on its own until 1914. See ibid, 264.

"that disagreeable — Wensley Family Archive, Box 174/4/3, Bishopsgate Institute, London. I am grateful to the Institute for permission to quote from this archive.

no sons now — The Wensleys lost both sons, Frederick and Harold, in the war. Jerry White, *Zeppelin Nights* (London: Bodley Head, 2014), 149–52.

107 Rue de Rome — Minutes of Acts of Marriage, Divorce Papers, NA.

The Magician — Wayne Andrews, *The Surrealist Parade* (New York: New Directions, 1990), 4.

"the glory — Stéphane Mallarmé, *Collected Poems,* 216, 217 (emphasis mine).

"Take your stick — Ibid., 222, 223.

"Skip, run and — Stéphane Mallarmé, *Œuvres complètes,* eds. Henri Mondor and G. Jean-Aubry (Paris: Éditions Gallimard, 1945), 106 (my translation).

"the postman's — Weinfeld, ed. and trans., *Collected Poems of Stéphane Mallarmé,* 94, 95.

number 89 — Gordon Millan, *A Throw of the Dice: The Life of Stéphane Mallarmé* (London: Secker and Warburg, 1994), 360.

"I dare not" — André Rodocanachi, "Stéphane Mallarmé et Méry Laurnet," *Bulletin du Bibliophile* IV (1979): 17. At least one of Mallarmé's private telegrams to Méry Laurent, a probable mistress of his, went astray. Laurent wintered in another apartment in the Rue de Rome. Millan, *A Throw of the Dice,* 236–37.

Alfred Adloff — Letter from Sara Wheeler to Madeleine Blocher-Saillens, Archives B-S. Adloff fought for Germany in the War, before becoming a POW, when he was held in England. Adloff went on to be a pro-Hitler industrialist and own several military paint factories, despite remaining a member of the Tabernacle. Madeleine Blocher-Saillens, *Témoin des années noires,* 134.

Detective of the Future — G.T. Crook, 'Detective of the Future,' *Daily Mail,* May 24, 1920. For further details, see Frederick Porter Wensley, *Forty Years of Scotland Yard: A Record of Lifetime's Service in the Criminal Investigation Department* (London: Kessinger Publishing, 2005 [1930]).

Flying Squad — Wensley was one of the first detectives to deploy cars. Anon, "Motor-Car Detectives," *Daily Mail,* September 22, 1920.

"whole of London — Weinfeld, ed. and trans., *Collected Poems of Stéphane Mallarmé,* 94, 95.

"grey sky" — Stéphane Mallarmé in a letter to Henri Cazalis, November 14, 1862, in Carl Barbier, ed., *Documents Stéphane Mallarmé,* 7 vols (Paris: Nizat, 1968–79), 6.67.

erstwhile neighbour — It is worth noting that Madeleine's elder brother, Emile Saillens (1878–1970), a close friend of Marie's sister, Sara, was acquainted with Henry-D. Davray (1873–1944), a literary journalist who, as a young man in the 1890s, used to attend Mallarmé's famous salon at his Rue de Rome apartment. Email to author from Blocher, March 8, 2018.

Marie times four — Mallarmé's sister was called Maria, and his mistress Méry Laurent was originally "Marie-Rose." Mallarmé was very aware of this accumulation of Maries (see Millan, *A Throw of the Dice,* 67), and so too are his commentators (see, for example, Weinfeld, ed. and trans., *Collected Poems of Stéphane Mallarmé,* 166, 244).

a violent red — Mallarmé himself compared, at the last, his face to that of "an exotic cockerel." Millan, *A Throw of the Dice,* 317.

"Why" — Stéphane Mallarmé, *Divagations,* trans. Barbara Johnson (Harvard University Press, 2007), 185. The original French translation appears in *Œuvres complètes,* 645.

"Does ... the poet" — Ibid., 272 / ibid., 406.

"a bequest — Weinfeld, ed. and trans., *Collected Poems of Stéphane Mallarmé,* 146, 168.

Société Littéraire Francaise — Meetings were held monthly. *The Recorder,* for Palmers Green, Winchmore Hill and Southgate, March 2, 1911, Enfield Local Studies & Archive.

"reading ... — Mallarmé, *Divagations,* 186 / *Œuvres complètes,* 647.

"modern experiments — Mallarmé in a letter to George Rodenbach, June 28, 1892, in *Correspondance,* eds. L.J. Austin, H. Mondor, and J.P. Richard, 11 vols. (Paris: Gallimard, 1959–85), 5.89.

"a book ... — Mallarmé, *Divagations,* 229 / *Œuvres complètes,* 381.

the postman — For more on this, see Jack D. Jones, *The Royal Prisoner Charles I at Carisbrooke* (London: Lutterworth, 1965), 88–89 and Charles Carlton, *Charles I: The Personal Monarch* (London: Ark, 1984), 329–32.

"Betrayed — Carlton, *Charles I,* 30.

"A rogue — See Jones, *The Royal Prisoner,* 88.

"K" for King — Ibid., 103.

King's own laundress — Ibid., 60.

"Switzerland — Mallarmé in a letter to Cazalis, June 3, 1863, in *Correspondance,* 1.89–90.

"Marie is a — Mallarmé in a letter to Méry Laurent, August 15, 1889, in *Correspondance,* 3.343. The letter refers to Mallarmé's wife Marie (neé Gerhard), who was German.

"Poor Marie — Mallarmé in a letter to Cazalis, December 4, 1862, in *Correspondance,* 1.60.

"The isolation is — Mallarmé in a letter to Cazalis, April 28, 1866, in *Correspondance,* 1.210.

St. Catherine — Writing in 1909, Marie remarks that "Sara appears to want to wear a St. Catherine's bonnet." She refers to the ancient French custom in which, on St. Catherine's Day (November 25), unmarried women who are turning twenty-five years of age attend a ball in a hat made specially for the occasion. Sara was 28 in 1909. Marie in a letter to Madeleine, [Summer] 1909.

"Do not read — Fanny Desmolins in a letter to Mallarmé, October 17, 1866, in Millan, *A Throw of the Dice,* 345.

"Marie says you — Mallarmé in a letter to Cazalis, January 7, 1864 in Rosemary Lloyd, ed., *Selected Letters* (Chicago: Chicago University Press, 1988), 28. Cazalis may have had grounds to question the status of Mallarmé's marriage if only because he and Marie had lived together for several months before any ceremony took place, which was a Catholic service on August 10, 1863 in London, far from all family and witnessed by one widow and a six year-old choirboy. Even then it took several months before the legality of the London ceremony was officially recognised in France. See Millan, *A Throw of the Dice,* 83, and Roger Pearson, *Stéphane Mallarmé* (London: Reaktion Books, 2010), 38.

"You'll tell me — Mallarmé in a letter to Cazalis, March 23, 1864, in *Correspondance,* 1.111.

"Marie was vexed — Mallarmé in a letter to Cazalis, March 24, 1871, *Correspondance,* 1.347.

"Why ... not — Mallarmé in a letter to Cazalis, May 21, 1866, *Correspondance,* 6.129.

Dr. Pinard — Dr. Pinard refers to Adolphe Pinard (1844–1934), an eminent Paris gynaecologist.

Dans la maison — Marie Schad in a letter to Madeleine, [Summer] 1909, Archives B-S.

"Do you remember — Eugène Lefébure in a letter to Mallarmé, August 1866, in Henry Mondor, ed., *Eugène Lefébure sa vie — ses lettres à Mallarmé* (Paris: Gallimard, 1951), 169.

A good deal — The Baptist Times and Freeman (July 23, 1915), accessed at British Library. I am grateful to the British Library Board for the permission to quote.

The blankets — The Women's League at New Southgate Baptist Church, the church attended by Marie and Johannes from 1905, collected and sent thirteen blankets to Baptist Church House. *The Baptist Times,* October 9, 1914, British Library.

worn in the middle — Ibid., October 9, 1914.

Baptist Touring Club — Ibid., August 14, 1914.

"All well" — Ibid., August 14, 1914. Engel translates as "Angel."

the Open Letter — Ibid., June 7, 1918.

another letter — Arthur S. Langley, of Stoke-on-Trent, in a letter to the Editor offering a five-month old "motherless" boy for adoption by a *Baptist Times* reader. *The Baptist Times,* October 9, 1914.

The Wilderness — Ibid., October 30, 1914.

The Monthly Visitor — This was a supply of evangelistic tracks and was regularly advertised in *The Baptist Times.* See, for example, October 1, 1915.

Poor Mr. Pearce — Ibid., June 16, 1916. The soldier in question was Corporal Bernard Pearce.

Revival at the Front — Ibid., July 9, 1915.

"Readers, please pray — Ibid., May 26, 1916.

"A great effusion — Ian Randall, *The English Baptists of the 20th Century* (London: Baptist Historical Society, 2005), 102.

"meetings with signs — The Baptist Times, April 14, 1916.

"We are witnessing — Mallarmé, *Divagations,* 201 / Œuvres complètes, 360.

"Meanwhile, not far — Ibid., 153 / ibid., 322.

"Your Venetian — Weinfeld, ed. and trans., *Collected Poems of Stéphane Mallarmé,* 86, 87.

"Perhaps, if — Ibid.

"*It will be* — Mallarmé, *Divagations,* 132 / *Œuvres complètes,* 304.

"*The floor avoided* — Ibid., 136 / ibid., 308.

"*She dance[d]* — Ibid., 129 / ibid., 303.

"*Step up!* — Weinfeld, ed. and trans., *Collected Poems of Stéphane Mallarmé,* 106, 107.

"*Ladies and Gentleman* — Ibid., 108–10 / *Œuvres complètes,* 109–11.

'*naked [and] framed* — Mallarmé, *Divagations,* 68 / ibid., 515.

'*to seduce* — Weinfeld, ed. and trans., *Collected Poems of Stéphane Mallarmé,* 66, 67.

Threaten to leap — According to Madeleine, Marie had agreed to facilitate his request for a divorce, "fearing that otherwise Johannes would commit suicide." *Le Journal de Madeleine Blocher-Saillens,* May 21, 1924, Archives B-S.

he who loses — Ibid. Madeleine also writes that Johannes "had lost his faith."

Tower Hill — For centuries, Tower Hill hosted public executions. Chautard's central office, at which Johannes worked, was located at 15/16 America Square, London EC3. The nearest underground station, if travelling from Palmer's Green, was (and is) Tower Hill.

'*useless head*' — Weinfeld, ed. and trans., *Collected Poems of Stéphane Mallarmé,* 146, 168.

'*If you wish*' — Ibid., 202, 203.

The flesh is sad — Ibid., 24, 25.

Johannes had read — Johannes was an avid reader. He is known to have loved, for example, the work of Victor Hugo and of Francis Brett Young. Indeed, in 1948, he briefly corresponded with the latter regarding Young's epic patriotic verse-novel on the history of Britain called *The Island* (1944), see Brett Young Archive, Cadbury Research Library Special Collections, University of Birmingham — FBY /1939 and FBY/3258.

The Rubber World — The full title is *India Rubber World.*

"*Army, French, rubber* — *India Rubber World* (New York: India Rubber Publishing Co.) 49–50 (1913–14): i.

"*Calendar Rolls* — Ibid.: ii.

"*War* — Ibid.: viii.

"*We want the* — See *Daily Mirror,* November 12, 1918.

"*Dancing Pump* — *India Rubber World* 49–50: ii.

"*Raincoats* — Ibid.: vi.

"*Slide Rule* — Ibid.: vii.

"*Definition* — Ibid.: ii.

Christian marriage — Stopes, *Marriage in My Time,* 25.

"*Umbrella* — *India Rubber World* 49–50: viii.

"*the Book*" — Mallarmé only got as far as planning the Book. For more on this, see Jacques Scherer, *Le livre de Mallarmé* (Paris: Gallimard, 1978). Here, what is being imagined is a more literal version of the Book, one containing all he ever wrote.

"*The virgin folds* — Mallarmé, *Divagations,* 229 / Œuvres complètes, 381.

one November — According to Dr. Stevens, of course, Marie "stated that she had not menstrated [sic] since November 1904." Medical Report, Divorce Papers, NA.

"*No Salvation* — *The Baptist Times,* May 5, 1916.

Holland. Scandinavia. — Naturalisation Papers, NA.

Rev. Joynes — William Joynes was the Minister at New Southgate Baptist Church from 1898 to 1926 and is cited, in January 1925, as stating that he had "known the Memorialist intimately for over 17 years through the latter being a member of his Church and meeting one another socially." Naturalisation Papers, NA.

an auditrice — Until one had undergone adult baptism, one attended the Tabernacle as, technically, an auditor rather than as a full member of the church.

"*an uncut page* — Mallarmé, *Divagations,* 227 / Œuvres complètes, 379.

"*It's only in* — Mallarmé in a letter to Cazalis, May 9, 1871, in *Correspondance,* 1.354.

"*He leaves the* — Mallarmé, *Œuvres complètes,* 436.

Because the paper — Weinfeld, ed. and trans., *Collected Poems of Stéphane Mallarmé,* 188, 189.

Within a stately — "The Angel of Peace," from the author's family archive.

Passport — Metropolitan Police Report, Naturalisation Papers, NA.

"for some time" — Weinfeld, ed. and trans., *Collected Poems of Stéphane Mallarmé*, 124, 125.

"a call at — Mallarmé, *Divagations*, 59 / *Œuvres complètes*, 494.

biannual doctoring — In 1916, the Summer Time Act was passed, which meant all clocks in Britain were set at Greenwich Mean Time plus one hour, a change extended for the duration of the War.

"a moment not — Mallarmé, *Divagations*, 61 / *Œuvres complètes*, 495.

"to annul — Ibid., 227 / ibid., 410.

"no one can — Weinfeld, ed. and trans., *Collected Poems of Stéphane Mallarmé*, 196, 197.

"heaven's beggars — Ibid., 2, 3.

"fondness for — Ibid., 124, 125.

"was obliged to — Mallarmé, *Œuvres complètes*, 439–40.

"alien tear" — Weinfeld, ed. and trans., *Collected Poems of Stéphane Mallarmé*, 38, 39.

"the song — Ibid., 24, 25.

"sad festivals — Ibid., 28, 29.

"to plough — Ibid., 16, 17.

"the Sky — Ibid., 22, 23. As Weinfeld observes, "the French language is unable to say 'sky' without simultaneously saying 'heaven.'" *Collected Poems of Stéphane Mallarmé*, 163.

"the trees are — Ibid., 83, 82.

"Dear Christian — Mallarmé, *Collected Poems*, 186–87.

"The Alien in — Baptist Times, August 6, 1915.

"castle of purity" — Mallarmé, *Œuvres complètes*, 443.

"this tomb" — Weinfeld, ed. and trans., *Collected Poems of Stéphane Mallarmé*, 198, 199.

"the Germans" — Mallarmé in a letter to Léon Cladel, August 28, 1875, in *Correspondance*, 2.71. It is worth noting that "as a consequence of the Franco-Prussian war in which [his friend] Henri Regnault and members of his own family were killed, Mallarmé resolutely refused to visit Germany, despite having a German wife." Millan, *A Throw of the Dice*, 351.

"not know what — Stéphane Mallarmé, *For Anatole's Tomb*, trans., Patrick McGuiness (Manchester: Carcanet, 2003 [1961]), 70, 71.

"he [Anatole] does — Ibid., 14, 15.

"I am perfectly — Mallarmé in a letter to Cazalis, May 14, 1867, in *Correspondance*, 1.240. For a brilliant discussion of Mallarmé's "I am dead," see Leo Bersani, *The Death of Stéphane Mallarmé* (Cambridge: Cambridge University Press, 1982).

"dead ... less" — Mallarmé, *Divagations*, 287 / *Œuvres complètes*, 418.

"my pockets are" — Mallarmé in a letter to Cazalis, June 4, 1862, in *Correspondance*, 1.30.

"One day" — Weinfeld, ed. and trans., *Collected Poems of Stéphane Mallarmé*, 92, 93.

pantomimic Pierrot — Pierrot's mimed performance of the murder of his wife is the subject of Mallarmé's short prose text, "Mimique." Mallarmé *Divagations*, 140–41 / *Œuvres complètes*, 310–11.

"little man" — Mallarmé in a letter to Odilon Redon, February 2, 1885, in *Correspondance*, 2.280.

"I hold — Weinfeld, ed. and trans., *Collected Poems of Stéphane Mallarmé*, 44, 45.

"I love being — Mallarmé, *Divagations*, 92 / *Œuvres complètes*, 521.

"future ghost" — Weinfeld, ed. and trans., *Collected Poems of Stéphane Mallarmé*, 48, 49.

"I [am] afraid — Ibid., 16, 17.

"A younger queen? — Johannes's second Marie is, as Madeleine points out, "seventeen years younger than" the first. She makes this point as early as May 1924, six months before the annulment. *Journal de Madeleine Blocher-Saillens*, Archives B-S.

"Let us forget!" — Mallarmé, *Divagations*, 247 / *Œuvres complètes*, 394.

"supreme adieu" — Weinfeld, ed. and trans., *Collected Poems of Stéphane Mallarmé*, 24, 25.

"terrible handkerchief" — Ibid., 94, 95.

"Please forget me" — Ibid., 26, 27.

"the shadow — Ibid., 194–96, 195–97 (my translation). The French is *ombre magicienne,* signalling a female magician.

"No one can — Mallarmé, *For Anatole's Tomb,* 20, 21.

Chapter Five

to see the — Oscar Wilde, "The Critic as Artist," (1890), in *The Complete Works of Oscar Wilde,* eds. Russell Jackson and Ian Small, 8. vols (Oxford: Oxford University Press, 2000–), 4.159.

To be born — Oscar Wilde, *The Importance of Being Earnest,* eds. Patricia Hern and Glenda Leeming (London: Methuen, 1981 [1895]), 19.

"have expressed" — Ibid., 66–67. It is worth noting again that Émile Saillens, brother of Madeleine and close friend of Sara, was acquainted with Henry-D. Davray. As a young man, Davray got to know Wilde during his final years in Paris and, indeed, attended Wilde's funeral. See Richard Ellman, *Oscar Wilde* (Harmondsworth: Penguin, 1987), 549. Johannes thus moved in circles that were not utterly removed from those of Wilde.

Mr. Melmoth — Oscar Wilde, *The Complete Letters of Oscar Wilde,* eds. Merlin Holland and Rupert Hart-Davis (London: Fourth Estate, 2000), 832, 912.

Hotel d'Alsace — For details of Wilde's last hours and Catholic baptism, see Ellman, *Oscar Wilde,* 549.

The feet of — Oscar Wilde, "The Doer of Good" (1894), in *The Complete Works of Oscar Wilde,* eds. Russell Jackson and Ian Small (Oxford: Oxford University Press, 2000), 1.174.

Immersion! — Wilde, *Importance of Being Earnest,* 35.

It is absurd — Wilde in a letter to Robert Ross, late March 1900, in *Complete Letters of Oscar Wilde,* 177.

I attended — Wilde in a letter to Robert Ross, May 31, 1897, in ibid., 866.

a Dissenter — The friends are Ross and More Adey. Ibid., 866.

Good heavens! — Wilde, *Importance of Being Earnest,* 59.

enthusiasm for baptism — Ellmann, *Oscar Wilde,* 18–19.

"a thing — For the complete quotation, refer to Wilde's *The Picture of Dorian Gray* (1890), in *Complete Works of Oscar Wilde,* 3.50.

I am grieved — Wilde, *Importance of Being Earnest,* 67.

The Riches and — *The Book of Common Prayer* (New York: The Church Hymnal Corporation, 1979 [1653]), 876.

I had no — Wilde, "Lord Arthur Saville's Crime" (1891), in *Complete Works of Oscar Wilde,* 8.71.

"refuted the views — Wilde, *Importance of Being Earnest,* 67.

But … I have — Ibid., 55.

Algernon, I forbid — Ibid., 67.

I beg your — Ibid., 61.

Explain — Wilde, *Picture of Dorian Gray,* in *Complete Works of Oscar Wilde,* 3.7.

Swiss variety — Amy Nelson Burnett and Emidio Campi, eds., *A Companion to the Swiss Reformation* (Leiden: Brill, 2012), 389–443.

New Jerusalem — This dream was most famously expressed in the Anabaptist seizure of the German city of Munster in 1534–35. Jonathan Dewald, *Europe 1450 to 1789: Absolutism to Coligny* (New York: Charles Scribner's Sons, 2004), 51.

The Third Baptism — Lamar Jensen, *Reformation Europe: Age of Reform and Revolution* (Lexington: D.C. Heath and Co., 1992), 109.

The fearful law — Oscar Wilde, *Vera; Or, the Nihilists* [1883], in *The Complete Plays* (London: Methuen, 1988), 572.

Pray go on — Oscar Wilde, "Lord Arthur Saville's Crime," in *Complete Works of Oscar Wilde,* 8.53.

entire mountain village — Burton Holmes, *Travelogues,* 10 vols. (New York: The McClure Co., 1905–1910), 2.283–92. See also Croal D. Thomson, *The Paris Exhibition 1900: An Illustrated Record* (London: The Art Journal Office, 1901), 233–38.

I am sorry — Oscar Wilde, *A Woman of No Importance,* ed. Ian Small (London: Bloomsbury Methuen, 2004 [1893]), 29.

frequently invoked — For a discussion of the use of the legend of William Tell in 1653, see Andreas Suter, *Der schweizerische*

Bauernkrieg von 1653. Politische Sozialgeschichte, Sozialge-schichte eines politischen Ereignisses (Tübingen: Bibliotheca Academica, 1997), 10, 92–93, 143–44.

Nothing — Ibid., 110.

Conditional Baptism — On November 29, 1900, Father Dunne records in the Register of St. Joseph Church that Wilde was "conditionally baptised by me." Wilde, *Complete Letters of Oscar Wilde,* 1225.

What on earth — Wilde, *Importance of Being Earnest,* 4.

One steamboat — Ellmann, *Oscar Wilde,* 548.

Can wordless hands — For a fascinating discussion of how Wil-de may have used his hands to communicate his desire for baptism, see Ann Astell, "'My Life Is a Work of Art': Oscar Wilde's Novelistic and Religious Conversion,'" *Renascence* 65, no. 3 (2013): 188–205.

looks like repentance — Wilde, *Importance of Being Earnest,* 57.

Explain — Wilde, *Picture of Dorian Gray,* in *Complete Works of Oscar Wilde,* 3.7.

If you are — *Book of Common Prayer,* 313.

I shudder at — Wilde, *Picture of Dorian Gray,* in *Complete Works of Oscar Wilde,* 5.45.

[But] it is — Oscar Wilde, *An Ideal Husband*, ed. Russell Jackson (London: Methuen, 2013 [1895]), 63.

"constitutes the — Alexander C.T. Geppert, *Fleeting Cities: Impe-rial Expositions in "Fin-de-Siècle" Europe* (London: Palgrave Macmillan, 2010), 62.

"palpable shams" — Ibid., 78.

Air Sports — Richard D. Mandell, *Paris 1900* (Toronto: Univer-sity of Toronto Press, 1967), 67–69.

Good heavens — Wilde, *Importance of Being Earnest,* 59.

La Maison de Rire — Mandell, *Paris 1900,* 65.

"Nature Disrobing — Ibid., 73.

Pray go on — Wilde, "Lord Arthur," in *Complete Works of Oscar Wilde,* 8.53.

Manoir à l'Envers — Philippe Jullian, *The Triumph of Art Nou-veau: Paris Exhibition, 1900* (New York: Larousse, 1974), 176.

To conclude — Wilde, "The Rise of Historical Criticism" (1879), in *Complete Works of Oscar Wilde,* 4.87.

Herr Hegel — Karl Marx famously claims that, with Hegel, "the dialectic … is standing on its head. It must be inverted." *Capital: A Critique of Political Economy,* trans. Ben Fowkes, 3 vols. (Harmondsworth: Penguin, 1976–81 [1867]), 1.103.

And who is — Wilde, *Vera; Or the Nihilists,* in *Complete Plays,* 52.

Trottoir Roulant — For a superb series of photographs of the electrically-powered "Moving Pavement," see Thomson, *Paris Exhibition 1900,* 271–76.

I cannot — Wilde, "The Happy Prince" [1888], in *Complete Works of Oscar Wilde,* 8.16.

November — The exhibition closed on November 12, 1900.

Nature — E.H. Mikhail, ed., *Oscar Wilde: Interviews and Recollections,* 2 vols. (London: Macmillan, 1979), 2.480.

"Here we have — Hebrews 13:14.

a warehouse — This is Blocher's understanding. Blocher in an email to author, August 21, 2015.

A thoroughly — Wilde, *Importance of Being Earnest,* 62–63.

Is that clever? — Ibid., 21.

The police should — Wilde, *An Ideal Husband,* 67.

It is what — Ibid., 111.

Oh that is — Wilde, *Importance of Being Earnest,* 20.

Jack? — Ibid., 36.

Twenty-eight — Ibid., 70.

Frederick Inderwick — Wilde, *Complete Letters of Oscar Wilde,* 820, 825.

UPON HEARING *the* — Appointment of Medical Inspectors, Divorce Papers, NA.

I do not — Oscar Wilde, *The Original Four-Act Version of "The Importance of Being Earnest: A Trivial Comedy for Serious People"* (London: Methuen, 1957), 52.

The … " city — Wilde, *Complete Works of Oscar Wilde,* 4.31.

Twenty years — Wilde, *Woman of No Importance,* 25

I hope marriage — Wilde in a letter to Charles Spurrier Mason, August 1894, in *Complete Letters of Oscar Wilde,* 603.

In married life — Wilde, *Importance of Being Earnest,* 9

The Sultan — Wilde, "A Ride through Morocco" [1886], in *Complete Works of Oscar Wilde,* 6.98.

"This is not" — Wilde, *Importance of Being Earnest,* 58

Keep your own — Merlin Holland, ed., *Irish Peacock and Scarlet Marquess: The Real Trial of Oscar Wilde* (London: Fourth Estate, 2003), 91.

[But] nowadays — Wilde, *An Ideal Husband,* 9.

Once a week — Ibid., 67.

Would you repeat — Holland, *Irish Peacock and Scarlet Marquess,* 50.

Have you been — Oscar Wilde, *Lady Windermere's Fan,* ed. Ian Small (London: Ernest Benn, 1980 [1893]), 34.

Schad … appears — Police Report, Naturalisation Papers, January 7, 1924, NA.

His … sister — Ibid., 2.

God has given — Wilde, *An Ideal Husband,* 99.

The Primitive Church — Wilde, *Importance of Being Earnest,* 32.

Christ — Wilde, "The Burden of Itys" (1881), in *Complete Works of Oscar Wilde,* 1.64.

The proper basis — Wilde, "Lord Arthur Saville's Crime," in *Complete Works of Oscar Wilde,* 8.55 (emphasis mine).

Yes, sir — Wilde, *Importance of Being Earnest,* 1–2

You read it — Holland, *Irish Peacock and Scarlet Marquess,* 106.

I admit — Wilde, *Importance of Being Earnest,* 68

My lord — H. Montgomery Hyde, ed., *The Trials of Oscar Wilde* (London: William Hodge and Co., 1948), 228–29.

May I say — Ibid., 339

Did you ever — Holland, *Irish Peacock and Scarlet Marquess,* 138.

I have carefully — Wilde, *Importance of Being Earnest,* 61–62.

falschen Briefen — Niklaus Landolt, *Untertanenrevolten und Widerstand auf der Basler Landschaft im 16. und 17. Jahrhundert* (Liestal: Verlag des Kantons Basel-Landschaft, 1996), 523.

Dear girl — Wilde, *Lady Windermere's Fan,* 15–16.

I don't like — Wilde, *Complete Letters of Oscar Wilde,* 1133.

The Swiss — Ibid., 1129.

the chastity — Ibid., 1139.

a married man — Uli was married in 1651. Andreas Heusler, *Der Bauernkrieg von 1653 in der Landschaft* (Basel: Neukirch'sche Buchhandlung, 1854), 70.

Dead? — Wilde, *Importance of Being Earnest,* 33

Gellert Hill — The site of the hanging, now part of a Basel suburb, can still be visited. I did so on a Sunday morning in late October 2017. I attempted a prayer.

July. The 7th — His death date is sometimes recorded as July 24, but that is according to the emergent Gregorian calendar, as opposed to the older Julian calendar.

Are you sure? — Wilde, *Woman of No Importance,* 28.

My wife — Wilde, *Picture of Dorian Gray,* in *Complete Works of Oscar Wilde,* 3.6.

Charles Wooldridge — Wooldridge's execution is the subject of "The Ballard of Reading Gaol" [1898], in Wilde, *Complete Works of Oscar Wilde,* 1.311.

There is nothing — Wilde, *Lady Windermere's Fan,* 17

Awful calendar — Wilde, "The Canterville Ghost" [1887], in *Complete Works of Oscar Wilde,* 8.90.

I will take — Wilde in a letter to Robert Ross [? late September 1899], in *Complete Letters of Oscar Wilde,* 165.

Basil Hayward — See the *Picture of Dorian Gray,* 1890 edition, *Complete Works,* 3.126. In the 1891 edition the death-date is 'the ninth of November.' The *Picture of Dorian Gray,* 1891 edition, *Complete Works,* 3.291. Basil is the artist who paints the portrait of Dorian Gray.

one half — "On November 13th, 1895, I was brought down here from London. From two o'clock till half past two on that day I had to stand on the centre platform at Clapham Junction in convict dress and handcuffed, for the world to look at …. For half an hour I stood there in the grey November rain surrounded by a jeering mob. For a year after that was done to me I wept every day at the same hour and for the same space of time." Wilde, *De Profundis* [1897], in *Complete Works of Oscar Wilde,* 2.187.

Heaven — Revelation 8:1. "And when He had opened the seventh seal, there was silence in heaven about the space of half an hour."

cannons — Mandell, *Paris 1900,* 88.

Were you with — Wilde, *Importance of Being Earnest,* 33.

Yes — Ibid., 67.

The Hanging Committee — Wilde, "The Grosvenor Gallery" (1877), in *Complete Works of Oscar Wilde,* 6.1.

[D]oes not [himself] — Wilde, "The Ballard of Reading Gaol," in *Complete Works of Oscar Wilde,* 1.196–97.

[Here] the shed — Wilde in a letter to Robert Ross, October 8, 1897, *Complete Letters of Oscar Wilde,* 956.

The weather — Wilde, *Importance of Being Earnest,* 42.

Whenever people — Ibid., 13.

The University — Wilde, "A Handbook to Marriage" [1885], in *Complete Works of Oscar Wilde,* 6.60.

A dissertation on — Wilde, "The Sphinx without a Secret" [1887], in *Complete Works of Oscar Wilde,* 8.79.

Professor of Massage — Hyde, *Trials of Oscar Wilde,* 21.

Criticism can recreate — Wilde, "The Critic as Artist," in *Complete Works of Oscar Wilde,* 4.201.

The only real — Wilde, "The Decay of Lying" [1891], in *Complete Works of Oscar Wilde,* 4.79.

Johannes ... turned — *Journal de Madeleine Blocher-Saillens,* May 21, 1924, Archives B-S.

how horrid — Wilde, "The Canterville Ghost" (1887), in *Complete Works of Oscar Wilde,* 8.84.

I beg — Wilde, *Importance of Being Earnest,* 61.

It is the — Wilde, "Canterville Ghost," in *Complete Works of Oscar Wilde,* 8.84.

The Permanence — Ibid., 8.85.

Mrs Schad states — Medical Report, April 16, 1924, Divorce Papers, NA.

The female mind — Thomas C. Stevens, *Diseases of Women* (London: University of London Press, 1912), 75.

152 Hertford Square — Wilde, *Picture of Dorian Gray,* in *Complete Works of Oscar Wilde,* 3.142.

"chemicals" — Ibid., 3.153.

"nitric acid" — Ibid., 3.313.

"an admirable — Ibid., 3.148.

"curious experiment" — Ibid., 3.145.

"the thing — Ibid., 3.137.

"Upstairs — Ibid., 3.193.

"The Indissolubility — Ibid., 3.xiv (emphasis mine).

Fell into the — Wilde, *Picture of Dorian Gray,* in *Complete Works of Oscar Wilde,* 3.349.

the very stairs — One can still see the stairs with one's own eyes, rather than just through Hopper's. This I did in May 2016. The church is still there.

Mr Hopper — Gail Levin, *Edward Hopper: An Intimate Biography* (Berkeley: University of California Press, 1995), 49.

the very church — This is Blocher's understanding. Blocher in an email to author, July 21, 2015.

How steep — Wilde, "The Critic as Artist," in *Complete Works of Oscar Wilde,* 4.171.

How steep — Wilde, "At Verona" (1881), in *Complete Works of Oscar Wilde,* 1.46.

Uli Schad is — Urs Hostettler, *Der Rebell vom Eggiwil. Aufstand der Emmentaler 1653* (Bern: Zytglogge Verlag, 1991), 332.

Every room — Wilde, "Comedy Theatre" [1887], in *Complete Works of Oscar Wilde,* 7.293.

Suddenly the — Holland, *Irish Peacock and Scarlet Marquess,* 227.

jump — Landolt, *Untertanen, Revolten und Widerstand,* 518, 523.

weep — Hostettler, *Der Rebell vom Eggiwil,* 384.

half-a-house — Jürg Ewald et al., *Nah dran, weit weg. Geschichte des Kantons Basel-Landschaft,* 6 vols. (Liestal: Verlag des Kantons Basel-Landschaft, 2001), 5.24.

It was a — Wilde, *Picture of Dorian Gray,* in *Complete Works of Oscar Wilde,* 3.101.

Families are so — Wilde, *An Ideal Husband,* 12.

[So,] what is — Wilde, *Importance of Being Earnest,* 71.

Most people — Wilde, *De Profundis,* in *Complete Works of Oscar Wilde,* 2.176.

Everyone should — Wilde in a letter to Ava Leverson, 1894, in *Complete Letters of Oscar Wilde,* 618.

I told [*Oscar*] — Wilde in a letter to Adela Schuster, December 23, 1900, in *Complete Letters of Oscar Wilde,* 1226.

The growth — Wilde, "The Decay of Lying," in *Complete Works of Oscar Wilde,* 4.100.

I am not — Wilde, *Importance of Being Earnest,* 27.

[*But*] *I should* — Wilde, *Picture of Dorian Gray,* in *Complete Works of Oscar Wilde,* 3.128.

Go … about — Ibid., 3.352.

You do? — Wilde, *Woman of No Importance,* 76.

"veritable Pentecost" — Randall, *The English Baptists of the 20th Century,* 51.

God hath — 2 Corinthians 1:22.

Is your name — Wilde, *Importance of Being Earnest,* 51.

Anything may happen — Wilde in a letter to Robert Ross, late March 1900, *Complete Letters of Oscar Wilde,* 1177.

Any woman — Wilde, *Importance of Being Earnest,* 14.

One always thinks — Wilde, *De Profundis,* in *Complete Works of Oscar Wilde,* 2.175.

An ideal husband — Wilde, *An Ideal Husband,* 140.

In Hell — Wilde, "The House of Judgement" [1881], in *Complete Works of Oscar Wilde,* 1.172.

A lot of — Wilde, *An Ideal Husband,* 21.

in Heaven — Matthew 22:30.

A passionate celibacy — Wilde, *Importance of Being Earnest,* 66.

Un-kissed kisses — Wilde, "Silentium Amoris" [1881], in *Complete Works of Oscar Wilde,* 1.124.

Love is never — Wilde, "Her Voice" (1881) in *Complete Works of Oscar Wilde,* 1.125.

To lose one — Wilde, *Importance of Being Earnest,* 18.

We hear nothing — Hostettler, *Der Rebell vom Eggiwil,* 492.

The Schads have — *Journal de Madeleine Blocher-Saillens,* May 21, 1924, Archives B-S.

Johannes sometimes — Ibid.

Marie has — Ibid.

Not a year — Wilde, *An Ideal Husband,* 33.

I beg your — Wilde, *Importance of Being Earnest,* 61.

Southwark, 1887 — W.T. Whitley, *The Baptists of London, 1612–1928* (London: Kingsgate Press, 1928), 133, 135, 167.

Stop! — Wilde, *Woman of No Importance,* 484.

Islington, 1813 — Whitley, *The Baptists of London,* 139, 196, 174.

Stop! Stop! — Wilde, *An Ideal Husband,* 111.

Croydon, 1797 — Whitley, *The Baptists of London,* 138, 169, 164.

Someone should — Wilde, *An Ideal Husband,* 71.

The Women's Emigration — Wilde, "Literary and Other Notes" [1888], in *Complete Works of Oscar Wilde,* 7.64, 386n.

Mrs Jekyll — Wilde, *An Ideal Husband,* 76.

He is in every — Wilde, *Salome* [1891], in *Complete Works of Oscar Wilde,* 5.720.

To Emmaus — Luke 24:13–35.

Did you kiss — Holland, *Irish Peacock and Scarlet Marquess,* 146.

I am unmarried — Wilde, *Importance of Being Earnest,* 70.

I am a celibate — Ibid., 67.

My life is — Wilde, *Lady Windermere's Fan,* 27.

I prefer living — Ibid., 76.

I am still — Wilde in a letter to Leonard Smithers, February 28, 1898, *Complete Letters of Oscar Wilde,* 1026.

I am not — Wilde, "ΓΛΥΚΥΠΙΚΟΣ ΕΡΩΣ," in *Complete Works of Oscar Wilde,* 1.127.

Love is never — Ibid., 1.125.

Chapter Six

She had become — Katherine Mansfield, *The Collected Fiction of Katherine Mansfield 1916–1922,* in *The Edinburgh Edition of the Collected Works of Katherine Mansfield,* eds. Gerri Kimber et al., 4 vols. (Edinburgh: Edinburgh University Press, 2012–2016), 2.251.

I want also — *Journal de Madeleine Blocher-Saillens,* September 2, 1925, Archives B-S.

The Daughters of — Katherine Mansfield, *The Edinburgh Edition of the Collected Works of Katherine Mansfield,* 2.266–83. Please note that, hereon, all quotations from Katherine

Mansfield (her fiction, her diaries her letters, her notebooks) are italicised.

Father would never — Ibid., 2.271

His watch still — Mansfield, *The Diaries of Katherine Mansfield,* in *The Edinburgh Edition of the Collected Works of Katherine Mansfield,* 4.387. The context here is "He is dead … but his watch still ticks."

There had been — Ibid., 2.281

There was a — Ibid., 2.233.

He was killed — Kathleen Jones, *Katherine Mansfield* (Edinburgh: Edinburgh

University Press, 2010), 247–49.

To the trenches — To J. M. Murry, [March] 19, 1918, in *The Collected Letters of Katherine Mansfield,* eds. Vincent O'Sullivan and Margaret Scott, 4 vols. (Oxford: Clarendon Press, 1984–96), 2.131.

After the War — Ralf Roth and Colin Divall, eds., *From Rail to Road and Back Again? A Century of Transport, Competition and Interdependency* (London: Routledge, 2015), 175.

Giant tyres — P. Schidrowitz and T.R. Dawson, *History of the Rubber Industry* (London: Heffer & Sons Ltd., 1952), 219.

One gets mortally — Mansfield in a letter to Richard Murry, August 9, 1921, in *The Collected Letters of Katherine Mansfield,* 4.262.

Not in Paris — According to one US contemporary reporter, "Paris police make no effort to enforce … speed limits for motor vehicles." Anon., "Studies in Traffic Taming," *New York Times,* April 7, 1929.

I would love — Mansfield in a letter to Anne Drey, [May 19, 1921], *The Collected Letters of Katherine Mansfield,* 4.231

Run into by — Katherine Mansfield, *The Collected Fiction of Katherine Mansfield 1898–1915,* in *The Edinburgh Edition of the Collected Works of Katherine Mansfield,* 1.176.

People do bang — Mansfield in a letter to Richard Murry, [February 16, 1918], in *The Collected Letters of Katherine Mansfield,* 2.74.

"A new way — Quoted in Adrian Rifkin, *Street Noises: Parisian Pleasure 1900-40* (Manchester and New York: Manchester University Press, 1993), 128.

If she — Mansfield, *The Edinburgh Edition of the Collected Works of Katherine Mansfield*, 1.218.

"Will you marry — Ibid., 1.142.

They were asked — Minutes of Acts of Marriage, July 4, 1905, Divorce Papers, NA.

They sounded married — Mansfield, *The Edinburgh Edition of the Collected Works of Katherine Mansfield*, 2.474.

On March 2nd — Jones, *Katherine Mansfield*, 98–103.

You can't advise — Mansfield in a letter to Richard Murry, [April 9, 1920], in *The Collected Letters of Katherine Mansfield*, 3.277.

Half-words — Mansfield in a letter to Richard Murry, [February 27, 1918], in *The Edinburgh Edition of the Collected Works of Katherine Mansfield*, 2.96.

Professor of Speech — In the 1911 Census, Bowden declares himself to be a "Professor of Voice Culture."

Man's vocal apparatus — Saussure, *Course in General Linguistics*, 10 / *Cours de linguistiques générale*, 18.

an accident — Saussure once remarked, in a lecture, that "language [langage] is in reality ... completely accidental." Joseph, *Ferdinand de Saussure*, 378.

Walking about a — Mansfield in a letter to Bertrand Russell [January 21, 1917], in *The Collected Letters of Katherine Mansfield*, 1.294.

A cinematograph[ic] figure — Mansfield, *The Edinburgh Edition of the Collected Works of Katherine Mansfield*, 1.228.

"Love in False — Ibid., 2.148

In London — For an excellent discussion of not only Mansfield's work as a film extra but her relationship to film as a writer, see Maurizio Ascari, *Cinema and the Imagination in Katherine Mansfield's Writing* (Houndmills: Palgrave, 2014).

"I feel ... that — Mansfield, *The Edinburgh Edition of the Collected Works of Katherine Mansfield*, 2.237.

Wrong house — Ibid., 2.211, 2.124.

False coins — Ibid., 2.124, 2.132.

[*The*] *old man* — Ibid., 1.442.

A fly … walked — Mansfield in a letter to Richard Murry, [November 15 1919], in *The Collected Letters of Katherine Mansfield*, 3.96.

An old man — Mansfield, *The Edinburgh Edition of the Collected Works of Katherine Mansfield*, 1.67.

Gare Saint-Lazare — Mansfield, *The Diaries of Katherine Mansfield*, in *The Edinburgh Edition of the Collected Works of Katherine Mansfield*, 4.97.

If … a fire — Mansfield, *The Edinburgh Edition of the Collected Works of Katherine Mansfield*, 2.503.

In Heaven — Mansfield in a letter to Raymond Drey, December 27, 1921, in *The Collected Letters of Katherine Mansfield*, 4.358.

"My Father's House" — John 14:12.

It [*is*] *…* — Mansfield, *The Edinburgh Edition of the Collected Works of Katherine Mansfield*, 2.422.

I saw myself — Ibid., 2.146.

Damnation take — Mansfield in a letter to Dorothy Brett, [May 1, 1918], in *The Collected Letters of Katherine Mansfield*, 2.168.

The frightening thing — Mansfield in a letter to Ottoline Morrell, [August 20, 1916?], in *The Collected Letters of Katherine Mansfield*, 1.276.

If [*only*] *Marie* — *Journal de Madeleine Blocher-Saillens*, May 21, 1924, Archives B-S.

Something had happened — Mansfield, *The Edinburgh Edition of the Collected Works of Katherine Mansfield*, 2.407.

missed so many — Robert Wheeler had once been a leading figure in the Tabernacle, but toward the end of his life he rarely attended. Blocher in a conversation with the author, Paris, July 7, 2015.

Father [*was*] *… there* — Mansfield, *The Edinburgh Edition of the Collected Works of Katherine Mansfield*, 2.273.

Knockings at the — Ibid., 4.440.

Every man — Mansfield in a letter to Ottoline Morrell, [February 21, 1919], in *The Collected Letters of Katherine Mansfield*, 2.302.

Coming into an — Mansfield, *The Edinburgh Edition of the Collected Works of Katherine Mansfield,* 1.450.

renounced England? — Ibid., 1.226.

In 1924 — Clifford Rosenberg, *Policing Paris: The Origins of Modern Immigration Control Between the Wars* (Ithaca: Cornell University Press, 2006), 53.

You're not married — Mansfield, *The Edinburgh Edition of the Collected Works of Katherine Mansfield,* 2.106.

a knock at — Ibid., 4.223.

Two shabby old — Ibid., 2.106.

"Madame does not — In France in the mid-twenties, this became a feminist, catchphrase response to the government propaganda designed to improve France's very low birth-rate. For more discussion on this, see Mary Louise Roberts, *Civilization without Sexes: Reconstructing Gender in Postwar France, 1917–1927* (Chicago: University of Chicago Press, 1994), 131.

down to the — Mansfield in a letter to Ottoline Morrell, [July 3, 1917], in *The Collected Letters of Katherine Mansfield,* 1.314.

I am sick — Mansfield, *The Edinburgh Edition of the Collected Works of Katherine Mansfield,* 1.148.

Harley Street — Ibid., 4.190.

Queen Anne Street — Ibid., 4.137.

One of those — Mansfield in a letter to Sydney Waterlow, March 16, 1921, in *The Collected Letters of Katherine Mansfield,* 4.193.

"the history of — Medical Report, Divorce Papers, NA.

told to undress — Mansfield, *The Edinburgh Edition of the Collected Works of Katherine Mansfield,* 1.337.

I [shall] go — Mansfield in a letter to S.S. Koteliansky, [October 18, 1921], in *The Collected Letters of Katherine Mansfield,* 4.299.

I hope to — Marie in a letter to Madeleine, [January?] 1909, Archives B-S.

Dr. Pinard — Adolphe Pinard (1844–1934) was "the uncontested master of French gynaecology." Marc Decimo, ed., *Marcel Duchamp and Eroticism* (Cambridge: Cambridge Scholars Press, 2007), 145.

that … thing — Mansfield, *The Edinburgh Edition of the Collected Works of Katherine Mansfield,* 2.10.

Supposing — Ibid., 1.197.

Frau Lehman's — Ibid., 1.179.

Aunt Martha — Mansfield in a letter to Richard Murry, [March 23, 1918], in *The Collected Letters of Katherine Mansfield,* 2.137. "Aunt Martha" was quite a common soubriquet for menstruation and certainly one used by Mansfield.

A train is — Mansfield, *The Edinburgh Edition of the Collected Works of Katherine Mansfield,* 4.149.

My husband — Ibid., 2.222.

Try for a — Mansfield in a letter to Dorothy Brett, [March 18, 1920], in *The Collected Letters of Katherine Mansfield,* 3.249.

wherever it is — Mansfield in a letter to Richard Murry, [March 2, 1918], in *The Collected Letters of Katherine Mansfield,* 2.101. The context here is, "the warm South, wherever it is."

perhaps Switzerland — Mansfield in a letter to Ida Baker, [March 18, 1921], in *The Collected Letters of Katherine Mansfield,* 4.197.

The Swiss Cure — Ibid., 4.93 n.6.

Charing X — Mansfield, *The Edinburgh Edition of the Collected Works of Katherine Mansfield,* 4.265.

I [am] … — Mansfield, *The Edinburgh Edition of the Collected Works of Katherine Mansfield,* 2.119.

I've never yet — Ibid., 2.117.

Without my clothes — Ibid., 2.118.

Can you aviate — Ibid., 2.40.

hoped to adopt — Mansfield in a letter to Richard Murry, December 4, 1919, in *The Collected Letters of Katherine Mansfield,* 3.133. The context is, "I want to adopt a baby boy of about one."

child called "Dicky" — Mansfield in a letter to Richard Murry, January 23, 1920, in *The Collected Letters of Katherine Mansfield,* 3.190.

Shadow Children — Mansfield, *The Edinburgh Edition of the Collected Works of Katherine Mansfield,* 1.125.

The Shadow Children — Mansfield, *The Poetry and Critical Writings of Katherine Mansfield,* in *The Edinburgh Edition of the Collected Works of Katherine Mansfield,* 3.57.

the valley — Mansfield in a letter to Richard Murry, [October 4, 1920], in *The Collected Letters of Katherine Mansfield,* 4.58.

I see you — Mansfield in a letter to Richard Murry, [December 11, 1919], in *The Collected Letters of Katherine Mansfield,* 3.153.

Summer of 1932 — The two boys were awarded compensation upon turning twenty-one years old; in Dicky's case, this was in February 1951. In April of that year he went to the High Court in the Strand to receive his compensation, £15 of savings certificates.

strange places — Mansfield, *The Edinburgh Edition of the Collected Works of Katherine Mansfield,* 4.320.

Friday 2nd March — Margaret Scott, ed., *The Katherine Mansfield Notebooks,* 2 vols. (Minneapolis: University of Minnesota Press, 1997), 2.187.

asked … indecent — Mansfield, *The Edinburgh Edition of the Collected Works of Katherine Mansfield,* 4.412.

as a rule — Ibid., 2.489.

no-one listens — Mansfield in a letter to Richard Murry, [November 2, 1919], in *The Collected Letters of Katherine Mansfield,* 3.65.

Doctors do talk — Mansfield, *The Edinburgh Edition of the Collected Works of Katherine Mansfield,* 2.191.

book for a — Mansfield, *The Collected Letters of Katherine Mansfield,* 4.74. A "rubber shop" was a shop that sold condoms and pornographic material.

"It is only — Stevens, *Diseases of Women,* 60.

Oh doctor — Mansfield, *The Edinburgh Edition of the Collected Works of Katherine Mansfield,* 4.354.

the beauty of — Mansfield in a letter to S.S. Koteliansky, [December 13, 1919], in *The Collected Letters of Katherine Mansfield,* 3.161.

the afternoon of — Mansfield, *The Edinburgh Edition of the Collected Works of Katherine Mansfield,* 2.385.

why had he — Ibid., 2.49.

average British husband? — Ibid., 1.198.

corset-box that — Ibid., 2.274.

advertisement — Ibid., 1.238.

Marie wants to — *Journal de Madeleine Blocher-Saillens,* January 25, 1905, Archives B-S.

Really — Mansfield, *The Edinburgh Edition of the Collected Works of Katherine Mansfield,* 2.352.

I wish — Mansfield in a letter to Richard Murry, [October 15, 1919], in *The Collected Letters of Katherine Mansfield,* 3.26.

knelt on [her] — Mansfield, *The Edinburgh Edition of the Collected Works of Katherine Mansfield,* 1.296.

wear a crucifix — Ibid., 2.187.

every wife has — Ibid., 1.187.

Our bedrooms — Mansfield in a letter to Richard Murry, [October 25, 1920], *The Collected Letters of Katherine Mansfield,* 4.85.

Were they going — Mansfield, *The Edinburgh Edition of the Collected Works of Katherine Mansfield,* 2.376.

Did you kneel? — Ibid., 4.321.

She was [though] — Ibid., 2.211.

She never undressed — Ibid., 2.353.

The Lord Jesus — The Keswick Week, 1925, 109–10.

The Question of — Mansfield in a letter to Sydney Schiff, [mid-February 1921?], in *The Collected Letters of Katherine Mansfield,* 4.181.

How much do — Mansfield, *The Edinburgh Edition of the Collected Works of Katherine Mansfield,* 1.237.

I suppose you — Ibid., 1.298.

I hold you — Ibid., 1.410.

Christian trap — Ibid., 1.237.

Edgar Brandt — Blocher, *Madeleine Blocher-Saillens,* 31.

"it was that — Fath, *Une autre manière,* 391.

One [did] read — Mansfield, *The Edinburgh Edition of the Collected Works of Katherine Mansfield,* 2.281.

The Lord has — This is cited in Blocher, *Madeleine Blocher-Saillens,* 93, 104.

Neither married or — Mansfield in a letter to Dorothy Brett, [October 27, 1918], in *The Collected Letters of Katherine Mansfield*, 2.284.

Not what I — Mansfield in a letter to Richard Murry, [November 30, 1919], in *The Collected Letters of Katherine Mansfield*, 3.127.

It was in — Blocher, *Madeleine Blocher-Saillens*, 68.

I do not — Mansfield in a letter to S.S. Koteliansky, November 28, 1915, in *The Collected Letters of Katherine Mansfield*, 1.255.

What are you — Mansfield, *The Edinburgh Edition of the Collected Works of Katherine Mansfield*, 1.333.

Someone … said — Ibid., 3.130.

[Though] you — Mansfield in a letter to S.S. Koteliansky, [March 29, 1915], in *The Collected Letters of Katherine Mansfield*, 1.173.

He heard her — Mansfield, *The Edinburgh Edition of the Collected Works of Katherine Mansfield*, 2.197.

A barrel-organ — Mansfield in a letter to the editor, *The New Age*, [May 25, 1911], in *The Collected Letters of Katherine Mansfield*, 1.104.

The … nuns — Mansfield, *The Edinburgh Edition of the Collected Works of Katherine Mansfield*, 2.106.

On the doorstep — Ibid., 2.197.

As the night — Mansfield in a letter to Jeanne Beauchamp, January 1, 1912, in *The Collected Letters of Katherine Mansfield*, 1.110.

Salvation Army — Mansfield in a letter to Richard Murry, [November 1, 1920], in *The Collected Letters of Katherine Mansfield*, 4.95.

I am not — Mansfield in a letter to Anne Drey, [May 19, 1921], in *The Collected Letters of Katherine Mansfield*, 4.232.

I … do — Mansfield in a letter to Richard Murry, [October 24, 1920], in *The Collected Letters of Katherine Mansfield*, 4.82.

I feel — Mansfield in a letter to Richard Murry, [June 5, 1918], in *The Collected Letters of Katherine Mansfield*, 2.219.

These modernist pastors — Blocher, *Madeleine Blocher-Saillens*, 93–94. The term "modernism" was, initially, used more as a theological than artistic term.

If you were — Mansfield, *The Edinburgh Edition of the Collected Works of Katherine Mansfield,* 1.48.

"an unknown woman" — Marguerite Wargenau-Saillens, *Ruben et Jeanne Saillens évangélistes* (Paris: Editions Ampelos, 2014), 134.

I … [once] met — Mansfield, *Katherine Mansfield Notebooks,* 2.7.

What Ultimate Cinema! — Mansfield in a letter to Richard Murry, [June 1, 1918], in *The Collected Letters of Katherine Mansfield,* 2.210.

The soldiers['] — Mansfield, *The Edinburgh Edition of the Collected Works of Katherine Mansfield,* 1.440.

Walking about — Mansfield in a letter to Bertrand Russell, [January 21, 1917], in *The Collected Letters of Katherine Mansfield,* 1.294.

She had her — Mansfield in a letter to Richard Murry, [April 25, 1920], in *The Collected Letters of Katherine Mansfield,* 3.292.

Rac[ing] along a — Ibid., 1.228.

I … [once] met — Mansfield, *Katherine Mansfield Notebooks,* 2.7.

On April 20, — Sara Wheeler, *Guérie par Dieu seul* (Paris: Les Bons Semeurs, 1936), 15.

"an absurdity — Ibid., 16.

reading in Genesis — Ibid., 23.

"in the arms — Ibid., 25.

"gliding — Ibid., 20.

"locked — Ibid., 25.

"was able to — Ibid., 27.

This — Mansfield in a letter to Annie Burnell Beauchamp, [November 20, 1907], in *The Collected Letters of Katherine Mansfield,* 1.32.

The driver — Mansfield, *The Edinburgh Edition of the Collected Works of Katherine Mansfield,* 2.218.

sat in the — Mansfield in a letter to Garnett Trowel, [October 16, 1908], in *The Collected Letters of Katherine Mansfield,* 1.73.

She leaned out — Mansfield, *The Edinburgh Edition of the Collected Works of Katherine Mansfield,* 1.345.

I'll … come and — Ibid., 1.513.

monster big — Ibid., 1.24.

Half-words — Mansfield in a letter to Richard Murry, [February 27, 1918], in *The Collected Letters of Katherine Mansfield*, 2.96.

Drowned men — Mansfield, *The Edinburgh Edition of the Collected Works of Katherine Mansfield*, 3.120.

I am only — Mansfield in a letter to Richard Murry, [May 8, 1915], in *The Collected Letters of Katherine Mansfield*, 1.178.

"Oh" — Mansfield, *The Edinburgh Edition of the Collected Works of Katherine Mansfield*, 1.307.

"Nobody is going — Ibid., 2.382.

at the door — Ibid., 1.246.

"miracles have not — Adloff in a letter to Arthur Blocher, February 4, 1918, Archives B-S. Adloff was, by this point, a prisoner of war and being held in Britain.

"It is" — Mansfield in a letter to Ottoline Morrell, [early May 1919], in *The Collected Letters of Katherine Mansfield*, 2.317.

one must have — Mansfield in a letter to Dorothy Brett, [December 19, 1921], in *The Collected Letters of Katherine Mansfield*, 4.341.

"night descended" — Wheeler, *Guérie par Dieu seul*, 8.

"a drowned person" — Ibid., 12.

"to stop everything" — Ibid., 19.

"a demon" — Ibid., 20.

We came back — Mansfield in a letter to Garnett Trowell, [October 16, 1908], in *The Collected Letters of Katherine Mansfield*, 1.73.

"the miracle" — Mansfield in a letter to Hugh Walpole, October 27, 1920, in *The Collected Letters of Katherine Mansfield*, 4.86.

one must have — Mansfield in a letter to Dorothy Brett, [December 19, 1921], in *The Collected Letters of Katherine Mansfield*, 4.341.

On January 9th — Claire Tomalin, *Katherine Mansfield: A Secret Life* (London: Viking, 1987), 236–37.

went upstairs — Mansfield, *The Edinburgh Edition of the Collected Works of Katherine Mansfield*, 4.334.

Every house ought — Ibid., 1.134.

John is downstairs — Mansfield in a letter to Virginia Woolf, [late April 1919], in *The Collected Letters of Katherine Mansfield,* 2.314.

another woman — Mansfield in a letter to Richard Murry, [October 20, 1919], in *The Collected Letters of Katherine Mansfield,* 3.35.

people [do] come — Mansfield in a letter to Dorothy Brett, July 29, 1921, in *The Collected Letters of Katherine Mansfield,* 4.256.

Chapter 7

It is not — Walter Benjamin, "The Present Social Situation of the French Writer" [1934], in Michael W. Jennings, Howard Eiland and Gary Smith, eds., *Walter Benjamin: Selected Writings,* 4 vols. (London: Harvard University Press, 1996–2003), 2.2.749. Originally published as Walter Benjamin, *Gesammelte Schriften,* eds. Rolf Tiedmann and Hermann Schweppenhäuser, 7 vols. (Frankfurt: Suhrkamp, 1972–1989), 2.782.

Dear Herr Wiesengrund — Benjamin in a letter to Theodor Adorno, in Theodor W. Adorno and Walter Benjamin, *The Complete Correspondence 1928–1940,* ed. Henry Lonitz, trans. Nicholas Walker (London: Polity Press, 1999), 41. Originally published as Theodor W. Adorno and Walter Benjamin, *Briefwechsel 1928–1940,* ed. Henry Lonitz (Frankfurt am Main: Suhrkamp Verlag, 1994), 58.

La Maison de Verre — For an excellent visual guide, see Olivier Cinqualbre, *Pierre Chareau: Maison de Verre (Maison Dalsace) Paris, France, 1928–32* (Tokyo: ADA Edita, 2012). For a brilliant exploration of the myriad subtexts that may be read within the Maison de Verre, see Emma Cheatle, *Part-architecture. The Maison de Verre, Duchamp, Domesticity and Desire in 1930s Paris* (London: Routledge, 2017). Of particular pertinence to this present book are the ways in which Cheatle: reads the house as a mirror image of Duchamp's "The Bride Stripped Bare"; speculates on the unknown history of the many women who would have attended the clinic; meditates on why Benjamin does not give the name of Dalsace in his letter to Adorno; and considers whether Benjamin's reservations regarding glass as a building material were a factor in his not giving the lectures.

many lecterns — The work "Schiller and Goethe: A Layman's Vision," written between 1906 and 1912, went unpublished in Benjamin's lifetime. Walter Benjamin, *The Storyteller: Tales out of Loneliness,* trans. Sam Dolbear, Esther Leslie, and Sebastian Truskolaski (London: Verso, 2016), 8 / *Gesammelte Schriften,* 7.638.

department — Benjamin in a letter to Gerhard Scholem, Bönigen, September 18, 1918, in *The Correspondence of Walter Benjamin, 1910-1940,* trans. Manfred and Evelyn Jacobson (Chicago: University of Chicago Press, 1994), 134. Originally published as Walter Benjamin, *Briefe* (Frankfurt am Main: Suhrkamp, 1978), 201.

"In Paris even — Benjamin in a letter to Carla Seligson, Freiburg, June 5, 1913, in *The Correspondence of Walter Benjamin,* 26 / *Briefe,* 56.

mass-produced — The work "Central Park," written between April 1938 and February 1939, went unpublished in Benjamin's lifetime. The full citation is: "in big cities, the woman appears ... as a mass-produced article [*Massenartikel*]." Benjamin, *Selected Writings,* 4.188 / *Gesammelte Schriften,* 1.686.

The arcade was — Walter Benjamin, *The Arcades Project,* trans. Howard Eiland and Kevin McLaughlin (Cambridge: Belknap Press, 1999), 37 / *Gesammelte Schriften,* 5.86

"Glass ... is — Benjamin, "Experience and Poverty" (1933), in *Walter Benjamin: Selected Writings,* 2.2.734 / *Gesammelte Schriften,* 2.217.

"In Paris — The work "The Paris of the Second Empire in Baudelaire," written in 1938 went unpublished in Benjamin's lifetime. Benjamin, *Walter Benjamin: Selected Writings,* 4.31 / *Gesammelte Schriften,* 1.557.

"I have been — Benjamin in a letter to Julia Radt, Paris, April 8, 1926, in *The Correspondence of Walter Benjamin,* 296 / *Briefe,* 419.

"The 'femme passante'" — Benjamin, "The Paris of...," in *Walter Benjamin: Selected Writings,* 4.46 / *Gesammelte Schriften,* 1.580

"The eroticist — Ibid., 4.25 / ibid., 1.547.

"Love at last — Ibid., 4.25 / ibid., 1.548.

"Taking a stroll — The work "Letter from Paris (2)," written November to December 1936, went unpublished in Benjamin's lifetime. *Walter Benjamin: Selected Writings,* 3.327 / *Gesammelte Schriften,* 3.495

"I walk up — Benjamin, "Paris Diary" (1930), in *Walter Benjamin: Selected Writings,* 2.1.346 / *Gesammelte Schriften,* 4.580.

"The triumphant encounter — The work "Even the Sacramental Migrates into Myth," written around 1923, went unpublished in Benjamin's lifetime. *Walter Benjamin: Selected Writings,* 1.402.

"Dora has opened — Benjamin in a letter to Gerhard Scholem, Paris, February 4, 1939, in *The Correspondence of Walter Benjamin,* 594 / *Briefe,* 802.

"I have just — Benjamin in a letter to Theodor Adorno, Boulogne sur Seine, December 4, 1937, in *The Complete Correspondence,* 234 / *Briefwechsel,* 305.

"The Black Mass — Benjamin, "Even the Sacramental...," in *Walter Benjamin: Selected Writings,* 1.403.

"The women we — The work "On the Concept of History," written between February and May 1940, went unpublished in Benjamin's lifetime. *Walter Benjamin: Selected Writings,* 4.390 / *Gesammelte Schriften,* 1.693.

"The ... women who — Ibid., 4.389. / ibid., 1.693.

"In ... Paris — Benjamin, *The Arcades Project,* 537 / ibid., 5.666–67.

"The only person — Benjamin in a letter to Gerhard Scholem, Paris, December 31, 1933, in *The Correspondence of Walter Benjamin and Gershom Scholem,* trans. Gary Smith and Andre Lefevere (London: Harvard University Press, 1992), 93. Originally published as Walter Benjamin and Gershom Scholem, *Briefwechsel 1933–1940* (Frankfurt: Suhrkamp, 1980), 119.

"Magical reading?" — The work "Doctrine of the Similar," written between January and February 1933, went unpublished in Benjamin's lifetime. *Walter Benjamin: Selected Writings,* 2.2.697 / *Gesammelte Schriften,* 2.209.

"Magical criticism?" — The work "Criticism as the Fundamental Discipline of Literary History," written in 1930, went unpublished in Benjamin's lifetime. *Walter Benjamin: Selected Writings,* 2.2.415 / *Gesammelte Schriften,* 6.173.

"I was once — Benjamin, "Berlin Chronicle," in *Walter Benjamin: Selected Writings,* 2.2.614 / *Gesammelte Schriften,* 6.491.

"It is — Benjamin in a letter to Gretel Adorno, Paris, January 17, 1940, in *The Correspondence of Walter Benjamin,* 625 / Gretel Adorno and Walter Benjamin, *Briefwechsel 1930–1940,* eds. Christoph Gödde and Henri Lonitz (Frankfurt am Main: Surhkamp Verlag, 2005), 399.

"I weave — Benjamin in a letter to Gerhard Scholem, Paris, April 5, 1926, in *The Correspondence of Walter Benjamin,* 295 / *Briefwechsel 1930–1940,* 418.

"The republic of — Benjamin, "The Present Social Situation of the French Writer" [1934], in *Walter Benjamin: Selected Writings,* 2.2.747 / *Gesammelte Schriften,* 2.780.

"I must express — Benjamin in a letter to Max Horkheimer, Paris, December 15, 1939, in *The Correspondence of Walter Benjamin,* 621 / *Briefe,* 840–41.

"It is less — Benjamin in a letter to Gerhard Scholem, Frankfurt am Main, c. May 20–25, 1925, in *The Correspondence of Walter Benjamin,* 266 / *Briefe,* 379.

"The conventional — Benjamin in a letter to Ernst Cohen, April 7, 1919, in *The Correspondence of Walter Benjamin,* 140 / *Briefe,* 208.

a book — The book is *Ursprung des deutschen Trauerspiels* (1928) translated as *The Origin of German Tragic Drama* by John Osbourne (London: Verso, 1998). In 1925 Benjamin submitted the book to the University of Frankfurt as his Habilitation thesis, a post-doctoral qualification needed for university teaching. In the end, he was advised to withdraw the thesis "to avoid the unpleasantness of public refusal." George Steiner, "Introduction" in ibid., 11.

"Nearly the saddest — The work "The Role of Language in Trauerspiel and Tragedy," written in 1916, went unpublished in Benjamin's lifetime. *Walter Benjamin: Selected Writings,* 1.59 / *Gesammelte Schriften,* 2.137. Benjamin is here remarking that a tragic drama, or mourning play (the more literal translation of *Trauerspiel*) is not quite the saddest thing in the world. He does not make clear what is.

"My wife — The Origin is "dedicated to my wife." Benjamin, *The Origin of German Tragic Drama,* 25.

"In the Princess — Benjamin, "Berlin Chronicle," in *Walter Benjamin: Selected Writings,* 2.2.609 / *Gesammelte Schriften,* 6.484.

"Sleeping Beauty — Benjamin in a letter to Gerhard Scholem, Paris, April 5, 1926, in *The Correspondence of Walter Benjamin,* 295 / *Briefe,* 418.

"A professor philosophiae — The work "Diary from 7 August, 1931, to the Day of my Death," written in late 1931, went unpublished in Benjamin's lifetime. Benjamin, *Walter Benjamin: Selected Writings,* 2.2.503 / *Gesammelte Schriften,* 6.443.

"In the universities — Benjamin, "The Life of Students" [1915], in *Walter Benjamin: Selected Writings,* 1.44 / *Gesammelte Schriften,* 2.84.

"Male impotence" — Benjamin, "Central Park," in *Walter Benjamin: Selected Writings,* 4.185 / *Gesammelte Schriften,* 1.683.

marital sterility — Jean Dalsace, *La stérilité* (Paris: Presses universitaires de France, 1962), 6–24.

"The enfer" — Benjamin in a letter to Alfred Cohn, Paris, July 18, 1935, in *The Correspondence of Walter Benjamin,* 493 / *Briefe,* 669.

"Pornography" — Benjamin, *The Arcades Project,* 855. Also appears in *Gesammelte Schriften,* 5.1024.

"More or less — Benjamin in a letter to Kitty Marx-Steinschneider, Paris, April 15, 1936, in *The Correspondence of Walter Benjamin,* 525 / *Briefe,* 711.

"Obtaining official — Benjamin in a letter to Alfred Cohn, Paris, July 18, 1935, in *The Correspondence of Walter Benjamin*, 493 / *Briefe*, 669.

"I have no — Benjamin in a letter to Gretel and Theodor Adorno, Boulogne sur Seine, October 2, 1937, in *The Complete Correspondence*, 219 / *Briefwechsel*, 298.

"Danton 9073 — Benjamin in a letter to Theodor Adorno, Paris, June 10, 1935, in *The Complete Correspondence*, 101 / *Briefwechsel*, 134.

"A dream Paris?" — Benjamin, *The Arcades Project*, 137 / *Gesammelte Schriften*, 5.198.

an aggregate of — Ibid., 410 / ibid., 5.517.

"The purer Paris?" — Ibid., 137 / ibid., 5.198.

Dalsace and wife — The Dalsaces moved to the département de l'Allier in central France, where Dalsace helped to organise the resistance. Cheatle, *Part-architecture*, 35.

too expensive — Dominique Vellay and Francois Halard, *La maison de verre* (London: Thames & Hudson, 2007), 146.

Paris — Benjamin in a letter to Gerhard Scholem, Paris, November 25, 1939, *The Correspondence of Walter Benjamin and Gershom Scholem*, 259 / *Briefwechsel 1933–1940*, 312.

We Are Not — Gilles Perrault and Pierre Azema, *Paris under the Occupation* (New York: Vendome Press, 1990), 12.

If I can't build — Benjamin in a letter to Florens Christian Rang, Berlin, September 28, 1923, in *The Correspondence of Walter Benjamin*, 209 / *Briefe*, 302.

"Nothing in the — Benjamin in a letter to Max Horkheimer, Paris, December 15, 1939, in *The Correspondence of Walter Benjamin*, 621 / *Briefe*, 839.

Benjamin's library card — Howard Eiland and Michael Jennings, *Walter Benjamin: A Critical Life* (Cambridge: Harvard University Press, 2014), 656.

the manuscript — Ibid., 667.

Like Madeleine — Blocher-Saillens, *Temoin des années noires*, 49–55. See also Blocher ed., *Madeleine Blocher-Saillens*, 132.

centrifugal force — Benjamin in a letter to Hugo Hofmannsthal, Tours, August 16, 1927, in *The Correspondence of Walter Benjamin,* 318 / *Briefe,* 449.

"They were afraid" — Blocher-Saillens, *Témoin des années noires,* 61. With all the fighting and bombing around Paris, there were, in fact, severe risks in leaving the city. As Blocher points out, Madeleine's escape was undertaken "at peril of her life." Blocher, *Madeleine Blocher-Saillens,* 132.

clowns making a — Benjamin, *The Arcades Project,* 524 / *Gesammelte Schriften,* 5.652.

In what time — The work "The Metaphysics of Youth," written between 1913 and 1914, went unpublished in Benjamin's lifetime. Benjamin, *Walter Benjamin: Selected Writings,* 1.10 / *Gesammelte Schriften,* 2.96.

We … are resurrected — Ibid., 1.12 / ibid., 2.99.

Jewish girl — This was in August 1943. Blocher-Saillens, *Témoin des années noires,* 174.

Yesterday, I went — Ibid., 78.

Herr Stutzel — Ibid., 62–65.

You look first — Benjamin in a letter to Gerhard Scholem, Paris, March 20, 1933, in *The Correspondence of Walter Benjamin,* 406 / *Briefe,* 567.

Herr Adloff was — Blocher-Saillens, *Témoin des années noires,* 134.

I flee — Benjamin in a letter to Theodor Adorno, November 2, 1937, in *The Complete Correspondence,* 222 / *Briefwechsel,* 288.

As one leafs — Benjamin, *The Arcades Project,* 549 / *Gesammelte Schriften,* 5.682.

To be found — Ibid., 48 / ibid., 5.99.

I.G. Farben produced — As Esther Leslie comments, "a mutual desire for synthetic rubber brought Hitler and I.G. Farben together." Esther Leslie, *Synthetic Worlds: Nature, Art and the Chemical Industry* (London: Reaktion, 2005), 169.

What are the — Benjamin, "Surrealism: The Last Snapshot of the European Intelligentsia" [1929], in *Walter Benjamin: Selected Writings,* 2.1.216–17 / *Gesammelte Schriften,* 2.308–9.

The gas-mask — Benjamin in a letter to Gretel Adorno, January 17, 1940, in *The Correspondence of Walter Benjamin,* 625 / *Briefe,* 842.

Green and violet — Benjamin in a diary entry, Ibiza, 1932, in *The Storyteller,* 36 / *Gesammelte Schriften,* 6.447. Fromms Akt was the brand name for a condom made from liquefied rubber by the chemist Julius Fromm who, as a Jew, fled Germany for England in 1939.

On a rubber — Benjamin, "Collection of Frankfurt Children's Rhymes" (1925), *The Storyteller,* 156–57 / *Gesammelte Schriften,* 4.795.

Three to be — This is June 27, 1942. Blocher-Saillens, *Témoin des années noires,* 136.

a yellow star — Madeleine makes clear that the young man was wearing *l'étoile jaune.* Blocher-Saillens, *Témoin des années noires,* 136.

Madame T. — Ibid., 138–41.

Monsieur T. abandoned — Ibid., 141. Madeleine believed he had done so.

Hitler is doomed — Benjamin in a letter to Gerhard Scholem, Paris, November 25, 1939, in *Correspondence of Benjamin and Scholem,* 259 / *Briefwechsel,* 312.

Try to see — As Madeleine writes, "we are trying to help him see God, His power, and the work [*l'œuvre*] He has for him to do in the camp." Blocher-Saillens, *Témoin des années noires,* 140.

largely formal — Madeleine wrote that, by the time they got married, Johannes had "lost his faith" and Marie "had only a formal piety [*piété de forme*]." *Journal de Madeleine Blocher-Saillens,* May 21, 1924, Archives B-S.

His return — In a sermon given at the Tabernacle on October 24, 1941, Madeleine remarks of the Second Coming, "everything seems to indicate that it is near [*proche*]." Blocher, *Madeleine Blocher-Saillens,* 167.

a New Testament — This is in November 1940. Blocher-Saillens, *Témoin des années noires,* 74.

"I dreamed — The work "Diary Entries, 1938" went unpublished in Benjamin's lifetime. *Walter Benjamin: Selected Writings,* 3.335 / *Gesammelte Schriften,* 6.532.

"Allow me to — Benjamin, *The Arcades Project,* 172 / *Gesammelte Schriften,* 5.233.

bookshops on the — Ibid., 922 / ibid., 5.1343.

"I have …grasped — Benjamin in a letter to Gerhard Scholem, c. September 10–12, 1933, in *Correspondence of Benjamin and Scholem,* 76 / *Briefwechsel,* 100.

"Gare Saint-Lazare — Benjamin, *The Arcades Project,* 831 / *Gesammelte Schriften,* 5.998.

"The mountains — Benjamin in a letter to Theodor Adorno, Paris, May 5, 1940, in *The Correspondence of Walter Benjamin,* 633 / *Briefe,* 855.

waving … to strangers — Benjamin, *The Arcades Project,* 843 / *Gesammelte Schriften,* 5.1101.

Pastor Feat — Blocher-Saillens, *Témoin des années noires,* 201.

The denunciations — Benjamin in a letter to Gerhard Scholem, Paris, December 7, 1933, *Correspondence of Benjamin and Scholem,* 89 / *Briefwechsel,* 115.

Dachau — Blocher-Saillens, *Témoin des années noires,* 201. Feat died on April 3, 1945.

In my thoughts — Benjamin in a letter to Gretel Adorno, Paris, December 14, 1939, *The Correspondence of Walter Benjamin,* 620 / *Briefe,* 836.

Theology … by whispers — Benjamin in a letter to Gerhard Scholem, June 12, 1938, in *The Correspondence of Walter Benjamin,* 565 / *Briefe,* 763. The German reads *Flüsterzeitung,* meaning "rumour newspaper."

The … night before — Benjamin, "World and Time," in *Walter Benjamin: Selected Writings,* 1.30.

the Pyrenees — See Eiland and Jennings, *Walter Benjamin,* 656.

I live on — Benjamin in a letter to Margarete Steffin, Paris, October 1935, in *The Correspondence of Walter Benjamin,* 510 / *Briefe,* 692.

The philosopher — Benjamin, *The Arcades Project,* 459 / *Gesammelte Schriften,* 5.572.

Last night — "Diary Entries, 1938," in *Walter Benjamin: Selected Writings* 3.335–36 / *Gesammelte Schriften,* 6.533–34.

Among the Jews — Madeleine mentions one particular Jewish woman who had thrown both herself and her child of eight from a window. Blocher-Saillens, *Témoin des années noires,* 138.

A leap from — The work "The Work of Art in the Age of its Reproducibility," written between 1935 and 1936, went unpublished in Benjamin's lifetime. *Walter Benjamin: Selected Writings* 3.113 / *Gesammelte Schriften,* 7.368.

Early on in — Blocher-Saillens, *Témoin des années noires,* 84.

"the telephone — Ibid., 236.

"Danton 9037" — This was Benjamin's telephone number at the time. Benjamin in a letter to Theodor Adorno, Paris, June 10, 1935, in *The Complete Correspondence,* 101 / *Briefwechsel,* 134.

"You misunderstood me" — Benjamin in a letter to Julia Radt, Paris, April 8, 1926, in *The Correspondence of Walter Benjamin,* 295 / *Briefe,* 419.

I ... informed — Benjamin in a letter to Gretel Adorno, Paris, April 7, 1934, in Walter Benjamin and Gretel Adorno, *Correspondence: 1930–1940,* eds. Christoph Gödde and Henri Lonitz, trans. Wieland Hoban (London: Polity Press, 2007), 92 / *Briefwechsel,* 138.

I was told — Blocher-Saillens, *Témoin des années noires,* 236.

I am standing — Benjamin in a letter to Gerhard Scholem, Paris, June 1, 1938, in *The Correspondence of Walter Benjamin,* 563 / *Briefe,* 761.

The gates — Benjamin, *The Arcades Project,* 845 / *Gesammelte Schriften,* 5.1013.

Thresholds ... — Benjamin, "Review: Franz Hessel, Secret Berlin" [1927], in *The Storyteller,* 105–6. Also appears in *Gesammelte Schriften,* 3.82.

Every second is — The work "On the Concept of History," written between February and May 1940, went unpublished in Benjamin's lifetime. *Walter Benjamin: Selected Writings,* 4.397 / *Gesammelte Schriften,* 1.704.

We have just — *Le Bon Combat* (Tabernacle Newsletter), written by Madeleine herself, Archives B-S.

The public — Benjamin, "The Path to Success, in Thirteen Theses, 1928," in *Walter Benjamin: Selected Writings*, 2.1.145 / *Gesammelte Schriften*, 4.349.

"The readiness — Benjamin, "Hugo von Hofmannsthal's Der Turm" [1928], in *Walter Benjamin: Selected Writings*, 2.1.105 / *Gesammelte Schriften*, 3.100.

"Court reduced — Benjamin, *The Origin of German Tragic Drama*, 93. Also appears in *Gesammelte Schriften*, 1.271.

"Shadows of kings" — Benjamin, *The Storyteller*, 7 / *Gesammelte Schriften*, 7.637.

"I noticed that — Benjamin in a letter to Gretel Adorno, Nièvre, October 12, 1939, in *The Correspondence of Walter Benjamin*, 615 / *Briefe*, 830.

The late Mme — *Le Bon Combat*, April 1948, Archives B-S.

"Its elongation — Benjamin in a letter to Gretel Adorno, Nièvre, October 12, 1939, in *The Correspondence of Walter Benjamin*, 615 / *Briefe*, 830.

"It was — The work "May to June 1931" went unpublished in Benjamin's lifetime. *Walter Benjamin: Selected Writings*, 2.2.484 / *Gesammelte Schriften*, 6.440.

"Please forgive — Benjamin in a letter to Theodor Adorno, Lourdes, August 2, 1940, in *The Correspondence of Walter Benjamin*, 639 / *Briefe*, 862.

"Storm of forgiveness" — Benjamin, "The Meaning of Time in the Moral Universe" [1921], in *Walter Benjamin: Selected Writings*, 1.287.

Afterword

the lives of — Woolf, *The Diary of Virginia Woolf*, 2.37.

What is laid — Kafka, *Aphorisms*, 27.

to see the — Wilde, *Complete Works*, 4.159.

The break with — Gregory Ulmer, "The Object of Post-Criticism," in *The Anti-Aesthetic: Essays on Postmodern Culture*, ed. Hal Foster (Port Townsend: Bay Press, 1983), 83.

Bibliography

Apart from the section for unpublished materials, each section below corresponds either to a particular chapter or to a particular location or theme.

Unpublished Materials

Johannes Schad Naturalisation Papers. The National Archives. NA: HO 144 / 6158.230293.

Le journal de Madeleine Blocher-Saillens. Archives Blocher-Saillens.

Schad v Schad Divorce Papers. The National Archives. J 77 / 2080.C450964.

Wensley Family Archive. Bishopsgate Institute, London. Box 174/4/3.

Titles relating to marriage and divorce

Bourne, Aleck. "Thomas George Stevens, Obituary." *Journal of Obstetrics and Gynaecology of the British Empire* 61 (1954): 123–25.

Dalsace, Jean. *La stérilité.* Paris: Presses universitaires de France, 1962.

Merrivale, Henry. *Marriage and Divorce: The English Point of View.* London: George Allen, 1936.

Stevens, Thomas C. *Diseases of Women.* London: University of London Press, 1912.

Stopes, Marie. *Marriage in My Time.* London: Rich and Cowan, 1935.

———. *Married Love.* Edited by Ross McKibbin. Oxford: Oxford University Press, 2008.

Titles relating to the rubber trade

Coates, Austin. *The Commerce in Rubber: The First 250 Years.* Oxford: Oxford University Press, 1987.

Firestone, Harvey Samuel. *The Romance and Drama of the Rubber Industry.* Akron: The Firestone Tire and Rubber Co., 1932.

India Rubber World. New York: India Rubber Publishing Co, 1913–14.

J.W.L. *Slave Stories in Rubber-Seeking.* London: Walter Scott Publishing, 1913.

Roth, Ralf, and Colin Divall, eds. *From Rail to Road and Back Again? A Century of Transport, Competition and Interdependency.* London: Routledge, 2015.

Schidrowitz, P., and T.R. Dawson. *History of the Rubber Industry.* London: Heffer & Sons Ltd., 1952.

Titles relating to London

Anon. "Motor-Car Detectives." *Daily Mail,* September 22, 1920.

Crook, G.T. "Detective of the Future." *Daily Mail,* May 24, 1920.

Randall, Ian. *The English Baptists of the 20th Century.* London: Baptist Historical Society, 2005.

Ross, Cathy. *Twenties London.* London: Philip Wilson Publishers, 2003.

The Baptist Times and Freeman. London: British Library.

The Recorder, for Palmers Green, Winchmore Hill and Southgate. Enfield Local Studies & Archive.

Wensley, Frederick Porter. *Forty Years of Scotland Yard: A Record of Lifetime's Service in the Criminal Investigation Department.* London: Kessinger Publishing, 2005 [1930].

White, Jerry. *Zeppelin Nights.* London: Bodley Head, 2014.

Whitley, W.T. *The Baptists of London, 1612–1928.* London: Kingsgate Press, 1928.

Titles relating to Paris

Anon. "Studies in Traffic Taming," *New York Times,* April 7, 1929.

Cheatle, Emma. *Part-architecture: The Maison de Verre, Duchamp, Domesticity and Desire in 1930s Paris.* London: Routledge, 2017.

Cinqualbre, Olivier. *Pierre Chareau: Maison de Verre (Maison Dalsace) Paris, France, 1928–32.* Tokyo: ADA Edita, 2012.

Geppert, Alexander C.T. *Fleeting Cities: Imperial Expositions in "Fin-de-Siècle" Europe.* London: Palgrave Macmillan, 2010.

Jackson, Julian. *France: The Dark Years.* Oxford: Oxford University Press, 2001.

Julian, Philippe. *The Triumph of Art Nouveau: Paris Exhibition, 1900.* New York: Larousse, 1974.

Holmes, Burton. *Travelogues.* Vol. 2. New York: The McClure Co., 1905–1910.

Levin, Gail. *Edward Hopper: An Intimate Biography.* Berkeley: University of California Press, 1995.

Mandell, Richard D. *Paris 1900.* Toronto: University of Toronto Press, 1967.

Marrus, Michael R., and Robert O. Paxton. *Vichy France and the Jews.* Stanford: Stanford University Press, 1995.

Rifkin, Adrian. *Street Noises: Parisian Pleasure 1900–40.* Manchester: Manchester University Press, 1993.

Roberts, Mary Louise. *Civilization without Sexes: Reconstructing Gender in Postwar France, 1917–1927.* Chicago: University of Chicago Press, 1994.

Rosenberg, Clifford. *Policing Paris: The Origins of Modern Immigration Control Between the Wars.* Ithaca: Cornell University Press, 2006.

Thomson, D. Croal, ed. *The Paris Exhibition 1900: An Illustrated Record.* London: The Art Journal Office, 1901.

Vellay, Dominique, and Francois Halard. *La maison de verre.* London: Thames & Hudson, 2007.

Titles relating to Paris Tabernacle

Blocher, Jacques E., ed. *Madeleine Blocher-Saillens: Féministe et fondamentalise.* Paris: Edition Excelsis, 2014.

———. "Ruben Saillens: Prophète Camisard." *Théologie Évangélique* 4 (2005): 72–78.

Blocher-Saillens, Madeleine. *Témoin des années noires: Journal d'une femme pasteur, 1938–1945.* Edited by Jacques E. Blocher. Paris: Les Éditions de Paris, 1998.

Fath, Sébastien. *Une autre manière d'être chrétien en France. Socio-histoire de l'implantation baptiste, 1810–1950.* Geneva: Labor et Fides, 2001.

Marrus, Michael R. "French Protestant Churches and the Persecution of the Jews." In *The Holocaust and the Christian World,* edited by Carol Rittner et al., 88–91. London: Continuum, 2000.

Passy, Paul. *Souvenirs d'un socialiste chrétien.* 2 vols. Issy-les-Moulineaux: Editions "Je sers," 1930.

The Keswick Week, 1925. London: Marshall Brothers, 1925.

Wargenau-Saillens, Marguerite. *Ruben et Jeanne Saillens évangélistes.* Paris: Editions Ampelos, 2014.

Wheeler, Sara. *Guérie par Dieu seul.* Paris: Les Bons Semeurs, 1936.

Titles relating to Switzerland

de Beer, G.R. *Escape to Switzerland.* Harmondsworth: Penguin, 1945.

Dewald, Jonathan. *Europe 1450 to 1789: Absolutism to Coligny.* New York: Charles Scribner's Sons, 2004.

Ewald, Jürg, et al. *Nah dran, weit weg. Geschichte des Kantons Basel-Landschaft.* 6 vols. Liestal: Verlag des Kantons Basel-Landschaft, 2001.

Gordon, Peter E. *Continental Divide: Heidegger, Cassirer, Davos.* Cambridge: Harvard University Press, 2010.

Haumann, H., ed. *The First Zionist Congress.* Basel: S Karger AG, 1997.

Heusler, Andreas. *Der Bauernkrieg von 1653 in der Landschaft.* Basel: Neukirch'sche Buchhandlung, 1854.

Hostettler, Urs. *Der Rebell vom Eggiwil. Aufstand der Emmentaler 1653.* Bern: Zytglogge Verlag, 1991.

Jensen, Lamar. *Reformation Europe: Age of Reform and Revolution.* Lexington: D.C. Heath and Co., 1992.

Joseph, John E. *Ferdinand de Saussure.* Oxford: Oxford University Press, 2012.

——. "He Was an Englishman." *TLS* (November 16, 2007): 15–16.

Landolt, Niklaus. *Untertanenrevolten und Widerstand auf der Basler Landschaft im 16. und 17. Jahrhundert.* Liestal: Verlag des Kantons Basel-Landschaft, 1996.

Lunn, Arnold. *The Swiss and their Mountains.* London: George Allen, 1963.

Mann, Thomas. *The Magic Mountain.* Translated by H.T. Lowe-Porter. Harmondsworth: Penguin, 1960 [1924].

Nelson Burnett, Amy, and Emidio Campi, eds. *A Companion to the Swiss Reformation.* Leiden: Brill, 2012.

Noyce, Wilfred. *The Alps.* London: Thames and Hudson, 1963.

Saussure, Ferdinand de. *Cours de linguistique générale.* Edited by Charles Bally and Albert Sechehaye. Paris: Payot, 1964 [1916].

——. *Course in General Linguistics.* Translated by Roy Harris. La Salle: Open Court, 1983.

——. *Écrits de linguistique générale.* Paris: Gallimard, 2002.

——. *Writings in General Linguistics.* Oxford: Oxford University Press, 2006.

Starobinski, Jean. *Words upon Words: The Anagrams of Ferdinand de Saussure.* Translated by Olivia Emmet. New Haven: Yale University Press, 1979:

Suter, Andreas. *Der schweizerische Bauernkrieg von 1653. Politische Sozialgeschichte, Sozialgeschichte eines politischen Ereignisses.* Tübingen: Bibliotheca Academica, 1997.

The Swiss Observer. London: British Library.

Titles relating to Virginia Woolf (Chapter One)

Woolf, Virginia. *Collected Essays of Virginia Woolf.* 4 vols. Edited by Leonard Woolf. London: Hogarth, 1966–67.

———. *Letters of Virginia Woolf.* 6 vols. Edited by Nigel Nicolson and Joanne Trautmann. London: Harcourt Brace Jovanovich, 1975–79.

———. *Mrs Dalloway.* Edited by Stella McNichol. Harmondsworth: Penguin, 1992 [1925].

———. *The Diary of Virginia Woolf.* 5 vols. Edited by Anne Olivier Bell. London: Hogarth Press, 1979–85.

———. *The Essays of Virginia Woolf.* 6 vols. Edited by Andrew McNeillie. London: Chatto and Windus, 1986–2012.

Titles relating to Franz Kafka (Chapter Two)

Gilman, Sander. *Franz Kafka: The Jewish Patient.* London: Routledge, 1995.

Hockaday, Mary. *Kafka, Love and Courage: The Life of Milena Jesenská.* London: André Deutsch, 1995.

Kafka, Franz. *Aphorisms.* Translated by Willa and Edwin Muir. New York: Schocken Books, 2015.

———. *Briefe an Milena.* Edited by Jürgen Born and Michael Müller. Frankfurt am Main: Fischer Verlag, 1986.

———. *Letters to Felice.* Translated by James Stern and Elisabeth Duckworth. Edited by Erich Heller and Jürgen Born. Harmondsworth: Penguin, 1973.

———. *Letters to Milena.* Translated by Tania and James Stern. Edited by Willy Hass. London: Vintage Books, 1999 [1935].

————. *Schriften, Tagebücher, Briefe. Kritische Ausgabe.* 16 vols. Frankfurt am Main: S. Fischer Verlag, 1982–99.

————. *The Diaries of Franz Kafka, 1910–23.* Edited by Max Brod. Harmondsworth: Penguin, 1972.

————. *The Trial.* Translated by Willa and Edwin Muir. Harmondsworth: Penguin, 1953 [1937].

Karl, Frederick. *Franz Kafka: Representative Man.* New York: International Publishing Corporation, 1993.

Titles relating to Surrealism (Chapter Three)

Andrews, Wayne. *The Surrealist Parade.* New York: New Directions, 1990.

Aragon, Louis. *A Wave of Dreams.* Translated by Susan de Muth. London: Thin Man Press, 2010 [1924].

————. *Le paysan de Paris.* Paris: Gallimard, 1953 [1926].

————. *Paris Peasant.* Translated by Simon Watson Taylor. Boston: Exact Change, 1994.

————. *Une vague de rêves.* Paris: Seghers, 1990.

Baker, Simon. *Surrealism, History and Revolution.* Oxford: Peter Lang, 2007.

Breton, André. *Break of Day.* Translated by Mark Polizzotti and Mary

————. *Le point du jour.* Paris: Gallimard, 1970 [1927].

Ann Caws. Lincoln: University of Nebraska Press, 1999.

————. *L'immaculée conception.* Paris: Editions Seghers, 2011.

————. *Manifestes du surréalisme. 1924–53.* Paris: Jean-Jacques Pauvert, 1962.

————. *Manifestoes of Surrealism.* Translated by Richard Seaver and Helen R. Lane. Ann Arbor: University of Michigan Press, 1969.

———— and Paul Éluard. *The Immaculate Conception.* London: Atlas Press, 1990 [1930].

Clair, René. *A Nous la Liberté and Entr'acte.* Translated by Richard Jacques and Nicola Hayden. New York: Simon and Schuster, 1970.

Decimo, Marc, ed. *Marcel Duchamp and Eroticism.* Cambridge: Cambridge Scholars Press, 2007.

Desnos, Robert. *La liberté ou l'amour!* Paris: Gallimard, 1962 [1927].

———. *Liberty or Love!* Translated by Terry Hale. London: Atlas Press, 1993.

Durozoi, Gérard. *History of the Surrealist Movement.* Chicago: University of Chicago Press, 2002.

Ernst, Max. *The Hundred Headless Woman (La femme 100 têtes).* Translated by Dorothea Tanning. New York: George Braziller, 1981 [1929].

Genbach, Jean (a.k.a. Ernest Gengenbach). *Satan à Paris.* Albi: Passage du Nord/Ouest, 2003 [1927].

Gengenbach, Ernest. *Surréalisme et christianisme.* Rennes: Imprimerie Bretonne, 1938.

Golding, John. *Duchamp: The Bride Stripped Bare by her Bachelors, Even.* London: Allen Lane, 1973.

La révolution surréaliste. 12 issues edited by Pierre Naville and Benjamin Péret (1–3), André Breton (4–12). Paris: 1924–29. Facsimile reprint. Paris: Jean Michel Place, 2004.

Mundy, Jennifer, ed. *Surrealism: Desire Unbound.* Princeton: Princeton University Press, 2002.

Nadeau, Maurice. *The History of Surrealism.* Translated by Richard Howard. Harmondsworth: Penguin, 1968 [1964].

Polizzotti, Mark. *Revolution of the Mind: The Life of André Breton.* London: Bloomsbury, 1995.

Sandro, Paul. "Parodic Narration in *Entr'acte.*" Film Criticism 1 (1979): 44–55.

Sanouillet, Michel, ed. *Marchand du sel, écrits de Marcel Duchamp.* Paris: Le Terrain Vague, 1959.

Sanouillet, Michel, and Elmer Peterson, eds. *The Writings of Marcel Duchamp.* Oxford: Oxford University Press, 1973.

Spieker, Sven. *The Big Archive: Art From Bureaucracy.* Cambridge: MIT Press, 2008.

Thévenin, Paul, ed. *Bureau de recherches surréalistes. Cahier de la permanence.* Paris: Gallimard, 1988.

Townsend, Christopher. "'The Art I Love Is the Art of Cowards': Francis Picabia and René Clair's *Entr'acte* and the Politics of Death and Remembrance in France after World War One." *Science as Culture* 18 (2009): 81–96. DOI: 10.1080/09505430903123040.

Walker, Ian. *City Gorged with Dreams: Surrealism and Documentary Photography in Interwar Paris.* Manchester: Manchester University Press, 2002.

Walz, Robin. *Pulp Surrealism: Insolent Popular Culture in Early Twentieth-Century Paris.* Berkeley: University of California Press, 2000.

Titles relating to Stéphane Mallarmé (Chapter Four)

Barbier, Carl, ed. *Documents Stéphane Mallarmé.* 7 vols. Paris: Nizat, 1968–79.

Bersani, Leo. *The Death of Stéphane Mallarmé.* Cambridge: Cambridge University Press, 1982.

Lloyd, Rosemary, ed. *Selected Letters.* Chicago: Chicago University Press, 1988.

Mallarmé, Stéphane. *Collected Poems and Other Verse.* Translated and edited by E.H. and A.M. Blackmore. Oxford: Oxford University Press, 2006.

———. *Collected Poems of Stéphane Mallarmé.* Translated and edited by Henry Weinfeld. Berkeley: University of California Press, 1994.

———. *Correspondance.* Edited by L.J. Austin, H. Mondor, and J.P. Richard. 11 vols. Paris: Gallimard, 1959-85.

———. *Divagations.* Translated by Barabara Johnson. Cambridge: Harvard University Press, 2007.

———. *For Anatole's Tomb.* Translated by Patrick McGuiness. Manchester: Carcanet, 2003 [1961].

———. *Œuvres complètes.* Edited by Henri Mondor and G. Jean-Aubry. Paris: Gallimard, 1945.

Millan, Gordon. *A Throw of the Dice: The Life of Stéphane Mallarmé.* London: Secker and Warburg, 1994.

Mondor, Henry, ed. *Eugène Lefébure: sa vie — ses lettres à Mallarmé.* Paris: Gallimard, 1951.

Pearson, Roger. *Stéphane Mallarmé.* London: Reaktion Books, 2010.

Rodocanachi, André. "Stéphane Mallarmé et Méry Laurnet." *Bulletin du Bibliophile* 4 (1979): 489–507.

Scherer, Jacques. *Le livre de Mallarmé.* Paris: Gallimard, 1978.

Titles relating to Wilde (Chapter Five)

Astell, Ann. "'My Life Is a Work of Art': Oscar Wilde's Novelistic and Religious Conversion." *Renascence* 65 (2013): 188–205. DOI: 10.5840/renascence20136539.

Ellman, Richard. *Oscar Wilde.* Harmondsworth: Penguin, 1987.

Holland, Merlin, ed. *Irish Peacock and Scarlet Marquess: The Real Trial of Oscar Wilde.* London: Fourth Estate, 2003.

Hyde, H. Montgomery, ed. *The Trials of Oscar Wilde.* London: William Hodge and Co., 1948.

Mikhail E.H., ed. *Oscar Wilde: Interviews and Recollections.* 2 vols. London: Macmillan, 1979.

Wilde, Oscar. *An Ideal Husband.* Edited by Russell Jackson. London: Methuen, 2013 [1895].

———. *A Woman of No Importance.* Edited by Ian Small. London: Methuen, 2004 [1893].

———. *Lady Windermere's Fan.* Edited by Ian Small. London: Ernest Benn, 1980 [1893].

———. *The Complete Letters of Oscar Wilde.* Edited by Merlin Holland and Rupert Hart-Davis. London: Fourth Estate, 2000.

———. *The Complete Works of Oscar Wilde.* Edited by Russell Jackson and Ian Small. 8 vols. Oxford: Oxford University Press, 2000.

———. *The Importance of Being Earnest.* Edited by Patricia Hern and Glenda Leeming. London: Methuen, 1981 [1895].

———. *The Original Four-Act Version of "The Importance of Being Earnest: A Trivial Comedy for Serious People."* London: Methuen, 1957.

———. *Vera; Or, the Nihilists* [1883]. In *The Complete Plays,* 515–78. London: Methuen, 1988.

Titles relating to Katherine Mansfield (Chapter Six)

Ascari, Maurizio. *Cinema and the Imagination in Katherine Mansfield's Writing.* London: Palgrave, 2014.

Jones, Kathleen. *Katherine Mansfield.* Edinburgh: Edinburgh University Press, 2010.

Mansfield, Katherine. *The Collected Letters of Katherine Mansfield.* 4 vols. Edited by Vincent O'Sullivan and Margaret Scott. Oxford: Clarendon Press, 1984–1996.

———. *The Edinburgh Edition of the Collected Works of Katherine Mansfield.* 4 vols. Edited by Gerri Kimber, Vincent O'Sullivan, Angela Smith, and Claire Davison. Edinburgh: Edinburgh University Press, 2012–16.

———. *The Katherine Mansfield Notebooks.* 2 vols. Edited by Margaret Scott. Minneapolis: University of Minnesota Press, 1997.

Tomalin, Claire. *Katherine Mansfield: A Secret Life.* London: Viking, 1987.

Titles relating to Walter Benjamin (Chapter Seven)

Adorno, Gretel, and Walter Benjamin. *Briefwechsel 1930–1940.* Edited by Christoph Gödde and Henri Lonitz. Frankfurt am Main: Surhkamp Verlag, 2005.

———. *Correspondence: 1930–1940.* Translated by Wieland Hoban. London: Polity Press, 2007.

Adorno, Theodor W., and Walter Benjamin. *Briefwechsel 1928–1940.* Edited by Henry Lonitz. Frankfurt am Main: Suhrkamp Verlag, 1994.

———. *The Complete Correspondence 1928–1940.* Translated by Nicholas Walker. London: Polity Press, 1999.

Benjamin, Walter. *Gesammelte Schriften.* 7 vols. Edited by Rolf Tiedmann and Hermann Schweppenhäuser. Frankfurt: Suhrkamp Verlag, 1972–89.

————. *The Arcades Project.* Translated by Howard Eiland and Kevin McLaughlin. Cambridge: Belknap Press, 1999.

————. *The Correspondence of Walter Benjamin.* Translated by Manfred and Evelyn Jacobson. Chicago: University of Chicago Press, 1994.

————. *The Correspondence of Walter Benjamin and Gershom Scholem.* Edited by Gershom Scholem. Translated by Gary Smith and André Lefevere. Cambridge: Harvard University Press, 1992.

————. *The Origin of German Tragic Drama.* Translated by John Osbourne. London: Verso, 1998.

————. *The Storyteller: Tales out of Loneliness.* Translated by Sam Dolbear, Esther Leslie, and Sebastian Truskolaski. London: Verso, 2016.

————. *Walter Benjamin: Selected Writings.* 4 vols. Edited by Michael W. Jennings, Howard Eiland, and Gary Smith. Cambridge: Belknap Press, 1999–2006.

Benjamin, Walter, and Gershom Scholem. *Briefwechsel 1933–1940.* Edited by Gershom Scholem. Frankfurt am Main: Suhrkamp Verlag, 1980.

Eiland, Howard, and Michael Jennings. *Walter Benjamin. A Critical Life.* Cambridge: Harvard University Press, 2014.

Leslie, Esther. *Synthetic Worlds: Nature, Art and the Chemical Industry.* London: Reaktion, 2005.

Miscellaneous

Carlton, Charles. *Charles I: The Personal Monarch.* London: Ark, 1984.

de Beistegui, Miguel. *The New Heidegger.* London: Continuum, 2005.

Damien, Pierre. *Lettre sur la toute-puissance divine. Introduction, texte critique, traduction et notes.* Edited and translated by André Cantin. Sources Chrétiennes 191. Paris: Les Editions du Cerf, 1972.

Derrida, Jacques, *Of Grammatology.* Translated by Gayatri
Chakravorty Spivak. Baltimore: John Hopkins University
Press, 1976 [1967].

———. *The Post Card.* Translated by Alan Bass. Chicago: University of Chicago Press, 1987 [1980].

Dickinson, Emily. *The Complete Poems.* Edited by Thomas H.
Johnson. London: Faber, 1970.

Ebbatson, Roger. *Heidegger's Bicycle: Interfering with Victorian
Texts.* Brighton: Sussex Academic Press, 2006.

Eliot, T.S. *The Complete Poems of T.S. Eliot.* London: Faber,
1969.

Fraser, Antonia. *Marie Antoinette.* London: Wiedenfeld and
Nicolson, 2001.

Hanna, Emma. *The Great War on the Small Screen: Representing the First World War in Contemporary Britain.* Edinburgh: Edinburgh University Press, 2009.

Hardy, Thomas. *The Complete Poetry of Thomas Hardy.* Edited
by James Gibson. London: Macmillan, 1976.

Heidegger, Martin. *Existence and Being.* Translated by Werner
Brock. Chicago: Gateway, 1949.

———. *Gesamtausgabe.* 102 vols. Edited by Friedrich-Wilhelm
von Herrmann. Frankfurt am Main: Vittorio Klostermann,
1975–.

Holmes, Sherlock. *The Penguin Complete Sherlock Holmes.*
Harmondsworth: Penguin, 1981.

Jones, Jack D. *The Royal Prisoner Charles I at Carisbrooke.*
London: Lutterworth, 1965.

Karmi, Ghada. *Married to Another Man.* London: Pluto Press,
2008.

Lehrer, Steven. *Explorers of the Body.* New York: Doubleday,
2006.

Maass, Joachim. *Kleist: A Biography.* Translated by Ralph Manheim. London: Secker and Warburg, 1983.

Marx, Karl. *Capital: A Critique of Political Economy.* 3 vols.
Translated by Ben Fowkes. Harmondsworth: Penguin,
1976–81 [1867].

Roberts, Colin H., and T.C. Skeat. *The Birth of the Codex.* London: Oxford University Press, 1983.

The Book of Common Prayer. New York: The Church Hymnal Corporation, 1979 [1653].

Ulmer, Gregory. "The Object of Post-Criticism." In *The Anti-Aesthetic: Essays on Postmodern Culture,* edited by Hal Foster, 83–108. Port Townsend: Bay Press, 1983.

"W. dreams, like Phaedrus, of an army of thinker-friends, thinker-lovers. He dreams of a thought-army, a thought-pack, which would storm the philosophical Houses of Parliament. He dreams of Tartars from the philosophical steppes, of thought-barbarians, thought-outsiders. What distance would shine in their eyes!"

— Lars Iyer

Printed in Poland
by Amazon Fulfillment
Poland Sp. z o.o., Wrocław

54556154R00201